By R. F. Delderfield

RETURN JOURNEY
GIVE US THIS DAY
TO SERVE THEM ALL MY DAYS
FOR MY OWN AMUSEMENT
THEIRS WAS THE KINGDOM
GOD IS AN ENGLISHMAN
MR. SERMON
THE AVENUE
THE GREEN GAUNTLET
A HORSEMAN RIDING BY

Seven Men of Gascony

R. F. Delderfield

SIMON AND SCHUSTER · NEW YORK

Copyright © 1949, 1973 by May Delderfield
All rights reserved
including the right of reproduction
in whole or in part in any form
Published by Simon and Schuster
Rockefeller Center, 630 Fifth Avenue
New York, New York 10020
Designed by Edith Fowler
Manufactured in the United States of America

1 2 3 4 5 6 7 8 9 10

LIBRARY OF CONGRESS CATALOGING IN PUBLICATION DATA

Delderfield, Ronald Frederick, 1912–1972
SEVEN MEN OF GASCONY

I. Title.
PZ3.D37618Se5   [PR6007.E36]   823'.9'12   74–4315
ISBN 0–671–21794–1

CONTENTS

AUTHOR'S NOTE

Most of the incidents recorded in the following pages are true, episodes written down at the time, or in after years, by officers and men of the Grand Army. The central characters are spun from fact, typical infantrymen of Napoleon in the years of the First Empire's decline. The greater part of the subsidiary characters, men like Marshal Lannes and Marshal Ney, are now enshrined in French history and their names are prominent on the Arc de Triomphe.

If the reader would like to know more concerning the careers of these remarkable men, the public libraries teem with current memoir and biography recording their deeds between the outbreak of the Revolution and the final debacle at Waterloo. They are worth contemplating, for men of their calibre are lamentably rare in the Europe of today.

Lannes was a dyer's apprentice whose gallantry earned him the title "Bayard of the French Army"; he was universally mourned when he received his mortal wound at Aspern, in 1809. Ney was the son of a cooper, called "Bravest of the Brave," who died facing a Bourbon firing-squad after Waterloo. The flamboyant Murat, son of an innkeeper, became a king before he also died in front of a firing-squad. Marshal Massena, once a smuggler, earned a military reputation second only to his chief, Napoleon. Marshal Bessières, darling of the Old Guard, died in action like Lannes, and was affectionately remembered by all the veterans. Marshal Marmont, another friend of Napoleon's youth, betrayed him and lived to regret it; Marshal Poniatowski, a Polish prince, was drowned escaping from Leipzig; Marshal Mortier, as popular as any, lived to hold high office under the Bourbons and was blown up by a bomb thrown during a Paris procession years after his master had died in exile. The others, Victor, Oudinot, Macdonald and the steadfast Eugène de Beauharnais, were equally colourful in their lives and in their deaths.

There were many high-ranking Imperialists who never received the coveted marshal's baton. Some of them are mentioned in these pages, men like Lasalle and Sainte-Croix, both dashing cavalrymen, and hard-fighting corps commanders like Reynier, Reille, Vandamme, Foy and Gérard; leaders of heavy cavalry like Montbrun and Milhaud, all men of mettle who enjoyed living and did not regret dying at the head of their battalions and squadrons.

Napoleon himself thought of them constantly during the six years' exile on St. Helena, and when he died his last words paid tribute to their gay courage. "I shall meet all my faithful companions in Valhalla," he said, but there were many faithful companions whose names he did not know but who nevertheless died for him, some willingly, some indifferently.

This book is only a fragment of the First Empire legend, and in writing it I intended to commemorate the gallantry and the hardihood of a million unknown men who marched, fought and died during the years when France challenged a continent.

R. F. D.

PROLOGUE

When Father Pavart climbed the uncarpeted stairs to the veteran's room overlooking the river he found the old man sitting in the window-seat, looking down on the crowd surrounding Peltier, the postillion. Peltier had just galloped across the bridge with the news.

Father Pavart was the one person in the village who was acquainted with the old fellow. The others had been discouraged by the veteran's incivility. He seldom gave any sign that he heard when he was addressed, and the woman who attended to his few wants and lived on the ground floor below seldom wasted time in endeavours to open a conversation when she came up with his meals or to mend the fire he kept going both summer and winter.

He was thought to have money, but none knew this for certain. Nobody was sure of his name, not even Father Pavart, who visited him occasionally. He had come to the village from a small town in the south, where he was supposed to have buried his wife a year or two ago. He was a commonplace-looking man, who might have been any age between fifty and seventy. He had an air of brooding and large, sad eyes. At times he appeared to be crippled with rheumatism and rarely left his room. His right hand had been maimed in some sort of accident. Two fingers were missing and the remainder were bent over a scarred palm, reddish and unsightly. The hand looked like a claw and did nothing to increase his popularity among the children.

He was supposed to have fought in the wars of the Empire, but he never told stories, like some of the other veterans in the district. He lived the life of a bad-tempered recluse, and Madame Friant, his landlady, often told neighbours that she would have turned him out long ago if he had not paid his dues in advance and in gold, on the first of every month.

Father Pavart was known to be on good terms with the old man, but he showed no disposition to enlighten the curious. After a few months Madame Friant's taciturn lodger was accepted as a newcomer who would never play any part in village life and consequently came to be ignored. Far from resenting this, he did all he could to encourage the villagers in their neglect. He spoke to no one but the priest and his landlady.

It was early in December, 1840, when Peltier, the postillion, flogged his lathered team across the bridge and pulled them up in the yard of the inn. All the way across the bridge Peltier had been shouting down to pedestrians. The first snow had fallen and the posthorses were badly blown. They had been driven much too hard along the main road from Rennes.

The veteran had seen the chaise when it first entered the byroad approaching the bridge on the far side of the river. He had watched its progress right up to the inn-yard and had seen François, the little inn's sole ostler, unlatch the boot and take out the mails and one or two packages. He must have wondered why Peltier's arrival caused such a stir. Everyone within earshot was running to talk to the postillion, who jumped down from his box and stamped about the yard, beating his hands together and turning to answer questions on every side.

It was then that Father Pavart entered the room; but the figure on the window-seat did not turn to greet him. The priest sat down in the one arm-chair and spread his gloved hands to the flames.

"He's come home," he said.

The veteran seemed to shiver slightly but continued to look down on the lively scene in the yard.

Father Pavart chuckled. He was a short, slight man, with a mahogany complexion and startlingly blue eyes. For a provincial priest who seldom moved out of a remote parish, he might be considered a highly intelligent man, and he usually got his own way with the most obstinate of his flock. He was notoriously garrulous. He never went to Paris, but he read all the papers and always knew everything that was going on in the capital and beyond. He was very friendly with the editor of the Rennes newspaper, who was a distant relative; the two occasionally visited one another and were known to correspond a good deal.

When the veteran made no reply Pavart went on: "Peltier's been telling them all about the funeral procession. The catafalque came down the Seine on a barge. There were torches and music. I should like to have been present myself."

As he said this Pavart squinted in the veteran's direction. He paused a moment, his eyes fixed on the old man's bent shoulders. He seemed to be pondering how best to broach the purpose of his visit.

Presently he said: "My cousin in Rennes wants you to write about him."

The old man spun round and stared into the priest's eyes.

"Me!"

Pavart affected not to notice the old man's agitation. He shrugged his shoulders.

"Why not? You could do it as well as anyone I know. You were there, were you not?"

"There are dozens of veterans in Rennes. There are one or two here, so I've heard."

"The men here are conscripts, Leipzig and Waterloo men. My cousin wants something better than that. I told him about you when we met during the summer. He is an unrepentant Bonapartist and often asks after you."

The man in the window-seat got up and moved towards the

fire. His height sometimes surprised strangers. When sitting down he appeared quite short. He carried himself loosely, as though to brace himself would have made his bones ache. His hair was thin and grey and he looked miserably under-nourished, although Pavart knew that Madame Friant fed him well enough. He came and stood on the worn hearthrug, looking down on the priest.

"I don't know why I ever told you anything," he said. "It wasn't because you were a priest. Priests were never of much account in the old days. We didn't see one from one campaign to another. I'm not in the habit of talking about the past. My wife and I made a pact the night of Waterloo."

"What sort of pact?"

"A pact to forget the past. It was our only chance."

The veteran pushed forward his maimed hand and with his left hand pulled out the grotesquely curled fingers and let them clench again. Pavart had seen him do this before. The habit fascinated him.

The priest let his imagination wander to Paris for a moment. He saw the silent throng lining the snow-covered streets to watch the funeral procession move towards the fantastic tomb they had prepared at the Invalides. He heard the slow, mournful strains of the bands, the shuffle of the plumed horses that pulled the funeral carriage, the creak of the carriage wheels along the precise lines of the procession. He had never seen Napoleon and he wished, with all his heart, to be in Paris at this moment. He looked at the veteran with a new interest. It gave him a pleasant shock to realize that the gaunt, nondescript man standing on the hearthrug had marched with the Emperor across the Danube plains and through the icy pine forests from Moscow to the Niemen. Great names, already part of a great legend, were as familiar to this man as the names of Peltier, the postillion, and François, the ostler, were to the priest. It had all happened more than a quarter-century ago when the half-crippled man before him was in the prime of his life. A greedy curiosity took possession of Pavart. He had mounted the stairs to make a request on

12

behalf of his editor cousin, whom he greatly admired; he determined now that the request should be made a demand.

"I should like you to listen to me carefully for a few moments," he said.

The veteran grunted and sat down on the rush-covered chair opposite, reaching for his pipe, a long, old-fashioned clay with a discoloured bowl. Pavart knew him for a heavy smoker.

The priest leaned forward, speaking earnestly.

"The First Empire is already a legend," he began. "It does not matter whether your memories are painful or pleasurable. Nothing can alter the attitude of the average Frenchman today or that of succeeding generations tomorrow, to the man who made that Empire and sustained it for nearly twenty years. People who were in exile like me, or those that were born after he went away, cannot be expected to measure the good or the evil of his influence on our country or on Europe. History a century hence may decide upon that, or again it may never arrive at a conclusion. What is important is that we Frenchmen build up truthful records from the testimony of men such as you. Whether you regard Napoleon as a living force or as a fiend now in his master's keeping is incidental. The fact remains that he and his generation belong to us, to France. New dynasties, new invasions, new theories, cannot influence that fact, much less alter it. It is for men like you to tell us what you yourselves know of those years. History is only important if, by surveying it, we are able to account for the past and shape the future. If you have suffered in the past, as I presume you have, then it is your duty as a Frenchman—"

Father Pavart broke off and coughed, feeling suddenly embarrassed. The man opposite was still looking towards him, but his melancholy eyes were quite vacant. Pavart knew that he was no longer listening to a word of the lecture. His unlighted pipe was still clutched in his sound hand.

The priest stood up and shook out the folds of his cloak. He felt slightly piqued.

"I'll call in again tomorrow," he said, and quietly left the room.

The veteran sat motionless in the uncomfortable chair until the fire had burned down to a dull glow, almost smothered in grey ash. Outside it began to snow again and large flakes cushioned themselves against the window-panes. He got up and stirred the fire, tossing on some more billets and ramming them down with his foot. Then he crossed over to his bed and, stooping, dragged a hair trunk from beneath it; throwing back the battered lid, he groped in the interior for some large clothbound manuscript books that lay submerged among the jumble of creased clothes and papers.

When he had carried the books over to the table and lit his oil lamp, drawing a chair up and leaning forward on his elbows he opened one of the books and flicked the first few pages. On every page there was a crayon sketch, but he did not examine any of them until he came to a page labelled "Lobau, June, 1809." It was a portrait group of six men, three sitting, three standing, against a background of blue sky and light-green foliage. He reached out, pulling the lamp a little nearer and studying the page intently.

He examined each face separately, giving it all his attention for minutes at a time, and then, going back to the right-hand man in the rear file, he began his scrutiny over again. He must have stared at the page for over an hour before he began to work through the book methodically, spending a considerable time on each sketch. The fire had burned down again, but he did not notice the chill that crept over the room or the layer of snow that piled up on the slate sill of the uncurtained window.

The house was very quiet. Madame Friant, the landlady, had been in bed nearly two hours when her lodger's head fell forward on the open sketchbook. The fire went out and the shabby room became as cold as a tomb.

Book One

PART ONE

The Danube

CHAPTER ONE

The night Gabriel's aunt died he went into her little sitting-room behind the shop and ransacked the old lady's escritoire. The drawers were locked and none of the numerous keys she wore round her neck would fit them. So instead all had to be forced with a toasting-fork.

There was no one left in the house after the doctor had gone and so Gabriel was able to take his time. He went through a forty-year accumulation of receipts and statements of accounts before he found the letter; the old lady had placed it at the bottom of a handsome little workbox which, unfortunately, also required the attentions of the toasting-fork.

It seemed to Gabriel that his aunt had wanted to make everything as difficult as possible. There would have been no necessity for a letter at all if she had shown the slightest willingness to answer some very natural questions regarding his birth and parentage, but the old lady's mind had been a little unhinged by the scenes she witnessed during the Terror in Bordeaux and she had been generally recognized in Agen, the town to which she fled, as eccentric, though not sufficiently so to prevent her from building up a flourishing little business as a pastrycook and confectioner.

Gabriel had lived there alone with her ever since he could remember and, as he grew up, he had assisted with the business, the two of them managing to live quite comfortably on the proceeds of a contract with the two local inns and a limited private clientele.

Gabriel was an odd, dreamy young man, who had a local reputation for excessive amiability but seemed to lack ambition. Families in the Agen district, some of whom had sent two and three sons to the wars since the annual levies were accelerated in the first years of the Empire, could never understand how it was that Gabriel never received his papers. At the time of his aunt's death he was thought to be twenty years of age, and all the lads of eighteen had been called. One of them, Alphonse Briand, the shoemaker's son, was already back with an empty right sleeve and a distressing habit of dribbling.

By the winter of 1808–9, with the war in Spain more than a year old, young men were scarce about Agen, and several mothers with marriageable daughters went out of their way to be agreeable to Gabriel when he called with a basket of his aunt's confectionery. Few made any progress, for although Gabriel was polite and even mildly affectionate towards customers, his thoughts, if he had any, were elsewhere, perhaps with his canvas-covered sketchbook and a favourite grassy nook on the river bank where he could watch both the stream and the main road on the long summer evenings.

He was known to read a good deal and had been a promising pupil at the school of the ex-priest Crichot. He and Crichot still remained on terms of pleasant intimacy, and an excellent crayon sketch of the latter, done by Gabriel during school-hours, continued to hang over Crichot's chimney-piece long after Gabriel had been forgotten in the Agen district.

It would not have been difficult for Gabriel to have found a pretty wife without the help of possible mothers-in-law. He had a frank, pleasing face, intelligent and kindly grey eyes, and a mop of unruly dark-brown hair. His complexion was dark, even for a Gascon, and his high cheekbones and vivid colouring gave him something of an alien look. His hands were long and his fingers sensitive, with neat unblunted fingernails. He was of medium build, but his shoulders were broad. Although he looked, and indeed was, in perfect health, he was shy and his reserve communicated itself to his voice, which was soft but pleasantly modulated. His shyness had been accentuated by the circumstances of his life, spent mostly alone with the eccentric old woman who passed him off as her nephew. Nobody in Agen believed in this relationship; some suspected Gabriel of being the old lady's son, fruit of a solitary youthful romance in the mad days of the Revolution. Had the pair been less inoffensive Agen would have pondered the question more intensively. As it was, the two soon merged into the life of the little town and were accepted, principally on account of Gabriel's amiability and the old lady's undeniably expert cooking.

Having forced the workbox, Gabriel broke the seals of the letter and took out several carefully folded sheets. He noticed that his hands were trembling, but a glance at the contents gave him a sense of anticlimax. None of the papers were in his aunt's unformed handwriting. All were covered with the formal, angular hand of Agen's notary, a fat little man who, as Gabriel recalled, had died some years ago. He experienced a momentary disappointment. Without knowing why, he had always imagined that the contents of the letter would belong to the period when Aunt Marie was in full command of her faculties and, therefore, able to set down the facts herself.

The will was there, and Aunt Marie's estate had been valued at just over eight thousand francs. Gabriel was the sole beneficiary. The letter itself was a dry statement of facts compiled by the notary, presumably at Aunt Marie's dictation.

He began to read.

First there was a brief introduction from the notary, informing him that his client, Mademoiselle Cléry, had issued instructions that the facts below were to be committed to paper and given to Gabriel after her death. The notary sounded somewhat apologetic. It was evident that Aunt Marie had given him a good deal of

trouble. The information was set down in paragraph form, the
first being the most important.

Gabriel read:

Item One. Mademoiselle Cléry asks me to inform you that,
in the first instance, you are not her nephew. Your mother's
name was Guillame and, as far as Mademoiselle Cléry is
aware, she came from somewhere in the Bayonne district.
To the best of Mademoiselle Cléry's recollection your father
was called Colonna and he was, for a time immediately preceding your birth, employed as a church decorator at Pauillac, in the Gironde. He was an Italian who had been engaged
by the de Courcey family to carry out certain repairs to a
chapel on the de Courcey estate, where your mother was
then employed as a still-room maid.

At this point in the narrative there was a bracketed comment
by the notary. It read:

(It would appear that Mademoiselle Cléry never met the
party Colonna but only heard of him through your mother.
He died, it seems, by falling from a scaffold inside the
chapel, his death occurring some months before your birth.
I feel it my duty to inform you that Mademoiselle Cléry
appeared to be very confused upon this point.)

Item Two. Mademoiselle Cléry further states that at this
time she was herself employed in the kitchens of the de
Courcey family and that she was present at the time of your
birth. Your mother, the party Guillame, died within three
days of the event and left no estate. Mademoiselle Cléry took
custody of the child and, at a later date, removed herself to
Agen following the flight of the de Courcey family to
England on the outbreak of the Revolution and the arrival
in Bordeaux of the Committee of Public Safety.

Item number two was not entirely news to Gabriel. He had
often heard Aunt Marie chatter, in her absent way, of her flight
from Bordeaux, and to the end of her life the old lady had been

convinced that the minions of Robespierre were still searching for her. Gabriel sometimes suspected that she had actually seen the guillotine at work when the Paris Committee came down to pacify the Gironde.

There were several other items about the business, and these clarified passages in the will.

The document concluded with a further comment from the notary, written, no doubt, to excuse the paucity of information contained in the earlier statement. Underneath Aunt Marie's shaky signature the notary had written:

· I feel it my duty to remind you that the above information cannot be regarded as accurate. You are well aware of Mademoiselle Cléry's incoherency, and it was only with considerable difficulty that I was able to marshal the facts contained herein. I was quite unable to place the date of your birth, but my own opinion is that it took place a year or two before the Disturbances, say in 1787–8.

That was all. Gabriel folded the letter with a feeling of inadequacy. He did not even know his age. His mother had been a still-room maid from the Bayonne district, his father an Italian church decorator who might have been called Colonna. It seemed hardly worth waiting a lifetime to learn these facts. He wondered what would have become of him if Aunt Marie had not been employed in the de Courcey kitchens when the party Guillame presented a dead Italian with a token of her affection.

Gabriel felt that he needed advice, and the only place he could seek it was at the house of the ex-priest Crichot, his schoolmaster. He put the letter in his pocket, locked the bakery door and went out.

He found Crichot just sitting down to his supper. The old man was known as a republican who held the Empire and all its glitter in emphatic contempt. He was a man of violent theories but gentle disposition. He took great pains with promising scholars, and Gabriel had always been one of his favourites.

Crichot knew all about Aunt Marie's letter. He read the statement through twice without interrupting his meal while Gabriel watched him nervously.

Finally Crichot pushed both letter and plate aside and began to pick his teeth with an ivory toothpick.

"Well," he observed at last, "and what are you going to do now?"

Gabriel said that he had no clear idea; continue the confectionery business, perhaps.

"Can you make cakes?"

Gabriel admitted that he could not. Aunt Marie had always been elaborately secretive about her recipes.

Crichot mused awhile. Presently he said:

"It's an odd thing, Gabriel. I've seen the ceiling paintings of the de Courcey chapel in Pauillac. If they were done by your father he was a man of considerable talent."

Gabriel observed that this was gratifying but thought it was more likely that Colonna had only been called in to restore existing work.

Crichot glanced at the sketch over the mantelshelf and then at Gabriel.

"Do you want to become a painter?" he asked.

As Chichot said this the younger man experienced an odd sensation. Until that moment he had always regarded painting and sketching as a pleasant pastime. It had never assumed much importance in his life but was merely a way of spending odd leisure hours when his duties as baker's roundsman were over for the day. But when the schoolmaster asked the question Gabriel was immediately conscious of an overwhelming desire to move away from Agen, to cross Europe, to cross the seas, to deepen an experience that suddenly seemed to him ridiculously shallow. He could not say why this was so. His entire outlook seemed to have been transformed in a matter of seconds. Before he could sort out his thoughts and answer the old man's question, the ex-priest asked him another which came as an even greater shock.

"Has it occurred to you why you have never been conscripted into the army, Gabriel?"

Strangely enough, his escape had never puzzled him. It occurred to him now that he might have been overlooked on account of the fact that his birth was not officially recorded. He mentioned this to Crichot, but the schoolmaster shook his head.

"That might have answered for a year or so, but you must be more than twenty and the levies are already two years ahead of the legal periods. Your aunt must have bought you off."

"Is that possible?"

"Perfectly possible. I don't know what it costs. The sum probably depends on the state of the local mayor's finances. There was a scandal about it over in Toulouse a year ago, but it still goes on. I daresay the State winks at it—a few hundred francs are worth more than a sickly boy here and there. Why don't you go and talk to old Latrec, the Mayor? He's always in debt with that huge family of his. It wouldn't surprise me if he hadn't made the first approaches to your aunt. I wonder how much you cost her."

A vivid memory flashed through Gabriel's brain. He had been sitting in his riverside nook one golden evening the previous summer, when his ear had caught the creak of wagon wheels coming up the main road from the frontier. He had scrambled up the high bank and stood there for an hour or more, watching a convoy of wounded toil into the town ahead trailing its rolling clouds of dust. The wagons were packed tight with pallid, silent men, men with their uniforms in tatters and filthy bandages showing through their rags. There seemed to be no end of them, and after a while Gabriel had begun to sketch the tail of the dismal procession. The carts and their contents had provoked no pity in him, only a determination to capture the sharp angles of the bones that jutted from the heaving flanks of the half-starved mules, and the almost comic helplessness of a soldier's arm lolling from the tailboard of the last ambulance. He had remained there until the light faded, and the result had been the best water-colour he had ever done. It possessed some indefinable quality, the lack of which made all his other work flat and unsatisfying. He had shown the sketch to no one, not even to Crichot.

23

"Father," he said at last, "would you say that I was a good painter?"

"I would say that you could become one," replied Crichot, glancing once more at his own portrait above the chimney-piece.

"What is required to improve myself? Practice?"

"Practice, yes," said the old man, "but suffering too. Suffering is more important than practice."

The young man smiled.

"Then I will go!" he announced, rising.

"Go where? To sea, to the Americas, to the Orient to beg your bread?"

"To fight for it," said Gabriel.

Crichot stared at him for a long minute through half-closed eyes.

"As a young fool with an untrained paint-brush, you might do a good deal worse," he said.

To volunteer for service with the Grand Army when he might have purchased at least another year's respite was certainly a mistake on the part of Gabriel Cléry-Guillame-Colonna, judging by the standards of his day and those of his neighbours. But this action had a certain amount of personal justification. However shy and reserved a young man might be, he needed the companionship of other young men; and, if the Emperor's wars continued, as there seemed every likelihood of their doing, it would not be long before he was the only young man in the district apart from the cripples and idiots.

To gain the companionship of men his own age it was inevitable that he should be drawn to the army wherein all the young men of Europe were gathered at that time. Furthermore, if Gabriel was anxious to travel, he would have found it difficult and dangerous to do so as a civilian on a capital of a few thousand francs. It is doubtful whether he would have got out of the department without an inspection of papers leading to some form of detention or of observation by a horde of officials, beginning with Fouché's police agents and ending with agricultural inspectors. The seas were closed by the British blockade, and his land progress east, west, south or north would soon have been checked by war. Even if his papers had been in order, as they must have been to enable him to cross any frontier at all, the appearance of an able-bodied young Frenchman without some sort of uniform would automatically have been questioned. Sooner or later Gabriel might have found himself charged with desertion and sent to drag a shot with the galley-slaves at Brest or Toulon.

In such circumstances Gabriel's act of volunteering cannot be set down as an error. His actions, however, both immediately before and after presenting himself at the Bordeaux depot, were certainly errors. In the first place, he paid his fare by stagecoach into the city, when he might have travelled free on the carrier's cart and arrived almost as soon. In addition, on being questioned by the recruiting sergeant, he admitted to some previous experience with firearms, the old dragoon, Marcel, having taken him shooting in the woods almost every fine Sunday since he was old enough to carry a fowling-piece. The sergeant soon put him to the test and he scored eight hits out of ten at the first practice. Henceforward Gabriel was carefully segregated from the other conscripts (there were no other volunteers) and, after the briefest of training periods, was sent overland to join a company of *voltigeurs*, sharpshooters attached to the Eighty-seventh Regiment of the line, then on active service south of Vienna. His arrival was timely. The Eighty-seventh was just going into action.

The greater part of Europe was going into action. Some thought it the climax of the post-Revolutionary wars that had been surging up and down the Continent, and the seas enclosing it, since that far-off July afternoon when a Paris mob stormed the Bastille. Those who did think so were poor prophets. The climax was still more than six years distant.

The Spanish Peninsula was aflame; English and Portuguese, indifferently assisted by Spanish levies, were battling with the French in half a dozen provinces. Farther east, Austria was making an unexpected bid for freedom and the Grand Army was pouring down the Danube Valley, its chief seeking a major action and a Habsburg bride. Russia was quiet for a while, licking the wounds of Austerlitz, Eylau and Friedland. Prussia was sullen after the debacle of Jena. Britain, her fleet blockading the coastline of Europe, was about to engage in another of her futile sallies on the Low Countries. The mountaineers of the Austrian Tyrol were engaged in an equally futile attempt to worst Napoleon.

The great and the defeated stood by watching, watching Spain and the Danube, hoping that the roar of battle would not end once again in a fanfare of Imperial victory trumpets and the boom of triumphant salvoes from the Paris depots. For seventeen years the fanfares and the salvoes had been the final notes of every attempt on the part of Napoleon's neighbours to arrest an annual extension of the French Empire.

Over in London the exiled Bourbons waited, and in Berlin the Prussian King waited. In St. Petersburg the Czar toyed with the idea of dividing Europe with an ex-artillery officer.

In the third week of May, 1809, the Grand Army was enjoying one of the last of its victorious sweeps across hostile territory, driving all before it in the fashion of earlier and happier campaigns.

Austria, beaten more than a dozen times since her first invasion of French territory during the Revolutionary Wars, had made another attempt to throw off the shackles. The attempt failed, but only just. On the evening that Gabriel combed the bivouacs in search of his regiment, six corps of the Grand Army were spread out along the right bank of the Danube, facing a concentration of Austrian troops, under the Archduke Charles, on the opposite bank. An attempt had already been made to cross the swollen river, and a bridge of boats had been constructed connecting the right bank with the large island of Lobau, the shores of which reached to within eighty yards of the enemy's bank. A second bridge over this narrow but turbulent neck of the stream was in the process of construction.

At advanced posts in the island were sections of two corps, troops of Marshal Lannes, the ex–dyer's apprentice of whom every Gascon lad had heard so much (he came from Lectourne, the nearest town to Agen), and the corps of one-eyed Massena, whose exploits were almost as colourful as those of Lannes and whose ability in the field was second only to that of the Emperor himself. The cavalry of the Guard was there, too, under Marshal Bessières, and the three marshals had already pushed detachments into the villages of Aspern and Essling, which were just visible where the Austrian bank met the edge of the plain.

It seemed to Gabriel, trudging across the crowded bridge to the island, that the entire male population of the world had been concentrated in this curve of the river. He would have liked to admire the scenery, which was refreshingly cool after his interminable journey across France and Germany. The evening sun was setting behind the woods of the opposite bank. The Danube, brown with flood water, seemed immense after the little Dordogne near his home. The early summer air was soft, and the thick foliage of the island was the greenest he had ever seen.

There was little leisure to enjoy the scene. In the first place, he was hard tasked to keep a footing on the bridge. Cavalry, infantry, artillery and baggage trains seemed united in a conspiracy to pitch him into the Danube. In his efforts to cling to the narrow causeway, he forgot his two overpowering preoccupations, lacerated feet and gnawing hunger. His last meal had been breakfast, thin soup and biscuit, issued at an artillery park four leagues from the bridgehead. His feet, after thirty-two days' marching, were still unhardened and felt almost liquid in their untallowed boots. His shoulders had ceased to ache under the weight of his knapsack and musket, but his cotton underclothes were clammy with perspiration, and the rim of his shako pressed like an iron clamp on his brow.

At last he got through the press at the end of the island and asked, for the hundredth time that day, for directions.

A sergeant of the Flying Artillery pointed towards the woods, where the undergrowth beside the track was beaten flat and the air was heavy with the scent of wild flowers, crushed under the wheels of ammunition caissons.

"The Eighty-seventh? They're in the forest somewhere. They came over before noon. They might be in action now; try the glades," and he nodded towards a wood on the right of the main track, where bivouac fires were already winking brightly and ribbons of blue wood smoke crept from beneath the low branches of the trees.

The glades were packed with armed men. Gabriel found there a riot of colour, the firelight sparkling on the brass casques of the dragoons and the gleaming silver of the cuirassiers as they lolled at ease beside their huge black horses. Blue and white of the grenadiers of the Guard, canary yellow of the Mounted Gendarmerie, green of the lancers, silver-grey of the hussars, a jostling, shouting, singing, sunburned multitude, some eating, some sleeping, a few cleaning their weapons for tomorrow's engagement, and over all such an air of exultant confidence that a man might have staked every franc he possessed on the issue of Napoleon's next hundred battles.

Along the line of bivouacs he wandered, peering at the numerals on the shako of every infantryman he encountered. Up and down, with the maddening smell of soup-kettles in his nostrils, directed here, redirected there, until his blistered feet seemed to have trudged over every inch of that teeming triangle of land. Dazzled by the setting of the sun and the glare of a thousand camp-fires, he felt himself growing light-headed and paused to lean heavily against the trunk of a great beech whose roots spread almost to the water's edge on the eastern bank.

A camp-fire, its jets of flame spurting horizontally under a large pile of freshly gathered brushwood, threw a flickering light round the roots of the tree. Sprawled on the margin of the blaze, wrapped in greatcoats and pillowed on knapsacks, were five young men, all sound asleep. He could hear their regular breathing above the regular clump-clump of the engineers' sledgehammers farther down the bank, and the ceaseless murmur of sound that rose from the green arcades stretching away to the main bridgehead. Between the two men nearest to him was a dog, a long-muzzled, grey-brown brute, with absurdly small ears that stuck from its head like two little tents. The dog also was asleep, its lean jaws resting affectionately across the calf of a sleeping man.

Gabriel saw all this and then looked beyond the men and the dog to a spit, made of two forked uprights and a bayonet for crosspiece. Turning slowly on a short length of chain attached to the bayonet was a large camp kettle, and as a spurt of flame shot up to its rim Gabriel saw the contents bubble and froth, as though stirred by an invisible hand from beneath the surface of the thickening stew.

He stood there a moment longer, crouched in the shadow of the tree bole. He saw a fresh series of bubbles form and burst round the edge of the cauldron. Then a soft whiff of the evening breeze blew in his direction and he hesitated no longer. Groping softly for his tin pannikin, he dropped to his knees and crawled towards the fire, moving an inch at a time, his pannikin barely raised above the ground.

He reached the circle of the fire, paused a few seconds, and then reached forward and upward, turning his back on the dog.

There was a snarl, a yelp and the crash of feet in the under-growth behind the tree. Gabriel pitched face foremost into the fire, his clawing hands almost upsetting the kettle as the dog buried its teeth in his shoulder. In the first moment of pain and terror, as the red-hot embers burned into the palms of his hands, and the dog's jaws tore at his thick epaulette, Gabriel was con-scious of a harsh, high-pitched voice shouting, "Off, Fouché, off, you brute!" and felt himself seized, thrust sideways and rolled beyond the fire, to be pinned down by half a dozen arms, one of which lay firmly across his throat, almost preventing him from breathing.

Every sleeper was sitting upright, and in the centre of the firelight stood a tall, thin sergeant, holding the yapping mongrel by its collar. The animal's strangled yelps seemed to melt into the background of sound that rose from the glade. Above the tree tops the moon sailed out, flooding the bivouac with dappled silver.

Gabriel glanced round at the ring of faces. They were fierce and challenging. Only the sergeant who was holding the dog seemed impassive. Gabriel noted, almost unconsciously, that the numerals on his shako were "87" and thought: "Here, then, are my comrades, the men I have marched two hundred leagues to join. Any one of them would slit my throat for a pannikin of dirty stew," and he struggled, pettishly, as a child might writhe in the grip of a brawny nurse and with as little result, for the arm only tightened its hold.

The sergeant released the dog, which slunk off into the shadows and continued to growl like a young wolf deprived of its prey. Then, sitting down on a log, he motioned to the men holding the thief.

"Let him go, it's only a conscript!"

The men released their holds and wriggled nearer to the fire, but none of them took their eyes off Gabriel, who sat back and sulkily sucked his burns.

"The dog's earned his supper," said a plump, red-faced young man with greasy black hair. "I told you he was worth taking along. Good boy, Fouché!" He foraged around for his pannikin and began to dip it into the cauldron, an example soon followed by the other four men, who, once the meal had begun, minded Gabriel no more than if he had been a field-mouse crouched at the roots of the beech.

The sergeant did not eat. He sat worrying his long stringy moustache and screwing up his nose, as though engaged in solving a mental problem of some complexity.

At length he came to a decision. Opening his knapsack, of rather more than regulation size, he took out a loaf, a clasp-knife and a small, battered tin bowl.

"Come over here, conscript," he said, while all the men stopped eating and looked at the sergeant with incredulous expressions.

Gabriel rose stiffly to his feet and warily circled the fire.

"When did you eat last?" asked the sergeant, beginning to carve the loaf into equal portions, some of which he tossed across the flames to the men.

Gabriel told him that he had not eaten since early that morning.

"Have you got any salt? You should have, you were issued salt at the depot."

Gabriel produced an oblong block of salt that had indeed, much to his mystification, been issued as part of his marching kit. He had not found occasion to use it and had wondered how he would do so, since it was as hard as stone.

The sergeant took the salt and bent over the stew, rubbing the block vigorously against the rounded edge of the bayonet.

"That will pay for your supper," he said. "Another time offer to trade. A conscript should always have something to trade with. Don't steal from your comrades. I've seen a man's ears cut off for less!"

He filled Gabriel's pannikin and tossed him a large crust. The stew was highly flavoured with garlic and seemed to have more solidity than most of those at which Gabriel had sniffed earlier in the evening. There was a jointed rabbit in it and the sergeant fished about until he found a piece of the meat, which he splashed into the recruit's pan. The bread was sour but fairly fresh. Gabriel ate slowly, trying to make it last. He never recalled a meal that was half as satisfying.

When the soup bowls had been scraped clean with tufts of wiry grass and the dog was crunching what was left of the bones beside the empty kettle, one of the men unstrapped a small fiddle from his knapsack and drew a three-inch bow from a waterproof covering made of untanned skin. While the other four and the sergeant lit their short pipes the fiddler, whom they addressed as Dominique, began to play.

It was a tune that Gabriel had never heard before. A wild, frolicsome air that might have accompanied the clash of a gipsy's tambourine. Sitting back against the tree, he cast a glance at the player. Dominique was scarcely his own age and had a heavy mop of blond hair. His mouth was loose and his eyes were dreamy and vacant. He seemed to enjoy his music, and his feet, which were stretched toward the recruit, twitched to the rhythm as though at any instant the man would leap up and begin to dance.

A delicious drowsiness stole over Gabriel, and with it came an odd sense of well-being and fulfilment. It seemed to him in some unfathomable way that the last hour had seen the transformation of his life completed, that he had marched all those leagues solely to take his place with these six men round a spluttering wood fire on an island in the middle of the Danube. He glanced again at the circle, at the vacant blue eyes of the shock-headed fiddler, at the chubby cheeks of the man who had praised the dog, at the meditative, unblinking stares of the others and, finally, at the hawklike profile of the sergeant, silhouetted against the glow of the next section's fire, his pipe jutting from the apex of his drooping moustache, his lean, sunburned cheeks puffing in and out at long regular intervals.

That was how Gabriel found the six men and added a seventh to their number. The section's corporal had been killed at Ratisbon a week or two before and they were to need him badly in the next two days, when the Grand Army received its first major check in the blazing villages on the plain across the river. That was when Gabriel discovered his principal error. A voltigeur is always stationed nearest to the enemy, just to make certain, for the benefit of the line regiments behind, that the enemy is still there. A voltigeur proves it by getting shot at.

CHAPTER TWO

Marching across the flimsy bridge at the head of his file of voltigeurs to take up positions in the granary of Essling, Sergeant Jean Ticquet experienced a qualm of misgiving. He had not served in fifteen campaigns and as many major engagements without learning how to draw conclusions from the close observation of facts. He had been uneasy all right, and this morning he found himself unable to share the exuberance of his little flock. If that young Jewish mountebank who called himself Emmanuel Jacobsen, for instance, had seen as many men blown to pieces as Sergeant Ticquet had, he would not, at this moment, be amusing the rest of the file by using his musket and bayonet as a drum-major's staff. Neither would the latest recruit, Gabriel Guillame, who had tried to steal soup the previous evening, be looking as though he were about to play a minor rôle in a May-time flower festival.

The dog Fouché also followed them into battle. Ticquet would have credited the mongrel with more sense.

The sergeant was old and wise in the ways of war, but his age and his wisdom had not endeared to him the whistle of approaching roundshot, it had merely trained his ear to the point of knowing when and when not to grovel in the nearest ditch. He was considered by his officers a brave and steady soldier, but Jean was well aware of the fact that there were many occasions, particularly of late, when he was neither brave nor steady, merely observant and extraordinarily lucky; so lucky that he had begun to wonder how much longer his luck would hold out against the determined efforts of the thousands of men who had had designs on his life during all these years. For Jean, now approaching fifty, had been fighting since he was twelve years of age. He was conscious that he had had an exceptionally long run for his loot.

He was a narrow-faced man, partially bald where his heavy shako had pressed for so long. His frame, above medium height, was painfully thin, so that his blue-and-white uniform hung on him loosely and looked as if the tailor had never intended it to fit. His height and thinness gave him a slight stoop, and without the artificial bolstering of red woollen epaulettes his shoulders looked rounded to the point of deformity. For all his emaciated body, however, he was as tough as a harness strap and as active as a mountain squirrel. Under fire he appeared to fold himself up like a clasp-knife and dart here and there with incredible swiftness. He had remarkably keen sight and could pick off a sentry at extreme musket range, aiming at the head and sending a long, drooping shot into the stomach or loins. He could march and fight on the barest subsistence allowance, and if the commissariat wagons were far behind, as they usually were when they existed otherwise than on muster rolls, he could often find a meal for himself and his file from a ruined cottage garden twice ransacked by the Guard. He seemed able to smell out water and vegetables. Marching along a highroad miles from any sign of habitation, he would suddenly disappear, picking up the line of march a league farther on with a haversack full of turnips or fruit. What was left of the file, after two campaigns in Spain and the present fighting on the Danube, worshipped him, as well they might. There was not one whose life he had not directly or indirectly saved during the last eighteen months.

34

He had learned the art of warfare in the hardest school in the world, the Republican armies of '92 and '93. He had fought under Marceau in La Vendée as private second class, and under Bonaparte in Italy as private first class. He had been a corporal in Egypt and was one of those reputed to have made a good haul by fishing for dead Mamelukes in the Nile. If he had indeed been lucky enough to hook a jingling body-belt, he must have abandoned the gold as unnecessary baggage in the march back across the Sinai Desert, for he went through the Marengo campaign in debt, although he subsequently sent some pickings to the widow and children of an old comrade sabred by the Russian Imperial Guard on the Pratzen Heights of Austerlitz. He was like that about money. If there was loot to be found he found it, but he never let it accumulate in banks like his miserly old chief, Massena. If it came to choosing between carrying a piece of church plate or a piece of cooked horseflesh, Jean threw away the plate. He had once existed for more than a week on a piece of horseflesh, but no one ever made a meal out of an ecclesiastical vessel.

He was a grim, solemn, practical man, not over-talkative, but friendly enough when his stomach was full and he could suck his pipe over the fire or watch the Jew, Emmanuel, dancing an eccentric, acrobatic measure to the scrape of young Dominique's fiddle. He was often over-indulgent with his charges, treating them with the heavy playfulness of a busy father who watches his family's games and listens to its prattle while pondering weightier matters of commerce and finance. He had never married, and he never even spoke to a woman unless it was Old Carla, the shapeless cantinière of the company. The two of them were cronies, having served together in all parts of Europe, and Jean had a real affection for the foul-mouthed old woman who had married, canteen fashion, at least three husbands from among his former comrades and was always plaguing Jean, in a half-humorous way, to become her fourth.

Jean's eyes were restless during the march from the bivouac to the tileworks. There was not a gun or a regimental disc that he missed, and he paid particular attention to the haphazard structure of the floating bridge stretching from the bank to the island. It looked to him, an expert layman in bridge-building, far too light a contrivance to provide the only thread between the main battle and the reinforcements. He said as much to Nicholas, the big man at his side.

Nicholas had been acting corporal since the idiot Raoul had got himself killed at Ratisbon the month before. Jean sucked his moustache in vexation at the thought of their latest casualty. Get killed, yes, in the line of ordinary duty, but why run across open ground holding the end of a scaling-ladder? Carrying scaling-ladders was not the business of a voltigeur. His work was to keep enemy heads down whilst the grenadiers planted the ladders. If Marshal Lannes had not been so stupid as to take hold of the ladder himself Corporal Raoul would never have laid hand on a rung and thereby left his head in the rampart ditch. Jean had seen too many men exchange their lives for a moment's glory. He was not that type of soldier. He believed in living as long as one could. God alone knew the chances of ultimate survival were sufficiently remote, without sticking one's head over the redoubt and drawing fire.

Nicholas laughed at the sergeant's misgivings.

"They'll have another bridge across here in a matter of hours," he said. "Besides, there's a dozen boats paddling upstream to gather in anything that's likely to pile up on the causeway."

Jean grunted and looked towards the boats, noting that they were manned by sailors. What in God's name was the Grand Army coming to that it should need naval men in the field? Was the Emperor losing his grip? Were the old days of infallible victory receding? If so, it was because men like himself were becoming used up. Hardly anyone serving in the company today had fought in Egypt; scarcely more than a dozen had been present at Jena or Eylau, if one discounted the officers. Where were they all, those jolly companions of a dozen years ago? Dead, most of them, buried along the banks of Italian rivers or under the rubble at Genoa and Saragossa. Dead of plague on the Jaffa road, or of cold and hunger in the Spanish mountains; and in their place were mere children like this new recruit, Guillame, boys who had never heard a shot fired save at a brace of pigeons and did not know the difference between the whistle of chain-shot and the whine of grape.

Yet, as he was bound to admit, most of them learned the trade soon enough. This latest batch, for instance, stood fire like veterans if you found them sufficient cover and prevented them from taking silly risks. This fellow Nicholas was reliable, too, although how it came about that a man of his education, who had taught school at home in Toulouse, was serving as a private at the age of twenty-eight was a mystery which Jean had never been able to solve. Some scrape or other with a woman behind it, he'd wager. Much good education did for a man! He had never learned to read or to write, but had never felt the lack of these accomplishments. He could have become an officer without them in the old, carefree days but had preferred to remain as he was. Half a dozen men to watch over was more than enough; what sort of fool was a man who wanted thirty?

Jean, by nature, a confirmed pessimist, always hoped that things would not turn out quite as badly as he expected. He switched his thoughts again to the campaign.

Over on the far side of the plain, and already shooting off at them from a village to the south, were a hundred thousand Habsburg mice. No Frenchman troubled himself about Austrian battalions. Still, there were a hundred thousand of them and, at a rough guess, two hundred and fifty guns. Against what? Less than two corps, he would say; not more than thirty thousand men. And all reinforcements and ammunition had to come over that single plank of a bridge!

He looked up as a group of horsemen cantered past the column. At sight of one of them his brown face brightened, and immediately he found himself taking a less gloomy view of the situation. There went Jean Lannes, once a sergeant in the Volunteers of Gers when he and Jean Ticquet had fought side by side in the eastern Pyrenees. Now the ex-sergeant was a marshal, with God knows how many titles and revenues allotted to him. Wealth and fame had not spoiled him, as most were spoiled. He still knew how to fight with the bayonet and still had wave and greeting for an old comrade. Ticquet carelessly answered the wave of the marshal's hand, catching, as he did so, a look of mute astonishment on the face of the new recruit, Guillame. What did the young idiot suppose? That a sergeant couldn't wave at a marshal?

The marshal reined in and leaned over his saddle-bow.

"Ha, there, you old scarecrow!" he shouted. "I didn't see you at Ratisbon."

"I was there," grunted Jean, "and saw you get my corporal killed with your damn fool monkey tricks! Why don't you leave such japes to the Emperor's brother-in-law!"

Lannes threw back his head and roared with laughter, and several of the older men in the staff group shared the joke. Everyone in the army knew the extravagant antics of Marshal Murat, King of Naples and husband of Napoleon's sister, who pranced about in front of the enemy waving a gold-tipped staff and issuing challenges to single combat. Everyone laughed, somewhat contemptuously perhaps, but they were glad enough when Murat's squadrons went thundering against enemy cavalry, scattering them like feathers in a gale. Moreover, the rainbow-hued cavalry leader was always a yard or two in front of the foremost trooper, and to the men of the Grand Army that meant more than a dozen Neapolitan crowns and their attendant revenues.

Jean Ticquet felt much better after the marshal had gone by, and shepherded his file into the yard of the granary at the extreme end of the village. In less than half an hour the place had been loopholed for musketry, not only on the south side, as Nicholas had advised (apart from fighting, he had an intense dislike of all forms of manual labour), but on every side, for Jean prophesied that their infantry would be driven from the main street during the course of the day and if this happened they could easily maintain themselves in the building. The stone granary was being properly garrisoned.

Jean's instincts were right, but all that morning it looked as if his gloomy prophecies would be borne away on the wings of victory.

From his loophole on the top floor of the tall building Gabriel stood with Manny, the jovial young Jew, and watched the progress of the battle without firing more than a few scattered shots. Roundshot smashed against the outer wall, but the range was too long to allow the balls to penetrate, most of the shots ricocheting from the edge of the yard below and flattening themselves on the second impact.

Over at Aspern, where the church tower was visible through the trees, all hell had broken loose as columns of Hungarian grenadiers and Croats flung themselves against the fortified houses of the village. Five times Massena's troops drove them back with appalling losses. At the sixth attack the voltigeurs, watching from Essling, saw bursts of smoke moving rapidly towards the river and noted the sergeant's frown.

"I hope they've got replacements down there at the bridgehead," he growled. "Watch out; here comes our turn!"

The Austrian batteries had been moved farther in, and a heavy salvo of eighteen-pounders thundered down on the wall by which they stood. One ball crashed through the roof and hurled a man across the dusty floor, flinging him, in shapeless huddle, on a pile of chaff in the corner.

"There goes Tinville," said the Jew, coolly aiming his musket at a blur of white figures moving towards them across the plain. "He owed me six francs. I must look for it when there's a lull."

Firing from behind loopholed masonry, it was easy enough to repulse the first suicidal attempt to drive them from their positions. Despite the increasing power of the enemy artillery, Boudet's infantry, which had held Essling most of the day, threw back the second, third and fourth attempts on the village, but soon after midday French ammunition began to give out, and Nicholas, who had been sent back to the river with Claude, one of the other youngsters in Jean's file, returned empty-handed. Nicholas climbed the wooden ladder to their loft and flung himself down with a curse.

"You were right, Jean," he admitted, "the bridge has caved in; there's a fifty-yard gap and not a ball cartridge to be had at the bridgehead. They're bringing it over by boats."

Jean shrugged and nodded towards the inert heap in the corner.

"Look for your six francs, Manny, and don't forget his cartridge belt."

The Jew crossed the loft and began to rummage, returning a few minutes later with reeking hands, a dozen rounds of ammunition and a cheap metal watch and chain. "He'd have liked me to have it," he said, pocketing the watch and throwing the cartridges into the common pool.

The sun beat through the jagged hole in the roof. Trickles of dislodged plaster cascaded down the cracked walls. They shot off the last of their ammunition, but it was insufficient to stem the flood of white-coated Croats who swept on past the granary and into the main street, which began spewing French infantry of the line, all, seemingly, without ammunition.

"Out! Out and cut them to pieces!" roared Jean. Gabriel now saw a far different man from the meditative pipe-smoker of the bivouac. His prominent cheekbones were flushed and his eyes were set in a fierce, pitiless stare. His voice, always high-pitched, rose to a shriek under the stimulus of wild excitement.

They followed one another down the ladder, across the mid-loft and down a second flight, falling over one another in crazy rivalry to be first in the open. Attacked from each side and meeting with a stiffening resistance lower down the street, the Croats began to give way. Gabriel never got within striking distance of them. Thrust aside on the first floor, he was last out of the building, and when he emerged into the street it was only to see Claude, the good-looking boy of their section, plunging his bayonet in and out of a prostrate body lying across the pump, killing it a dozen times over and laughing into the bloodied stone basin, his face distorted with savage delight. Gabriel, the painter, noted these things, but it was not until long afterwards that he pondered them and by that time he knew more about Claude's tragi-comic hatred of all Austrians.

On the outskirts of the village Jean and a few other veterans were working like madmen to prevent the inexperienced infantry from pursuing the Croats back to their lines. Their efforts were only partially successful.

Before the French could rally into groups Uhlan cavalry had ridden up to their infantry's assistance, and Gabriel, watching the sabres rise and fall with practised rhythm, saw men, a moment since drunk with victory, run here and there like terrified hens, throwing down their muskets and trying in vain to shield their heads with their arms. Infected by their panic, he doubled back to one of the cottages, ran up the short ladder and into a room at the back. Panting and terrified at finding himself alone, he flopped down on the floor and listened to the thumping of his heart.

He must have been there the best part of an hour. No French came back into the house. Once, when he peered cautiously over the low window-sill, he saw the street full of Austrian cavalry, picking their way over the dead and behaving as though the battle was won.

Over at Aspern he could hear the roar of guns and guessed that the village was being retaken. Once, when he heard the tread of feet in the room below and the jabber of a foreign tongue, he nearly fainted from fear of being discovered alone, armed and unwounded. He would have surrendered had he dared descend the ladder, but he knew that to show himself in the street would mean instant death. Jean had informed him that men seldom took prisoners in street fighting; it was too inconvenient.

So he lay there on the bare wooden floor, not daring to move. His eyes roved over the shabby little room and his mind dwelt for a moment on its contents and the family whose home it had been, perhaps less than a week ago. There was a big double bed, a broken cane-bottomed chair, a peasant woman's cotton dress and straw bonnet and a home-made crucifix over the window. The furniture was pathetically awry. The black and gnarled beam across the ceiling led him to think that the cottage was old, probably the home of generations of men and women who had stayed at home and tilled the fields and never wished their neighbours anything but good harvests and fruitful marriages.

The bed fascinated him. He shut his mind to the horror of the street below and tried to think of all that the heavy, canopied couch had meant in the lives of the people who had lived in this house. It was a plain, solid piece of furniture, hand-made by a craftsman who did not believe in frills and fancies. Gabriel pondered on its functions, sleep, love, childbirth and death. How many times had it been a marriage-bed? How many times a death-bed? Who had sewn the gaudy patchwork quilt that looked so incongruous on its plain, unpolished surface? Where had the mattress gone, if there had been a mattress? Probably at this moment it was stuffed into one of the lower windows to serve as a barricade.

There was a slight scraping on the ladder in the room below. Someone was ascending, a man alone, moving with caution.

A dozen plans raced through Gabriel's brain: to flatten himself against the wall behind the trapdoor and brain the man as his head rose above the level of the floor, to surrender on a pledge of clemency, to scramble through the tiny window into the yard, to pretend to be dead or badly wounded—that was best, to sprawl on the floor, stop breathing and lie perfectly still until the Austrian had glanced round the room and made certain that there was nothing worth the trouble of carrying away.

He lay on his face and then, realizing that this would expose his back to the man's weapons, rolled onto his side, twisting his legs and arms in a grotesque pose and half-closing his eyes.

A shako appeared from below, followed by the head and shoulders of a bearded man of about Jean's age and with Jean's hardbitten features, but with a much heavier growth of hair on his face. He had small, piglike eyes, inflamed with powder and lack of sleep. There was a vivid white scar running slantwise across his forehead, the slash of a sabre in some half-forgotten battle of the past. A veteran, this one, a man as old and cunning in war as the sergeant who had befriended him by the camp-fire the night before.

Gabriel lay still and let his jaw sag, fixing the man with the glassy stare of the dying.

The Austrian paused, as though mildly surprised at finding a Frenchman in the room. Then, reassured by Gabriel's empty, loosely clenched hands, he mounted the remaining rungs of the ladder and stepped into the room. He crossed the floor, muttering something to himself, and immediately dropped on his knees and began rummaging in the recruit's tunic, running expert hands through his pockets and strewing Gabriel's few personal belongings on the floor.

Gabriel wondered if the man was really taken in or if he assumed that the prostrate Frenchman was merely wounded and helpless. The effort of holding his breath made his ears sing and his eyes fill with moisture. The man seemed to be an age rummaging down his left side.

The Austrian knew his business. He wasted little time on pockets but was rapidly thumbing the lining of the Frenchman's waistcoat. Almost immediately he grunted, having felt the out-line of the ten gold pieces that Gabriel had sewn into the lining. The looter sat back on his heels and whipped out his sabre, applying the point to the seam of Gabriel's waistcoat and ripping it up in a single movement. The touch of the gold seemed to excite him. Gabriel felt his breath on his cheek. He began to squeeze the coins through the tear in the cloth.

Gabriel could not have said what it was that suddenly stirred his indignation to the point of submerging his fear. It might have been the fellow's roughness as he tumbled the unresisting French-man this way and that in an endeavour to extract the money as quickly as possible, or it might have been Gabriel's sudden appre-ciation of an opportunity which would last no more than a few seconds.

The grenadier's chin was within an inch or two of Gabriel's

shoulder and was turned conveniently sideways, presenting an ideal target. Gabriel did not pause to think out his action. Had he done so he might have reflected that the Austrian would probably stab or shoot him the moment he ceased to be preoccupied with the gold.

The recruit merely obeyed an impulse. Hoisting himself to a sitting position, he swung his fist and struck the man on the side of the head with all the force he could muster. The Austrian rolled sideways across Gabriel's knees, overbalanced and partially stunned by the unexpectedness of the blow.

Gabriel knew then that he must kill this man, kill him within a few seconds or be killed there and then, struck through and through with the man's sabre, left to rot in this dismal little room perhaps for days, until burial parties came to toss him into the street and drag him off to share a pit with all those other mutilated corpses in the sun-drenched street outside.

A mad rage overwhelmed his fear. It was like a barrel clapped on a candle flame. He whipped his musket from the bed, where he had flung it in the first moment of panic on entering the room, stood over the man on the floor and drove the stock hard into the face, striking again and again and uttering sharp animal noises with every blow.

The man's face seemed to sink under a red torrent. His legs contracted feebly and automatically, as in helpless protest. Gabriel remembered the same thing happening to a clumsily butchered calf in the slaughterhouse at Agen, when he had called in one morning with some of Aunt Marie's cakes. He re-called the calf's mild eyes rolling up at the slaughterman, making the same unspoken plea as this man's legs. When all movement ceased Gabriel let fall his musket and sat on the bed, his hands upon his knees. He watched a dark pool of the man's blood crawl like a blind-eyed reptile into the dust-choked cracks of the plank floor. He was quite unconscious of the renewed up-roar in the street, of shots, screams, shouts and the confused clatter of iron hooves on the cobbles. He sat there a long time, stupefied and speechless, his gaze riveted to the spreading pool but somehow remote from the huddle of limbs at his feet.

He was roused from his stupor by the movement of a wood louse which crawled out from the skirting-board and commenced a purposeful journey across the floor. Gabriel wondered what the insect would do when it reached the pool, whether it would turn back or make a detour round the edge of the trap to reach its destination. It did neither. It stopped on the brink, then gingerly edged forward until all its legs were engulfed in the flood. Then it stopped again, its feelers weaving, the amber glitter of its back fixed in a sunbeam. It seemed to Gabriel to be drinking.

The thought struck him like a blow on the head. With a shriek he leaped to his feet, seized his musket and scrambled through the trapdoor. The gold coins slipped from the rent in his waistcoat and cascaded silently into the straw of the room below. He flung himself into the street, not caring whether the village was in the hands of friend or enemy, driven only by an overwhelming desire to rub shoulders with living men again, to hear voices and shouting, to take part in fresh slaughter, to be killed if need be, but in the company of others. Anything rather than remain up there alone with a faceless thing and an amber insect that drank its blood.

He ran straight into the arms of Nicholas, who held him by his belt and screamed above the hideous din:

"Keep to the houses—the heavies are coming!"

Ten squadrons of Nansouty's cuirassiers swept by, big men on huge horses, a torrent of steel, their crested helmets dipping left and right as their long, straight swords flickered at the last of the flying Croats, pinning them among the debris of shattered artillery wagons which the enemy infantry had been trying to erect as a barricade.

Down the winding street, where the road ran to the river's edge, tossed the sea of horsehair plumes. The last rays of the setting sun danced on a thousand steel casques. Nothing could stem that tide, not the thrusts of squadrons of Hungarian lancers, nor wedges of white-coated grenadiers, flung in to cling to the last few house on the edge of the plain. The Austrian columns were rolled up and hurled back on their supports, but the cuirassiers did not press the pursuit. Their charge had been a measure of desperation. A huge floating mill, set on fire by units of the enemy higher up the stream, had drifted down and crashed through the frail bridge to Lobau. What was left of the two advanced corps of the Grand Army would have to fight for fingerholds on the Austrian bank of the river.

CHAPTER THREE

Several of the houses were on fire and the shattered village was lit by the glare of flames that no one attempted to subdue.

The voltigeurs were bivouacked in the churchyard, their arms and equipment piled against the leaning stones, the men sound asleep in hollows between the turf mounds.

The south wind, blowing freshly up river, rolled clouds of yellowish wood smoke over the exhausted infantry, laid in ragged rows along the road to the bridgehead.

Nicholas sat, his back to a tombstone, sucking an empty pipe, watching the others preparing their evening meal, a piece of horseflesh hacked from the carcass of an Uhlan's well-groomed mare. They were broiling the meat in a cuirassier's breastplate, the communal kettle having been holed by a sharpshooter on the outskirts of the village.

Nicholas was too depressed to forage for tobacco. The pungent smell of powder, sweat-soaked uniforms, wood smoke and roasting meat made him cough and splutter. The stench sickened him, mentally more than physically, stirring anew the disgust he had long felt for his fellow men when judged en masse, opening up old wounds that had ached intermittently ever since he had slipped out of his lodging the night when old Cicero found him in Camilla's arms.

For a moment or two he thought about Camilla—the scent of her dark hair, the sweetness of her breath on his cheek that night when he had first taken her into the little summer-house at the bottom of the garden. She had been lovely, enchanting, but not worth the price he had paid for those few stolen hours. How could she have been, when he had loved and respected her husband, for all his elderly pedantry and barbarous foreign tongue?

Nicholas had come to Cicero's straight from university, almost penniless and without much hope of ever earning more than would be sufficient to maintain himself. The old fellow had liked him from the start, devoting hours of his time to extra tuition in the long library over pipes and brandy. Another smell came back to Nicholas, weaving through the stinging smoke of the camp-fire and burning houses, the smell of old leather and old books, a library that might have been his by this time, for Cicero had not long to live and it was unlikely that Camilla would have given him any children.

The house, the school, the beautiful inlaid Italian furniture, all would have been his. Camilla would have been eager to marry him the moment the breath was out of the old man's body. They could have settled down there for the rest of their lives in an atmosphere of luxury, elegance and learning, Camilla indulging her fantastic whims for garden architecture, himself browsing in the library, entertaining the parents of his wealthier pupils, secure and relaxed with the best of the world at his feet. Instead he had a graveyard for a couch, shared with half a dozen courageous, easygoing boors, who were even now preparing his supper of scraps cut from a dead warhorse such as he would not have flung even to Chita, Camilla's snuffling little bitch, in the world now closed to him forever.

Nicholas wondered if he genuinely regretted having betrayed the gentle Cicero, or whether he merely regretted his benefactor's discovery of the sordid little intrigue. Perhaps he ought to have

48

restrained her and insisted upon a mutual exercise of patience. Patience, with Camilla! One might as well try to reason with a squadron of Hungarian hussars bearing down on an isolated foot soldier. How could any man of flesh and blood have unlocked those long, white fingers when they twined together behind his head and pressed his mouth closer and closer to hers? How could any man but a eunuch have resisted the soft pressure of her chiffon-clad body that last night when she had come to him in his room? He was a fool to have gone on blaming himself all these years. Better to have cursed her for her stupidity and blind, possessive lust. If he had resisted, how long would it have lasted? How long before Camilla, having taken possession of him and of everything the old man left, would have gone down by moonlight to the pool at the bottom of the garden, intent upon snaring some other young fool, as he had been ensnared when she swam to him, naked and laughing, across that expanse of moonlit water the first night he held her in his arms?

Nicholas spat and jammed his cold pipe into his greatcoat pocket. What was the use of regretting? What use travelling back to a bitter-sweet dream of the past? It was over, finished, which was more than could be said of this criminally conceived battle that seemed likely to cost the lot of them their lives before another twenty-four hours had passed. Would any of them care if it did? Would Old Jean, who had learned by this time that violent death must find each one of them in turn when at last his luck ran out?

Nicholas glanced at the circle round the fire. Jean sat brooding about the battle and looking as if his doglike faith in the Emperor's tactics had been shaken, as the faith of everyone in the army was being shaken by this campaign. Dominique, the half-idiot boy from a farmyard on the slopes of the Pyrenees, was already scraping out a tune on his infernal fiddle. Dominique would fight and fiddle until a charge of grapeshot sent him and his violin to hell. And there, at his elbow, leaned Claude, his face still black with powder smudges.

Nicholas wondered about Claude. How long it would be before

the boy's republican dream was shattered? What interminable arguments they had had about it in billet, garrison and bivouac. Yet Claude still insisted that Napoleon's misson was to humble the autocracies of Europe and impose a régime of liberty, equality and fraternity on every community between Portugal and Moscow. The naïveté of the man! What did he suppose the Emperor would do with his throne when opposition was liquidated? Step down from the Imperial dais and offer it to a charming assembly of peasants' spokesmen and ignorant artisans? Claude had been steeped in revolutionary propaganda from earliest childhood. Nicholas marvelled at the amount of blood that had flowed in front of the man's eyes without washing his dream away. Claude's grandfather had been hanged in Bordeaux years ago because he took a fancy to one of the de Courcey pheasants. He hadn't even eaten the pheasant; but it had been hung beside him, with a warning to others, nailed to the gibbet. The old man's family had enjoyed themselves for a short space when the Revolution came to the Gironde, but the boy's father had marched off with the local deputies to build the new France in Paris and had gone to the guillotine, along with Barbaroux and the other Girondists, leaving nothing but a pile of debts and a burning conviction that the Revolution, if it was to succeed, must be buttressed by reason and a whole bookful of dogma. Claude had inherited the tradition and was now fighting for it through the person of the Emperor. Claude realized that Napoleon's patchwork Empire fell a little short of his father's dream of an Ideal State, but he contrived to hope. One day the last foreign autocracy would crash and a new dawn would gladden the hearts of men. When he heard talk like this the savant Nicholas sneered, dismissing the man as a typical product of years of rhetorical anarchy.

The former schoolmaster began munching his ration of meat, tearing at the red gristle with white, even teeth, smearing his short brown beard with blood and wood ash, his eyes and brain busy on the two remaining members of the file, Emmanuel, the dark-skinned Jewish acrobat, and Louis, the coachman's son from Gers.

50

Emmanuel had all the exuberance of the fit and the feather-brained. His supple body, which had vaulted and tumbled in every fairground between the Loire and the Mediterranean sea-ports, had retained its litheness in the active life of a sharp-shooter during the past two years. He had Jean's tough fibres but could dance to Dominique's fiddle with the grace of a gipsy girl, gyrating and leaping, always with the same merry grin and backward toss of his greasy blue-black hair. He turned everything to a joke, reducing semi-starvation, intense heat, paralysing cold, death itself to terms of the absurb and ludicrous. Nicholas liked him better than any of them, saving perhaps old Jean, for whose steadfastness and skill the schoolmaser had a profound if detached admiration. Jean realized that Manny, as they affectionately termed the Jew, was good for the file. He made them forget that life would never offer anything else but this endless marching and skirmishing towards a nameless grave on a confused battlefield. Manny had not received much beyond hard knocks and a bed under a stall, with scraps to eat when the crowd was drunk and easily amused. Here, in the army, one had licence to steal. The men were expected to live on the country and to take what they could find in the way of food and trifling valuables. He had never regretted his enlistment during a dead season at Arras.

Louis, the last of the group, was different. Louis loved horses and seldom thought of anything else. His father had driven the Orléans-Bayonne coach for more than twenty years and had often taken his son on the box beside him for a couple of stages, sending him back to their cottage by the carrier whom they passed on the return journey. For hours and hours the boy had kept his eyes fixed on the shining backs and heaving flanks of his father's horses and had longed, above everything, to own a horse of his own. The wish remained a dream. Louis's father had been killed in a collision with a furiously driven post-chaise out-side Angers, and the family had broken up to seek livelihoods elsewhere. Louis had applied to join several regiments of cavalry, but somehow luck always went against him, and all Nicholas's carefully written applications on his behalf were either lost or ignored. He was still trying, and even now, when he ought to have been eating his supper, Nicholas saw him staring beyond the churchyard wall, watching a party of hussars dam the muddy brook for the purpose of watering their horses.

Nicholas wiped his greasy fingers on the skirts of his coat and looked across at their latest recruit, the dreamy young man who called himself Guillame, and who said he could paint. He wondered what had happened to him earlier that day when the young fool strayed from the company, and was left behind in the counter-attack. The boy had looked almost happy when they set out that morning, marching down the street behind Manny, who had been playing drum-major with his musket. Later he had seemed to face the granary bombardment bravely enough, although that was by no means the worst he could expect in a voltigeur company. Then he had disappeared for an hour or two and when Nicholas found him, during the cavalry charge, he looked as though he had been gazing at some unutterable horror. He wasn't eating either; his portion of broiled horseflesh lay untouched on his tin plate.

Nicholas yawned and stretched his big limbs. Ah, well, he'd learn, no doubt, as they'd all had to learn. Killing was a trade. Anyone could acquire the art if he could manage to stay alive for a week or two.

Dominique was playing one of his wild, freakish tunes and nobody saw a group of officers leave the church tower and stroll towards the group. A short, thickset man in a loose-fitting riding coat came forward and stood at the edge of the group, listening. For a moment nobody took any notice of him; only Nicholas glanced up sourly and looked quickly away again.

Presently the little man said: "Play 'Watch Over the Safety of the Empire.' "

Dominique complied and Nicholas noticed that, as he began, some of the men round the fire made an attempt to struggle to their feet, but were motioned to be still by a swift, nervous gesture. On each side of them the chatter of men round the fires

52

subsided to a mutter. The moon sailed out from behind a bank of cloud and helped the flickering fires to light the scene. As the tune wailed on, the Emperor's hands, stretched behind his back, beat a nervous tattoo one upon the other.

When Dominique came to the final bar he let fall the fiddle, overcome by sudden embarrassment. With the same jerky movement a plump hand plucked at the pocket of the white kerseymere waistcoat and emerged with finger and thumb holding a gold piece. The coin spun into the farm-hand's lap and Dominique, a peasant's avarice sweeping away his shyness, groped for it, bit it and thrust it hurriedly into his knapsack pouch.

The pale face seemed to glow for a moment. There was absolute stillness. Then the Emperor said: "Anyone here from Egypt?"

Nicholas saw Jean's face light up. The sergeant sprang to his feet.

"The Pyramids and Acre, sire!"

"And before that?"

"Lodi and Rivoli, five wounds."

The plump hand reached forward and gently tugged the sergeant's ear.

"Look after the children tomorrow, they need you as much as I do!"

There was a swift step on the loose gravel of the path and Napoleon rejoined his officers.

Deep in the shadow Nicholas ground his teeth. "That's how he does it," he hissed to himself, "a gold piece, an assumed interest, a small avalanche of accurate detail. Suppose he had stood in my shoes three years ago, would he have had Camilla, house, property and all, without being discovered in bed with the woman?"

Before he settled himself in the grassy trough between the graves, Nicholas looked at the recruit once again and found that his expression had changed. The tense, strained look had gone. The boy was staring after the Emperor with an expression of alert intelligence in his eyes. Nicholas thought: "He'll go the same way. Another Jean in the making; but he won't survive as long as Jean if he lets himself be overrun by counter-attacks."

A drowsy silence settled in the bivouacs. Here and there a man groaned in his sleep. Over at Ebersdorf a solitary gun barked off at the shattered bridge. The clump-clump of the engineers' hammers was its sole accompaniment.

CHAPTER FOUR

The remains of the two corps limped back across the bridge to Lobau, leaving two-thirds of their number dead or prisoners on the right bank of the river.

All the next day they had fought. Aspern had been retaken five times, Essling six. Marshal Lannes was among the mortally wounded, and Jean Ticquet, who had been distributing the last ammunition within a pistol shot of the marshal when the ricochetting three-pounder struck him in the knees, had helped to carry the marshal to the bridgehead on a litter of boughs and muskets.

The Gascon marshal had forbidden his stretcher-bearers to use the blood-stained cloak of his old friend, Major-General Pouzet, who had been killed shortly before Lannes received his own agonizing wound. There were tears in Jean's eyes when he glanced at the bloody pulp of the marshal's legs. He did not need a surgeon to tell him that Lannes would never fight again.

Jean helped one of the marshal's aides-de-camp to strain some of the brackish Danube water through a silk shirt and give the sufferer a drink. With the maiming of Lannes all Jean's forebodings returned to him.

Shortly afterwards they received the order to retire and crossed to the island. The veteran sergeant was disgusted to witness grenadiers of the Guard throwing their busbies into the water, convinced as they were that the tall bearskins drew enemy fire. Jean found it another sign of rot setting in, but he said nothing and shepherded his little flock back to the glade they had occupied before the battle. After all, he had grounds for personal satisfaction. In the two days' struggle he had not lost a man.

Just before the voltigeurs passed over, a short string of wagons had edged its way across the bridge. In the last of them was Old Carla, the cantinière of the Second Battalion. The wagon was driven by her sixteen-year-old daughter, Nicholette.

Old Carla was dying, dying of her pain.

Carla's pain was the subject of ribald jokes in the Eighty-seventh. It was as famous as Murat's coxcombery or Massena's avarice. She had been attached to the regiment for nearly nine years now, and veterans like Jean could remember the pain for as long as they could remember Carla. She often talked about it, describing and boasting about it, telling them that one day it would kill her. She was fond of speculating on its cause. Was it the stone of a date or the pip of an orange that remained in her stomach and was gradually sealing her bowels? Or was it a delayed poison administered by one of her long-dead husbands, slowly moving towards her heart? It came on her suddenly and nearly always at an inconvenient time, just before or during a battle, when she was particularly busy preparing her cart for bivouac-time. It gripped her stomach like the pincers of a giant crab and squeezed until the moisture ran from her eyes and she had to fight for breath. Sometimes it lasted for hours and sometimes for hardly more than a few moments. In the beginning it had come at rare intervals, but lately, particularly since her return from Spain, its visitation had been alarmingly frequent. Since crossing the Danube three or four days ago it had been practically continuous and was only eased according to the amount of brandy she swallowed. She lay back on a bed of looted cavalry cloaks and gasped with rage and frustration, for Nicholette, despite the girl's shrewdness, was too inexperienced to run the canteen as it should be run if steady profits were to be made. The pain had already robbed them of a thousand francs in this campaign.

This time Carla knew she was dying and had told Nicholette as much.

"Drive back to the island," she said, "there's nothing more here. They've begun to retreat!"

Nicholette waited four hours for a place in the stream of men and vehicles, and during the interval Carla tried to take her mind off the pain by asking a hundred questions, all of them relating to the progress of the battle. Nicholette answered her tersely. She had been reared on the battlefields and did not think the pain very important. She was bored with it anyway, her mother having chattered about it for years. She knew that it would soon pass off and that the old woman would climb back into the driving-seat again.

Nicholette was slim and dark, but already a matured woman. She had straight thick hair, piled in tight coils at the back of her small head. Everything about her was small, neat and solemn. Carla could not swear to her father, but rather favoured a Southerner whom she dimly remembered as having been killed in Dumouriez's last campaign in the Ardennes. Seventeen years ago would make it about right. Before that it would have been Mouton, the armourer, and afterwards Henriot or Big Hervé, her favourite. She often thought it odd that she had conceived only once and on that occasion a daughter, not a son who could follow the regiment. Carla never craved Nicholette's affection, and had, indeed, beaten her often enough until the girl grew strong enough to knock the old woman down with a single blow. But their partnership had worked well enough during the last few years, and her mother admired Nicholette's cool handling of men.

In the last year or two a good many men had looked her over when they slammed down their sous for a jack of cheap wine or a glass of Carla's famous black coffee. Some of them had tried a

57

little gallantry, but something in the frigid stare of the girl's hard brown eyes soon sent them away with a shrug or a light-hearted curse. Several of the officers had tried their luck and one of them, a foppish young hussar who aped Lasalle's studied careless-ness of attire, had told Carla that the girl was sexless. Carla did not think so. In the past she had often looked at her daughter's wide red mouth, at the graceful curves of her prematurely adult figure, and indulged in lazy speculation about her future. There were so many men and so few women. Nicholette could afford to wait a year or two before she took a husband. Carla hoped it would be someone from the infantry, the Eighty-seventh prefer-ably, for she herself had never married outside the regiment. It seemed disloyal, and in a freakish way that she could never have explained to herself Old Carla was proud of the Eighty-seventh. It was as good and better than most of the line regiments and had seen as much hard fighting since Valmy as any unit in the army.

Carla lay back on her pile of cloaks and looked at Nicholette's straight back. The girl handled the wagon well in this press, beating off a stream of mounted gendarmes who were trying to edge her off the causeway, flicking her whip this way and that in the surge of men and vehicles fighting to keep their places on the loose planking. She watched the girl with a touch of maternal pride, and her thoughts returned to the immediate future. The pain clawed and wrenched at her abdomen with every lurch of the unsprung vehicle and she decided that when they reached the island bivouacs she must send for Old Jean, the sergeant she had always felt would have made such a reliable husband but who had always rejected her proposals with the slow, maddening grin of a confirmed bachelor. Carla wondered what Jean had done about women all these years. Nothing, perhaps; some men didn't, though these were few enough in Carla's experience. Not that she had ever wanted Jean to climb into the wagon with her. Nobody had stirred the faintest desire in her since a Prussian cannon ball took off Big Hervé's head in the fighting round Hohenlinden years ago, but a cantinière, especially a young and attractive one like Nicholette, was obliged to find herself a regu-

58

lar husband and replace him as soon as he was killed; otherwise there was always trouble, brawls and bickerings about the drop-board, spilled wine, sword cuts and inquiries by the provost. If a woman married, well, that was an end to it until next time. The men of the regiment respected a canteen marriage as rigidly, perhaps more so, than civilians adhered to a union performed by a priest. Carla wondered, between spasms of pain, why civilians found it necessary to go to all that trouble to get married. Here in the camp you chose a man, opened a cask of the best wine, indulged in a song and dance or two and climbed into the cart with him there and then, leaving the guests outside to drink themselves stupid or stagger away to their fires, whichever they preferred. After that you followed your man until he was either killed, maimed and discharged or had made enough money to buy himself a transfer to a civilian unit and set up business in a garrison town like Strasbourg or Dresden. If you were unlucky enough to have a child, and the child was tough enough to survive its first few weeks, you did one of two things: you either reared it, as she had reared Nicholette, and taught it the tricks of the trade or you claimed your bounty and sent the infant back to one of the military orphanages in France and forgot the whole incident. There was no need to tell Nicholette this, she had known it all before she had reached the age of ten. The simplest thing, of course, was to make sure you didn't have children. The best of them were an encumbrance on the line of march and they invariably impaired your health at a time when you needed all your reserves for the rigours of a campaign. She remembered old Annette, the mountainous cantinière of the 103rd. She had produced an infant in every campaign and was known in the regiment as "The Factory." Her carelessness had brought its penalty in the end, for Annette had been drowned the year before in a Spanish mountain torrent, trying to save her youngest, whose father she couldn't have named for a thousand gold napoleons. Carla had lectured Nicholette on the moral of Annette's end, but the girl had only smiled her sour smile, as if to say: "Don't worry, you old fool, that could never happen to me!"

They pulled in under the trees, not far from the bridgehead, and Carla told her daughter to go back to the river and watch out for Jean Ticquet and his voltigeurs. The girl went, leaving Carla with her pain and her satisfied memories.

The sergeant came to the cart just before midnight. He excused his delay on the grounds that he had been snaring rabbits for the evening soup.

"There's a million of them around," he said. "I never saw such a place for rabbits. Old Massena was thrown by his horse when it stumbled in one of the holes over there. He's out of action now for a spell and Jean Lannes is finished. This is a bad business, Carla."

He settled himself on one of the lockers and looked down on the woman, whose sweating face glistened in the dim rays of the smoke-grimed lantern that swung from the canopy.

Carla said: "I'm moving on, Jean!"

"What is it, the pain?"

She nodded, unable to speak for a moment as a new spasm shook her flabby body.

Presently she said: "I want you to get Nicholette married. It's best that way. I don't want her causing trouble with the regiment the minute they've tumbled me into the ground."

Jean was thoughtful for a moment and sucked hard at his pipe.

He did not assure her that she was not dying, knowing her well enough to be certain that she was the best judge of that. Neither did he offer to get a surgeon. He knew they were all too busy to come to a cantinière.

"Can't Nicholette get herself a man?" he asked. "She's sixteen."

"She won't do it, doesn't seem to mind one way or the other, but I'd like her to be with your file. You could keep an eye on her then. Why don't you take her yourself? She's a good girl if you don't mind a bit of temper now and again."

Jean chuckled. "I'd sooner have you, Carla," he said and meant it, for in spite of the sour stench that rose from the sick woman's bed he felt a surge of affection for her, the comrade of

60

so many lively years and a woman who had never withheld a drink from a man if he happened to be dying or out of cash. First Lannes, now Old Carla. It had been a bad day.

"Find someone in your set, then," she told him. "They're all young, aren't they, and I'll wager there isn't one of them that won't get a dry throat when he lays hold of Nicholette for the first time!"

Jean agreed that this was probably true, but he felt vaguely irritated by the proposal. The file was enough trouble without a sixteen-year-old girl tacked onto it. The girl, of course, could fend for herself when there was fighting, but a wagon this size was a damned nuisance on the march, hardly worth the extra comfort it afforded if the weather turned against them and, as often as not, a positive menace on a retreat, for the vanguard of the enemy always made for a canteen, where they were likely to find both wine and money once they had disposed of its defenders.

Carla was finding difficulty in speaking now. The jolting journey across the bridge had exhausted her, and Jean's seamed face appeared to recede in a halo of winking lights.

"Get her in here," she gasped, and Jean, after passing Carla the brandy bottle, drew open the canvas curtains and called the girl from her seat on an empty cask near the small fire she had built.

Nicholette climbed into the wagon and casually sponged the sweat from her mother's face. After a gulp or two from the bottle Carla grew more composed.

"I've been telling Jean," she said, "you've got to get married!"

A smile flickered about the girl's wide mouth. "I know that," she said, and Jean could not help noticing the soft bloom of her cheeks and the graceful lines of her neck and shoulders as she bent over the older woman. He decided that Carla was right. Any of them back in the bivouac would be mad about her, but not one of them would be able to manage her, if he knew anything about the strength of the woman's jaw or the firm, almost savage lines of her mouth. She would have had a man before this if she had wanted one.

Carla went to sleep for a short while and Jean sat on, smoking his pipe over the cantinière's fire. He accepted a jug of Bordeaux wine and pocketed the small plug of tobacco she gave him.

Presently the girl spoke.

"I'll have the curly-headed one!" she announced.

Jean resisted an impulse to laugh.

"Claude Dupont?"

"That's him."

It was like a child choosing a doll from a shop-window, but a very determined child, Jean decided, one that would rave and shout and kick if any doll but the one she had selected was placed in her arms.

"Suppose he's not agreeable?" grunted Jean, disliking the whole business, which now struck him as a fitting climax to a thoroughly unsatisfactory battle.

The girl smiled into the fire. "He's agreeable all right," she said, recalling Dupont's hungry glances every time she served him at the drop-board of the cart.

Jean knocked out his pipe. "It won't do like that," he told her. "They'll have to choose straws!"

The girl looked straight at him. "I don't mind how many straws they choose, but you'd better make sure Claude Dupont gets the right one."

Jean got up and went back to his bivouac. The file was asleep, utterly exhausted after its exertions since dawn. The mended kettle turned slowly on the improvised spit. The men hadn't even waited to eat supper.

The sergeant went over to the nearest horse lines and returned with a handful of straw, selecting half a dozen stalks and breaking them into differing lengths. He preferred straw for a lottery; grass broke too easily and then there were frantic disputes. He held five straws firmly in his clenched palm, and the longest, the sixth, he pushed forward between his finger and thumb. Then he woke them, one by one, touching Claude first.

CHAPTER FIVE

All went as Jean had planned. The canteen wedding was held in the company's glade within a few hours of Carla's burial. Jean would have waited a day or two, but the girl did not seem to mind and Jean soon persuaded himself that Carla was the last woman in the world to sentimentalize over such a matter. Besides, after the two-day battle across the river the men were in an unpleasant mood and it would not have been safe to let Nicholette stray far from the company bivouacs.

Old Carla had died within a few hours of the lottery. Jean, who had lain down to sleep with the others after supper, was awakened by the girl shortly before dawn. She told him to hurry and he got up and ran through the long, wet grass to the wagon.

He found Carla in a delirium from which she never emerged, and sat down on the locker to wait for the end. There was nothing that he could do. Carla was beyond the relief of the brandy bottle and no one knew better than Jean that it would have been quite useless to go over to the medical camp and ask for a surgeon. They were all too busy with wounded officers, while their orderlies were engaged in patching up any rankers with a fair chance of recovery.

Jean sat down and listened to Carla's wanderings. Some of the names she muttered stirred his memories. Once a grim smile crossed his lean face, for Carla croaked out the name of Denis O'Sullivan and tagged it with a picturesque curse. Jean remembered Denis, an Irish volunteer who had died of cholera in the siege of Genoa nine years back. Carla never forgave O'Sullivan for dying, he had owed her four hundred francs, and she couldn't even get at the body, for Genoa was ringed with enemy forces and soon afterwards surrendered. Jean remembered how Carla had cursed when a straggler came into the camp with the news after Marengo. She had known that O'Sullivan was shut up in the town but thought her money safe enough. The Irishman's death infuriated her, and, with a woman's logic, she never felt the same about the Emperor again for keeping them all hanging about before the battle instead of marching directly to the relief of the town.

Just as it began to get light the gross body under the sheepskin gave a shudder and the coarse features of the old woman relaxed. Jean covered her face with one of the cloaks and went out to make arrangements for the burial, taking the girl along with him to the bivouac. The reveille had sounded and Claude was astir brewing coffee. The recruit, Gabriel, was blowing embers of the fire, and both looked slightly sheepish when Jean arrived with Nicholette in tow.

The girl looked at her bridegroom frankly, but Claude looked away. Gabriel bustled off into the woods for more fuel.

The lottery had been a mild business after all. Jean found that only three of the six men showed any inclination to take it seriously. Of these three, one, the schoolmaster, Nicholas, tried hard to conceal his feelings in the matter. Jean thought that he seemed miserably anxious to demonstrate that he cared nothing which straw he plucked. He did not deceive Jean, however, who knew him far better than he supposed, and the old sergeant was mildly shocked by the man's eagerness. He had always supposed

64

that education lifted a fellow above that sort of thing. He could have sworn that Nicholas would have given a year's loot to win.

Emmanuel, ex-acrobat, showed a purely professional interest in the woman. He was always determined to try his hand at the fairs again when he left the army, and was inclined to think that Nicholette might have been trained as a partner in a black-magic act. She certainly would have looked attractive in scarlet tights, disappearing and reappearing inside a coffin, or being apparently dissolved in a few spirals of sulphur. His business instincts were not aroused by the prospect of a canteen. Emmanuel Jacobsen knew better than to tie himself to unwieldy stock-in-trade. He liked to carry his wares on his back and sleep on them. There would be times when the wagon would be out of sight.

The eagerness of Gabriel, the recruit, had also surprised Jean. He noticed how the young man's hand had trembled when he drew his straw. Jean could not have known that Gabriel, going down to the river to draw water on the second morning of the battle, had seen Nicholette combing her thick hair on the driving-seat and that their eyes had met for a second as he came up the bank, bowed under the weight of the two leather tubs he carried. He had stopped, in sheer amazement at seeing a woman in the wagon park. Framed in the oval canopy of the vehicle, with the rising sun sparkling on the swift current behind, she reawakened in him his old urge to paint, to capture something of the movement and colour of the crowded scene on the white pages of the bulky sketchbook that made his knapsack so unmanageable. It was the first time he had wanted to paint since leaving home. The vision did something else for him. The glow of the girl's pink cheeks and the strong, graceful line of her neck helped to obliterate the memory, not twenty-four hours old, of an amber-backed insect wading in a pool of blood. It was comforting to find how rapidly that memory, which he could have sworn would have dogged him to the grave, could be wiped out like a scribble on a slate by new scenes and sensations. The previous night it had been so vivid that he had shuddered to look at the portion of horsemeat they splashed onto his plate. Then he had seen Napoleon, the short, pale-faced author of it all, the arbiter of every man's fate, the cold, concentrated brain behind the whole sprawling Empire. Looking at the man, as he stood listening to Dominique's tune, Gabriel had felt curiously dwarfed, as though he were in the presence of a god neither good nor evil but magnificently indifferent, not only to the fate of men but to the fate of nations. And with this feeling came an odd sense of completeness to supplement that of the first night by the campfire. All the major pieces of the new mosaic that was now his life had been fitted into place; the pale-faced man who dispensed gold pieces for badly played tunes was the missing centrepiece.

Then had come the second day's battle, a nightmare of smoke and heat and screaming roundshot. And, after that, sleep by the fire in the glade, to be awakened and told that he could draw straws for the cantinière with the brown eyes and the thick black tresses.

Claude Dupont had not known of his pre-selection. The sergeant had explained the reason for the ballot in the briefest terms and thrust his hand holding the straws in the direction of the sleepy men; it had been easy to get the right man to pick the longest piece, but Jean thought it best not to tell him but to let him imagine merely that he had been lucky. It was good for a soldier to think himself lucky, and Jean felt certain that the girl herself would never tell him that he was her choice.

Claude felt strangely elated at the prospect of the rôle he was to adopt now that the earth had been trodden down on the old woman's grave, and they broke open the casks by the firelight that evening. He was a shy young man and his experience with women was more than usually limited. There had been a few boy-and-girl encounters in the hayfields, before he was drafted into the army, and, after that, a few minutes with a laconic harlot in a small town on the road to Saragossa. The latter experience had sickened him, as well it might, for the woman reeked of garlic and had been well past her prime. Claude had visited the brothel with Manny when both were drunk, and afterwards he had amused the Jew by being violently sick on the way back to bivouac. Now, clumsily busying himself with the coffee, Claude stole a glance at Nicholette as she sat watching him from a seat on somebody's knapsack. She seemed to him outrageously cool about the whole business.

He had been conscious of her for more than a year now, and he had often wondered if Old Carla had treated her roughly in that ramshackle wagon of theirs. He had often talked to her when she seemed to him only a child, swilling out buckets and stacking up pyramids of leather cups, while they stopped beside the road during a long march. But since she had matured—and it struck Claude that she had matured almost overnight—he had never been able to bring himself to address her.

Several of the linesmen came over to the voltigeurs' bivouac for the wedding. They all knew Carla and her daughter and had heard that a cask of the old woman's Burgundy would be broached. Old Jean went out and trapped a brace of rabbits, and Nicholas, the best shot of the party, did better still, lying in wait in the sedges and killing a wild duck, whose dying outcry caused such a commotion that Austrian outposts on the east bank fired a volley into the wooded spur of the island.

By ten o'clock most of the party were roaring drunk, and of this majority a dozen or more had eaten or danced themselves into an exhausted sleep in the long grass. Emmanuel, the Jew, was still sober. No amount of liquor seemed to have much effect on him. Grinning, he covered the drunkards with greatcoats and sat down to scrape out the stewpot and roasting-tins. Old Jean motioned to Dominique to put away his fiddle. The sergeant got up and looked in the wagon, showing no surprise when he found that it was empty. Then he locked the deep wine cupboards and lay down to sleep.

Earlier in the evening Jean had performed the gipsy wedding rite, cutting the wrists of Claude and the girl and binding their right hands together with a piece of dirty bandage which he took from his tunic pocket. He did this as though in jest and the ceremony was greeted with cheers and laughter, but deep in his heart Jean did not jest. To him, who had lived in the camps the

67

whole of his life, the ceremony was as binding as a marriage in a church. He had witnessed many weddings, and not one had been sanctified by a priest. To Jean the blood tie signified the willingness of a man and a woman to campaign together, to share the last scrap of food and to breed if they were so inclined. Of all the garbled utterances, half savage, half civil, that he made at a canteen wedding, only the phrase "till death us do part" meant anything. Sooner or later death was certain to take one or the other, not in the fullness of time, but tomorrow, or the day after, or next spring. Nor was the man more likely to go than the woman. The incidence of death among cantinières was as great, proportionately, as among front-line infantry regiments. Old Carla had lasted well and Jean was bound to admit that, young as she was, her daughter appeared to have learned most of the tricks of her trade. He could not say the same for Claude. The boy was too absent-minded to last long under present conditions.

After the blood-letting Claude and Nicholette sat together on the outskirts of the circle. Neither consumed much wine, the girl because she was naturally abstemious, the man because he felt rather foolish and nervous. There was a good deal of badinage and a spate of stale jokes. Some of the linesmen nodded significantly towards the wagon, as though they expected, and rather hoped, that he would carry her in there at once. Someone crawled over and tied a set of harness bells on the axle-tree, while Claude grinned and pretended not to mind.

Just before the moon came up, and immediately after Manny and Gabriel had damped the fire down with armfuls of fresh wood, Claude felt a slight tugging at his wrist. He turned and looked down upon the girl sitting beside him. She met his glance steadily and her head inclined towards the thicket behind them. He got up, as unobtrusively as possible, and followed her down the narrow path, away towards the northern point of the island.

When they were clear of the bivouac he took out his clasp-knife and cut the bandage that coupled them. She glided on ahead, moving as though she was familiar with the outgrown track. He followed in silence, noticing that they inclined towards the bank and kept away from the long curving row of fires that winked and spluttered through the trees to the west.

She led him to the head of a steep gully carved out by a brook seeking the main stream. There was just light enough to see their way down, and at the foot of the cleft, where the current ran turgidly, Claude saw a small raft. The girl stepped aboard, motioning him to follow. She cast off and the current took them gently downstream a few hundred yards, until the raft grated on the shingle beach of a tiny islet, barely forty yards from Lobau. Here she jumped ashore and took him by the hand. A few yards from the water's edge he saw a tent which he recognized as Carla's store, a complicated affair of hoops and spikes that she sometimes erected to protect her wine from the weather when the regiment had been stationary for a few days.

An odd sense of pride grew in him. The girl, his wife, had conceived and planned this refuge. His head spun with the wonderment of it all, the girl's slyness, her resource, the manner in which she had effected their escape from the bivouac and from the joyless choice of waiting until every guest was dead drunk or spending her wedding night in the wagon, surrounded by intoxicated practical jokers.

The more he thought about it the greater was his respect for the girl, but with this feeling came a qualm of inferiority, a sense of being led and controlled. He wondered if Old Jean knew Nicholette for what she was, a woman capable not only of planning an undisturbed wedding night in the midst of a beaten army, but possessing sufficient strength and will to catch or build a raft and to transport and erect this unwieldy tent on an island in the Danube, then to guide her lover to it in almost complete darkness.

The moon came out as they entered the tent, and its wan light revealed the cosiness of the interior. There were one or two cooking utensils, an iron stove, a small cask of wine and a soft bed of bracken spread with a new horse blanket.

She sat down and looked at him. He noticed that her eyes were shining and her lips were parted. He could hear her breathing. Outside it seemed unnaturally still. Only the swirl of the water or the faint rustle of the night breeze in the woods broke the silence.

"We can stay here until the day after tomorrow," she said, and as he opened his mouth to protest she smiled and shook her head vigorously. "I've arranged it with Jean."

With her smile and the gleam of her small, even teeth he suddenly became aware of her as a woman. A great wave of tenderness swept over him. His mouth went dry and his heart hammered at his ribs. Reaching out gently, he laid his palms on her shining black hair, and at his touch she shivered. The movement inflamed him; he seized her by the shoulders, holding her fiercely and kissing her mouth, eyes and cheeks. She did not return his kisses, but seemed abstracted. Presently she freed herself and moved across the tent. His disappointment was so keen that he almost cried out.

He heard a prolonged rustling and a sound that might have been a woman's laugh, choked back and smothered. The moon above the open flap of the tent rode in behind a cloud as she moved back to the couch. Her thick hair, freed of pins, brushed his cheek; she was bending over him. Her naked body glowed in the pale light and he held her close, speechless with pride and gratitude.

CHAPTER SIX

For more than a month the steady clump of sledge-hammers and the dry rattle of limber chains were heard in Lobau. The island was transformed into a vast fort, bristling with nine hundred large-calibre guns, hedged round with rampart, redoubt and complicated systems of abattis.

Under the combined effects of strong sunshine and ceaseless physical labour the morale of the army improved. Emperor and marshals were everywhere, planning the forthcoming assault. Dressed as sergeants, Napoleon and Massena strolled down to the river and bathed opposite Enzersdorf, General Sainte-Croix following as a private. Splashing in the water, half a musket shot from indulgent Austrian sentries, they selected the spot for a night crossing. There was to be no repetition of the slaughter opposite Aspern-Essling.

The voltigeurs became pioneers for the month. Stripped to the waist, the seven men worked with mattock and wheelbarrow at the gun emplacements on the northern tip of the island. It was hard but invigorating work. In the fierce sunshine everyone tanned to the colour of dull bronze.

Gabriel became accustomed to encounters with Napoleon and

the veterans of his staff. They often appeared at the emplacements, asking questions, joking about rations, promising lively days in the near future.

One morning, when the seven infantrymen were sitting down to their midday soup, the Emperor himself came through the bushes and called across to Nicholas. The ex-schoolmaster had finished eating and was in the act of raising a long-necked wine bottle to his lips.

"I hope the wine is good, soldier!" said the Emperor, with one of his pale smiles.

Nicholas lowered the bottle and wiped his mouth.

"It ought to be," he grunted, "there's our cellar!" and he nodded towards the river.

The Emperor's brows contracted. He moved into the centre of the group, checking a general movement to rise with an impatient gesture of his small hand.

"I ordered the distribution of four thousand bottles of wine to this division only yesterday!" he said quietly.

Nicholas grinned, sourly. Under his tilted shako, worn to protect him from the fierce beat of the noonday sun, he looked raffish and comical, like a character out of a camp burlesque.

"It's gone the way of most of our wine, sire," he said, and, rising, picked up his spade and began to dig.

The Emperor made no reply, but stood there a moment longer, fidgeting with his riding-switch. Then he turned and walked away. An infantry colonel accompanying him remained long enough to scowl at the oblivious Nicholas, who went on digging. "Time somebody told the Old Man," he muttered to Jean when the group had gone out of earshot.

The same night an officer of the Guard came down to the bivouac for a statement from Jean about the detachment's wine supplies. Jean told him the truth. There had been no issue since before Aspern.

Two days later there was a court-martial, attended by the Emperor in person. Four commissary officials were found guilty

72

of misappropriation and shot. Nicholas volunteered for the firing-party. Louis and Dominique went over to see the fun.

Towards the end of those arduous but pleasant days on Lobau Gabriel painted his first portrait group of the file. The sketch survived and was among the best found in the hair trunk. It is strangely symbolic of the First Empire, like the study of the young dragoon whom Gabriel sketched later on the road into Portugal.

The six men are grouped against a background of summer foliage with the formality popular in daguerreotypes of later generations. Three are standing, three sitting or kneeling. Sergeant Jean occupies the central position in the back row, and the melancholy droop of his thin moustache, a soft growth that would never answer to wax no matter how determined the owner might be to emulate the Guard, converts the sergeant's warlike stare into the expression of a disillusioned clown. It is a solemn face, but there is unexpected gentleness about the mouth, and although the cheekbones are prominent, helping to make the upper part of the face lean and harsh, the chin is as small and rounded as a woman's.

On Jean's right is Nicholas, his more genuinely hardbitten features accentuated by the rakish tilt of his shako and its broad chin-strap. His powerful shoulders are slightly stooped, as though to bring him more closely in line with the slighter figure of Jean, and his square ruthless jaw is dark with the stubble of a three-day beard.

Cross-legged in the foreground is the Jew, Emmanuel, his swarthy, mobile features grinning into the eye of the artist with an expression half impish, half genial; an attractive, likeable face with unsmiling eyes.

Beside him, on one knee, appears the farmhand, Dominique, and Gabriel must have posed this picture, for the young man's fiddle has been placed in his hand and the bow is resting lightly across Manny's shoulders.

Claude Dupont, bridegroom of a few days, is the only member

of the group wearing full uniform. Perhaps he had just come off guard duty, for he carries musket and fixed bayonet, or perhaps he dressed specially for the sitting. He was the only member of the file who studied his personal appearance. He recurs farther on in the sketchbook and is always well turned out, as though he were proud of his profession. It is easy to see why Nicholette chose him. He has a softness of feature lacking in the others, but, for all that, is sufficiently masculine to please any woman, even a woman like the cantinière's daughter, with an army to choose from.

Louis, the coachman's son, is not looking towards the artist. Perhaps he had seen a thoroughbred straying out of the cavalry lines, for Gabriel has caught his expression of mild abstraction, as though Louis had shouted: "Hurry and finish, Gabriel, I'm going down to the hussars' bivouac before supper!"

But Gabriel took his time and went on painting until the light failed and blue wood smoke began to drift through the glades where a hundred and fifty thousand men cooked and quaffed and sharpened swords against tomorrow's new challenge to survive.

The sketch is dated July 3rd, 1809.

At 9 A.M. on July 5th a violent storm broke over the teeming island. In a tempest of rain and wind the French columns assembled opposite Enzersdorf and defiled across a bridge that seemed to take shape actually under their blundering feet, so swiftly and silently was it built. By the time the storm had blown itself out seventy thousand men were across the river, and the reserves followed, turning the flank of the Austrians' entrenched positions from the rubble of Aspern and Essling and marching on over the field where, six centuries before, the armies of the first Habsburg had struggled for a throne.

On the following day the battle began in earnest, battalions hurling themselves at one another through fields of breast-high corn, squadrons of glittering cavalry galloping across the plain under a cloudless sky, adding the thunder of their hooves to that of a thousand guns.

All day the battle swayed across the Marchfield, Davout and Oudinot's grenadiers carrying the villages on the right, Macdonald, son of a Highland exile, earning his baton and the Emperor's long-withheld favour by a suicidal attack on the centre. Fifteen hundred from Macdonald's sixteen thousand marched out of that battle.

On the French left, where the voltigeurs fought alongside Boudet's infantry of the line, old Massena slowly yielded ground to the enemy's main attack, sitting all day in an open carriage amid a tempest of shot, calmly directing a withdrawal to lure the enemy within range of the Lobau batteries. All day the miserly old Italian sat there, his thin knees spread with maps. Vainglory, obstinacy or both had caused him to choose four white horses for his carriage, well knowing that such an entourage would attract fire. His coachman Pils kept his place on the box, constantly steadying the plunging animals. The marshal sat there, massaging his injured thigh, rubbing his chin and screwing up his one sound eye, as though he were turning over a gardening problem in one of the ornate summer-houses on his country estate.

The issue of the battle was never in doubt. It was combat after the old style, stirring the veterans' memories of Marengo, Austerlitz, Jena and Friedland, but the artillery fire was weightier and more destructive than at any of these battles, and the losses, on both sides, were proportionately heavy.

Marshal Bessières, charging at the head of the Guard, after Macdonald had carved his way through the Austrian centre, was hurled from his horse by a cannon ball but escaped with a slight wound. Other high-ranking officers were not as lucky. At the end of the action three generals had been killed, twenty-one wounded. Among the dead was the dashing Lasalle, whom Louis, an excellent judge in such matters, considered the best horseman in the army.

The victory was complete and Austrian resistance collapsed, but there had been a moment on the French left when the infantry feared for another Aspern. Forced back along the river banks, raked by crossfire and harried by heavy cavalry, Boudet's light troops had been almost cut to pieces. Bernadotte's Saxon corps broke under the strain and fled in all directions, mercilessly sabred by the Austrian cavalry. The voltigeurs of the Eighty-seventh were sent up in support, firing their first shots of the day, forming a square and shouting to the fugitives to take refuge in their ranks. The Saxons, however, were too demoralized to heed advice that might have saved their units from extermination. They swept over and through the squares, opening up lanes through which the Habsburg troopers pranced and slashed.

Old Jean was used to this sort of horseplay and minded it no more than skittles. He kept his file in a close knot at the crest of a little knoll, and this spur of resistance soon attracted a company, which presented a hedge of bayonets to the plunging horsemen. When the troopers went after easier game Jean ordered a retreat, before the Austrian infantry could come up in support of their cavalry. The file moved back to the reserves, where it had the satisfaction of watching the Austrian attack crumple under point-blank fire from the heavy batteries on Lobau, batteries the volti-geurs had helped to erect.

Across the plain Davout's guns were firing beyond Wagram church tower, and Jean said that the battle was won. The breathless infantry sorted themselves out, officers standing up in their stirrups and calling out the numerals of various units that had become intermingled in the mêlée.

It was then they discovered that Nicholas was missing.

What remained of the fighting had swept far to the north. Masses of cavalry were taking up the pursuit on the smoke-shrouded horizon. Gabriel saw them galloping into the haze like squadrons of centaurs, riding on the errand of some savage deity bent on ravaging the earth.

In the middle distance large patches of corn were ablaze, and the soft wind carried the crackle of flames down to the river bank. Jean said:

"Nicholas is out there; they weren't taking prisoners."

Manny and Louis gathered a pile of branches cut down by grapeshot, and each of the group took one of the boughs for fire-beating. Jean obtained an officer's permission to collect the wounded and they spread out fanwise and moved off across the plain, walking slowly within twenty yards of one another.

It was not long before they encountered wounded soldiers with shattered limbs, who moaned and writhed among the blood-ied cornstalks. Men called piteously in German and French, but the file moved on, heading for the scene of their late encounter. They did not turn aside for strangers. They were looking for Nicholas.

He had been separated from the others by a spate of fugitives, which bore him away from the low hedges until he was able to fight his way free and stand alone in the trampled corn. On every side Austrian troopers were cutting away at the Saxons, none of whom made any serious attempt to defend themselves beyond the futile raising of arms to shield their heads from the sabres.

One of the horsemen rode at Nicholas, a small, red-haired trooper with broken front teeth. With a guttural oath he brought up his horse and cavorted round the infantryman, his small eyes ferreting here and there for an opening in the Frenchman's guard. Nicholas gave him no leisure to find one. He dropped on one knee and lunged upward, driving his bayonet, with the whole of his strength, into the horse's belly. The animal screamed and flung its bulk sideways, away from the agonizing point. Los-ing his seat, the trooper fell forward on his face in the corn. Before he could brace his knees for a spring Nicholas had driven his weapon through the back of his neck. The horse, mad with pain, plunged into a struggling group a few yards distant, spilling them in all directions and gushing blood as it ran.

Nicholas liked this sort of thing. Only when fighting for his life, living second by second as now, had he no opportunity to brood. If there had been fighting every day he would have en-joyed soldiering. Violence had a soothing effect on his brain. Every time he fired his musket at point-blank range, every time he lunged at warm flesh with bayonet or sabre, he felt that he was paying off an old score. He was able to despise war as an art but to enjoy the actual business of killing. He was not naturally cruel, nor did he fight for a creed like Claude or, in another sense, Old Jean. He fought because he had a contempt for mankind and he liked to express that contempt by bayonet thrusts. He preferred killing with the bayonet. It was more personal and direct. It was quick, often merciful, and it had a certainty lacking in the discharge of fire-arms at whatever range. Nobody recovered from one of Nicholas's bayonet thrusts.

Two other troopers cantered across and he awaited them unflinchingly. One he shot through the chest. He was no conscript and had not discharged his musket in the general volley at the top of the slope. The man fell forward in his saddle, his sabre swinging free on its swordknot, his fingers clawing at his mount's sweating neck. The other horseman pulled at his reins and drew a pistol. Nicholas dropped his musket and ducked under the horse's belly, the bullet tearing through the blue wool of his epaulette and searing the lower part of his shoulder.

The Austrian twisted this way and that, flailing the air with his blade, cursing like a madman. Nicholas ran in under the weapon and seized the man by his tunic, bracing himself to tear him from the saddle and finish the issue on the ground. He never knew whether he succeeded in doing this. A distant roaring filled his ears; the man he held was torn from his grasp and seemed to disappear into nothingness. Lights rocketed up from the trampled corn and hung, like flaming castles, in front of his eyes, telescoping themselves into new and more terrifying flashes that seemed to detonate an inch from his face. When their searing light had faded he was lying in the corn, his feet across the man he had bayoneted. He could see and hear but he could not move or speak. He lay there listening to the distant roll of cannon fire and the confused outcry of the battle as it rolled away down the slope towards the tip of Lobau.

For several hours he lay perfectly still while all sense of the present left him, giving in its place an odd and not unpleasant

78

sense of detachment. He found himself thinking about trivial, inconsequential things, the glossy shine of Camilla's hair, the delicate tracery of a ribbon-backed chair in old Cicero's red study, the smallpox craters on the face of Old Jean, the scent of lilacs, overpoweringly sweet, in the ruined garden of a château that they had occupied during a rest period after Friedland. All these things seemed important to him, the sum total of life as he remembered it. Reflection upon them gave him great serenity and he became almost feverish in his anxiety to keep the train of contemplation moving, fearing blackness and oblivion if it were checked or broken.

Overhead the sky began to recede and grow less blue. A light wind stirred in the cornstalks. Carried on the wind, faint and incredibly far off, came the sound of battle, but Nicholas did not recognize it as such. To him it was a summer sea, sucking and swishing along the fringe of a wide, pebbled bay and sparkling under a noonday sun. It was easy enough to slip off his shirt and breeches, as he had done so many times on the edge of Cicero's lake, and to plunge headlong into the shimmering water, certain of the moment of ecstasy to follow.

For a long time he splashed in the pool, and so vivid was the mirage that he could see his tumbled clothes on the mossy bank near the summer-house. Then the wind stirred again and this time it brought with it a smell of burning.

At first he thought the smart in his nostrils originated from one of the gardener's bonfires. Griot, Cicero's lame gardener, was always burning rubbish under the chestnuts near the boundary wall. Then Nicholas knew that the smell could not come from Griot's bonfire, for he felt the hot breath of the flames in his face and the smoke was so close and pungent that it made him splutter.

The cough jerked him back to reality. It shook his body and reopened the wound in his shoulder. Feeling the blood flow down his arm, Nicholas wondered, idly, why a shoulder wound should have paralysed the whole of his body. He forced his brain to

79

think back over the last of his encounters. He could remember the bullet wound with perfect clarity, but after that nothing at all.

Gradually full consciousness returned to him. He knew that he must have been injured in the cavalry mêlée. He knew, approximately, where he was lying and even began to assess his chances of being picked up, realizing that this depended upon the issue of the battle. Then he tried to remember how the battle had been going when this peculiar numbness struck him down, but the effort was too great and he turned his attention to the smoke, which seemed to be growing thicker every moment, trickling through the firm bases of the cornstalks and drifting immediately above his face, blotting out what remained of the sun. A brown mouse, piping its protests, ran across his chest, where it suddenly halted and peered to left and right, as though trying to make up its mind which direction to take. Nicholas looked ino its startled eyes and smiled, thinking how desperately it appeared to be in need of advice and sympathy. Finally, still squeaking, it ran down his leg and disappeared. There was silence again.

Then a great puff of smoke drifted across his face and he forgot the mouse in a new fit of coughing. This time the pain racked his entire body. "I am dying or perhaps I am dead," he thought.

This knowledge did not shock him. The bridge connecting present with past seemed to have been almost painless save for that one sharp spasm. But, at that moment, a sudden panic seized him lest he should be denied a final glance at the past, and should enter upon a new experience without calm and reasoned assessment of the old.

"I must fix my mind on a single point, as one does when a ship is beating out to sea," he thought. A whole series of images flashed through his brain, carrying him back through youth and boyhood to childhood, but to none of them would the sliding hook of his consciousness hold fast and he was whirled back on the immediate past again, to Lobau and the events of the last few days.

Then he remembered Nicholette as he had seen her sitting demurely beside Claude during that absurd wedding carousal. Her ripe mouth smiled at him indulgently, as though she had just looked into his brain and read what was written there, as simply as he had read his pupils' copybooks in the old days at Cicero's. He knew then that he had outgrown Camilla and that this canteen trollop could more than fill her place at any time when she wished. He knew that if Claude were killed he could begin now to live again. The bitterness of the years had been drained out of him here, among the bruised corn.

It was Louis and the mongrel Fouché who found him, with the flames licking the upturned soles of his boots and the low blanket of smoke covering him like a shroud. The dog began to bark furiously, and Louis, slashing at the horseshoe of fire with his leafless branch, shouted to Gabriel, who was moving in alignment twenty yards nearer the river.

A little knot of them dragged him clear of the flames. He was stiff and his face and neck had a peculiar mottled appearance like that of a man long drowned. Jean came over and knelt beside him, his lower lip biting at the end of his moustache.

"Finished?" asked Manny, awaiting the sergeant's verdict.

Jean tore away the bloodied tunic, exposing the shoulder wound. He gave a low cry of satisfaction.

"That may have saved him," he told them. "He's got a violent concussion. A fair-sized ball must have passed clean through his shako. I've seen it happen before. This discoloration is due to shock; the jerk must have all but broken his neck."

Gabriel noticed that the broad leather chin-strap of Nicholas's shako had cut its way into the flesh. The top of the shako was beaten flat and the stiff leather had buckled, like a concertina. They examined the shako with interest. Jean said that the flow of blood from the bullet in his shoulder wound gave the man a chance. They made a litter of their boughs and carried him back to the wagon. Nicholas was placed in the care of the girl, who went about the business of tending him with the same unhurried self-assurance that she displayed in everything else they asked her to do, cooking meals, cleaning arms, making a bivouac. She might be Claude's wife, but she was still a collective possession also.

Skilfully she cleaned out the shoulder wound and cut Nicholas's wrist to draw off more blood. Gradually the discoloration about the face and neck began to fade, and in less than a week the girl drove him into Vienna. The voltigeurs took him to a convent in one of the outer suburbs, close to the ammunition park which they were detailed to guard. None of them trusted docors or hospitals. They would have kept Nicholas in the wagon had this been possible, but garrison work meant that Nicholette would be busy and it would have been unfair to burden her permanently with a sick man. So two of them went to see Nicholas every morning as they came off guard. When the ex-schoolmaster asked for books they went over to the Schönbrunn library and helped themselves. The others waited, whilst Gabriel selected something suitable. He was the only other member of the file who could read.

CHAPTER SEVEN

Gabriel explored Vienna in the company of Emmanuel, the Jew. He could hardly have found a better guide, for Manny had attended the Viennese fairs half a dozen times and knew every street, every market and most of the cheaper cafés.

Gabriel had received money from Crichot, and together they spent freely. Their guard duties were not exacting, for Vienna was full of troops awaiting the signing of the peace treaty. The voltigeurs were under arms every other night, but the rest of the time was their own and they made the most of it, drinking the sweet local wine in the gardens, listening to better, if less appreciated, music than Dominique provided, flirting with the friendly Viennese, who seemed to bear the French no grudge on account of the recent campaign or their defeats and humiliations of the past fifteen years.

The hospitals were pest-houses of sick, verminous men. Hundreds of labourers were required to dig graves for the dead, both in Vienna and on the Marchfield. At the Schönbrunn Palace the marshals gave a series of balls, and the Emperor's civil staff were already whispering of a marriage that would make Napoleon's late enemy his father-in-law.

Old Jean was more than usually depressed when he heard of the Austrian marriage. Like most of the veterans he was attached to the Empress Josephine. The army regarded her as a symbol of victory, dating back to the early Italian campaigns, when Napoleon, as an experimental general of twenty-six, had turned aside from his mountain of maps to dash off impassioned love-letters to his ex-courtesan wife in Paris, the woman who cost him a king's ransom each year in clothes and jewels, but whose warm smile and regal dignity had won the goodwill even of the gossips in the salons.

Claude Dupont shared his sergeant's pessimism. To him Josephine was symbolic not only of victory but of the Revolution. She had lived in Paris prisons through the last stages of the Terror, and her husband, who had gone to the guillotine, had known Claude's father when the latter came up from the Gironde as a deputy to share in the blithe business of making a new society in which all men were equal. Claude had been brought up to detest Habsburgs. One member of this accursed family with whom the Emperor now saw fit to unite represented the system that had brought his grandfather to the gallows for stealing a pheasant. How could a free France hope to profit by such an alliance? He went in to have a long talk with Nicholas on the subject, but the schoolmaster, wan but fast recovering his accustomed irony, only lay back on his sweat-soiled pallet and laughed.

"Hang on to your republican dream, Claude," he told the young man. "It's all you've got!"

Claude was detailed to join a guard of honour for the Arch-duke Charles when he visited Imperial Headquarters for the armistice preliminaries. He saw the punctilio observed by the hundreds of gold-braided flunkeys bowing and bobbing round the members of the staffs, and he recalled Nicholas's caustic remark when the two of them had witnessed a similar function at Tilsit two years before. "A million Frenchmen died to get rid of all this!" Nicholas had muttered. Claude felt the same misgivings, only now they were the more acute, for at Tilsit he had at least

84

seen the King of Prussia treated like a wilful schoolboy.

Neither Manny nor Gabriel bothered themselves about politics. Manny went off on his own now and again, to sample the Viennese brothels, but he was never able to persuade Gabriel to accompany him. The young man was far too absorbed in the colour and bustle of Vienna, the first capital city he had ever visited. He applied himself to the German tongue and became fairly fluent. He sketched odd corners of the older part of the town and invariably attracted a crowd of curious urchins to his sketchbook. He carried out a small commission for a café proprietor, who paid in wine for some mural decorations, and he wandered with a watchful eye along the lines of the relaxed army, observing and storing up his impressions for the future.

One hot afternoon while on twenty-four hours' leave he hired a punt, poling his way into one of the many backwaters that flowed into the main stream above the bridge. It was on this solitary occasion that he found Karen.

Not far from the centre of the city, the buildings on each side of the narrow stream gave place to a string of flat meadows, broken, here and there, by an overgrown copse. He had tied up his punt in the shade of an overhanging bank crowned by a clump of dwarf oaks and alders, all in rich green leaf. The low-hanging branches formed a green cave, concealing the punt from the opposite bank, where the shallow stream spread itself into a tiny bay hemmed in on all sides by foliage.

Gabriel was lying here, too lazy to take up brush or crayon, when a gentle splashing attracted his attention. He looked across the stream and saw a small herd of cows wading into the water, their stumbling hooves stirring up the mud and sending out a ring of gentle ripples that splashed softly against his punt.

After the last animal had entered the water he saw their drover, a buxom, sunburned girl of about eighteen, with honey-coloured hair swinging in long, thick plaits to her waist.

He watched, idly, as the girl slipped off her heavy clogs and sat down on the bank, dabbling her feet in the stream and humming to herself as she leaned back on her hands and watched the cows drink their fill. There was a pastoral perfection about the scene that delighted Gabriel. Its appeal lay in its very ordinariness, the contented cattle revelling in the cooling ripple of the water, the dappled pattern of sunlight on the still leaves, the girl's relaxed contentment as she wriggled her pink toes in the stream. Cautiously he reached for his book and began to sketch.

Gabriel's original study of Karen is one of three sketches, among a total of close on four hundred, in which a layman can discern real merit. Some of the others are good, particularly his early work in the camps, and a few are arresting, like the crayon drawing of the young dragoon called "Remount Demand," but this picture excels by the charm and freshness of the cowslip bank upon which the girl is sitting. Her head is thrown back, displaying a strong neck but unexpectedly delicate chin. Her figure is that of a peasant, prematurely developed by ceaseless toil in the fields, a woman who would be middle-aged within eight or nine years. The features, however, have a delicate bourgeois caste, and the eyes, blue as the Austrian sky, have a sparkle that makes the stream ripple and the drowsy summer air hum with the music of bees. It has a simple title. Gabriel signed it "Cowherd, Vienna, August, 1809."

The girl sat there for close on half an hour, oblivious of Gabriel sketching from his ambush in the alder clump. Perhaps this is why the picture has such appeal. It is the only portrait in the book for which the subject did not pose.

When Gabriel was putting the finishing touches to his portrait, smiling to himself with satisfaction at having completed it without advertising his presence, the girl seemed to recollect her work on the farm, a white building which was just visible on a low plateau immediately above the woods. Suddenly she stood up and waded into the stream, calling to her cows and driving them round to the path.

One beast was loth to go. Instead of responding to her cries it waded beyond her depth and stood flank deep in the current, cropping the bushes within inches of Gabriel's punt.

A mischievous impulse seized the young Frenchman. Tearing

the page from his book, he reached out and drove the corner of the stiff paper onto the animal's horn. The cow, startled by the movement, shied away from the bushes and stumbled back to its own side of the stream, with the sketch hanging incongruously over its left ear.

From his screen of alders Gabriel grinned at the girl's astonishment. He saw her hestitate a moment and glance both left and right before stepping forward to snatch the page from its peg.

She studied it for a moment, flushing with pleasure; then, holding the drawing to her breast, she turned to run up the path in the wake of her cows. Gabriel pushed off from the bank and sent the punt skimming through the leaves half-way across the stream. He called: "Wait, please wait!" in his best German.

She stopped, indecisively, at the foot of the incline. He stood up and waved and the flat-bottom skiff lurched, throwing him head foremost into the shallow water. Above the splash he heard her peal of laughter.

She retraced her steps down the path as he waded ashore. A pair of kingfishers, disturbed by the commotion, returned to their scrutiny in the iris clump by the water's edge. He dragged the punt onto the tiny beach and sat on the thwarts, dashing the drops from his hair.

The girl looked at the drawing again. Smiling, he held out his hand, but she shook her head vigorously and held it close to her laced bodice.

"I shall keep it!" she told him firmly.

"I will make another and a better one."

"When?" He detected an eagerness in her voice and it flattered him.

"Now?"

She shook her head. "I have been here too long. There is work at the farm. Come," she held out her hand, "I will dry your clothes while you eat."

The simplicity of the gesture and her childlike assurance touched him. He recalled a comment of Old Jean's when they had passed a group of peasants whilst marching in from Wagram: "No wonder we beat these people. They are babies at war."

He took her hand, wondering how the palm of a peasant should be so soft. It was like the hand of a burgher's daughter in Agen, a girl groomed and petted for a wealthy marriage. But she had no intention of letting him leave the punt without his sketch-book and crayons. Happily he tucked them under his arm and followed her up the gully to the farm.

The farm was a small, ramshackle building of four rooms, built of cob and thatched with local reed gathered beside the stream. In the large tiled kitchen there was a warm smell of baking bread and chicken mash. A tall, strongly built woman with a wealth of dark-chestnut hair was making pastry near the open window. The cowherd went up to her and handed her the drawing, saying something in a dialect which Gabriel could not understand. The tall woman gave an exclamation of pleasure and at once broke into a torrent of speech. From their gestures Gabriel concluded that they were discussing the picture. The young woman went through a pantomime of the recent en-counter, ending in an amusing reconstruction of Gabriel's tumble into the water. The tall woman threw back her head and laughed, showing strong white teeth. Gabriel stood by the stove, conscious of a new sense of peace and serenity.

Presently the woman dropped back into the Viennese dialect he understood and bade him sit down and eat. They gave him two monstrous pasties, flavoured too highly with garlic but far tastier than any of the food he had bought in the cafés during the last few weeks. His shirt and breeches dried on him as he ate and washed down the pasties with a draught of heady local wine.

When the sun began to get low an elderly man, gnarled and white-haired, came into the kitchen. He showed no surprise on seeing Gabriel, but there was another lengthy inquest on the picture, which the girl had propped against a large copper jug on the table. When the old man had finished his meal he offered Gabriel a pipe and tobacco. They sat and smoked and drank home-brewed beer. The cowherd, Karen, hovered delightedly in

88

the background and Gabriel noticed that her eyes constantly roved back to his drawing. Presently the tall woman fetched his sketchbook and thrust it into his hands.

"Make a picture of my father," she asked him.

Gabriel took out his crayons and carefully selected three or four colours.

"I will make a picture of you all," he told them.

Gabriel remained at the farm that night, sleeping on a truss of sweet-smelling hay in the loft above the byre. The combined effects of the wine, the beer and the old peasant's strong tobacco had rendered him pleasantly intoxicated by nightfall. Underneath him the cattle stamped and rustled. As sleep came to him he heard the distant ripple of the stream at the foot of the gully, and he thought how gentle life could be if it were not for the rattle of sidearms and the shrill blare of the cavalry trumpet. Once in the night he awoke with a cry of terror. He had seen a large, amber-coloured insect wade into a pool of blood and stop, its feelers hovering over a shapeless thing huddled on the dusty floor. He almost sobbed with relief when he reached out and touched the fragrant hay and saw the white stars winking through the open casement of the loft. Then he fell to sleep again, this time dreamlessly.

The girl Karen called him in the morning, shouting his name from the cobbles in the yard below. He jumped down, shivering slightly in the keen morning air, and breakfasted on fresh rolls, served with strong black coffee. He offered money, but it was refused indignantly, and when he enquired after the old man, anxious to thank him for his hospitality, Karen told him that her father and her sister, Louise, had already gone to the fields and would not be back until they came for their noonday meal. He asked her if he might come again, bringing a friend, and she agreed eagerly, adding that he was to be sure and bring his sketchbook. She came down to the punt with him and placed his book reverently in the bows.

He took both her hands, smiling down at her.

"You are very happy here," he said.

She looked into his eyes and saw that they were strikingly blue in the strong morning sunlight.

"Yes," she said simply, "we are happy enough."

As though moved by a simultaneous impulse they embraced, gently and without passion, as two children might. He climbed into the punt and she gave it a playful push with her clogged foot. He looked back and saw her smiling as he poled himself downstream.

All hours of the day, whenever he could escape from his duties in the city, Gabriel spent sketching and working on the smallholding, helping Karen or her sister with their livestock, feeding the hens, repairing outhouses, sometimes painting scenes of farm life, the simplest of which never failed to delight the two girls and earn the solemn appreciation of their father.

Karen was the only child of a second marriage and was ten years younger than Louise, her stepsister. There was a boy, Karl, by the first wife, but he had been called away by the conscription decree of four years ago and they had heard nothing of him since he left, for he was unable to write so much as his name.

For a time, particularly during harvesting or when one of the cows calved, the old man had missed his son's slow, stubborn strength, and the farm, a sub-tenant's holding from a large manor farm higher up the river, had shrunk to a few fields of maize and barley and an acre or two of pasturage beside the backwater. The goats roamed the plateau, and the poultry, which included a flock of fine geese, scratched about the yard and in the copse behind the cottage. The family lived simply, seldom leaving their fields and rarely travelling as far as Vienna, less than three leagues distant. They worked from dawn until dusk, and after supper they went to bed. They had no immediate neighbors, for the soil on this side of the river was too poor to attract the more ambitious farmers. The old man paid his rent in kind, driving a two-wheeled cart laden with mixed produce over to his landlord's farm at stipulated intervals. Gabriel reflected that the life of such sub-tenants had undergone no important change during the past ten centuries. Dynasties came and went. Wars surged up and down the Danube Valley and occasionally the younger peasants were forced to take part in them. But, sooner or later, all who survived found their way back to the fields to go on ploughing until they became too crippled with rheumatism to stir from the fireside. Karen's father, Stepan, had perhaps half a dozen years of active life ahead of him. One day, he said, Karl would come back, or one of the girls would marry and her husband would probably agree to some arrangement concerning the future of the farm. Louise, his elder daughter, had given birth to a child years ago. He could not say who the father had been, probably one of the men who came in to help with the harvesting before casual labour died out under the strain of successive conscriptions. Gabriel asked what had become of the child. The priest took it, Stepan told him; Louise had been too busy to nurse it after they had called his son into the army.

The old man looked into the fire a while. Suddenly he said: "Why don't you take her? She'd make you a good wife and she's as strong as a bull. Why don't you stay here? It's better than marching about the country with nothing but roots to eat half the time. Or perhaps you would rather have Karen? She's not such a good worker as Louise, but she milks well. The cows like someone with a soft hand who isn't in too much of a hurry."

Gabriel would have chuckled inwardly if this invitation had been made a month or two ago, but now he found himself giving it serious consideration. Desertion, at this short distance from the camp, was practically an impossibility, but there were other means at his disposal. With his aunt's money, which old Crichot continued to forward in methodically spaced driblets, he could purchase a discharge, if he went about it with sufficient care and gave bribes to the right people. An old friend of Jean's had managed it only a month ago, cashing in his accumulated loot and setting himself up as an innkeeper at Innsbruck. Why not? It was better, as Stepan pointed out, than marching about Europe eating roots; it was infinitely better than getting killed, or maimed, or rotting in a damp fortress as a prisoner of war awaiting one of the inevitable gaol epidemics.

Perhaps Gabriel was feeling the reaction of the recent campaign. In the army the veterans had a saying: "A man fights best in his first battle." After two major engagements Gabriel had had enough war. It seemed to him that he had lived through a whole lifetime since that day, barely eight months ago, when he had buried Aunt Marie and set off for the recruiting depot at Bordeaux. He sometimes asked himself if he had found what he sought in the colour and movement of the camps, and in the easy companionship of his six comrades, but he could never answer this query to his own satisfaction. It depended so much on the mood of the moment.

The sun-drenched landscape of the Danube Valley inclined a man towards lotus-eating. For a brief space he had resisted the inertia, but he found it increasingly difficult to return to billets after off-duty periods at the farm. During the hours he spent with Karen his happiness was complete and he sketched easily and well. Her health and simplicity were a twin inspiration. He did a crayon study of Karen milking in the byre, a shaft of sunlight striking through the broken tiles and lighting her head with a golden halo. He caught her turning half sideways and smiling up at him through the haze of vapour rising from the cow's flanks.

There is another sketch of her in a hayfield, beside the backwater, and here she looks less simple, almost coquettish. Her startlingly blue eyes are half closed, and a cornstalk droops from her red mouth. It is an idealized picture, not so carefully done as the original sketch from the alder clump, but with the same quality of innocence, as though artist and sitter were two children romping in a sweet-smelling clover field.

In after years Gabriel often wondered whether the old man, Stepan, had dropped a hint to his elder daughter after his invitation to Gabriel to become one of the family.

One night when, tired out with hay-raking, Gabriel had climbed the ladder to his bed in the loft, he was awakened by a heavy rustle in the hay at his side. Too drowsy to take alarm, he reached out and touched a woman beside him. His disappointment was intense when he heard the voice of Louise whisper: "It's me, Gabriel!" He lay silent whilst she held him in her arms, too sensitive about her feeling to resist. She was gone again by morning and Gabriel felt cheated as he drank the coffee that Karen prepared for him. He said nothing to her, but on his return to the camp he told Manny, who threw back his head and bellowed with laughter.

"It's time you took me out there," he said, and Gabriel thought the idea a good one. That afternoon he punted the Jew up the winding backwater and presented him to the family. The Jew's eyes sparkled when Louise served their supper. Gabriel thought that she must be aware of his subterfuge, for she paid the Jew special attention. After that Manny always accompanied him and all three of the peasants made him welcome.

As the summer passed, and the first leaves began to fall in the tall beechwoods behind the cottage, Gabriel felt a new, more intense fascination for the place. One afternoon when he and Karen had been tending the goats on the hillside he suddenly turned to her and covered her face with shy kisses. She returned them and laid her sunburned cheek against his, making little sounds, like a young mother soothing a child. He too felt like a child, crying for comfort, not to a pretty peasant girl but to all the women in the world whose sons and lovers buckled their belts and bandoliers about them and marched out to play the child's game of war. He dared not tell her that earlier in the day the Eighty-seventh had received orders to break camp and move up to the north-west, where Massena was assembling a vast army for the Spanish Peninsula. For the first time since he had enlisted he hated his military obligations. He felt he could have stayed here in this field forever, holding this woman to his breast.

When the sun went down they wandered silently back to the cottage. A stranger was sitting at the table, wolfing an omelette. He glared balefully in their direction but said nothing. A homemade crutch rested against his chair.

"It's Karl," Louise told them, "back from the hospital at Litz. He's been discharged."

Gabriel saw that the peasant's right leg was missing. His thigh ended in a knot of dirty bandages and a leather pad, kept in place by an ugly network of tapes that reached up to a sword-belt buckled round his waist. The wound and its amateur appliances looked obscene. The Frenchman observed that the man's face was worn with pain and fatigue. He ate as though he had not seen food for days, hardly pausing to glance at the strangers or his stepsister, but reserving the whole of his concentration for the food they ladled onto his plate.

Karen went over and kissed him on the forehead, while the old man talked to him about the farm. Manny sat in the chimney seat, looking somewhat uncomfortable. Once or twice he glanced sharply in Gabriel's direction, and Gabriel sensed the warning hint in his eyes.

When at length the two voltigeurs climbed the loft to their bed, Manny said: "Damn the fellow! Why couldn't he die and be done with it! He's no use here, Stepan will have to feed him for nothing!" Then, as though relenting, he added, "Poor devil, he's quite mad."

Gabriel felt a surge of fear for the trio in the cottage. He asked Manny: "Did you tell Louise that we were leaving in the morning?"

"No, let them be; it's just as well we are leaving. There's murder in that fellow down there."

"What can we do?" said Gabriel.

"Do?" Manny grunted, so far from his usual good humour that he seemed almost a stranger. "We can't do a thing. This time tomorrow we'll be a dozen leagues away." And then, more drowsily, "Damn the fellow, he's spoiled my last night with the woman, unless she has the sense to come out here in spite of him."

He dozed off then, but within an hour Gabriel heard a creak on the ladder. He sat up, unreasonably alarmed, and reached out to shake Manny, who was a heavy sleeper.

It was only Louise, however, and Manny gratefully pulled her down in the hay beside him. For a time Gabriel heard them talking in low whispers. Unable to sleep again, he got up, dressed and went out.

He went into the yard and leaned on the gate, inhaling the soft night air, yearning for the warmth of the girl's body, the scent of her hair in his nostrils, but prevented from going round to the back of the cottage and calling her name by a gnawing anxiety which he could not explain. Finally he vaulted the gate and climbed the hillside to the spot where he had lain with her that afternoon. He stood there for a long time, looking down at the faint glimmer of the starlight on the tiny bay where he had seen her first.

Down in the fold of the hillside, where the cottage crouched in the deep shadow of the woods, he saw a sudden spurt of flame, then another and then a shapeless white glow that almost dazzled him, lighting up the barn and the outbuildings as if it were day.

He cried out and began to run, stumbling down the uneven slope, slipping and rolling in the furze bushes and among the rabbit warrens. It seemed an endless time before he flung himself into the yard, scratched, bruised and sobbing for breath. The whole cottage was now a whirling mass of flames, spitting showers of sparks that had already ignited the barn, where the hay flared up like pitch. He could hardly see the cottage walls for the thick clouds of smoke that caught at his throat and sent him reeling against the byre. Inside he heard the outcry of terrified cattle.

He tore open the byre door, but no animals stampeded into the open. He had forgotten, in his wild panic, that the cows were chained to an oak bar that ran the length of the outhouse. He hovered a moment, uncertain what to do, and then leaped the fence and ran round to the back of the cottage. There was no sign of the girls or of Manny. He plunged across the little vegetable patch and laid his hand on the iron latch of the back door. The heat was terrific and he was blinded by smoke, choked by the pungent smell of burning wool where sparks were smouldering in his epaulettes.

Then he heard a scream and a confused medley of sounds. A huge shower of sparks soared up in his face and a man's arm was flung across his throat, dragging him back, across the vegetables, towards the woods. He clawed at the arm with all his strength, but it held on like the bite of a steel trap. The glare of the fire faded and the merry roar of the flames was shut off, as though somebody had slammed a heavy door on them. He lost consciousness.

When he regained his senses he was sitting with his back to a tree and Manny was kneeling over him, forcing the neck of a small bottle of brandy between his teeth. The raw spirit made him retch and he gulped for air.

Presently the brandy had its effect and his brain cleared. He looked round and saw the Jew, naked except for his shirt, sitting back on his haunches and regarding him with an expression of mild concern.

"I thought you were gone," was all he said.

They were silent for a while. Finally, Gabriel nerved himself to ask the question: "Were any of them saved?"

Manny shook his head and slowly massaged his bare thighs.

"After we got down Louise ran in at the front. I tried to stop her, but she's got a punch like a mule's kick." He rubbed the side of his jaw, and Gabriel, in the soft light of the glow from below, noticed that his face looked lopsided. "That cripple must have fired the place," Manny added. "He hopped out for a moment with his clothes alight. He was still holding a faggot and screeching like a fiend. I didn't see either of the others. He'd probably staved in their heads before he put his torch to the place. You'd have gone, too, if I hadn't caught you."

"I wish you had let me try," Gabriel said quietly and suddenly began to sob.

Manny made no attempt to comfort him. He got up abruptly.

"I'm going to forage around for some breeches," he said. "I might come across something." Then he stooped and flung a bulky object at Gabriel's feet. "I brought this out of the loft when I jumped into the yard. God knows why; it just happened to come to hand."

It was Gabriel's sketchbook. Gabriel considered the incongruity of Manny's act of salvage. Two men and two women burned to death. A farm and its livestock charred to a cinder. Yet here was his sketchbook, not even soiled by drifting smuts.

Manny came back to him after a time. He had found a sack in one of the outhouses which had been saved from utter destruction by its wide drinking trough, filled to the brim before supper that evening. Tearing a hole in each corner of the sack, he slipped the course garment over his loins, belting it with a strip of linen wrenched from the hem of his shirt.

"Let's march," he said, leading the way down the narrow path to the moored punt, and Gabriel experienced another shock in the realization that Manny had already thrust the tragedy into the back of his mind. To the Jew the gutted farm and its charred bodies were already as far away as the grenadier whom Gabriel had killed in the bedroom of the cottage at Essling. To Manny the incident was sad, but not overwhelmingly so. It was another unpleasant stage on the journey, a patch of mud they had not been able to circumnavigate on the march, a musket with a broken stock that had to be tossed aside on the route.

A great cloud seemed to rise up and blot out Gabriel's brain. He sat in the punt and watched the Jew skilfully poling his way through the shadows. Last night there had been Karen, a girl with blue eyes and honey-coloured plaits, who had held his body close to hers in the coarse grass on the hillside. Today she was gone, along with all those huddled forms that he passed and repassed in the village street at Essling and in the cornfields at Wagram. Tomorrow this indifferent Jew maybe, or Dominique the fiddler, or Old Jean, or himself, would cross over into the ranks of the newly dead and join the countless army of those who had once watched the sun setting on a bank of campion and cow-parsley, who had once smelled roasted meat and tasted the tang of the sea, had savoured wine and women's kisses. There

97

was no end to this process, and no beginning. A few short years of heat and cold, struggle and relaxation, hunger and satiety, a constant swing from one extreme to another, with nothing outside the pigmy limits of these crude contrasts.

He began to understand the fantastic but cunningly disguised melancholy of it all, and the constant staving off of the inevitable by the parrying instinct. On the retina of his memory he saw an image of a Saxon infantryman, one of those harried by the Austrian cavalry in the charge near the river. The fellow had been slashed by a dozen sabre cuts, his bare head was streaming blood, but he did not surrender life and lie down to die. Instead he kept running to and fro, like a worried ant, until even the callous troopers ceased to waste further blows on him and turned their attention to others. Then, with a sort of grotesque grace, like a savage in a symbolic dance, the man sank down and bowed his shoulders in death. The impulse to go on living was as unreasoning as it was universal. Gabriel wondered why nobody troubled to think it out, why sick men, numb with pain, stricken with wounds and disease, should nerve themselves to get up and struggle a few yards farther down the road, looking, with miserable envy, after their comrades, whose time had not yet come and who went on acting as though it never would come, right up to the final moment.

Before they reached the outskirts of the city he thumbed idly through the book that lay upon his knees. His thumb moved a loose page and he took it out. It was his first drawing of Karen. Two days before he had asked her to lend it to him for retouching and she had done so reluctantly. He fingered the jagged edges of the rent made in the corner of the page by the cow's horn. The playful moment seemed infinitely far off, something half-remembered from his childhood. He resisted an impulse to drop the sketch into the rippling water. Instead he pushed off the clip that gripped the pages and clamped the torn sheet in its place.

Manny straightened his back. He looked absurb standing there in the stern, draped in his piece of sacking and the tatters of a shirt.

"The Devil take that cripple," he said lightly. "Unless I can lie well enough I shall have to pay for a new uniform. Here, take the pole now, we don't want to attract attention."

He steadied the punt while Gabriel moved across and took the pole. As it began to grow light they passed the first of the suburbs. The streets were already astir. Far off, in the grounds of the Imperial Palace, they heard the shrilling of a bugle as the Young Guard got under arms. A wagon, piled high with golden barley, splashed across the ford, heading for the main road to the north. Manny glanced after it, his lips pursed in a soundless whistle.

"It's time we made a move," he said. "Hurry, we'll make it before reveille."

Gabriel plunged the ten-foot pole into the weeds. A spot of water fell onto the buff covers of his sketchbook. Behind them the stream curved into the trees, and high above the thinning foliage he saw a small black cloud, stationary in the pale sky.

PART TWO

The Tagus

CHAPTER ONE

Massena's army, eighty thousand strong, was marching down the broad metalled highway to Salamanca. For more than twenty leagues the motley caravan extended, winding back towards the frontier like a blue-and-silver snake, sending up clouds of choking dust that hung motionless above the route, marking out the army's crawling progress to the watchful guerrillas posted along the chain of mountain observation posts that looked down on the valley of the Douro.

Napoleon, impatient of sterile campaigns in the Peninsula, and irritated by the continued presence of a small British force that refused to be driven back to its transports but remained to put new heart ino the fanatical resistance of the Spanish peasantry, had made a decision. Regiments of the Young Guard, freed from service in Austria by the recent conclusion of peace, finally sealed by the Habsburg marriage, had been refitted for service in Spain. Line regiments, thoroughly rested after their brief but arduous campaign on the Danube, had been sent across Europe in relays of four-horse wagons, picking up recruits en route. Heavy cavalry under the bearded Montbrun, the light horsemen of Sainte-Croix and thousands of baggage wagons made up the cavalcade that wound its way over the Spanish frontier and down into Portugal.

At its head rode the reluctant Massena, worn out by twenty years of active service, longing for retirement and leisure to count his hoarded millions and toy with his latest mistress. This pretty lady was obliged to follow the line of march, and did so resolutely enough in the becoming uniform of a light dragoon. Veterans who passed her were not impressed; she was one more non-combatant mouth to feed in a country made desolate by three years' ferocious warfare and populated, outside the big towns, by bands of ruthless partisans who swooped down on stragglers and small convoys and outdid the Turks of happier campaigns in the variety of the methods they employed to despatch their prisoners.

Behind Massena rode his unruly lieutenants, choleric, red-headed Ney, the sardonic Reynier, softly spoken Foy and General Junot, already a little unbalanced by a wound in the head, all of them envying Marshal Soult and the others who had buried themselves and their self-supporting armies in far-off Spanish provinces, where they ruled like independent kings, out of reach of the War Department in Paris and cut off, by distance and guerrilla activity, from the hand that sought to co-ordinate this sprawling war.

The army hated Spain. Most of the veterans had served in the earlier campaigns in the Peninsula, and had communicated their dislike to the footsore conscripts and to those soldiers whose garrison duties had kept them, fat and contented, in the well-stocked fortresses of Germany or the sunny billets of Italy. There was no loot to be had in these wretched little villages, which hardly broke the monotony of the main road. An hour's lagging behind the column meant almost certain death, and death with the refinements of Oriental torture. There were few women to be found, most of them having fled to the mountains or starved to death on the untilled farms of the plains. Food was scarce, even at this early stage of the expedition. Draught horses and mules were almost unobtainable and beyond the reach of any but high-ranking officers with money to burn. The sun was pitiless, a fierce African sun far different from the golden sunshine of the Danube. It struck down on chafed shoulders as though it were an active ally of the Spaniards, intent on withering the French columns before they had accomplished half the distance between the Pyrenees and the Portuguese frontier. Several men in the Eighty-seventh went down with heatstroke and died, raving, in the stifling villages along the route. Others, with festering feet, lay in the springless wagons, happy to be carried along to the nearest hospital and not abandoned to the knives of the Navarrese and Castilian partisans.

The voltigeurs marched in Ney's division, sometimes acting as skirmishers along the flanks of the tortured columns, beating the open country and now and then surprising a ragged marksman, who would rise from the scrub and run like a hare toward the mountains.

Old Jean was more cheerful than usual. He had served under Ney in several campaigns in the past and had implicit faith in the Alsatian's courage and tactics, although he held a poor opinion of his ability to handle anything larger than a corps. Jean had fought in Spain under Lannes in 1808. He knew the Spanish and their crude methods of warfare. He reiterated the officers' warnings to the young troops about the folly of straggling and was sometimes seen, like a grizzled sheepdog, hovering up and down the line of march, ordering this man to carry a weaker comrade's musket, that man to fall out and grease his feet with a special preparation of tallow and goose fat, stored in an earthenware jar in Nicholette's wagon and used sparingly for bad cases of blistering.

Nicholette's canteen travelled with the company, the file taking turns to ride on the box and tailboard. Fouché, the mongrel that had followed them from the Danube, panted along in the shade of the rear axle. The file had become attached to the dog and shared their food with it, but during the march down from the Pyrenees Fouché's need was for water and he drank greedily at every ford. Nicholette, who held the reins of the two Flemish horses, seldom showed signs of the common fatigue, setting up her trestles at every bivouac and selling the light Spanish wines which she and Claude had managed to purchase at Tolosa, soon after they passed the Pyrenees.

Claude was morose during the march. He was beginning to wonder whether the girl had tired of him during their long stay in Vienna. She was still dutiful and there had been no open quarrel, but he could never rouse in her responses equal to those of the first few weeks after the wedding. She seldom spoke to him except about business or routine duties in connection with the wagon and horses. Sometimes, when he sat beside her during his spells on the driving-seat, he realized that her mind was far away, moving purposefully along the lanes of a dream world where there were no uniforms, no battles, no dust-choked men to be served at each halt in the endless trek.

Occasionally he caught her looking at Nicholas in a queer, concentrated way, and the first quirks of jealousy nagged him. Nothing had happened, however, to confirm this suspicion. She talked to Nicholas more than to any of the others because Nicholas usually had more to talk about. Very occasionally he made her laugh, and Claude, hearing her laugh for the first time, decided that he did not like the sound. It was a harsh rattle, like the sudden tug of a chain coupling on an artillery caisson rusty from disuse.

He realized dismally that he knew no more about the woman now than on the night when she had sat beside him during the wedding carousal. She had never spoken her thoughts or described her feelings. She had no convictions about anyone or anything. Yet, despite this reticence, she always managed to convey the impression that she had already drawn her own conclusions about all of them, not only the members of the file but the army, the generals, the campaign and the war.

It was uncanny that she never seemed to feel pain, heat, fatigue or even thirst in this Devil's country. She was neat and competent in everything she did, and if she was required to do something beyond her physical strength, which was not often, she never attempted it but quietly asked him to accomplish the work and then came to inspect the results.

Claude sometimes wondered if she would have a child; whether, in this event, it would break down her reserve and improve their relationship. She did not, apparently, do anything to prevent conception, but more than a year had gone by since their marriage and her figure was still as slender and graceful as on the day he had first seen her helping Old Carla to scour the wagon in Dresden. He was not anxious to be a father. What could one do with a pregnant woman on a trip like this? And even supposing that she was able to have the child in one of the strongly held towns between their present position and Portugal, what would they do with an infant in arms during a retreat or a general attack?

He knew that she would never willingly abandon the canteen. When it came to money she had the tenacity of a Norman small-holder. He did not know how much money she possessed or even where it was hidden, if she carried it with her, which he felt was likely. It must, he thought, be a considerable sum, for Old Carla was known to have made steady profits over a number of years. As he lay beside her in the hooped tent throughout the stifling nights, Claude wondered if she would ever trust him as he felt that he ought to be trusted. After all, it was she who had chosen him when she might have had the pick of a thousand men. By this time he was aware of the facts regarding Jean's straw ballot. She had whispered them in his ear during that first idyllic night on the islet. He had been immeasurably gratified at the time, but now he sometimes wondered whether other considerations had directed her choice. Perhaps she did not want a man who would require anything more than her body. Perhaps she cherished her solitary thoughts and had an active aversion to sharing them with anyone.

The march was proving a lonely one for Claude. Jean was often at some distance from the company and rejoined them only when it bivouacked. Louis and Nicholas scouted on the right flank, Claude pairing with Dominique on the left. The farmboy chattered like a magpie and went hallooing over the rocks in pursuit of stray Spaniards, as though he enjoyed moving at the double under full equipment and the scourge of a noonday sun.

Gabriel and Manny were farther to the rear, having been assigned as guards to a column of would-be deserters, conscripts marshalled at Pau after individual attempts to evade service.

Apart from wrist fetters the men were no longer shackled. Escape in this countryside was impossible now that the army was well inside Spain. On arrival at Salamanca they were to be split up among various units, but the company's orders had been to keep them under close guard and secure them at night, until they could be absorbed into regiments where they would be under permanent observation.

Captain Vidal, the company's senior officer, was a strict disciplinarian. Obeying the letter of his commands, he had the men marched under guard and each night, after supper, saw them yoked together in batches of twenty by lengths of light chain carried in one of the ambulances. Captain Vidal had won the Legion of Honour at Raab after more than twenty years' active service. He was a ruthlessly efficient soldier, and if he had been given his way he would have shot the prisoners en masse before they left France. To clutter up the march with a mob of men who had already done their best to evade service, nursing them along in the slender hope that one or two, finding no alternative, might turn out to be good soldiers in the end, seemed to him the outside limit of idiocy. So he dispensed with outlying flank guards and enclosed the conscripts within an oblong of veteran infantrymen. He also made sure that his charges were not overfed during the march.

The inclusion of Gabriel and Manny in the escort was due to an unusual incident, in which both were unwilling participants. Just before leaving Valladolid the two voltigeurs had ordered a dinner in a tavern kept by a Frenchman. The remaining members of the file were on duty and unable to enjoy Gabriel's hospitality. On reaching the inn they found more than a dozen soldiers eating in the general room. Among the diners, sitting in an alcove by himself, was Captain Vidal.

The meal was a bad and very expensive one. Just as they were about to pay their score and depart, the innkeeper, a portly, florid man with an air of self-importance less than justified by the quality of his entertainment, came into the room and announced, in a threatening tone, that someone present had stolen more than a dozen of his silver spoons. Ignoring the indignant denials, he despatched a serving-man forthwith to fetch the nearest provost.

Captain Vidal told the innkeeper that this was unnecessary, and announced that he, as senior officer present, would search everyone in the room. Vidal was respected in the ranks, and each man submitted without demur to close scrutiny of his kit and pockets. The spoons were not discovered.

By the time the search was concluded two junior provost officers had arrived, and Vidal explained what had been done. The innkeeper, refusing to be satisfied, insisted on a second search, this time in the presence of the provosts. Again the kits and pockets of nearly twenty men were turned out on the floor. As the last man was being searched the innkeeper's wife, a thin, sour-faced Spaniard, entered the room. She announced, in a casual tone, that the spoons had been found. They had been mislaid in cleaning.

Vidal quietly unbuckled his sword-belt and laid it on the table. Manny, who knew Vidal well, plucked Gabriel by the sleeve. "Watch this, it's going to be good!" he whispered.

Vidal advanced softly towards the landlord. The infantry captain was a short, well-knit man, renowned in the regiment for agility and physical strength. At Raab, where he had won his decoration, he had run up a sloping beam like a monkey, gained the ramparts and thrown two artillerymen into the moat, after which he turned their eight-pounder onto a field-gun a short distance away and dismantled it with a single discharge. He had high, arched brows and a sallow complexion, with prominent cheekbones and a small, clipped moustache; this combination of features made him look satanic when he scowled. In the regiment he was known as "Lucie," short for Lucifer.

Speaking very quietly, Vidal said: "You seem to have made a mistake, fellow!"

"I have and I apologize," said the landlord, but, not liking the expression in the captain's eye, he began to edge towards the kitchen door, closely followed by his wife.

"An apology is not enough," said Vidal bluntly. "You have insulted the soldiers of the Empire, the men to whom you owe every sou of your ill-deserved prosperity. I cannot allow this to pass for an apology. There must be atonement!"

With a sudden bound he reached the innkeeper and floored him with a terrific blow between the eyes. The man's wife screamed and two or three tapsters ran in with cudgels. A general movement among the troops, who had been watching the scene with growing satisfaction, was checked by Vidal.

"If any man intervenes I'll have him arrested," he shouted. Then, picking up a chair, he stepped over the dazed host and rushed at the group of tapsters standing near the kitchen door. In less than a minute the chair was smashed to fragments, one tapster lay bleeding and unconscious on the floor, and the remainder had fled into the street, shouting for gendarmes.

Vidal dropped the splintered chairback and returned to the landlord, who was rising unsteadily to his knees. On his way the captain drew his sword from the discarded belt. The hostess rushed to the window, screaming for help, while Gabriel thought her husband as good as dead.

But Vidal had no intention of murdering the man. He tossed away the sabre and grasped the heavy leather scabbard, swinging it above his head and bringing it down with enormous force on the civilian's plump shoulders. At the second blow the man began to bellow, adding his roars to the shrill screams of his wife and the laughter of the troops ranged round the walls. Wherever the victim crawled and darted Vidal moved in pursuit, keeping up a fierce tattoo of blows on the landlord's head, neck and shoulders. He continued to flail the man thus until he lost consciousness and lay with his face in the sawdust. The moment he ceased to move Vidal sheathed his sabre, buckled on his belt and gave the order to march. As he left the room he called to the hysterical wife:

"That will teach you to be more careful about confusing soldiers with petty thieves!"

"There goes a man," said Manny joyfully, following Vidal into the street.

Vidal wrote their names in his notebook as a precaution against civilian prosecution, but nothing further was heard of the incident. An hour later Vidal was given charge of the conscript column and sent his orderly for Gabriel, Manny and the other voltigeurs to join the escort. They all set off together down the Salamanca road.

At the first halt Manny called Gabriel on to one side.

"Follow me!" he said, leading the way down the column to a small clump of trees, where the conscripts were sitting in their irons.

Manny halted in front of a sturdy prisoner who was sitting cross-legged on the grass, smoking the broken stub of a pipe. He was a gipsy-like man of about thirty with an enormous amount of hair showing through the tatters of his shirt.

"Hullo, brother?" Manny said, with a wry grin.

The prisoner looked up and smiled back at him, showing no surprise at the recognition.

"I saw you two leagues back," he told Manny. "How are you going to get me out of this?" He raised his manacled hands and winked.

Manny considered. "How did you get into it?" he asked.

The conscript gave up trying to light his pipe and yawned, stretching out his hands and letting them drop suddenly so that the chain rattled.

"I got into a fight with gendarmes in Blois," he said. "I ought to have known better. They took me to the watch-house and asked for my papers." He let out a loud, derisive laugh, as though the very idea of his possessing satisfactory papers caused him vast amusement.

Manny laughed, too. "He's a kinsman of mine," he told Gabriel. "We teamed together for more than a year in the Low Countries."

The provost's whistle shrilled and the column shuffled to its feet. Gabriel looked along the line of sullen, defeated faces. Only the gipsy appeared to take his situation philosophically.

Manny had an abstracted air during the next day's march. He seemed to be turning over a problem and Gabriel suspected that the problem had some relation to the plight of Andreas, his kinsman. At night Manny went along with some rations and a half-bottle of wine. He also gave the prisoner a little tobacco borrowed from Old Jean.

A short march beyond Alaejos, when the army had split, one half to take the main road and the other, consisting chiefly of draught horses and baggage wagons, to follow a parallel road that gradually deteriorated, Manny woke Gabriel as they lay beside the bivouac fire. They had camped in a half-deserted village, but the night was warm and they preferred the open street to vermin-infested houses.

"I'm going to pass Andreas a farrier's file and let him take his chance," he said. "We'll be handing them over and rejoining the main body tomorrow."

In low tones Gabriel did his best to dissuade the Jew.

"If Lucie finds out that one is missing he'll halve the column and comb the whole country," he said.

Manny chuckled. "He'll never catch Andreas once he's off the chain. I've known that monkey dodge the gendarmes of a whole department for years on end. And he's safe enough from the guerrillas; Andreas can speak better Spanish than a Spaniard."

Gabriel shrugged and said nothing. He was familiar with the Jew's obstinacy, and knew that the young man considered it his plain duty to do what he could for an old comrade in trouble.

The following morning, when they were about to set off, the escort sergeant reported one of the prisoners missing. Captain Vidal, already half a day's march behind the main column, cursed violently in Italian, his favourite medium for fluent blasphemy.

He went into the cattle compound, where the prisoners had been housed, and personally checked the tally. They showed him the neatly filed links of the gipsy's chain. Manny stood by expressionless. Gabriel made himself scarce and found employment at the far end of the column.

Anyone less resolute than Vidal, any officer to whom the army was more of a profession and less of a religion, would have written off Andreas then and there, but Vidal had the Pau Commandant's manifest in his pocket and on that manifest one hundred and fourteen recalcitrants were listed. Not one hundred and thirteen, or one hundred and fifteen, but one hundred and fourteen, of whom Andreas, now off the chain, was one.

Vidal rubbed his blue chin. The man could not be far. There was no food to be had between their present position and Salamanca, a day's march to the south. The fugitive would not make for the cities, which French troops garrisoned and others were traversing every day. Neither would he push on into Portugal, for his intention must, ultimately, be a speedy return to France. What would he do? What would Vidal have done in his place? Hang around the fringe of the village and wait until the column had moved on, then slink back and beg or steal the means to carry him north of the main road.

He turned to the escort sergeant.

"Take eight men and keep out of sight. Wait here until to-morrow and see if he turns up. If he doesn't, push on after us at top speed. If you catch him you can share this," and he spun a gold Napoleon in the air, catching it and returning it to his breeches pocket. Vidal was probably the only officer in the French army who valued a deserter in gold.

The sergeant thought it a pity that such a good soldier should be going stark, staring mad. He said nothing, however, and selected a patrol of eight. Manny was the first man called.

The main column handed over the conscripts and picked up the army route once more at the crossroads, a short day's march farther on. Massena had ordered two days' rest, in order to allow time for the rearguard to come up and to conduct a general overhaul of wagons, many of which were breaking down under the severe strain of the Peninsula roads. Gabriel rejoined his file and they lay up in the scrub. Dominique shot a stray goat during one of his hide-and-seek rushes with the guerrillas, and the regiment shouted with laughter when they saw him picking his way to the road with the carcass slung across his shoulders. Many of the jokers were glad of the pickings, however, when Old Jean had filled the communal kettle.

At noon on the second day a sergeant staggered past the bivouac, looking for Captain Vidal. Gabriel barely recognized the man whom the captain had left in command of the detachment three days earlier. His uniform was in tatters and his hands and face were covered with scratches. He walked as though he had been bastinadoed.

Gabriel went after him for news of Manny and the fugitive conscript, Andreas.

"A curse on the conscript," muttered the sergeant. "Lucie was right; we should have shot them all in the mountains. My detachment was ambushed and wiped out. I only escaped by a miracle. In the name of God take me to Lucie and let me sleep."

They took him to Lucie and heard his tale. The detachment had waited at the village for a day and a night, but there had been no sign of the runaway. At dawn the next morning a local man well disposed towards the French had offered to guide the party by a short cut over the spur of the mountain. They would be within sight of the main road all the way, and the Spaniard had come to them seeking protection, saying that his wife had been French and that the peasants in the village had threatened to kill him the moment the troops moved on. He led them straight into the hands of the irregulars, barely five leagues out of the village. The other seven had all been killed or taken. The sergeant himself had only escaped by leaping over a precipice and rolling hundreds of feet down the mountainside. The guerrillas must have assumed that he was dead, for after firing a few random shots in his direction they moved off to one of the passes.

Vidal's lip jutted. "I ought to have you shot for incompetence," he growled. "Could you guide a party to the spot?"

"Easily, it's not half a day's march from the camp," said the sergeant, looking ruefully at his feet.

"Get the company under arms," said Vidal.

In less than an hour the voltigeurs of the Eighty-seventh were marching back over the road the guard party had travelled. The sergeant, his wounds bandaged, rode Vidal's horse. The captain followed, riding a tall mule which soon abandoned its attempts to unseat him.

An hour before sunset on the second day they reached the scene of the encounter, a narrow track worn in the lower slopes of the mountain. One or two items of equipment, too worn or broken to be salvaged by the Spaniards, were all that was left to mark the fight. Following the sergeant's directions, they marched into the pass higher up the slope.

It was a gloomy place, shut in by towering crags, broken through by outcroppings of granite that jutted, like broken teeth, from the gritty soil. The valley was flooded with the red light of the setting sun. Gabriel shivered involuntarily.

They did not have to search far. A short distance up the valley, where the guerrillas had judged themselves safe from any immediate pursuit, the company rounded a bend and disturbed a flock of carrion birds. They rose heavily and flapped away to ledges nearer the summit, blinking down malevolently on the little column of men toiling up the mountain path.

On a flat rock, where the shelf widened, the voltigeurs found their comrades, six of them, with bullet wounds and throats cut, spread naked for the mountain eagles and laid in a neat row, as though the Spaniards had planned an obscene parody of parade-ground precision.

The men began to curse. Captain Vidal examined the corpses, then ordered a party of men to get busy with mattocks, scratching shallow graves in the space between the flat rock and the towering mountainside.

"There's one missing," the sergeant told him. "The Jew, Jacobsen!"

In the fading light Gabriel scruinized each vacant face. Manny was not there.

The thought occurred to him that Manny had deserted, too, and found means to join his fugitive kinsman, but this idea Gabriel dismissed as wildly improbable. If Manny had intended to go he would have slipped away with his kinsman when Andreas had filed his fetters. He had accompanied the detachment up to the moment the main column moved off, and obviously in so small a party the sergeant would have missed him on the march.

His conjectures were interrupted by a loud cry from a voltigeur higher up the path. Men began running in that direction, forming a ring round a gnarled, twisted tree that clung, by some miracle of hardihood, to a crevice in the rocks just above their heads. Fastened to the tree by his hands, through which had been driven two strong nails, his ankles roped a few inches above the ground, was a naked man.

The last rays of the sun, dipping behind the rugged horizon of mountain peaks, fell on a pallid face and a mop of tight black curls. The body was Emmanuel Jacobsen's; some freak of agony had twisted his wide mouth into a dying grin, a grin neither defiant nor resolute but with a sidelong twist of the lips that made even Vidal and other veterans turn their eyes away.

Claude spoke first, his voice dry and unnatural.

"Why single him out? Why Manny?"

Old Jean laid down his musket and crossed over to the tree, methodically unfastening the rope that held the ankles.

"Manny was a Jew," he said, his voice trembling; "some of these Spaniards have long memories."

They took him down and buried him alongside the others. Old Jean climbed on a voltigeur's shoulders and gently prised the

nails from the splintered palms, easing the iron out of the blood-
ied wood as though Manny was alive and would still feel pain.

Captain Vidal spurred on the gravediggers with a steady spate
of blasphemy. The men sweated in spite of the chill wind that
soughed through the valley with the going down of the sun.
When the sparse soil had been stamped down the company received the order to march, not westward towards the main body,
but north-east, to the village. Soon after the march began the
sergeant guide collapsed. He was tied to the saddle and the march
continued. Vidal did not need a guide for the remainder of the
journey. He followed the winding track, his mouth set in a
savage line, and behind him trailed the company, more than a
hundred strong. They had forgotten equally their weariness and
prospects of an evening meal.

The little column burst into the village within a few hours of
leaving the pass. The Frenchmen went from house to house,
dragging men, women and children into the street. Torches were
lighted and the entire population was paraded in the miserable
little square. The men, not more than twenty of varying ages,
were sullen. Some of the women screamed, dragging sleepy
children this way and that, turning and spitting at the men who
drove them forward at the bayonet point. Vidal massed them in
a hollow square in front of the one sizeable building in the place,
a squat stone-built storehouse. Then he climbed onto the wooden
steps with the voltigeurs drawn up at the rear of the civilians,
and asked, in halting Spanish, if anyone present understood
French. There was complete silence, except for the occasional
wail of a child.

At length two of the men pushed forward a man of about
thirty.

"This dog understands all right; I remember him well enough.
He tried to sell us some wine," said one of the original escort.

Vidal wasted no time in parleying. He addressed the man
crisply, his metallic voice ringing across the square.

"I shall give you one minute to hand over the guide who led
my detachment across the mountain path!" he said. "If, at the

end of that minute, he is not delivered up to me I shall shoot all the men present, one after another, until there is no male Spaniard in the square!"

He took out his watch, a handsome silver timepiece which Gabriel had often seen before, and held it steadily in the palm of his hand. The torches guttered in the stiff breeze. Somewhere at the back of the crowd a woman began sobbing. Men shuffled their feet in the thick dust. The minute seemed endless.

Vidal brought the period to an abrupt close. He drew out a heavy, brass-mounted pistol, cocked it and, pointing it directly at the Spaniard's head, pulled the trigger. The report shattered the silence like a salvo of siege guns and the man dropped dead at the captain's feet. A half-naked woman flung herself out of the crowd and across the twitching body of the Spaniard. Vidal recharged his pistol and barked an order at Old Jean to marshal the firing-squad.

Gabriel hung back and Old Jean did not look in his direction, choosing instead Nicholas and five other veterans of the company. They formed up in front of the storehouse steps, other voltigeurs seizing and pushing forward three more men, two greybeards and one hardly more than a boy. The latter fell on his knees and began to pray.

The square began to seethe. At several points little isolated struggles commenced, where voltigeurs held back men and women who tried to writhe out of the circle of torchlight. Some of the children, sick with the terror they read in the eyes of their parents, became hysterical and added their cries to the maddeningly insistent lament of the woman kneeling over the corpse.

Gabriel's senses reeled with the horror of the scene. The whole agony of the human race seemed to rise from the little mob enclosed in the hollow square. Vidal, calmly priming his pistol, looked like a uniformed demon.

As the first wave of horror passed, Gabriel felt curiously alive to the ghastly symbolism of the picture—a whole people crucified, nailed, like Manny, to a tree in a wilderness. He looked left and right for some answering feeling in the eyes of his comrades, but found none. Claude, holding a guttering torch, with his musket crooked under his right armpit, met his glance and his eyes seemed to say: "What's wrong with it? They crucified Manny, didn't they?" Gabriel sought out Old Jean, standing with the firing-squad. The sergeant's face was expressionless. This was not new to him, a man who had witnessed the sack of a dozen towns and fished for dead Mamelukes in the Nile. Dominique, his bayonet at the back of a bowed peasant of more than eighty, was actually grinning, as though taking part in a hideous game played out under the portals of hell. Louis, beside him, looked solemn enough. Perhaps his love of horses lent him some compassion for the human sheep they were slaughtering, or perhaps, like Claude, he was remembering Manny's grin. Nicholas stood beside Old Jean, his musket levelled at the boy on his knees in the dust. Gabriel had sometimes heard Nicholas recite from the Iliad, on Lobau, after Dominique had put away his fiddle and only Gabriel remained awake round the camp-fire. He wondered how it was that a man like that, who had known culture and came from a respectable bourgeois family, could stand there in a ring of torchlight and shoot a grovelling boy scarcely older than those he had once taught in school.

Gabriel's thoughts were cut short by the volley. The two men dropped, but the boy, apparently only wounded, suddenly leaped to his feet and sped across the square, bursting through the ranks of the villagers and disappearing into the shadows beyond.

The boy's action seemed to snap the spell. The crowd became unmanageable and surged to and fro, breaking on the steps of the storehouse, where Gabriel caught a final glimpse of Vidal laying about him with his sabre, shouting to the men to use their bayonets. Few did. Perhaps they had sickened of slaughter, or perhaps they were merely dazed by the uproar and confused in the unsteady light. In less than a minute the square was clear of civilians, but one side of the wretched street was ablaze and the voltigeurs had rallied round the store. Vidal, stabbed in the side, was being supported by two men. Gabriel felt Jean plucking at his sleeve.

"March," he hissed, "before the fire brings in the guerrillas."

They began to retreat towards the open country. They had gone barely a league when sharpshooters began to fire on the column from the rocks on each side of the track. They lost four men, including Vidal, shot through the head, and carried away three others lightly wounded. By dawn they were within sight of a main camp.

Trudging along beside Gabriel, Louis said: "I wonder if Manny had any money on him."

CHAPTER TWO

On the twenty-third of September, 1810, the French army halted in the valley of the Mondego, beneath the towering escarpment of Busaco. Between them and their goal, Lisbon, lay the British army and its allies, Portuguese militia who had yet to smell powder.

Massena's army, wasted by sickness and thinned by the siege of Almeida and the garrisoning of towns en route, was reduced to something under sixty thousand men. Morale was exceptionally bad. Endless marching, dwindling rations, and the relentless hostility of the countryside had done less to sap the confidence of men who had won victories for nearly twenty years than the opinions expressed by veterans in the ranks, men like Old Jean who were the barometers of the battalions and who now distrusted their commanders. It was common knowledge in the army that Massena was at loggerheads with his lieutenants, Ney, Reynier, Foy and Junot. Rumours of furious quarrels trickled down to the ranks through the gossip of staff orderlies and headquarters guards. Ney was said to have insulted Massena's mistress in front of junior staff officers.

When the retreating British made a desperate stand, the French bivouacked at the foot of their precipitous position. Rumour went round that there would be a battle in the morning, but Jean scoffed at the idea. A frontal attack on a lofty ridge held by an unbeaten enemy would be suicidal, he declared.

In spite of Jean's denial, there was battle in the morning. Without any effort to turn the enemy's flank, as Jean said they must if they were to continue the pursuit, the French corps were flung headlong up the slopes of Busaco ridge, right onto the bayonets of the redcoats and caçadores defending the summit.

The result was precisely as Jean predicted. All the dash of the French sharpshooters and all the dogged courage of the massed columns of Ney and Reynier proved only a prelude to a bloody repulse.

Fighting in the van of the Sixth Corps, urged on by Marshal Ney himself, hatless and clambering from rock to rock as the voltigeurs prised the British riflemen from the hillside, Jean, Nicholas, Dominique and Gabriel gained the summit, only to receive the full blast of a point-blank volley fired by English guards who rose up from ambush immediately in front of them.

The head of the French column withered away under a deadly and accurate fire. Jean got a ball through the fleshy part of the thigh, and Nicholas, flinging his musket to Gabriel, carried the sergeant down the steep slope on his back, rolling him behind a boulder in the valley and returning to keep the cautious pursuit away from close range.

At midday the attack was called off. The French army crawled back from the dry stream-bed, leaving over five thousand killed and wounded out on the sunny slopes.

Jean they dragged back to the lines, and Louis, who could vet men as well as dogs and horses, heated a knife and dug out the ball from the sinews of his leg, Gabriel giving the veteran a scarf upon which to bite whilst the clumsy operation was in progress. After that they poured brandy into his wound and mouth, and the sergeant, his lean face waxen under its mahogany tan, went into an exhausted sleep under an awning of greatcoats rigged up to keep off the afternoon sun.

The men sat around and talked gloomily. Louis, who had gone back to the cavalry lines for water, returned with more bad news. Nicholette had struggled into camp, but one of her horses had broken a leg on the last incline. Unless they could find a replacement not only would the wagon have to be abandoned, but Jean's chances of survival were negligible. The British were already striking camp and continuing their march. If the French went in pursuit what would happen to the canteen and to Jean?

After dark they held a conference. Jean was lifted into the wagon and Nicholette joined them in bivouac. Over on the right Montbrun's cavalry reserve was already breaking camp, to lead the way round the left flank of the British through a pass that had been found after the useless slaughter of the frontal attack.

"What in the name of God is the matter with them?" growled Nicholas, after a lieutenant had passed on orders to prepare to resume the march in the morning. "What's to be done with the wounded in this desert?"

They soon learned of headquarters' plans regarding the wounded. All those too sick to be moved were to be abandoned, without a guard.

"I'll see them in hell first," said Louis, glancing towards the wagon, where Dominique and Gabriel were raising the haggard Jean and coaxing him to drink the broth they had made from a ration of horseflesh.

"We've got to get hold of another horse or a mule," said Nicholas.

There was a short silence. Each of the group knew that the acquisition of a horse or a mule was an impossibility. Back at Almeida fantastic prices had been asked for draught animals. Here, where hundreds of officers were numbered among the wounded, the price would soar even higher.

"The Carolini brothers followed me in!" said Nicholette.

Nobody made an immediate answer. Each of them knew of

the Carolini brothers and of their reputation for sharp practice and hard bargains. The brothers were three Italians who had held a canteen licence for almost as long as Old Carla. They were a tough, hardbitten outfit who were reputed to make immense profits, partly on account of ruthless pricing, and partly because they were never more than half a day's march behind the army. Their equipment, renewed every year and transported in strongly built wagons pulled by two teams of four mules, enabled them to keep on the tail of the columns as few camp-followers could. Only Old Carla had kept pace with them, and the rivalry between the old woman and the Carolinis was implacable. It had flared into hatred on many a battlefield, where Old Carla had often challenged their prices. On one occasion they had endeavoured to overturn her wagon and drain off her wine. One of them, Gino, still carried a scar from a bullet wound received in this encounter.

When the old woman had died on Lobau the Carolinis rejoiced. Assuming that the canteen would be sold, they came over to the voltigeurs' bivouac to make an offer. Nicholette, who had inherited her mother's hatred of the trio, told them that a hundred times the sum offered would be insufficient to put her out of business, if that meant selling out to the Italians. Gino had grinned, scratched the scar on his cheek and run his eye over her slight figure.

"I'll give you two months," he told her.

That was more than a year ago and Nicholette was still trailing the army, often a league or two ahead of the Carolinis, despite their eight mules to her two horses. She had the advantage of a lighter wagon and less personal baggage. The Carolinis travelled in comfort.

Claude pondered. "How much can we raise?" he asked.

Gabriel shook out his belt. He had just over a hundred francs in gold. The others pooled two hundred between them. Claude looked at his wife and wondered how much Jean's life would be worth to her. She said nothing for a few minutes, but Claude guessed that her brain was already a battlefield, avarice struggling with loyalty to her mother's oldest friend in the regiment.

"Double it, Nicholette!" he coaxed.

Nicholette's eyes flashed, and the others could not miss the scorn in the look that she gave him.

"Six hundred! Do you think that the Carolinis would part with a mule for six hundred? Are you mad? Are all of you mad?"

Nobody answered her. All of them felt that the sum she volunteered was her own business. Gabriel glanced towards the wagon. He realized that the sergeant's life hung on this woman's whim.

Nicholette rose and threw a blanket over her shoulders.

"I'll offer them two thousand," she said. "Nicholas, you'd better come along with me."

The two of them moved across the rough ground to the Carolinis' bivouac, where their two wagons stood side by side and their eight mules were tethered in a group round a stunted oak. Nicholette carried a heavy canvas bag over her shoulder. Watching them leave, Claude felt a qualm of jealousy about Nicholas, but it was swamped by wonder at the extent of the girl's generosity. Two thousand francs! The profit of weeks of hard work! Louis moved over to inform Jean of their decision.

Gino Carolini saw Nicholette approach and guessed her errand. He had passed and recognized her dead horse on the way up to the ridge. He called to his brothers, Luigi and Aldo, who were sitting in the baggage wagon, finishing their supper. The three of them stood by their fire, grinning.

"You should feed your horses, Nico," shouted Gino. "They won't travel this country on chaff!"

Nicholas swore softly. He felt an intense desire to seize Gino Carolini by his narrow shoulders and smash his head against the big round boulder beside the lowered shafts. As always when he encountered Jews, sutlers, hucksters and canteen-men or any of the rabble of camp-followers who drifted along in the wake of the battalions, picking their bones like the carrion birds he had seen squatting near Manny's cross, a surge of hatred such as he never felt for the enemy rose in his throat and almost choked him. Nicholette must have sensed this, for she gripped his wrist, enjoining silence.

"I'll give you two thousand, a third of it in gold, for one of your scarecrows!" she began, nodding towards the mules.

Gino bellowed with laughter. His brothers, small, insignificant men compared with the tall rascal who led them, echoed his laughter as schoolchildren laugh at the jokes of authority.

Nicholette stopped on the far side of the Italians' fire.

"Two and a half?" she said, her voice flat and harsh.

Gino shook his head.

"All my mules are good mules," he said. "Besides, what should I do with a mule short in this purgatory?"

Nicholette sat down and turned out all her money onto a flat stone.

"Five thousand. That's my limit."

The smile left Gino's mouth, but Nicholas saw that it still lurked in his eyes.

"Not for ten thousand!" he said, and turned away, his brothers following.

Nicholas felt a void in the pit of his stomach. Resolutely he thrust from his mind the prospect of leaving Jean on the bare hillside when they broke camp in the morning. Nicholette was silent for a moment. Then she jumped to her feet and called: "Gino!" across the fire.

The big Italian, who had begun to move away, swung round and looked at her. There was hatred in every line of his swarthy face.

"I've got more than eleven thousand with me," said Nicholette, speaking very slowly and distinctly. "You can have it all and I'll throw in my stock! I want only the wagon."

"No, by God!" shouted Nicholas, and even Gino Carolini opened his mouth in surprise. His brothers looked up at him with the expressions of hopeful curs when promised a particularly large bone. Eleven thousand and the stock for one mule! They felt sure that he would accept.

Gino came back and sat down on the shafts, looking at the

girl steadily. "Not even for that, Nico, not even for that!" Nicholas could hardly believe his ears, but Gino went on. "Suppose I took the money. Suppose I took the stock. A bargain, you'd say, wouldn't you? Something like fifteen thousand for one mangy mule? Well, so it would be to most people. I'm a bad business man to reject it. But am I? What would you do when we got to Lisbon? You'd get money from somewhere and start up again. You'd hitch one of my mules to your cart and follow me around, year after year, slandering my reputation as your whore of a mother used to, undercutting my prices until I had to lower them below the fair profit line, all because of you and your damned outfit! No, Nico. I'm not a bad business man; I'm a good one. I never choke myself swallowing a tasty morsel. Let us get into Lisbon first. Then maybe I will sell you a mule, if one of mine goes lame!"

Nicholette and Nicholas saw the futility of further bargaining. They got up, went back to the bivouac and told the others what had occurred, only keeping it from Jean, who seemed to be running a high fever. He tossed about in the wagon and grumbled to himself unceasingly.

English riflemen, the best marksmen in the world, had been crawling down the slopes and sniping at sleeping men. The sky was overcast and the moon often invisible behind thick banks of cloud. Jean moaned in his crude litter. A sense of oppression hung over the bivouac.

After the others had lain down to sleep Nicholas and Nicholette went on talking in low voices.

Gabriel, relieving Nicholas as guard, noticed that the schoolmaster did not coil himself down with the others when Gabriel took his place by the shafts. Instead he leaned his musket against the wagon and unfixed the bayonet, thrusting the naked blade into his belt. Then he unstrapped his shako and tossed it onto the driving-seat. Nicholette was still astir inside, hunting through one of the lockers for clean bandages. Nicholas said nothing, either to her or to Gabriel. The latter watched him move off into the deep shadows towards the horse lines. He thought, "Nicholas now?" The penalty for stealing a baggage horse was death within one hour of pronouncement of sentence.

But Nicholas did not approach the horse lines or the artillery park. He turned left when he was fifty yards from the wagon, and crossed the open patch of scrub in the direction of the Carolinis' bivouac. When he saw the outline of the two wagons he threw himself down in the heather and crawled, an inch at a time, towards the Italians' dead fire.

The moon sailed out from behind a cloud to reveal Luigi Carolini, sitting with his back to the big wheel of the larger wagon, smoking a cheroot. The periodical glow of the cigar was the only source of light when a fresh bank of cloud masked the moon. Behind him, Nicholas could hear occasional challenges of the sentries and the restless stamp of cavalry horses tethered in lines. In front, where the canteen mules were tied, it was very quiet. A high-pitched snore, Gino's or Aldo's, issued from the wagon.

Nicholas kept his eyes on the cigar end. With this as pivot he inched round in a wide and silent arc, finishing up on the far side of the vehicle, close to a low bank by the oak where the mules were tethered. He could no longer see the red cigar glow, but he knew the position of the big wheel and crawled forward until he was able to pass beside it and under the wagon on the side farthest from the Italian. He heard Luigi begin to hum, probably in an effort to keep awake. Nicholas, crouching within a few inches of the man's back, reached for his bayonet, but then thought better of it and slipped his hand into his breeches pocket for a piece of cord. Finding a short length, he waited for the moon, concentrating on his own soundless breathing.

Presently, when the moon appeared, Nicholas saw the Italian's head, resting against the spokes. He thrust both hands, one holding the cord, through the spokes and swiftly joined his fingers an inch in front of Luigi's face, jerking the cord tight and bracing his knee against the lower part of the wheel. So rapid was his movement that Luigi's humming broke off in the middle of a note. All that escaped from the Italian's mouth was a sharp hiss, his final breath.

Nicholas held on to the cord until the man's body had ceased to twitch. Then, reaching through the wheel, he eased the corpse to the ground. He listened for a moment, but no sound beyond that of a snore came from the wagon. He crawled back to the bank and, again, waited for the moon. As it sailed between two banks of cloud he swiftly cut the tether of the nearest mule and moved off to the right. The animal followed, uncomplaining. At a safe distance Nicholas climbed on its back and rode it over to the voltigeurs' lines. At the bivouac he awakened everyone and called a council of war.

There was a great deal to be done before it was light. Louis shaved the mule's back down to the base of its tail and then cropped its long ears. This done, he heated a ramrod and branded a rough diamond on the animal's wincing shoulder. Having buried the shorn hair, Louis then stoked up a brazier fire inside the wagon and shod the mule with shoes from Nicholette's harness box. It was difficult to disguise a mule, but he did his best, and had it harnessed beside the surviving horse before reveille.

At first light the forward sections of the army began to move, surging slowly along a rough track that ran over the spur of the mountain, driving the British sharpshooters before them. But long before the voltigeurs had left the camp area a provost rode up with Gino Carolini at his heels. The wagon, in which Jean was lying, came to a halt. The file gathered it as Gino coolly identified his mule.

"This one," he told the provost, "and I demand the arrest of all of them as thieves and murderers."

The provost cursed. Halted here, the wagon was blocking the line of march. Men and horses were beginning to pile up behind it, and the two corporals of the provost's squad were fully occupied directing the flow.

"Where's your sergeant?" demanded the lieutenant of Nicholas.

The schoolmaster jerked his head towards the wagon, and the provost glanced over the tailboard. Nicholette addressed the harassed provost from her driving-box.

"Do you arrest people on the word of that liar?" she asked. "Where's his proof?"

A party of infantrymen gathered round the group. The Carolinis were not popular. The onlookers soon caught the drift of the dispute. "Bayonet the bastard!" advised someone.

Gino Carolini was not to be deterred by the hostile attitude of the men. Methodically he began to unhitch the harness of the mule, whilst the provost, his attention temporarily distracted by the traffic block, stood by in indecision.

Gino did not get very far with his task. Nicholette reached for her long whip.

"Move away from that mule, Gino!" she warned him, but the Italian ignored her.

The lash whirled above the wagon canopy and cracked down on his bare neck. He dropped the piece of harness that he was holding and screamed. His hand shot to his belt and pulled at the butt of a small double-barrelled pistol. Seeing the weapon, some of the men around him began to jostle and the startled team jerked forward, scattering the group round the shafts. The provost jumped onto the box and pulled hard at the reins. For a moment the wagon lurched and swayed about the rough track. Above the shouting Gino screamed, "Thieves! Murderers!" Gabriel, Louis and the others hung around the shafts and tailboard, uncertain what to do whilst the provost occupied the box. Gino's pistol went off in the scrimmage, but the ball injured nobody, for Nicholas had grabbed his arms from behind.

Suddenly the violent lurching of the wagon ceased and the struggling group round the shafts melted away. Only the file, Nicholette, Gino and the provost remained. The undirected movements of the wagon had brought its wheels up onto one of the low banks, and the track was partially cleared. A group of brilliantly dressed officers had reined in beside the vehicle.

One of them, a red-headed middle-aged man in the uniform of a marshal, edged his horse forward.

"What's the trouble?" he asked.

The soldiers in the group immediately recognized Michel Ney and were silent. Once more Gabriel thought: "This is it; this is where Nicholas leaves us."

Under the marshal's terse directions they broke down part of the bank and moved the wagon onto the level scrub. Ney's staff officers returned to the road and directed the columns onward. Caissons of the Flying Artillery began to trundle past. Standing by the wagon, Gino poured out his tale, his hand constantly returning to massage the thick red weal on his neck. All his cool deliberation now gone, he was almost incoherent with rage. The marshal heard him out, the provost officer opening his sabretache and jotting down a few random notes. Nicholette said nothing, sitting up on the box, chin in cupped hand.

"Escort this man back to his canteen, Lieutenant," said Ney at last, and to Gino, who opened his mouth to protest, "You'll get justice all right. I'll investigate the matter myself."

Gino went reluctantly, one of the provost's men accompanying him back along the bank towards his wagons. Ney's grey eyes roved over the file and finally settled on Nicholas.

"Are you in charge?"

"I suppose I am, the sergeant's out of it for a spell!"

"Come into the wagon," said Ney, and swung himself from the saddle, tossing the reins to the single aide-de-camp who had remained.

The marshal and the corporal climbed the tailboard and sat facing one another on the lockers, with the pallid Jean between them. The sergeant was lying on a truss of straw stolen from the cavalry lines by Louis during the night. Jean was conscious and recognized Ney with a quiet smile.

"This is a bitch of a campaign; what's happened to us lately?" he said.

Ney grinned and a current of sympathy seemed to pass between the two men.

Nicholas noted it and hoped. He said: "The sergeant was at Hohenlinden."

"We fight better in low temperatures," the marshal said, and scratched his chin. He turned from contemplating the sergeant to Nicholas again. "Why didn't you buy that mule?" he asked. "The girl has money; all these people have money."

"She offered him eleven thousand and all her stock," growled Nicholas.

Ney looked incredulous. "She did? Why?"

"Her mother was an old friend of the sergeant's. She's like that—one of us."

Ney nodded. After sixteen years' continuous warfare he knew all about canteens and canteen rivalry. He recalled Old Carla, and his mind went back to an evening more than five years ago, on the night after Elchingen, when he had dismounted outside this same wagon to chat with a dying man, an old friend of his boyhood, to whom Carla was giving wine. He did not tell Nicholas that this was the reason why he had stopped after recognizing the wagon by its bizarre tailboard decorations. The marshal had a memory for that sort of detail.

All he said was: "Eleven thousand and stock!" And then, "Wounded were to be abandoned!"

Nicholas blazed out and Old Jean stared at him incredulously. There were times when this ex-schoolmaster addressed officers as if they were stupid children.

"Go on, then, arrest me and the girl, arrest the lot of us. Six men who win your battles count for less than an Italian civilian's mule! That's justice! Give him back his mule and leave a man like Jean, good for a hundred more fights, to be cut to pieces by the Portuguese! That's logic, that's about all the logic you get in the army nowadays. No wonder things aren't going so well with us!"

Ney's initial astonishment gave place to amusement. He suddenly bellowed with laughter and stood up. Nicholas noticed then that one of his epaulettes was new, contrasting oddly with its faded and tousled twin. He remembered seeing the marshal half-way up the slope on the day before, after his left epaulette had been torn away by point-blank musketry fire.

"You found the mule straying," he said quietly. "An English mule, perhaps, that broke loose during the battle. The English artillery mules have a distinguishing brand, a crown over a blank scroll. Much the same as our own Westphalian Hussars, I believe!"

He winked down at Jean and, climbing out of the wagon, swung himself into his saddle again and spurred down the bank, calling to the provost and his aide-de-camp to follow.

Before they eased the wagon back onto the track Louis went over to the hussars' horse lines and came back with a branding-iron. The smell of singed hair tickled Jean's nostrils as he lay listening to the endless shuffle of marching feet along the dusty track. Gino's mule brayed, protesting against the indignity of two brandings within six hours.

The file and wagon moved off down the scorching road to Coimbra.

CHAPTER THREE

They got Jean to Coimbra hospital, with the four thousand five hundred sick and wounded who had struggled thus far. The old sergeant's wound was healing satisfactorily. His fever had burned itself out during an agonizing day in the wagon as the army struggled along congested tracks towards the city.

Autumn weather had set in and it rained every day. The British did not make another stand. They hastened their steps toward Lisbon, where, presumably, their transports were waiting. The pace of their retreat gratified Jean as soon as he could sit up and ask for news. Massena, hoping to wipe out earlier failures by a grand coup which would result in expelling the British forces from the Peninsula, hurled his advance guard down the muddy tracks in a strenuous effort to maintain contact with the British rearguard.

The army approached Coimbra through a barren, devastated countryside. All round the city and beyond it villages had been burned and evacuated. Food stocks had been destroyed or carried away. Continuing the advance, the Eighty-seventh often marched for days without encountering a single Portuguese civilian. Irregulars of the militia kept up sniping attacks on the flanks, and occasionally the dragoons brought in a sulky prisoner or two, but there was no food, no dry billets, little enough fuel and, worst of all, no loot worth its carriage on the march.

"This is the toughest campaign of the lot," Old Jean told them the day before they parted.

"There'll be worse before the whole damned Empire topples over," growled Nicholas.

The group were missing Manny's high spirits and often referred to the dead man.

"God knows what he would have found to chuckle at in this country," said Claude, with a glance at the dismal sky.

Even Dominique's fiddle refused to call a tune. In the constant wet weather of the long march down Portugal the threads of the bow had gone slack and flabby. Dominique tried to replace them with hair, cut from the mane of a cuirassier's mount, but the substitute was not effective, and the farmhand solemnly wrapped the useless instrument in its oilskin and tucked it back into his knapsack. He could not nerve himself to throw it away and it weighed little enough in any case.

Jean did not want to be left at Coimbra, but Nicholas and the others thought it best. It would be some time before the sergeant could walk, and the pace of the final advance on the capital was likely to be too hot, even for Nicholette. Her horse and mule were sadly underfed. Fodder was almost unobtainable in a country swept clean by the redcoats and their fanatical allies.

The voltigeurs hurried on with the rest of the light infantry. Hardly were the columns out of sight when the Portuguese militia swooped down on the hospital, overwhelmed the inadequate guard and carried every wounded Frenchmen a prisoner to Oporto. Only the presence of an English commander prevented an orgy of throat-cutting. The file did not learn of Jean's capture until later. In the meantime they had worries enough of their own.

Nobody in the French army, from the Commander-in-Chief downwards, had the slightest inkling of the presence of vast lines of fortifications, erected by the British with Portuguese labour, in the area of Torres Vedras outside Lisbon. Every pass, every gully had been blocked and fortified. The mountains bristled with guns. A chain of small forts, each of which would have defied the assault of an army corps, ran like a granite necklace round the lower slopes of the bare hills.

The French army swung to the left and ranged along the twenty-two miles of fortifications. There was not a chink anywhere. The British retreat had come to an end. Snug in their impregnable lines, the enemy sat down to await the inevitable starvation of the army which had harried them all the way from the frontier. Massena stayed on for several months, but his invasion was virtually over on the day that he came within range of the lines. A single glance was enough to tell the old warrior that a frontal attack was out of the question. He would lose two-thirds of his men without getting so much as a footing within the first line of defence. If, by some miracle, this could be carried, there were others within it, and a well-fed, well-equipped company to defend every bastion.

Outwardly Massena did not despair. He regrouped, built cantonments, sent out strong foraging parties for food, despatched messages for help to France and to every other independent commander in the Peninsula. Inwardly, however, he knew that the game in Portugal was over. Years later he said to Wellington, his opposite number, "You turned every hair on my body white!" It was not an overstatement.

In the first days of autumn the voltigeurs found themselves billeted in the ruins of several small towns along the banks of the Tagus. The countryside around had obviously been rich and fertile, but it was no longer capable of supporting a single company for more than a few days. Fruit had once been plentiful there, but now the harvests were ruined. Millions of plovers soared over the rotting olives. Vines had not been stripped and the figs shrivelled on the trees. In the string of villages and small towns along the river there were no sheep, no goats, no chickens, no men and no women.

British gunboats patrolled the wide river, keeping up a desultory but highly annoying fire on the main road and causing a good many casualties.

When the weather mended for a while Gabriel sometimes forgot his hunger in admiration of the country, the broad strip between the river and the hills encouraging him to take out his sketchbook and make three or four hasty impressions of the sweep of orange trees, lemon groves and oleanders, under a vivid blue sky. But by far the most interesting page in this section of his book is a lively sketch of the barriers, where the hostile camps merged and the voltigeurs sometimes took a turn at sentry-go.

The relationship between the infantry of both armies was cordial. The British did not want to come out, not, at least, until Massena's troops were sufficiently thinned to make victory certain, and the French were resigned to their rôle of simulated siege. Every private in the ranks knew that it was only a question of time before they were forced, by hunger and excessive wastage, to retreat to the Spanish frontier. Then it would be their turn to be harried over the mountain ranges that lay between them and the modest refitting and revictualling depots of occupied Spain. A sort of careless stupor descended on the victors of Austerlitz and Friedland. Down at the barrier they did not even bother to return shots fired at them during the first days of the siege. The British soon showed themselves ready to live and let live. When the trumpeter sounded a morning summons officers and men of the two armies exchanged newspapers while some of the redcoats, after a brief exchange of raillery, tossed over navy rum and ship's biscuits to their scarecrow opponents. Gabriel's sketch shows a grinning British sergeant, his flesh straining at the buttons on his red tunic, his black shako pushed back from a broad , sunburned face, handing a bottle to a melancholy sergeant of the Eighty-seventh whose blue greatcoat hangs on his shoulders as upon a peg. The sketch is entitled "Villafranca, October, 1810." It is a vivid commentary on the situation existing in the camps, but Gabriel's titles reveal no sense of humour. Manny might have called it "The Taking of Lisbon," but Manny was dead and lay in his shallow grave high up on the slopes of the bleak sierra. His lighter suggestions are missing from the later pages of the sketchbooks.

Some of the voltigeurs of the Eighty-seventh were soon to enjoy British hospitality for a more prolonged period. In mid-November the surviving members of the file were taken prisoner. For the best part of two years they remained out of the war.

One of the British gunboats had been sunk by a lucky hit from a shore battery, on the outskirts of the town. The vessel went down in fairly shallow water, and at low tide part of it could be seen lying exposed. The crew had made off downstream in dinghies and, the ebbing tide favouring them, were soon back within their lines.

Captain Tinville, the good-natured but somewhat stupid successor to the ruthless Vidal, decided that an attempt should be made to salvage anything of value on the gunboat. He therefore ordered one of the sergeants, an obtuse Breton named Soutier, to detail a reliable file to punt out to the wreck at low tide, employing home-made rafts for the journey. Nicholas and his file were allotted the task.

Soutier was no Sergeant Jean. A veteran recently promoted, he tried to cover lack of self-confidence with a maddening reiteration of the word "orders." Once something was "ordered" Soutier considered that his responsibility ended with the passing on of instructions to the men in the ranks. The blunt rejoinder "Orders!" met any remonstrance, however reasonable.

Soutier told Nicholas to take his party across the dead water of the river opposite their billet and carry out the salvage before nightfall. He forgot that at this particular hour the full tide would be sweeping downriver to that section of the lower estuary held by the enemy. If the work were left until morning the incoming tide would greatly reduce the force of the current and probably enable the job to be performed without much risk or difficulty.

Nicholas stated this somewhat obvious fact, but Soutier shrugged his shoulders.

"Orders," he explained.

Nicholas pointed to the current racing past the half-submerged gunboat.

"We'll never anchor these rafts in that flood," he told Soutier. "Orders!"

Nicholas grunted and, assembling the men, told them to take off most of their equipment and their boots. His own group boarded the largest of the rafts, the others distributing themselves among the remaining craft. The rafts were pitiful substitutes for boats. Not a single river craft of any kind had been overlooked by the British in their preliminary inspection of the banks prior to retiring within their fortified lines.

They poled out to the wreck an hour before sunset, and, as Nicholas had predicted, it proved almost impossible, once they approached midstream, to check their progress down the river with the makeshift anchors supplied. The two lighter rafts were swept past the gunboat like corks and only managed to make the friendly bank by united efforts of their crews and of a line of voltigeurs on the shore, who saw their distress and waded shoulder deep into the water to form a rescue chain. Even so, two of the men were drowned.

Nicholas avoided similar failure by grappling the wreck as they surged past its protruding stern. The five of them hung on grimly, forcing the raft alongside so that Nicholas could clamber aboard. So swift was the flow of the river, swollen by weeks of autumnal rains, that Nicholas doubted whether the wreck would hold its position if it was shifted on the river bed by the movements of half a dozen men. So he ordered the others to remain on the raft while he himself crawled forward, looking for anything which he could wrench free and toss to them. There were some sealed jars of rum in the stern lockers, three of which he transferred. He also got an anchor and a sopping bundle of charts which he had no opportunity to examine in the precarious position he occupied on the sloping deck.

Gabriel advised him to jump aboard and abandon the rest of

the salvage. At that moment a British patrol, on the left bank, opened fire with an eight-pounder. The first ball plunged into the water not a dozen yards from the wreck.

It began to rain heavily, and the downpour beat in their faces. Over on the French bank a horde of voltigeurs were dancing and gesticulating, presumably advising immediate return. The British gunners fired again. This time the shot screamed over their heads and fell just short of the group on the bank, causing a hurried surge up the beach.

Nicholas glanced over his shoulder, to see four strained faces and four pairs of hands clinging desperately to the grappling line. He crawled backwards down the canting deck of the gunboat and dropped back onto the raft, which was already showing signs of disintegration. They cast off and were whirled down the river. A third shot crashed into the exposed side of the wreck and, through the driving rain, they saw the vessel heel over and disappear.

"Orders!" said Nicholas, but only Dominique gave an answering grin. The others were clinging to the loose planking for their lives.

The end came like a crash of thunder. Spinning madly in the boiling water, the raft piled up on a snag a hundred yards or so from the French bank. The shock threw Claude and Gabriel into the water. Claude, who could not swim a stroke, let out a piercing shriek, and as the timber splayed out on the surface of the river the other three grabbed at planks. Instead now of a single unit, five men rushed away downstream, Gabriel swimming strongly with the current, Claude thrashing the water to reach a fragment of salvage, while Louis and Dominique still clung to the largest section of the raft.

Nicholas, swirling past astride a beam, was carried within inches of Claude and, reaching out, grabbed him by the collar of his tunic, almost losing his hold on the plank with the jerk. In that brief second Nicholas thought of Nicholette and wondered whether she would thank him for saving her husband's life. He doubted it. Lately he had noticed her indifference towards the boy whom she had married on Lobau. Claude was a gentle man, and once the boy's physical charm began to cloy, as it eventually must with a woman as tough and resolute as Nicholette, she had probably found him very tedious. Perhaps this was why she seemed to be turning elsewhere. As he struggled in the water, with one arm wrapped round the skimming beam, his free hand straining at Claude's collar, Nicholas's brain swiftly formulated this reflection but did not record it. He was concentrating on a physical crisis. Instinct told him to hang on to the collar and he did hang on, until Claude, struggling for his life, and sacrificing it to his struggles, slipped from his comrade's grasp and was whirled downward and outward, into the main stream of the torrent. He rose once or twice, a bluish clot on the brown flood, before finally sinking to be tumbled along the muddy bed by playful undercurrents and flung at last on the wrinkled flats of the left bank, where a party of caçadores found him next morning and rifled his sodden clothes.

Claude never knew that a human hand had reached out to save him. His last conscious impression was of the splintering crash when the raft struck the snag, and the split second of stark terror that succeeded the collision. After that he fought for life without knowing it, beating the water or, it might be, the air with arms that were suddenly leaden. There was a great roaring in his ears, like the boom of the waterfall high up the Garonne where he had often fished as a child. Then, through this tumbling wall of sound, he had a fleeting vision of Nicholette, turning and reaching out her hand to him as they stepped onto their islet in the Danube, but her mouth was not smiling as it had smiled that summer evening. It was as set and grim as when she told them that the Carolini brothers had followed her into camp and that the purchase of a mule was inevitable. That was all he knew, that and the roaring, cramping, murderous cold.

The other four made the right bank at some distance below the barrier, cut off from their comrades, who ran along their side of the river shouting and calling through the storm. A British naval piquet dragged them, half-dead, from the water. They had been saved by the sweeping curve of the river, which had carried all four of them into shallower water where they were just able to grasp at the ropes and oars held out by the bluejackets.

They were laid on the bank and a fifteen-year-old midshipman gave each of them a generous tot of rum, before packing them off to the prisoners' compound and ordering the Portuguese guard to see them fed. The midshipman came along to see that his orders were carried out, and it was as well for the survivors that he did. Caçadores did not believe in wasting good food on half-drowned Frenchmen, even though inexhaustible supplies of beef and pork came in by lighter from the British men-o'-war in the harbour three times a week.

They remained in the compound for more than a week, during which period they were treated with consideration by the British, with indifference by the Portuguese. Prison food, however, was twice as nourishing and about four times as plentiful as the diet of their own officers inside the French lines. All that they saw through the stockade of their compound confirmed them in the opinion that a single dash from their fortifications by these well-fed, well-drilled Englishmen would hurl the starved and ailing French back along every track and lane leading to the Spanish frontier. It was only here, inside British lines, that a Frenchman could accurately assess the wreck of Massena's campaign. Gabriel, who discussed these things with Nicholas, could only conclude that Lord Wellington was either excessively cautious or else unaware of the true weaknesses in the enemy's ranks.

The prisoners were loosely guarded. Few of the French among the hundreds inside the compound had any desire to escape back to their own lines. They were well content to be fed on the beef, pork and biscuits of the besieged. Through the palings of the stockade they could see the life of the city going on very much as usual—regiments of green-clad Portuguese being drilled by sweating English officers and sergeants; lines of sleek transport horses moving up from the quays, their glossy hides in significant contrast to the raw-boned mules that staggered about the French cantonments; crate after crate of stores and ammunition going up to the regimental depots; two-horse wagons, piled high with brand-new muskets and equipment, straining up the incline to the citadel, in readiness for the spring advance.

Louis stared gloomily at the dragoons' horses as they were taken out to the beaches for exercise. "God help our cavalry when the redcoats do strike camp!" was his comment.

Good food and ample opportunity for relaxation had the effect of raising the spirits of the four voltigeurs. They were cast down, but not unduly so, by the death of Claude. They had received no definite news of him but were convinced, on talking it over among themselves, of his drowning in the Tagus. One morning Gabriel saw a British sergeant whom he had met at the barrier, and asked him to inform the voltigeurs' piquet of their capture and of Claude's probable death. Their fate would be of particular interest to Nicholette, who now would have to cast around for a new section. None of them worried much on her account. They knew Nicholette too well for that, and there were too many files in the Eighty-seventh that would be only too delighted to appoint themselves her unofficial escort for the remainder of the campaign. A claim on a canteen, in this particular war, was worth six months' arrears of pay.

Only Nicholas smouldered a little at the thought of the cantinière hitching herself to a new team. Claude was dead and Nicholette had to find herself a new husband. Who was better qualified for the vacancy than he? Yet, as things were, they were unlikely to see one another again. Nicholas was one of the few soldiers in the Grand Army who was convinced that these interminable wars could cease only with the overthrow, and possibly the death, of the Emperor. Talk along these lines had often brought him a sharp warning from Sergeant Jean, to whom such an outlook smacked of blasphemy.

When they had been in the compound for about a fortnight, an officer who spoke fluent French came round and selected the fit men for transportation. Two of the empty transport vessels in the harbour were returning to Plymouth for fresh stores, and every transport took back a batch of prisoners. This sort of traffic had been going on intermittently for years, shiploads of stores to Lisbon, shiploads of prisoners out. Ironically citing the Paris *Moniteur*, Nicholas remarked grimly that, for an army constantly being pushed into the sea, the British seemed to teach an unconscionably large number of Frenchmen to swim. The newcomers soon discovered, however, that a large number of the captives were deserters.

The prisoners were escorted down to the lighters by a guard of marines, very trim in their scarlet and gleaming black. On the way the shuffling column passed a handcart in which a half-naked and badly wounded man was being trundled along by a pair of Hanoverian footguards. The casualty's back was a bloody pulp.

Glancing in the direction of the handcart with faint interest, Louis raised a query. "Where are they using grapeshot? I haven't heard any artillery."

Nicholas laughed harshly.

"That isn't a grapeshot wound. The man has been flogged, practically to death, I should say."

Louis and the others looked after the cart with a new interest.

"Why didn't they hang the poor devil?" asked Gabriel.

"His offence wasn't a capital one," Nicholas told them. "The British are great believers in discipline and they've only two methods of enforcing it, the noose and the lash."

During the ensuing voyage they discovered that Nicholas knew a great deal about the British. He had specialized in English literature at his university and was less surprised than most Frenchmen by the strange inconsistencies of the race. He knew, for instance, that an island that had fought against France for seventeen years, in defence of freedom of the seas and constitutional government, still kept many of its children at work for sixteen hours a day, sometimes for a weekly pittance, often enough for nothing at all but a few meals and a communal bed. He knew that the sailor who leaped the bulwarks of French men-of-war, wielding a cutlass against what he considered the intolerable tyranny of the French Emperor, whom he knew from his cartoons and broadsheets as "Boney, the Robber Baron," had most probably been torn from his native village by the press gang and flogged into becoming one of the finest seamen in the world. He knew also that in England a standard of living far higher than that enjoyed by the wealthiest aristocrat who fell by the guillotine during the Terror could flourish side by side with abject poverty and semi-starvation. Nicholas spoke much of these things, but he did not neglect to remind his friends that the very men who were born and reared under these conditions possessed an independence of spirit and a consciousness of race superiority exceeding that of an Imperial Guardsman. He accepted this as part explanation of the continued survival of Britain against the organized might of a Continent dominated by the plump little man who had jocularly asked after their wine on the island of Lobau.

Kept informed by Nicholas's flow of laconic comment, and directed by the schoolmaster's unusually strong powers of observation, Gabriel, Louis and even Dominique rapidly adjusted themselves to their new surroundings. In this way Nicholas partially filled the vacancy left by Old Jean, whom they had all loved as boys in their teens will love and admire a wise old uncle who shares in their games and their adolescent enthusiasms.

Old Jean, however, was not so far off as they imagined.

Gabriel always looked back on their reunion with the sergeant as one of the keenest pleasures of all those years of hardship and vivid mental experiences.

Most of the time during the voyage up the coast of Portugal and across the Bay of Biscay, the prisoners were penned below, the sergeants having been carefully segregated from other ranks in obedience to what appeared to the French a fantastic notion of class prejudice on the part of the British, and nowhere more punctiliously observed than on board one of His Majesty's ships. During the early part of the voyage Louis and Dominique were very sick. The food was of far poorer quality than that served up in the compound at Lisbon, and the crowded space between decks grew unbearably stuffy and noisome. The ship's captain, however, was a man on loan from the East India Company and did not observe the discipline on board that might have been expected from a regular naval officer. He allowed the prisoners to exercise in batches for approximately one hour each day. The voltigeurs usually managed to go on deck together, and by the time the transport was cruising up the coast of France, with its escort of two frigates bobbing contemptuously inshore, Louis and Dominique had recovered and no longer implored the stolid marines who served their food to end their misery with blade or bullet. They reeled up on deck and swallowed great gulps of the stinging sea air, groping their way up to the handrail that divided the prisoners' walk from the forecastle, where some of the half-naked tars were amusing themselves and a curious crowd of Frenchmen by dancing a hornpipe.

One of the sailors, sitting cross-legged on a hatch-cover, was scraping away with a home-made fiddle, and Gabriel, who had followed the others forward, noted the rapt expression on Dominique's pale face as he watched the cavorting bow of the fiddler squeaking out a rhythm, without much melody, for the slapping feet of the dancers. Gabriel saw that Dominique had momentarily forgotten his troubles in an inarticulate yearning to tuck the home-made fiddle under his chin and play once again some of the gipsy tunes that he had improvised all the way from the Danube to Coimbra. Gabriel nudged Nicholas, who nodded his understanding.

The moment the dance had finished the schoolmaster elbowed his way to the rail and addressed the fiddler. The other Frenchmen showed their appreciation of the dance by shouts and applause.

"My mate here, he's a good fiddler, will you let him try?"

The tar looked surprised, but a big boatswain who had been lazily watching the dance whilst keeping a wary eye on the ragged crowd by the rail nodded his approval.

"Give it to him, Taffy," he said with a grin, "and see if the Froggies can fiddle any better than they can handle topsails in a gale!"

Dominique took the fiddle, handling it as though it were a

fragile piece of porcelain. He tucked it under his chin and drew the bow across the strings, producing a trial note or two.

"Come on, Froggy," called the genial boatswain, and he motioned Dominique over the rail onto the hatch-cover.

Dominique hesitated, glancing shyly at the crowds of men in the forecastle, but Frenchmen pushed him forward and suddenly his diffidence left him and he began to play.

He chose the tune which Gabriel had heard him fiddle that first evening in the Lobau bivouac. Listening, Gabriel reflected that it was a melody reaching beyond frontiers; it had in it something of the folk-music of all nations. It was violent, provocative, boisterous as a March wind in the trees; it had a theme that had never been committed to manuscript, but although he knew that it existed nowhere outside Dominique's head, Gabriel felt it belonged somehow to his own boyhood and to days in the sun and rain along the winding course of the river. It moved him deeply and it must have had the same effect on everyone present, for there was complete silence on the crowded deck, the seamen and prisoners standing amazed that a shock-headed lout could coax such a tune from the grotesque little instrument.

The owner of the fiddle was dumbfounded, finding it difficult to believe that he had sat on that very hatch-cover and carved the fiddle from fragments of a staved-in sea-chest, using only a few odd strands of catgut and a spoonful of glue begged from the ship's carpenter.

Gabriel saw the big boatswain turn away and look down at the choppy water. Some of the Frenchmen wept openly.

The tune came to an end as suddenly as it had begun, and Dominique, conscious of the impression he had made, flushed and quickly thrust the fiddle back into the unresisting hands of its owner. As he did so a storm of cheering broke out over the forecastle and Dominique found himself surrounded on all sides, some men reaching out to thump his narrow shoulders, others grasping his moist hands to reinforce a shower of extravagant compliments.

In the middle of this confusion, which had begun to alarm

both the officer of the watch and the corporal of the marine escort, Gabriel heard a high-pitched voice calling his name. He looked round, but could see no one that he recognized in the mob of prisoners and seamen. Yet there was no mistaking that unnaturally shrill voice. He called to Nicholas, who was watching the scene with one of his bitter smiles, a smile which did much to express his contemptuous pity for these monkeys whose pigmy enthusiasms he was forced to witness.

At that moment a spare figure forced its way through the press, and two long, sinewy arms clutched Gabriel round the neck. Nicholas's smile was instantly replaced by an expression of delighted astonishment. He bounded forward with a loud cry.

"Jean! Dear God, it's *Jean!*"

The old sergeant thrust one arm over Gabriel's shoulder and seized Nicholas by the hand. Dominique, catching a glimpse of the sergeant through his circle of admirers, burrowed through them like a fugitive stoat and began to caper about the deck, uttering shrill cries of welcome.

Gabriel noticed that Jean was weeping unashamedly. The music and the sudden recognition of his lost children was too much for him. He did not weep as easily as most Frenchmen, but on this occasion he made no attempt to wipe away the tears that coursed down his prominent cheekbones, features concerning which Nicholas had often said: "Are you *sure* that your father didn't campaign in China, Jean?"

The officious corporal of marines began to hustle them back to their cage, and Old Jean, hastily slipping off his tattered coat, the sleeve of which betrayed his rank, crowded in with the others, jabbering away like a fishwife while he tried to shake four pairs of hands at once.

In the artificial twilight of the pens they exchanged stories. Nicholas told the sergeant of their march in the rain to the British fortifications, of the hopeless weeks of mock siege and the disaster near the wrecked gunboat resulting in the death of young Claude.

Jean looked solemn for a moment.

"I wonder what's happened to Nicholette," he said.

"She'll manage all right," replied Nicholas, and Gabriel thought that he detected a note of harshness in his voice, an eagerness to dismiss the topic of the slight, unsmiling woman in her rackety old wagon. He knew Nicholas very well by this time, and, looking at him now, he felt that he had learned his secret.

They had all pondered about the future of Nicholette during the last few weeks. Gabriel had something of Claude's awe for the woman, but, unlike Claude, his admiration of her extended beyond the physical. Plodding along the wheel ruts during the march across Spain and Portugal, he had often glanced up at her erect figure on the driving-box with a mixture of wonder and affection, marvelling that such a small frame could endure all that she did without an occasional wail of discontent. If she had been less attractive as a woman, he could have dismissed it as one of those freaks of circumstance that occur, from time to time, in all fields of human action. As it was, with her clear skin and healthy, pleasing figure, she could have taken her place at any time in the establishment of a senior officer in one of the larger garrison towns. Or, if she preferred security, she could easily have married into one of the civilian branches of the army and settled down to comfortable bourgeois life. Even whilst thinking of this, however, Gabriel concluded that either of these callings would have been too flabby and too isolated for Nicholette. Reared in the camps, on the move from earliest infancy, her only home the wagon or the bivouac (with slightly more expansive but equally temporary dwellings during the limited periods of garrison work that fell to the light infantry), Nicholette seemed to crave movement and the rough comradeship of men. This regiment, this company and, above all, this particular file represented for Nicholette the home, family and husband of a normal woman. Her childhood and girlhood had been abnormal; her womanhood followed the same course. Gabriel, whose artist's eye was a shade keener than the eyes of the others, with the possible exception of

Nicholas, had long since discerned that a lifetime of physical discomfort could never make Nicholette unhappy. Nobody who had grown up with Old Carla would expect anything from life but hard knocks and constant exertion.

He turned from his reflections to listen to Old Jean. The sergeant's tale was simple enough. After the capture of the Coimbra hospital he had been carted off to Oporto. He was more fortunate than most in that his wound had almost healed. He thus survived a journey that accounted for hundreds of the more seriously wounded men, to spend a dismal period of confinement in a crowded warehouse which had been converted into a ramshackle prison by the jubilant Portuguese. British supervision had done little to ease the plight of the prisoners. Up at Oporto English officers were few and appallingly overworked. They were faced with the task of welding the Portuguese levies into an army capable of facing the French. It was a grave responsibility. The British were not unaware of the fact that, however underfed and ill-equipped Massena's veterans were, they could still scatter a Portuguese army with a single charge.

At length British frigates took the surviving prisoners aboard and ran them down the coast to Lisbon, where they joined the voltigeurs' convoy. Jean felt his captivity more keenly than the younger men. To him capture was still a disgrace, however much it might be excused by circumstances. He had been wounded nine times in various campaigns but had never before been taken prisoner. His only consolation was that at the time of capture he was not under arms. But he was immensely cheered by reunion with his file. It restored his sense of responsibility, and, with men whom he could trust at his side, there was always the possibility of escape, even from England.

He did not return to the sergeants' cage, though it was far less crowded than the den occupied by the other ranks. He sat propped up against a bulkhead, puffing at the same old broken pipe, the fumes from which did nothing to sweeten the poisonous atmosphere of the prisoners' hold.

Every day, when they were let out for exercise, the big boatswain beckoned to Dominique to climb over the rail and play a few tunes. For his services the British fiddler gave him a few handfuls of tobacco when he returned the fiddle.

That was how Old Jean managed to smoke all the way to Plymouth Sound.

PART THREE
The Otter

CHAPTER ONE

They did not go to the hulks, those living hells concerning which rumours had penetrated as far as the French cantonments outside Lisbon. The hulks, at this stage in the war, were reserved for prisoners with a bad record, earned either in attempts to escape after breaking parole or on account of violent conduct in their places of confinement. Conditions aboard these beached, verminous vessels were indescribable. Men lay and rotted with scurvy and semi-starvation. Murderous assaults upon guards were frequent. Prisoners often went mad and leaped overboard at high tide, or hanged themselves with strips torn from their rags.

The new prison at Dartmoor, specially built to receive French prisoners of war, was already full. Commenced in 1806, it was not yet complete, but all the blocks so far erected were crammed with soldiers captured in Spain and the Low Countries and with sailors from the French privateers and coasting vessels which had fallen into the hands of the blockading squadrons.

The disposal of the new convoy of prisoners taxed the Plymouth Commandant's ingenuity. He had had frequent requests from big landowners in the district for agricultural workers and labourers. Army recruiting, together with the activities of the press gang, and the constant migration of rural populations to the manufacturing towns were rapidly draining the farms and the smaller coastal communities of their manpower. Landowners in the West Country asked if they could engage paroled prisoners for routine work on their estates, and the military commissioners of various districts had been given permission to use their discretion in the granting of such requests. One such appeal had been sent in by Lord Rolle, a powerful landowner of East Devon, whose principal seat was at Bicton.

Lord Rolle's letter was placed on the Commandant's desk a day or two after the new convoy had discharged. His Lordship was asking for two hundred men for special work in the East Devon area. He particularly wanted engineers, men with a knowledge of dyke building.

There were not more than a dozen engineers among this latest batch. There were, however, a large number of men anxious to give their parole.

Old Jean and Nicholas had a lengthy argument on the subject. Jean was strongly against the giving of his parole. He was determined to escape as soon as a chance offered itself. Nicholas took a more cynical view. Escape, he said, was practically impossible anyhow, and even if it proved successful it only meant prompt despatch to one's regiment and a resumption of the old familiar round of marching, starving, fighting and, ultimately, dying.

The younger men were inclined to agree with the corporal. Spain had drained away their enthusiasm for a military life, and the humane treatment of the British up to this point encouraged them in the belief that there were far worse fates than that of a prisoner of war in England—the fate of a free man in front of Torres Vedras, for instance.

They ended by compromising. Jean, on behalf of the group, gave his parole for six months, comforting himself by the reflection that he would need this period to assess the chances of escape and to accumulate the means of making it likely to succeed. A few days later they all were packed into farm wagons and sent off under a light guard to Exeter. Here, in the castle yard, they were sorted for various assignments. One of Gabriel's gold pieces, still snug in the broad leather belt which he wore waking and sleeping, ensured that the five of them were not split up. With nearly two hundred other men, the voltigeurs joined a column for Bicton Park, a large enclosure on the East Devon coast, midway between the little coastal towns of Sidmouth and Exmouth. They were housed temporarily in large stables behind the red brick mansion, and Lord Rolle himself came down with Mr. Duke, a neighbouring landowner, who required men for the execution of a scheme long dear to his heart.

The prisoners, working under expert supervision, were detailed to erect a long, curving bank at the mouth of the River Otter, a shallow stream which had once seen a considerable amount of wool and wine trading to and from the Continent. There were two villages close by, Otterton, about a mile and a half up the river, and Budley, slightly to the west of its neighbour. Until comparatively recent times, both had been important centres for wool distribution, while returning vessels imported Continental wines. Now the villages were dwindling communities, their decay being due to the accumulation of a vast pebble ridge which all but sealed the mouth of the river. In summertime the stream was unnavigable for vessels of more than a few tons burthen.

Mr. Duke, who owned most of the manors in the district, had won over Lord Rolle to his scheme of clearing the river mouth and restoring this channel of local prosperity. He planned to build a large earthen breakwater, running inland from high-water mark west of the river, and thus to confine the tidal water to a limited area. He had great hopes that this would have the effect of deepening the little estuary and opening it up once again for larger vessels; Birmingham contractors informed him that the pebble ridge could be cleared away as soon as the breakwater had been completed.

Local inhabitants were more sceptical. They considered Mr. Duke a harmless crank and were perturbed by the invasion of two hundred Frenchmen. Fed for years on atrocity stories of the Napoleonic soldiers in Europe, they looked upon the ragged column as a horde of savages turned loose in their midst. Deputations were sent to Lord Rolle and Mr. Duke to protest against this open invitation to ravage the district. Such prejudice did not endure. Within a matter of weeks, the paroled Frenchmen were accepted as men whose savagery was limited to frog-eating.

In the early spring of 1811 the first spadefuls of earth were turned and a curious gathering of farmers, gamekeepers and fishermen stood about watching the commencement of the bank with interest, and the usual rural jests. They dubbed the enterprise "Dukey's Folly."

Jean and his four companions were billeted in a hayloft on the Bicton estate. Every morning except Sundays they marched without escort to the Otter marshes and went to work with pickaxe and mattock. Each night, when the sun was setting over the wide expanse of Channel that faced them, they stacked their tools in the storehouse of the resident engineer, who occupied farmhouse lodgings on the river bank, and marched home again to their loft.

It was a pleasant, humdrum life and they were not sorry that they had taken Nicholas's advice and given their parole. Food, in this agricultural district, was plentiful and wholesome, while the work, although physically hard, was no more arduous than building gun-emplacements on Lobau. All five of them, greatly reduced in weight by the rigours of the Spanish campaign, began to put on flesh again so that "Dukey's Folly" was popular enough among the French, whatever local people might think of its comic futility.

As warm spring days succeeded the drizzle of winter, and the south wind bent the rushes and flags along the diggings, Gabriel came to love the soft Devon land. He often thought of his sketchbooks, still in the common locker of Nicholette's wagon, and wondered if she would take care of them during the inevitable retreat into Spain. He began sketching a little with pieces of charcoal, but paper was hard to obtain. None of the rustics possessed any and he made no serious attempts at drawing until he

154

persuaded Nicholas to approach the local parson, who came over from Budley once a week to inspect the progress of his patron's scheme.

The priest, who was a good-natured fellow, returned a few days later with his saddle-bag crammed with scrap paper. Gabriel thanked him and that afternoon, during a rest period, executed one of his best landscapes, a view of the high red cliffs rolling away to the west, gashed by a series of little gullies that the local people called "goyles," long, deep clefts running down to the beach, their steep sides covered with brambles and gorse. The sketch is one of two that he brought away from England.

Summer brought a riot of colour to the overgrown banks of the Devon stream. Ragwort, speedwell, convolvulus, campion sprouted everywhere amid the tangles of cow-parsley and wild briar. Kingfishers flashed from rock to rock, and screaming gulls sailed upstream in their ceaseless hunt for eels. Back in their billet when the day's digging was over, the French arranged concerts, occasionally attended by Lord Rolle and his lady and often by the beaming Mr. Duke, who was rapidly becoming a Francophile, so delighted was he with the progress of his scheme. Dominique had found time and materials to make another fiddle. Scores of curious cottagers came into the barn and guffawed uproariously when he capered a Gascon dance to his own accompaniment.

At harvest-time all work on the bank ceased by Mr. Duke's order, the men being put to work in the fields instead, and afterwards regaled, in the manor barn, with quarts of rough Devonshire cider that sent scores of the Frenchmen staggering to their huts and lofts shouting snatches from the songs that had helped them over weary leagues in Poland and Bohemia or through the passes of the Spanish sierras.

Long afterwards Gabriel looked back on these months as the most contented of his life. He could have wished that they would go on forever and told Jean as much. The old sergeant looked glum.

"You too?" he queried, in a low voice.

Gabriel began to argue, but the veteran cut him short with an impatient wave of his hand.

"It's well enough for you, all of you," he admitted, "but for me—I've followed the drum since I was a boy. A man can't change that so easily at my age. I'm starved for the sound of a cavalry trumpet. I stand here, week after week, swinging a pick when I ought to be shouldering a musket. I've been with HIM ever since he was a fledgeling in Italy, and I can't help wondering what he's got up to since that lunatic campaign in Portugal."

The sergeant resumed his digging and Gabriel looked at him with a tolerant smile, ignoring the gesture of a plump artilleryman at work in the same trench. The artilleryman, who had overheard the conversation, significantly tapped his forehead.

To know Jean was to understand the years of unbroken success that attended French arms up to that unlucky day on the banks of the Danube in 1809.

Nicholas put it into words: "Men of Jean's generation were caught by the flood tide of the Revolution. Almost all of them went out with the volunteers to fight the professional armies of the old régimes. What happened? A miracle, perhaps. They smashed those armies, time and again, and chased them home to their own capitals. You can't wonder that they learned to consider themselves invincible. Their battalions stormed across Europe half-naked, shoeless, sometimes dangerously short of firearms. Instead of artillery they used revolutionary slogans, they sang the 'Sambre et Meuse.' "

Gabriel interrupted. "Jean doesn't identify himself with the Revolution," he pointed out. "He despises it!"

"He identifies himself with Bonaparte," replied Nicholas, "and that's the same thing under an imperial mantle. Every man of Jean's generation feels that he shares personally in the glory of conquest. Don't ask me to explain their idea of glory. Perhaps it's a substitute, in men like Jean, for the land-hunger of mediæval Jacks, for education or for avarice. I don't know; I only know that there have always been Western Europeans who have grown up and grouped themselves round a lucky adventurer. Caesar had his tenth legion; Gustavus Adolphus his pikemen; the English despot Cromwell had his psalm-singing cavalry; Bonaparte his Old Guard and the grognards, like Jean. Napoleon knows all this. He knows that this Empire of his is a thing of gilded tatters, held together by one thread. When the thread wears thin and breaks, as it must sooner or later, the whole thing will fall to pieces in less than a year. I advise you to stay here and watch the climax from a safe distance. Then you can go home and help to gather up the pieces, if the Habsburgs and Romanoffs leave any lying about!"

Nicholas spat on his leathery hands and swung his pick into the soft red earth.

They all renewed their parole, Nicholas willingly, Jean grudgingly. The sergeant could see no prospects of escape, and as the months wore on, his nostalgia for the camp seemed to grow less acute and he began to take professional interest in the technical aspects of the task upon which they were engaged. The long breakwater was taking shape, curving away across the river basin towards the thatched roofs of Otterton, occasionally crumbling under the lash of the autumn gales but always rising again and penning the floodwater into the bell-mouth of the little estuary. Mr. Duke rubbed his hands gleefully and cracked jokes in execrable French as he walked up and down along the lines of docile labourers.

A fine autumn followed the dry summer. All along the river banks the dwarf oaks and their skirts of tangled undergrowth turned myriad shades of bronze and russet. There was an invigorating nip in the air and a complementary quickening of rhythm in the line of picks and mattocks along the trenches. Gabriel painted often. Sometimes he tried to sketch a sunset over the purple hills on the far side of the Exe, sometimes applied himself to a portrait, a detail of the River Otter's course, or a study of the heavy brown rollers surging up to the foot of the low cliffs at the completed end of the dyke wall.

Gabriel was more than content with his fate. Quick to acquire languages, he learned to speak English with the accent and idiom of a Devonshire farm-labourer. At night, over supper, he listened a good deal to Nicholas, whose fluent English gave him the key to many local problems and to the topics of conversation men discussed in the cider-houses at Otterton and Budley. Nicholas told them about the press gang, and of the remarkable extent to which the whole population, high and low, were involved in the business of smuggling. Now and again he got hold of a soiled broadsheet from one of Mr. Duke's more affable stewards and read them items of news from the Continent. It was in this way that they heard of Massena's retreat into Spain and of the birth of Napoleon's son, the King of Rome. Jean received the latter news with immense satisfaction, Nicholas with the grim comment "That settles the matter. We'll be here for the rest of our lives!"

It was Louis, considered the luckiest of them all, who ultimately cut the cable that bound them to this soft landscape. The jolt was dramatic and unexpected.

They had been in England for nearly a year when Louis left the diggings for a job much closer to his heart.

One morning as the five of them were tramping to work they were suddenly herded into the hedge by a fierce little man in a red coat, sitting a huge dappled thoroughbred. A moment later pandemonium broke out immediately ahead; the five Frenchmen watched with astonishment a pack of yelping hounds tear through a gap in the hedge and pour into a coppice of larch trees on the opposite side of the road. Nicholas told them that it was a fox-hunt, the favourite winter sport of English squires and their yeoman tenantry. Louis's expression grew wistful as his eyes turned from the magnificent mare of the huntsman to the string of splendid horses that fell into file behind the gap and streamed across the road in pursuit of the pack. The crisp air rang with the shouts of the riders and the continuous baying of the hounds as the hunt crashed through the yellowing undergrowth almost on the brush of the fox. There was something gloriously exhilarating in the scene—the huntsmen's scarlet weaving its rich pattern against the dark green and gold of the copse, the flushed faces of the excited horsemen, oblivious of everything but the thrill of pursuit, the glitter of bridle chains and stirrup irons— that stirred in Jean memories of the plateau of Jena, where, early one morning, he had watched a light-cavalry charge after the exhausted infantry had spent all night dragging guns into position for the cannonade which was to dissolve Prussia's clumsy legions in a cloud of battery smoke.

When the horsemen had crashed into the copse Louis said: "God, they know how to breed!"

They walked on in silence and Gabriel thought that he had not seen Louis so pensive since the night when he had watched him cropping the ears of the mule stolen to save Jean's life after Busaco.

Within a few hundred yards of the diggings they turned off and filed down a steep lane enclosed in the high, overgrown banks that were so common a feature of the place. At the end of the lane they came upon a lame mare, its reins held by a woman in a voluminous grey riding-habit. The huntress appeared to be in a bad temper. She was biting her thin lips with vexation and cursing in a deep voice. Gabriel noticed that her brow was still damp with perspiration and her skirts were splashed with mud.

As the voltigeurs reached the end of the lane a broad-shouldered horseman cantered up, riding a cob. Seeing the woman, he reined in and shouted: "What is it, Lucy? A shoe?"

Lucy Manaton, one of the hardest riders to hounds in the West Country, scowled at him.

"That damned bar at the Rectory Gap, Roger. Somebody gets thrown every time we come through there. Why doesn't Duke have his property attended to, curse him? A horse will be killed there some day!"

"Are you hurt?"

The woman laughed and, displaying her fine teeth, she looked almost pretty. Four of the Frenchmen glanced at her with interest. Living between billets and diggings, they seldom saw any women except one or two solid-looking girls on the farms. Nicholas observed that the woman seemed to have a dash of the French about her. Her hair, fastened in tight, coiled plaits, was jet black, like Nicholette's. Her figure, in the becoming riding-habit, was straight and beautifully proportioned. She had not the usual look of the outdoor woman; her complexion was pale, her features pleasingly small and well made. Only her voice, unnaturally harsh and masculine, suggested the fact that she lived almost exclusively among men and horses, leaving her large house and adjacent farms in the high beech woods behind Knowle to the care of an unsupervised staff. For even when Lucy Manaton was at home she was generally to be found in the stables.

The burly rider, Roger, swung himself out of the saddle and glanced at the mare's injured foreleg, running his large hand lightly across an extensive graze. The cursory examination was expertly done, but even so the animal winced.

Louis had barely glanced at the woman. He watched the man set down the hoof. The animal would not allow the injured leg to rest on the gravel.

"You'd better get Burdock," the man said shortly, and climbed back into his saddle.

"Burdock's more than a mile away by now!" muttered the woman, impatiently shrugging her shoulders; then, to the mare, "Come on, Roxy, you won't hear the halloo for a month or more!"

Louis went over to the horse and lifted the leg again. The woman opened her mouth to protest, but whatever she had been going to say was checked by the expression on Louis's face. It was that of a young mother bending over a sick child. Even Old Jean noticed it and grinned.

"Come on," he said to the others, with a swift sidelong grin in Louis's direction. The four of them went down the lane and left him bending over the mare.

Presently the Frenchman looked up. He knew very little English and began to grope for the right words. Lucy Manaton cut him short, speaking perfect French.

"What is it you need?"

Louis told her that he wanted a pair of scissors and a roll of bandage.

"I have them here!" she said and, opening a small saddle-bag, took out a pair of groom's trimmers, packed in a small leather folder along with other stable equipment. Louis took the scissors and began to trim the wound. Lucy Manaton watched, fascinated by the speed and accuracy of the Frenchman's fingers. Roxy, the mare, remained statuesque. So did the burley horseman, leaning forward over his saddle-bow. He knew Roxy's temper and, knowing it, marvelled. The mare might never have been touched by any man save this silent young Frenchman.

When the edges of the long wound had been shaved Louis splashed it with running water from the gutter brook. The horse trembled slightly, but remained still. Lucy Manaton bent and, whisking the hem of her skirt over her knees, tore a long, broad strip from the edge of her short petticoat. Louis reached for it without a word. The burley man laughed.

"You're in good hands, Lucy; I'll move on and join the others!"

"You needn't bring Burdock!" she shouted as he applied his spurs and cantered off down the muddy lane.

Louis finished the dressing in silence and Lucy Manaton watched him, a quiet smile puckering the corners of her hard mouth. Squire Branton, who had known Lucy since she was a child, always said that her horses inherited that mouth of hers within a week of entering Knowle stables. Nobody but Lucy could ride her horses and Lucy liked it that way. A horse had broken up her marriage with the young fop Vince a year before. He had been thrown by Roxy's sire and had gone out, bruised and sullen, and shot the animal in its stall. The grooms said that Lucy would have cut his throat if he hadn't packed up and gone off to London the same night. Nobody regretted the departure of Vince Manaton. Everybody knew that the marriage was certain to fail. Vince rode like a City alderman, and in the eyes of the local gentry and farmers this was a far more serious offence than his absurb foppery and extravagance. Now he was in London, aping the bucks at the clubs of St. James's, and living far in excess of the allowance that Lucy gave him to stay away from her.

Lucy was an odd, impulsive creature, with even more of the characteristics of her French mother than of her fox-hunting father, Squire Lammater. Hardly anybody remembered her mother, whom the Squire had brought home after his Little Tour. She had died within a year or two of the marriage and the Squire had been left to bring up Lucy alone. He taught her to ride, to judge horseflesh, to swear and to intimidate servants. For the rest she had managed as best she could under a French governess who was so terrified by the Squire's oaths that she did not speak in his presence throughout the twenty years of her servitude.

It was not until many weeks later that Jean, Nicholas and the others learned about Lucy Manaton. Louis went back to Knowle with her the morning that he doctored Roxy. She was so impressed by his skill and by the mare's docility under his hands that she told him to stay in the lane whilst she approached the foreman engineer of the works and bullied the officer into allowing her to borrow Louis for the day. The same afternoon Lucy rode over to Mr. Duke's seat at Otterton and obtained his permission to employ Louis as a groom. There were nearly a score of horses at High Knowle, most of them thoroughbreds, and the stable staff were notoriously overworked. Mr. Duke, dubious of the legal position, went over to Lord Rolle at Bicton and asked if it were permissible for a private person to employ a prisoner of war in this capacity. Lord Rolle had been an old friend of Lucy's father and instantly gave his assent. One man would make no appreciable difference to the progress of Dukey's Folly down at the river mouth.

So Lucy went back to High Knowle with an official-looking document bearing Louis's name and prisoner's number. She found her new groom engrossed in a tour of the stables, passing from stall to stall, patting shining flanks and stroking soft muzzles. If he had been asked to choose an occupation from every vacancy in Europe Louis would have elected to stay at High Knowle as groom to Lucy Manaton.

They gave him a billet in a loft above the stables, but he did not use it much. Every time a horse coughed he was down the ladder like a man escaping from a blazing building. His enthusiasm was considered somewhat eccentric by the other stablemen, but his undeniable skill and quiet good humour soon won their friendship. They called him "Froggylad" and left it at that. Not only did he relieve them of a vast amount of work and with the utmost cheerfulness, but he seemed, in addition, to have a soothing effect upon their mistress, whose tantrums had sometimes driven them all to stupefy their senses at the cider jack.

Louis did not quite forget his comrades at Bicton. Two or three times a week he borrowed a cob and rode over of an evening, taking with him a supply of highly flavoured pasties specially made for him by the wife of one of the gamekeepers, a mountainous, motherly soul called Aggie. Aggie's sister, Thirza, as thin and sour as Aggie was fat and expansive, disapproved of the bakings and of Frenchmen in general and told Aggie not to be such a fool. All English prisoners in the hands of the French, she declared, were fattened, killed off and made into pasties. Everybody knew that the French Emperor, Boney, encouraged cannibalism. Had she not seen pamphlets depicting Napoleon and his men toasting captured children on their bayonets before a camp-fire? Aggie listened to Thirza, but was not impressed. She believed well of everyone, even of Napoleon, and if he was as bad as everybody said it must be because he had had a wicked mother.

The autumn and winter passed uneventfully. Spring came in and with it weeks of rain, flooding the diggings and bringing the work to a temporary standstill. Day after day the men had to abandon tools and take shelter along the bank under the dwarf oaks.

Old Jean's spirits touched bottom and even Nicholas became unreasonably depressed by the continual drizzle and the dripping countryside. Gabriel was unable to paint out of doors and after a few attempts at portraits flung his sketchbook back into the shot box which they used as a communal kit-locker. Dominique alone remained cheerful. During the long periods when the men were not able to work and were amusing themselves with wood-carvings which they sold for a few coppers to local families, he was asked to fiddle a good deal. He even learned half a dozen English tunes, including "Robin Adair," "Allan Water" and "Early One Morning." He also sang one or two West Country folk-songs about pigs and lovesick shepherds. His rendering of these in the original dialect, blended with a strong Gascon accent, was received by the English technicians with loud laughter. Dominique did not mind this; he took it for applause, which indeed it was in the circumstances, for laughter meant encores and Dominique fiddled until his fingers were raw.

Meanwhile at High Knowle something happened which cost Louis his job.

Lucy Manaton had taken to spending a good many of her evenings in the stables. She had, indeed, always crossed the yard at least once in the interval between her lonely dinner and retirement to bed, but during the latter part of the winter, when the weather was so bad, several of the horses had been sick and Louis was kept up most of the night for the best part of a month.

Looking down from her bedroom in the west turret of the rambling old house, Lucy often saw the gleam of Louis's horn-lantern through the open upper half of a stable door. One night, unable to sleep, she slipped on a bodice and skirt, took a bottle of wine from the kitchen table and crossed the yard to the stables. She found Louis sitting on a milking-stool beside Patch, the sturdy pony that they used for the dog-cart when Harris, Lucy's aged butler, had occasion to drive into Exeter to market.

Lucy had been restless during the past few weeks. Vince, the husband for whom she now felt nothing but vague contempt, had been pestering her again for money. He had lost a good deal at cards and she had been obliged to mortgage one of the estate's larger farms in order to clear his debts and give him a fresh start.

Her lawyer warned her that this sort of thing could not continue. Although she spent hardly anything on herself—she was never seen out of riding-habit, and even these clothes were so frayed and stained that they were a standing joke in the neighbourhood —her expenses were heavy at High Knowle and Vince had run through something like four thousand pounds since they had parted. She persuaded the lawyer to write Vince a letter telling him that he could expect no further help from his wife in excess of his usual quarterly allowance. If he went on spending he would have to return home and see about selling up. Although the ultimatum was her own idea, Lucy approved the letter unwillingly. The prospect of putting her horses up for auction made her sick with dismay.

It was only recently that she had become conscious of her isolation. She had been content to live in a world of her own, a world in which her horses were allied with memories of her stamping, swearing father and a house full of half-drunken men. She had never resented the way her father had treated her. He was a man and she expected men to be coarse and stupid. But her father had at least been a man in the physical sense, a fearless horseman, a two-and-a-half-bottle toper who knew how to use his fists in a community passionately devoted to the Fancy. She had once seen him stand up for a dozen rounds with Hammer-Toe Charlie, the Bristol smith, who had fought one hundred and four rounds against the Cornish favourite over at Crediton.

In his brusque way he had been kind to her and had shown infinite patience in teaching her to ride when she was a child of six. Had he lived he would never have let the family marry her off to a weakling like Vince mainly because his father had a seat in Parliament. She had never liked her husband, nor had he ever made the slightest attempt to win her affection. There had been a few dismal months of heavy drinking and furious quarrels, then that frightful scene when he went out and shot poor Hannibal. She still dreamed of that night, and since the incident Hannibal's stall had always been left empty. She passed it now, on her way down the flagged alley towards the winking lantern hooked above the stall where the young Frenchman sat with fat little Patch.

Louis looked up and smiled when he saw her. He was not surprised by her visit. There is an implicit understanding between people who share their feeling for horses. Lucy thought him almost handsome with half his face in shadow and the yellow light of the candle flame falling on his dark curls and thin, intelligent face. He looked young, eager and gentle and she felt exhilarated by their kinship. Because of him the image of her French mother's portrait in the hall stirred in her mind.

She poured some wine into a small beaker that she found on the shelf above his head. He sipped gratefully and it struck her that he looked excessively tired. He could not have had much sleep since Patch had begun to ail. When he set down the beaker she refilled it and said: "Did you have any supper tonight?"

"Aggie brought me a pasty."

"Pasty!" She spat the word. Her father had been a wonderful trencherman. She had seen him eat four of Aggie's pasties after a heavy dinner of beef, game and damson pie. He had always eaten pasties absently, as though they were wafers served with the junket.

She went out across the yard again. It was still drizzling and the house was a black mass except for the weak light of a pair of candles in her own room. She groped her way into the stone kitchen and lit the oil lamp with a glowing faggot taken from the hearth. There was just enough light for her to find half a cold chicken, a few slices of fat pork and two cold baked potatoes on one of the slate shelves of the pantry. She heaped the food onto a serving plate and carried it back across the yard, setting it down on the edge of Patch's trough. She had forgotten to bring a fork. Louis took out his clasp-knife—the knife Aggie's husband had given him to replace the one confiscated by the British provost in Lisbon—and sliced the meat. She thought that he handled the chicken bones more like a woman than a hungry man. He picked the meat from every bone, washing down

166

the meal with another beaker of wine. She noticed this time that it caused a slight flush.

They talked about Patch, and Louis said that the pony had greatly improved. He had given her two pills the day before and had watched her sweat. The fat little mare seemed comfortable enough in her deep layer of straw. He stroked her nose and she nuzzled his fingers every time they approached her nostrils. Lucy reflected that all the horses in the stables showed pleasure when this lean young Frenchman came near them. She felt curious to know about his origins.

"Where did you learn all this?" she asked him.

Louis told her about his father and about the Bayonne coach-run. He spoke of a happy childhood in the cottage which the family had shared with a coach-guard, behind one of the larger posting-houses on the frontier highroad. There had been a constant flow of traffic to and from Spain, and even in the small hours coaches rattled into the yard and teams were changed during the brief halts. He drew a vivid picture for her of steaming greys, stripped of their harness, trotting contentedly into the warm stables and standing loosely at their troughs, munching hay while the boy Louis stood on a box and rubbed them down. He described his father stamping out of the cottage at 2 A.M. on a frosty morning, looking huge in his multi-frilled driving cloak and low-crowned beaver, his broad face almost masked by a long woollen scarf wrapped round and round his neck and stuffed between the wide lapels. He told her about cold, dark rides south-west and north-east, with the rain beating in their faces and their feet numb under the driver's bearskin rug, of canters along the white road on long summer evenings, with the red sun on the vineyards and fine dust trailing like smoke from the hooves of the second pair of trotters. The wine made him unusually talkative. He described attempted highway robberies on lonely stretches of road, and an occasion when he had lain prone on the footboard and loaded pistols for his father throughout an hour-long attack by highwaymen firing from the woods. The guard had been killed and one of their leaders shot in its traces, but Louis's father had kept up the fight until reinforcements arrived in the form of the southbound coach.

Lucy listened enthralled. He was showing her another world, in which men and even children fought and sometimes died for their daily bread. She led him on to describe the battles along the Danube and in Spain. He told her of Manny, crucified high up in the sierras, and of Claude, swept away in the Tagus flood. She asked him a hundred questions about Nicholette the cantinière, and he laughed at her expression of amazement when he told her that he had often seen Napoleon during the Austrian campaign.

The drizzle had ceased and a watery sun was rising when she saw him stifle a long yawn. At once she became insistent—he must go to bed and stay there until midday at least. Frampton, one of the stable hands, would be at work in less than an hour and he would watch over Patch. The pony was asleep anyhow and would not need watching much longer.

She returned to bed herself and slept quietly until the afternoon.

When she awoke she thought with pleasure of the previous night. It puzzled her to discover how soothed she had been by the encounter. She rode Roxy through the damp woods and across the seeping thickets of Shortwood Common, and found herself wishing that she had asked him to accompany her. It was a pleasure to see how well he sat a good horse.

The next day she did ask him to accompany her and when he hesitated she blushed and covered her embarrassment by shouting the order at him in her hoarse man's voice. He only smiled and began to saddle the horses. Together they rode out towards the coast road, Lucy riding a little in front.

Her flash of temper disappeared the moment they were clear of the beech woods, and she challenged him to a race. The pair of them thundered across the common, thigh to thigh, until they were checked by the broken ground of the cliff warrens. After that they rode out every day, but, despite local gossip, which Lucy seemed to encourage by purposely taking the road through the village, their relationship remained that of mistress and servant. Louis still called her "madame" and never spoke unless he was first addressed.

March came and the woods round High Knowle were splashed with primroses. Thrushes sang in the thickets, rabbits started from the undergrowth when their horses stirred the shroud of dead leaves along the forest rides. There was a sweet smell in the glades, and from a knoll crowned by tall trees over at Hayes, near the cob-and-thatch farmhouse where Lucy told him the English colonist Raleigh had been born, Louis could glimpse the glitter of the Channel. They rode up there often. In the solitude their relationship seemed less strange, more like that of a man and a woman devoted to the same things, to open air and strenuous exercise.

He was standing there one afternoon, his back to a tree, holding the reins loosely so that his horse might crop the sweet grass, when she thought that she detected a trace of sadness in his expression. She gave him a swift smile.

"Homesick, Louis?"

He gave an answering smile and shook his head.

"I've been very happy here," he told her. "I've no wish to go back!"

She was unreasonably delighted and for all her powers of self-control could not help showing it.

"I'll keep you here, always!" she said, and came close to him possessively, as though at any moment the naval commissioners who distributed prisoners might leap out from behind the bushes and bundle him into a wagon for the port of repatriation. She knew that there was no real danger of his going back. The war with France had been in being for as long as either of them could remember and it seemed likely to go on forever.

He found himself moved also, more than he had been moved by anything since they had found Manny nailed to the tree in the mountains. He detected a mild scent, subtler and more elusive than the perfume of the flowers at their feet. He did not know that she had lately taken to dabbing her ears and throat with the stopper of a half-empty bottle of French perfume found in her old governess's trunk years ago. She had never used perfume before, despising the women who did so at the Bicton hunt balls which she had unwillingly attended in the past.

He only said: "You've been very kind to me, madame!"

She detected a flutter of nervousness in his manner and for one moment thought that he was about to swing back into the saddle. The slight movement that he made swept away the final restraint of the barrier she had been trying to maintain between them during the last few weeks. She caught his arm and pulled him round to face her.

"Don't ever go back, Louis, never, never!"

He stared down at her and for a moment she read panic in his eyes. Then his expression softened and he swallowed, deliberately, as though half-choked by tenderness. The movement of his throat was a sign to her. She flung her gauntleted arms around his neck and pulled him down to the clumps of primroses and violets, to the pine needles and the tatters of the old year's beech leaves. As she covered his face with kisses he saw that her eyes were wet. He buried his lips in her dark hair and whispered half-articulate endearments in her ear. He was nearly twenty-one, but war and poverty had denied him women, even the slatterns of the camp. He had often wondered what he would say when fond, caressing words were expected of him; now he discovered that these things said themselves. He held her close, thrilled by her trembling.

Left to themselves, their two horses ambled lower down the slope in search of richer grass.

CHAPTER TWO

They did not keep their secret for more than a week. Dodger, fat Aggie's husband, saw them one morning whilst he was emptying rabbit gins up on the common. Dodger was a simple old man and after a moment's open-mouthed scrutiny slunk off through the fir coppice to discuss the matter with his wife. Aggie was profoundly shocked. She had been reared in the feudal atmosphere of a remote country house, and it seemed to her incredible that her mistress, odd and wayward though she had always been, should lie in the grass with a French prisoner, presumably of the labouring class. She was wise enough, and kind enough, however, to say nothing about it to anyone, but her husband was not so discreet. He told Frampton, the groom, and soon the outrageous affair was common knowledge both in the household and in the village. Thirza, Aggie's unmarried sister, was horrified and she sought various counsels on the matter, finally acting on those of Mr. Grimshaw, a crony of hers who was employed in Mr. Duke's estate office and was thus able to write.

Lucy Manaton must have known that everyone in her world was aware of her infatuation, but she did not appear to care.

She sensed that it could not last very long, that something would happen to separate them forever, but she accepted this as part of the price she paid for the hours spent in Louis's arms and the warm spring days they spent together in the saddle, riding as far afield as Salcombe and Topsham. The pretence of decorum which they kept up in the immediate vicinity of High Knowle was dropped the moment they had ridden beyond the normal range of stray acquaintances.

Lucy felt that it was worth any risk to have someone like Louis to talk to after all her years of utter loneliness, and his shy, inexperienced lovemaking had stirred in her a physical appetite which she had thought Vince had killed during the first ugly week of their marriage. She wondered, calmly, whether she would have a child. The prospect did not alarm her. At the back of her mind she welcomed the possibility. It would be something to fling in the face of Vince if she ever saw him again, to make him look ridiculous and to pay off the score still owing on the murdered Hannibal; it would also be something by which to re-member this gentle boy, who looked at her and stroked her cheek as though she were a goddess. Perhaps that was why he held such an attraction for her. She had never known a gentle man. All the men in her life had been either violent and uncouth, like Vince and her hunting companions, or servile and sexless, like old Harris the butler or Dodger at the lodge gates. On the few oc-casions that her father had kissed her his breath had reeked of liquor, and Vince, on those few nights when she had slept with him, had used her roughly enough to cause her acute physical pain.

A month went by and the idyll endured. Louis discovered with dismay that his conquest had altered his relationship with the other servants. Some of them became shy in his presence, treating him almost as though he was master of the house, but the majority made no attempt to hide their surliness and hardly spoke to him. He did not know whether he was in love with Lucy Manaton. He only knew that he liked being near her and riding behind her, watching the easy rhythm of her carriage and the sun patterns moving across her cheek as they walked their horses through the woods of an April afternoon. He enjoyed their embraces, but it was always she who began them. He would have been content to edge his horse alongside Lucy's mare, Roxy, and let his fingers touch Lucy's across the saddle-bow. He liked to hear her laugh. It was a strange contrast to her harsh voice and nowadays she laughed often at the broken English that she encouraged him to practice. He stopped riding over to Bicton to see Jean and the others. He felt that if he did he would have to tell them what happened, and the prospect of doing so filled him with embarrassment.

Now that the nights were growing milder Lucy always came down to the stables as soon as the servants had retired to bed. Twice she asked him to enter the house by the back door and come to her room, but he refused. Some instinct left over from his days in the skirmishers' line checked him from entering unknown territory, and he said it was better that she should come out to him. She teased him, but complied, and they would sit, often simply holding hands, at the open window of his loft, looking out on the dark mass of the woods behind the paddock and speaking little.

It was an odd courtship and sometimes both of them had an uncomfortable feeling that they must appear a little ridiculous. It was only their physical need for one another which kept this from becoming embarrassingly obvious.

One night in early April she left him shortly before dawn and climbed the stone staircase to her room. She lit the candles of her heavy candelabra and began to undress, humming softly to herself as she unpinned her hair. She was standing there in her shift when she heard a floorboard creak. She spun round, thinking, for one happy moment, that he had broken his rule and followed her upstairs. A sallow, elegantly dressed young man stood on the threshold of the room, regarding her with an unpleasant, crooked smile. She started back against the fluted bedpost.

"Vince!"

He strolled into the room and she stared at him. All her contempt and loathing for the man, blunted by nearly two years' separation and thrust into the back of her mind by the happiness of the past few weeks, flared up again, like a smouldering fire fed with pitch. He stood there a moment longer, enjoying her utter dismay. Then he flung a single word at her.

"Whore!"

She noticed now that he held a light riding-switch pressed closely against his leg, and the moment he saw that she had seen it he sprang forward, lashing out at her with the full power of his arm. She dodged the first blow, which whipped against the bedpost. The next second he was upon her and the switch slashed mercilessly at her bare legs.

The pain made her gasp, but it drove out her fear. Throwing herself across the wide bed, she groped for the empty ewer that stood on her marble-topped wash-stand between the bed and the narrow casement. She tried to scream, but the cry stuck in her throat. She felt choked with murderous rage so that she hardly felt the repeated blows on her neck and shoulders. Grasping the ewer by its long, curved handle, she swung it like a flail. It struck him with shattering force on the right temple; like a puppy crushed by a blundering foot he gave a kind of yelp and fell sideways across the bed, the switch dropping from his hand. She saw the fingers that had held it twitch convulsively and curl.

In the brief struggle the candelabra had overturned and the room was in darkness. She suddenly felt sick and steadied herself against the bedpost.

Somebody was stirring below, and old Harris, the butler, feebly called out something that she could not catch. She stood there beside the open window, trembling and sobbing, still holding the ewer in her right hand. The man on the bed lay very still.

Harris knocked.

"Who's there, m'lady?"

His voice, unsteady with fear, forced on her mind an awareness that had left her the moment Vince entered the room. She seized a cloak from the back of the chair and flung it over her shoulders, wrapping the folds across her quivering body. Harris opened the door and peeped in. In the light of his single candle he looked like a tired old gnome. He opened his mouth and stared at the bed.

"It's the master," he said foolishly.

Her mind made an attempt to grapple with the situation. She thought: "Louis! I must get Louis away! Vince didn't come on his own. He must have been sent for. I can manage Vince. I've silenced him already, but they'll take Louis!"

She picked up the candelabra, lit a candle from Harris's flame and held it directly over Vince's head. There was no blood, but she saw a large blue bruise on the temple. She realized then that she was still holding the ewer and that Harris had transferred his startled gaze from the bed to her.

She said: "Call Frampton and some of the others. Take him downstairs, he's hurt!"

Then, without another glance at Vince, she went out, down the stairs and out across the yard to the stables. She went in and climbed the vertical ladder to Louis's loft. The effort made her breathless. She began to sob again and cursed herself for the weakness. Stumbling across the bare floor to the corner where Louis's pallet lay, she reached forward, grasping him by the shoulder and shaking him violently. He sat up instantly.

"What is it?"

As she gasped out her story he listened silently.

"You must get away now," she insisted.

"Where can I go?"

She hadn't thought as far as that. Where could he go? He was a prisoner of war and whether Vince was dead or merely stunned there was certain to be a hue and cry. Louis must leave the house. Chivalry on his part would avail them nothing. It could not help her and it might result in his own death. Vince might not be able to ride, but he was an excellent shot. She had seen him, so drunk that he could hardly stand, firing pistols at lighted candles and extinguishing them in three out of every four attempts. She knew Vince; he would never be satisfied until Louis was dead. He had a weak man's vanity and, where pride was involved, the obstinacy of a trapped stoat. If he was dead, then the law would be called in and for Louis it would mean the hulks or worse.

Across the yard the house had sprung into life. Lights moved up and down, there were calls and the clatter of wooden clogs on the old stairs.

Louis did not have to be persuaded to leave her to face the outcome alone. He was fully conscious of his helplessness as a prisoner of war, and if he were found there and arrested, it would only make matters worse for her. As it was, nobody could prove that they had been lovers. It might even be dismissed as a piece of malicious gossip. It was kinder to Lucy to leave at once.

Lucy Manaton was thinking clearly now and had fought down her sobs. During the struggle her brain had been clouded by hate, but once she had made up her mind that Louis must be whisked from the house her brain began to work over the possibilities that offered themselves. Like every other person living along the Devon coast she was quite familiar with the extent and practice of the smuggling trade. She knew most of the local characters who took an active part in the galley and fishing-smack traffic that plied to and from the Continent. She knew that within a few miles of Knowle men could be found who were ready to convey escaped prisoners across the Channel, providing that they were sufficiently well paid for the risks. A group of French officers had escaped that way from the Plymouth area less than a year ago. But she must have time to work out a plan.

Louis checked her flow of ideas.

"You'd better tell my friends," he said.

"Friends?"

"The sergeant and the others at Bicton."

As he said this, Louis experienced a sudden longing for the company of Jean, Nicholas, Gabriel and Dominique. Always before, when there had been difficulty and danger, they had acted as a group. Alone he felt peculiarly helpless, like a child lost on a racecourse.

As her panic subsided, Lucy had the first glimmering of an idea. "I'll get you away by sea," she said. "I know people round here who can arrange it."

His sense of helplessness made Louis obstinate.

"I can't go without my friends," he said.

She snapped back at him: "Don't be such a fool. Louis. The more that go, the more difficult it is to arrange."

"I won't go without my friends," he repeated. "We've always been together, I couldn't leave without them."

His expression confirmed her in the knowledge that it would be futile to reason with him. She would only be wasting precious time.

She said: "I'll find your friends and make arrangements. Go up to the knoll and stay out of sight until I come to you. Quickly! Go now!"

As they slipped down the ladder, Louis first, he touched her hand in the darkness of Hannibal's empty stall. He reached forward to kiss her, but she was too impatient and propelled him towards the door with both hands.

"Please hurry, I'll come to you, I promise!"

He ran across the yard and climbed the broken palings of the paddock, disappearing rapidly into the belt of woods. She stood for a moment looking after him and then glanced up at the sky. It was almost light and within an hour the prisoners would be trudging along the road from Bicton to their work on the breakwater. She ran into the hall, threw off her robe and took a fur-lined cape from the cloakroom, slipping her bare feet, splashed with the mud of the yard, into a dirty pair of riding-boots. Then she clumped upstairs, with Harris calling after her, and threw herself into some clothes, descending again in less than a minute.

Harris caught her by the arm.

"I wish you'd look at him, m'lady. I've tried him with brandy but—"

"I'm riding for Dr. Ellerman now!"

She flung the remark over her shoulder and hurried out

177

towards Roxy's stall. The butler looked after her stupidly, startled out of his old wits and still only half awake. A moment later he heard the clatter of hooves in the yard.

Lucy knew that she would recognize Old Jean and the others, for she and Louis had met the group going to and from the diggings on several occasions during their recent rides, and once she had attended a barn concert to hear Dominique play. She rode to the diggings at full gallop, but it was yet too early and she found them deserted. Turning, she began to pick her way slowly up the lane to the place where Louis had bandaged Roxy's injured leg. She passed several groups of men, but her presence there at that early hour did not excite much attention. One or two of them greeted her respectfully and she lifted her crop in acknowledgement.

At the main road she turned right and walked Roxy slowly back towards Bicton. Just before reaching Budley crossroads she encountered the four voltigeurs, shuffling along in couples, hands in the pockets of their tattered greatcoats and heads down to the keen north-west wind. They looked up at her, and Old Jean nodded a greeting. She reined in to the hedge and beckoned. Jean stopped and came over to her.

"Tell the others to move on," she told him.

He knew instinctively that her presence had something to do with Louis. He was accustomed to thinking and acting quickly and he called across to the hesitating trio. "Move on, Nicholas; I'll catch you up!" Then he turned back to her inquiringly. "Is it Louis?"

She nodded. "He told me to find you; he's in hiding."

Jean sucked his teeth. It flashed across his mind that here was something he had expected. He looked at Lucy Manaton with impatience. She had no right to have taken Louis away from the file for her own convenience. Didn't she understand that anything they did was done together as a unit?

"What are you going to do?"

"I'm going to get him over to France!"

"France!"

Jean's heart began to beat furiously. Was this the answer to all his ponderings on the subject of escape? Gabriel still had money and they had heard that passages could be bought from the smugglers; but one couldn't go without the others, while the bribe for five would be prohibitive.

She solved his problem.

"How easily can you leave your billets tonight?"

He chuckled. Years seemed to fall from his lined face.

"As easily as walking out. There are no guards, we're on parole."

"And the others?" She had never spoken to the man before, but she was quite certain that any attempt to split the group would be useless.

"They'll all come, I promise you; five of us, counting Louis."

"Do you know a clump of trees called Shortwood Knoll? It's about two miles from here, at the head of the common?"

He knew it, having made it his business to study the locality during the past fifteen months.

"Be there at eleven tonight, all four of you!"

She clapped spurs into Roxy before he had time to reply, and galloped off down the main road towards Bicton. He stared after a moment, his heart throbbing with joy. Then he moved on after the others and caught them up where the lane opened onto the diggings.

"How's Louis?" asked Nicholas casually.

"He's coming over with pies tomorrow," Jean said and picked up his spade. He was not going to have them chattering in the open. He had waited fifteen months and he could wait another twelve hours.

Lucy did call at Dr. Ellerman's as she passed his bow-windowed house in Budley, but only to leave a message asking him to go as soon as possible to High Knowle. She told the doctor's housekeeper that someone there had had a fall. It could all be explained later.

179

She did not return towards home but hurried along the coast road for another two hours or more, stopping only when she had reached a tumbledown cottage at the junction with the cart-track leading down to the village of Beer. Here she dismounted and knocked. A short, enormously thickset man wearing a striped shirt and tight breeches, supported by a highly decorative belt, opened the door. As the man recognized her his heavy features rapidly assumed a respectful expression. He bowed, his bulk making the gesture faintly comic.

"Thank God you're at home, Jack!" said Lucy, and without waiting for his invitation she entered the low-ceilinged room. It was so crowded with furniture and seafaring knick-knacks that there was barely space enough for the two of them to sit.

The fat man closed and bolted the door. His expression relaxed and he winked deliberately. When he smiled, his fat face seemed to dissolve, scores of creases gliding across the moist skin like eels stirred in a bucket. He had small but astonishingly bright blue eyes, set wide apart. His nose was short and decisive. His clean-shaven mouth was wide and humorous, and his bare arms, as thick as table legs, were grotesquely tattooed. He sat down on a stool, which creaked under his weight, and smacked his bulging thighs.

"What is it, m'lady? Brandy, lace . . . I've a good bit of stuff here straight from Lille, came in on the *Wanderer* night afore las'! A risky run it were. I wasn't on it myself, but Dick Crosbie told me they fetched up agin a cutter—"

She stopped him with a gesture.

"I want you to take something out, tonight!"

He whistled and then winked again.

"And what would a lady like you want with export trade?" he asked bluntly.

"Prisoners! Five of them!"

He shut both his eyes, spread his huge palms on the skin-tight nankeen of his breeches and blew out his lips, making a low, hissing sound.

"Prisoners!" He did not pursue the question. Jack Rattenbury had not built up a business unrivalled between Weymouth and Dartmouth by enquiring too closely into the motives of his high-class customers. He seldom enquired at all. He had expressed his surprise and that was all. His mind was already busy with figures, risks, cutter patrols, blockade sentinels, tides, wind and all the other factors requiring expert consideration.

"Prisoners is dangerous!" he said finally.

Lucy did not take her eyes off him.

"I'm paying a dangerous price," she said.

For the best part of a minute Jack rubbed his nose. Suddenly he screwed up his face so fiercely that his bushy eyebrows met in a long, even hedge.

"Ten guineas a head!" he announced. "Couldn't do it for less!"

He waited, ready to bargain. He had run prisoners in the past for eight and would have dropped as low as seven for Lucy Manaton. She was the daughter of the old Squire, one of his best customers in the days when he was young and spry in the trade and the coast blockade had extended only as far as the Hampshire border.

Lucy disappointed him. She did not bargain. "Fifty guineas the lot, but it must be tonight, fair or foul!"

He cocked an eye up at the window as though gauging the weather.

"You'll be wanting us over your way for sartin!" said the smuggler, by way of an epilogue to the conversation.

"I'll have them down at Sherbrook Goyle by one o'clock," Lucy promised, and, rising, unbolted the door and passed through the trim little garden to the fence where Roxy was tethered. She mounted and rode off without another word.

The others located Louis easily enough. It was two hours after dark and he was lying concealed in a thicket on the edge of the knoll. He called out when he recognized Jean's high-pitched voice and the deeper mumble of Nicholas replying. He told them nothing until he had eaten a crust of the bread they had carried with them. He had been ravenously hungry lying up there since first light, scanning the narrow path for signs of pursuit. He had seen no one but an odd ploughman and an old woman gathering faggots in the wood.

They exchanged stories and Louis accepted Lucy's decision as realistically as he had taken her first advice earlier in the day. There was no sense in hanging about waiting for more trouble. It did not occur to him that she might be making a great sacrifice. Their relationship had been intimate and affectionate, but he, no less than she, had been fully aware of its impermanence. To Louis, and to all of them, she had always remained a British aristocrat, with her full share of civic rights, whereas they, as alien prisoners, had no rights at all. Jean said that from what he had seen of her he judged Lucy Manaton capable of steering herself clear of trouble. He knew nothing of the harsh inconsistencies in the character of the local squirearchy, where a woman might command the respect of her neighbours under almost any circumstances except that of preferring a foreigner to an Englishman as bedfellow. Nicholas, who knew the English, had a vague suspicion that all would be far from well with Lucy if it once became known that, in addition to taking a Frenchman for a lover, she had engineered their escape, but he kept his thoughts to himself. It would do no good to worry Louis at this stage and make things more complicated for them all.

Now that they were on the point of escaping, Nicholas raised no objections. As the second spring in England had advanced he had been growing almost as restless as Jean. The season had stirred in him vague memories of Nicholette, which he had thought buried long ago, or perhaps it was merely his old urge to uproot himself and return to living on the edge of danger, the characteristic which made him prefer the life of a private soldier whilst fully aware of its utter futility. Gabriel and Dominique took their lead from Jean. Both of them had grown to look upon the lean old soldier as infallible. Their trust was partly faith, partly habit. They knew that Jean would keep them alive as long as he could. He had done that with all his subordinates ever since they had made him a sergeant in the camp at Boulogne, nearly a dozen years ago. If Jean had any scruples about breaking his parole he said nothing about them. A chance like this was too good to miss. His first duty was to his regiment. So they packed their kit, and nothing was said when he gave orders to march.

There was far too much to carry away and they jettisoned a good deal, including Gabriel's English sketchbook. He tore out two of the water-colours and folded them in neat creases between some oiled packing paper salvaged on the diggings. One was a view of the Exe estuary, looking south-west. The other was a portrait of a rosy Devon child who had often come down to the bank during their rest periods and looked curiously over the Frenchman's shoulder as he sketched. The portrait was called "Nellie, England, 1811."

The men stretched themselves in the thicket and tried to sleep. There was no immediate danger of pursuit, for Louis was the only one who would be missed until the working-parties were checked on the following morning. Jean would have liked a pipe, but he resisted the impulse. They would all want to smoke if he did, and five pipe bowls would be dangerous.

They lay quiet, watching the moor by the usual bivouac sentry spells. It was astonishing how naturally they slipped back into the old campaign routine. It was as though their period as prisoners of war and dyke labourers had been the occupation of a single day, a routine task in a dull campaign, and now they were back in the vanguard, the army's feelers for an enemy lying out in the boisterous darkness ahead. Before he slept Jean cocked an eye at the sky. There was no moon, only a glimmer of stars. The wind was fresh, but not too gusty for a voyage in an open boat if it had an expert seaman at the helm.

Just before midnight Gabriel, who was on watch, heard a pebble rattle on the bridle path below the knoll. He held his breath, listening, and strained his eyes into the darkness. A moment later an indistinct mass showed on the extreme edge of the moor. As it approached, Gabriel saw that it was a single individual, riding a small horse. He woke the others and they waited. The rider came straight for the clump in which they were concealed and stopped. They hesitated, wondering if they should take a chance.

Presently the figure dismounted and Gabriel, who had the keenest sight, noticed a swirl of skirts. He told Louis, and the coachman's son wriggled into the clearing and stood up. They saw him exchange a few words with the woman before he returned to them.

"It's Lucy herself," he told them. "We have to follow the pony and no one is to speak; there may be dragoons on patrol nearer the coast."

They passed, in single file, down the slope to the path, the woman riding ahead. They followed the track along the edge of the hill, turning to one side where it joined a sunken lane, noisy with dead leaves, which cut through a dense plantation of firs and undergrowth. This track was their guide until it left the wood on the right and plunged down into a cleft between two towering red cliffs running downhill to a shallow ford. The pony splashed gently through the water and they followed suit, all but Jean gasping audibly as the running water reached their knees.

The narrow road became a black tunnel as the cleft narrowed and the tall trees met overhead. Jean, who went first, could not even see the pony's tail five yards ahead, but followed the light crunch of its hooves on the gravelled surface.

Presently they emerged into the open again with the wind in their faces and heard the suck of the waves below. They were on the edge of the cliffs above Sherbrook Goyle, and there the pony halted. The little mare, Patch, had trodden this same track a hundred times, always in virtual darkness. Lucy had purchased her from a partner of Rattenbury's and she was familiar with the smugglers' road.

They waited at the cliff top for five minutes, but no patrol went by. The wind seemed to drop as they began to pick their way down the landslip to the beach. A zigzag path had been cut, probably by an earlier generation of East Devon smugglers, in the treacherous sandstone, but winter gales had made dangerous inroads into the two-foot ledge. In some places it was hardly more than a narrow shelf, and stakes had been driven into the wall of the cliff to assist the passage of heavily laden men on their way up from the cove below. Their guide was now on foot, having left the pony on a rocky platform a short way down the slope. She picked her way unerringly, bunching her skirts in her right hand, steadying herself with her left, and not once looking behind to see if they followed.

They blundered along at her heels, grasping one another's greatcoat skirts, moving like a crocodile of blinded sappers groping their way back from the walls of a beleaguered town. Jean marvelled at the woman's uncanny instinct. He did not know that Lucy's father, although Chief Magistrate in the district, had been the smugglers' patron most of his life and that his daughter's childhood had been spent clambering up and down these very cliffs in search of gulls' eggs. Lucy recalled all this as she descended; it pushed the thought of the still figure on the bed at High Knowle deeper and deeper into the unaired corridors of her mind.

They reached the cove at last and found Rattenbury sitting on a rock, a few yards from his moored craft. Lucy Manaton went over to him, leaving the Frenchmen in a knot at the foot of the cliff. Gabriel saw something pass from the woman's hand to the portly smuggler, and saw the latter casually stuff whatever it was into his belt and then beckon.

Four of them went aboard. Rattenbury's boat was a trim eighteen-footer, with a furled foresail. Its crew consisted of Rattenbury and a boy hardly more than fourteen years of age. The boy, saying nothing, pointed to where they should stow themselves. There was a fresh sea running, and down there with the water breaking in creamy surge along the narrow shore the night seemed much less dark.

Lucy had taken Louis's arm as he walked into the shallows, and he stopped, fighting down an unreasonable embarrassment.

The woman must have sensed this, for she drew away slightly and said in a steady voice: "You'll get home all right. Jack says it's an easy run."

"Where are they taking us?" asked Louis, more for something to say than out of curiosity.

"Jack says he'll try and make a Normandy bay that he knows, but it might have to be Jersey. You must leave it to him."

He hesitated, trying to force himself to say a few words of thanks, regret, gratitude, but nothing suitable came to his lips.

The smuggler got up and splashed into the water. Louis threw his arms round the woman and felt her shiver, as though his touch could hardly be borne. He wondered dimly what had happened between them since the night before when they had lain, like boy and girl lovers, in the warm straw of his loft, but he could find no answer. He had no experience in love. He said the first thing that came into his head and realized instantly how foolish it must have sounded.

"I shall miss the horses, Lucy."

Perhaps it was the best thing he could have said. His gaucherie seemed to melt something inside her, for she laughed aloud and threw up her chin to kiss him.

"They're waiting, Louis; go now."

He kissed her lightly and stumbled down the sliding bank of pebbles. His feet seemed to make an unconscionable noise. The smuggler's boy was leaning over the bows, skilfully steadying the boat in a foot of swirling water. Louis climbed in and sat amidships, but the smuggler prised him out and pushed him forward, muttering a string of unintelligible oaths. The voltigeurs looked back as the little vessel bobbed away from the beach and saw Lucy Manaton standing, her skirt spread in the wind. She was not waving, just looking after them.

As darkness closed on the boat, she turned and trudged up the difficult slope, suddenly overwhelmed by physical fatigue. Two hours later she arrived home to hear that Vince had died without recovering consciousness. She made no comment to Dr. Ellerman, who had been hastily summoned again by old Harris. She did not even notice his odd look, but climbed the stairs, flung herself on the bed and was asleep instantly.

A mile out to sea, Rattenbury's boat *Kestrel* dipped through choppy water, heading due south. Louis and Dominique were curled up in a large locker in the bows. Jean and Gabriel lay astern, both holding long boarding-pistols, their hands cupped over the hammers to shield the priming-pans from flying spray. Rattenbury had said that there was a hundred-to-one chance of running across a cutter, and if this happened they were to fire without waiting for a challenge. When it came to a matter of business Jack recognized no flag. His attitude was logical. One might as well be hung in chains for a dead preventive officer as hauled back into the King's Navy for running a pound of contraband.

Nicholas sat with the boy near the mast, now straining under four square yards of canvas. He was elated and stimulated by the swirl of the water, the salt smart in his nose and throat and the cold rush of the empty sky. He thought: "Nicholette—she ought to have been a fisherman's daughter; this is her world." At the thought of her a wild longing filled him, and a tenderness that he could not understand.

Book Two

PART FOUR
The Niemen

CHAPTER ONE

Endless columns of men were shuffling across Europe, heading ever east. All day long over the sunny roads hung a cloud of fine white dust. Regiments which had not crossed paths since the days of Jena and Friedland, before the Spanish madness split the veteran columns of the Grand Army, intermingled as they debouched from country byroads onto the main highways to Dresden, Mainz, Strasbourg and the other principal garrison towns of the Empire. All the Imperial arsenals were working in triple shifts. Remounts clattered into the depots in jostling bunches, their outriders cursing the baggage drivers when the slow progress of the wagons caused inevitable bottlenecks. The infantry marched stolidly north-east to Danzig and Königsberg, stripping the summer countryside of its fruit, spreading in a slow-moving tide through the rich German plains towards the banks of the Niemen. The Emperor had decided on his Russian adventure, and his assault column was the largest that Europe had seen since Persian Darius led his hordes west across the Bosporus.

There were men from every Western nation in the ranks. King Murat's flamboyant Italians from the south, Davout's well-disciplined Germans from the north, old campaigners from Spain and glad to see the last of the pestilential Peninsular War, Belgians, Hollanders and Rhinelanders, Westphalians from King Jerome's cardboard kingdom, Saxons, Württembergers and eager Poles, the latter foreseeing their country's independence as the outcome of the Russian campaign; men of every creed, talking every language, a polyglot army, but an army for the most part of doubtful loyalty and untested skill.

The survivors of the voltigeur companies of the Eighty-seventh were there, rearmed and reorganized, thrown in to bring the Ninth Regiment of the line up to strength. More than half the company had perished in Spain and Portugal, a large proportion of them during the disastrous retreat from Torres Vedras. Massena, called home in disgrace, was no longer their chief, but Ney had been forgiven for his insubordination and summoned to take over the advance guard, to which the Ninth Regiment was attached. They pushed on ahead, leaving the long, burdened columns to drag themselves to the starting-point days behind schedule, their strength already reduced by a strange sickness among the horses, due to the use of unripe rye as fodder. The voltigeurs did not know what was happening behind them. Had they done so they might have wondered if this were to be another Portuguese debacle, planned only on a much vaster scale. It was rumoured that more than half a million men were on the march against the Czar and that the Emperor was determined to root him out of his Muscovite capital.

Jean and the rest were there, and the old sergeant looked askance at the motley regiments which they overtook on the march. "It used to be quality," he grunted, "nowadays quantity counts for more!"

The five of them had crossed the Channel without incident, hearing nothing but some distant English voices in the dawn mist, and the smuggler, Rattenbury, had deposited them on a Normandy beach, leaving them to find their own way to the nearest depot, which happened to be Caen. Here a good many explanations had been necessary, but after a week of delays and forced marches, followed by a fortnight's halt at Lille for a refit, the little party had come up with their regrouped unit in Louvain.

The old town was crammed with troops, all making their way to the rendezvous at Dresden. They had picked their way here and there, recognizing no one, a tiny unimportant eddy lost in a flood tide of horse, foot and artillery, until Jean had chanced across Sergeant Soutier, the man who had replaced him when he had been left behind in hospital at Coimbra in the autumn of 1810. Soutier was the man who had been indirectly responsible for the disaster that overtook the party detailed for salvage on the Tagus. Nicholas remembered him well. He was now sergeant-major. All the survivors of the company had been promoted. Promotion was easy in a motley horde composed chiefly of recruits whose experience of gunfire was limited to the routine spatter of a practice shoot. Soutier expressed great surprise on seeing the five men.

"You're still listed as prisoners on my muster roll," he told them.

"Orders," said Nicholas sardonically.

Soutier pretended not to remember. He took them back to the bivouacs of the Ninth and handed them over to a young lieutenant of the second company. Jean noticed that the boy had not even grown a moustache, having left St.-Cyr before his course had been completed. The sergeant commented that if the Emperor was short of veterans he must be shorter still of experienced officers.

Jean was offered a commission. He was flattered but turned the offer down.

"I'm too old for that sort of nonsense," he said to Gabriel. "Imagine me learning to draw maps at my age. I can only sign my name with a squiggle."

"If they want officers as badly as I think they do they'd soon teach you to read and write, Jean," Nicholas told him. "I could do it myself if you'd let me."

Jean chuckled, amused at a vision of himself sitting down with a slate at the bivouac fire after supper.

"I'm well enough as I am. You'd none of you last a month if I weren't here."

Later the others discovered that Nicholas had been offered promotion to the rank of sergeant, but he too had refused. He said nothing about the offer. They found it out only as a result of a casual conversation between Gabriel and the paymaster's clerk.

During the march eastward they made continued enquiries for Nicholette. According to some of the men she had managed to get her wagon back from the Peninsula, and later, early in the spring, Sergeant-Major Soutier seemed to remember seeing her in Mayence. They went down to the artillery park and questioned some of the transport drivers. One of them confirmed that she had been in Mayence, but beyond that they could learn nothing. The regimental rolls could not help them; cantinières were not shown on the muster.

The regiment joined up with Ney's corps in Strasbourg, where they were paraded for review. Nearly everyone had been re-equipped, and the marshal rode slowly along the ranks with a satisfied expression. He seemed to hesitate a little abreast of the voltigeurs, and Nicholas fancied that he caught the Alsatian's eye. Perhaps he recognized the corporal and remembered the dispute over Gino Carolini's mule, or perhaps the twitch of the marshal's lips was imagination on Nicholas's part. He passed on without saying anything beyond a gruff "Well enough, colonel!" to the officer in command. Ney was never lavish with parade-ground praise, but, unlike many of the senior officers, he kept his eyes open during the battle and was seldom far from the upturned heels of the most advanced skirmisher. The men knew this and were satisfied. The deserving usually got recognition from the marshal himself and were not obliged to scan the tedious distinction lists issued by corps headquarters.

"If we're with Ney we're for it again," was Nicholas's comment when the battalion received orders to dismiss.

"We'd have been better off in Oudinot's corps on the flank," said Old Jean. "Those rascals won't get any farther than Poland."

But nobody believed that Jean meant what he said. They all knew that after eighteen months' inaction the sergeant was itching to be out with the advance guard again.

They were slopping through Dresden in thin summer rain when it happened.

The long greatcoated column marched head down, muskets at the underarm trail in an effort to keep the water from the locks. They looked like a vast muster of duck-shooters splashing along the street on their way to a shooting party.

A convoy of canopied wagons, ambulances and sutlers' vans had been forced into the shallow brook at the side of the road in order that the advance guard might have a clear passage through the city. As the voltigeurs passed there was a minor commotion beside one of the wagons. A lean dog, barking furiously, sprang from under the shafts of the listing vehicle and dashed into the ranks, lashing its plume of a tail and doubling its body in a frenzy of excitement.

The group wavered, disconcerted by the plunging animal. Louis spun round with a shout of recognition.

"Fouché! It's Fouché!"

Hearing its name, the dog stopped dead, head lowered between its muddy paws.

"Fall out!" shouted Jean, dashing the rain from his face. The five of them broke ranks and gathered round the dog. Fouché began to whine and whimper, while Louis bent and patted its sopping coat.

"There, boy, there . . . where's Nicholette? Where is she?"

"I'm up here!"

She was smiling down on them from the box of the wagon, her shoulders hunched under a dripping cloak, her dark hair sticking in a maze of small tendrils to the taut skin of her prominent cheekbones.

Nicholas leaped onto the step of the wagon and flung his arms round the girl.

"Good old Fouché, good boy, Fouché!" he laughed, hugging her.

"I'd seen you," she said quietly. "I wouldn't have let you go by."

Old Jean hurried ahead and told Sergeant-Major Soutier that they would be falling out for a spell.

"As long as you pick us up again by the time we break camp tomorrow," said Soutier, and then, grinning, "I shall expect a bottle of Moselle, Jean!"

They waited for the road to clear and then edged the wagon into a field on the far side of the brook. The rain ceased and a watery sun came out. Gabriel found part of a harrow in an old barn and they soon had a camp-fire going. They sat around it baking oatmeal cakes and watching Nicholette prepare a celebration stew. Onions and potatoes went into it, and a scraggy chicken which Nicholas cornered in an isolated pen on the outskirts of the town.

It was a lavish meal and they all enjoyed it; Nicholette broached her last two bottles of Madeira, left by a wounded hussar as part payment for a three-day lift across the León plain during the withdrawal from Spain. After supper they had leisure to look at her and were pained, though not surprised, by her thinness. She was still as agile as ever, but her prominent features gave them the impression that she had but recently recovered from a long illness. There was not much stock in the wagon, but the team and vehicle were brand-new.

"I shall restock in Königsberg," she told them. "I got more than half the money out of Spain!"

She smiled at them and Gabriel noticed that months of strain had not succeeded in ironing out the two dimples he had noticed that first afternoon when he had seen her watering her horses in the Danube. Nicholas noticed them, too, and felt strangely warmed. He tucked her hand into his damp greatcoat pocket and she left it there, folded within his. Old Jean beamed and Dominique began to unlace the waterproofing of his original fiddle. She had

196

kept it for him. It needed new strings but was otherwise intact. He could easily repair it in a German town.

Nicholette told them her story. After their capture and Claude's death, the English sergeant whom they had met in the compound had carried out his promise and taken their message to the barrier beside the river, so that she was not long in doubt about their fate. She did not attach herself to any other group, although she had several offers. When the retreat began she pulled out in advance and got a good start, marching with a company of the Young Guard. She chose this unit because she knew that the retreat would be a difficult one, and the Guard seemed the safest bet under the circumstances. She got as far as the frontier without much trouble, although they were attacked once or twice by guerrillas in the mountains and lost a number of men. The Guard had used the canteen as an ambulance, and after leaving Portugal it had been a canteen only in name. They had lived on salted mule during the march and judged themselves lucky. Most of the regiments had no transport left to slaughter.

Nicholette would have lost her own horse and mule had not a senior officer been included among her patients. She drove the old fellow all the way to Almeida, where he died, much to the company's annoyance, for they remembered the abandoned men who with the use of his space in the wagon might ultimately have recovered.

The wreck of the army from Portugal was regrouped under Marshal Marmont. Nicholette said that there had been a flare-up in the ranks when Massena was recalled in disgrace. Everybody who had been to Portugal knew that no general, not even the Emperor himself, could have made a success of the campaign, and the troops admired Massena's doggedness. Only that old miser could have succeeded in getting any of them back into Spain, while Marmont was full of amateurish ideas about a new offensive against Wellesley. He fought several battles, which did nothing except reduce his available strength, then finally marched off to the aid of Soult, in sunny Andalusia. This made him popular with all ranks. Soult's veterans had looted Andalusia down to its last piece of church plate, but at least its climate was bearable.

Nicholette did not follow the army south. She had caught some sort of infection at headquarters and after a long spell in a filthy hospital crawled out and decided to nurse herself in the wagon. The remains of the regiment had returned to France, so that when the general recall was issued she attached herself to the Flying Artillery and marched back with them to the border. She had come across stragglers of the Eighty-seventh in Bayonne and again in Tours and Mayence, but had left them to refit. At the latter town she bought a new outfit and moved eastwards towards Dresden, first depositing seven thousand francs with a banker in Strasbourg. The rest of her money had been used up in the purchase of a good wagon and three strong draught horses. The group thought it a magnificent equipage. Each of them was touched by her loyalty in not accepting one of the many chances she must have had to join up with a Guard or cavalry unit. Instead she had resolved to rejoin the voltigeurs, but owing to their absorption into a new regiment had had some difficulty in finding them. She spoke lightly of her steadfastness.

"I like the light infantry, they don't hang about!"

Nicholas and Nicholette were married by a priest in Königsberg.

None of the others was greatly surprised by the event. Nicholette had re-attached herself to the group after the Dresden reunion, and her choice of Nicholas was obvious. If she was to stay with them she would have to marry someone, and Nicholas was the senior after Old Jean, who said he would have preferred the galleys to marriage at his age.

What did surprise them, however, and other men of the company, was the formality of the occasion. Nicholas would have none of the canteen wedding nonsense that had characterized the ceremony on Lobau. If he was marrying, he said, he would be married conventionally. He was not a savage, and, although they were all in the army, Nicholette was a woman of means and there

198

might be civil claims to be considered in event of his or her failure to return from Russia. Only a dozen of them were invited to the wedding. Old Jean gave the bride away and Gabriel was principal groomsman. Afterwards they sat round the wagon drinking a good deal of the light German beer, and Dominique played a tune or two. It was almost like a bourgeois union in a provincial town without the guests and their wedding gifts.

Gabriel watched Nicholette very closely throughout the day and was puzzled by her serenity. She had always been the sort of girl to accept life, however hard it might be, as it found her day by day, but now he thought he saw a change. There was something in her demeanour amounting almost to demureness, especially when he caught her looking up at the bearded Nicholas, who swung his legs from the tailboard and sipped his long metal flagon of beer with a nonchalance suggesting that he had been a bridegroom on a dozen previous occasions. Gabriel wondered if Nicholette had always preferred him, whether her marriage with Claude had been mere physical attraction on the part of a curious sixteen-year-old virgin. Nicholette, who was only nineteen now, looked a mature woman of thirty and in some ways seemed even older than Jean, who was in his early fifties. At all events, both Nicholas and the girl seemed happy about the arrangement, and Gabriel was interested to note that he did not experience the qualm of jealousy he had felt at the first wedding. When it began to grow dark the four of them left the couple sitting on the tailboard of the new wagon, talking little, looking quietly out across the bare hills dotted with bivouac fires. Old Jean belched as he lay down beside their fire within hailing distance. He unbuckled his broad leather belt and lit up his stub of pipe.

"It's a good match," he told Gabriel, "they're fond of one another."

Back on the wagon Nicholas leaned against the bulge of the canopy strut and pulled Nicholette's dark head down onto his broad chest, gently stroking her hair. He was filled with a tenderness that he had never previously experienced. His reason told him that this marriage was ridiculous. He was an educated man and she an illiterate waif, not a trollop like most of the camp-followers but nevertheless the daughter of a whore who had never been able to remember the name of the girl's father. She had qualities—pluck, resolution and loyalty, but most cantinières had those things and he had not married her on that account. The fortunes of war, and an impeccable physique, had left her far better endowed with goods than he would ever be, but it was not for her wagon and her seven thousand francs at Strasbourg that he had married her, either. He wondered if it was because he needed a woman, somebody permanent to satisfy the periodical hunger that pricked him whenever he remembered Camilla all those years ago. He thought not; he had gone eighteen months without a woman in England, although he had had plenty of chances among the farm girls of Devon.

He could not answer the question and knew that he never would be able to answer it. Nicholette was just part of an environment to which he had become lazily accustomed. She occupied almost the same position as Old Jean and the three boys, Gabriel, Louis, Dominique. She fell into place in the background of war; she was a habit, prevailing, established, in the customary scheme of things like the smell of wood smoke, the champ of the horses in the cavalry lines, the rumble of artillery caissons, the rattle of musketry, the deeper chorus of fourteen-pounders. She was as familiar to him as an occasional skirmish in the undergrowth, and the touch of her hand, in spite of the fact that he had never remembered touching it until their chance reunion in Dresden, now seemed as habitual to him as his grip on a musket butt or on the hilt of his sword bayonet. Yet there was something fragrant about her, a feminine fragrance that all these years in the company of coarse men and hardship had never succeeded in destroying. Her pale skin showed no trace of the burning Spanish sun, she always looked neat in her high-laced bodice and full grey skirt, and the scent of her hair reminded him of the stocks that had once grown so freely in old Cicero's garden. She knew when to hold her tongue and did not chatter about silly, unimportant things as had every other woman he had known, including Camilla. He wondered, without excitement, how she would respond to his lovemaking and guessed that she would be dutiful and no more. He did not want her ardour; it would have embarrassed him. He felt protective and old, almost as though he had been her nameless father returning from some half-forgotten battlefield of nearly twenty years ago. After the first few months of his army career Nicholas had never really had any serious regrets about the past. Tonight he realized that something like this was bound to have happened to him sooner or later. He was now legally married to a cantinière and wedded, by preference, to a nomadic life in the ranks, condemned to wander up and down Europe until a bullet or a sabre singled him out and gave him the answer to all the questions he had been asking himself since childhood.

But in the meantime he was well enough satisfied. He had comrades, robust health and enough food and drink for present needs. He also had this child with fragrant hair and an odd regard for him that amounted almost to respect. He looked down on her with a quiet smile.

"I've always wanted you, Nicholette, all my life."

She said quite simply, "We ought to have known it before, Nicholas," and the answer filled him with a great content.

CHAPTER TWO

Not long after the wedding and shortly before the order for a general advance on the Niemen was issued they lost Louis—but not as a casualty. Louis got his wish. After more than three years in the infantry an order came through transferring him to the Danzig Dragoons, the new regiment raised by Davout especially for service in Russia.

Louis never ceased to long for a horse of his own; his association with the English thoroughbreds had made him determined to do everything in his power to transfer to a cavalry regiment on his return to the army. His heart had never been in the duties of a voltigeur, but Old Jean said that he would make an excellent trooper. His love of horses ensured this, since there was nothing wrong with him as a soldier. After Nicholas he had been the best marksman in the company, and the Danzig Dragoons had been issued the new short-muzzled carbine, accurate up to three hundred yards.

Although delighted with his change, Louis parted from his friends with genuine regret. He would have loved to enrol them all as troopers, but Nicholas railed at him good-naturedly when he expressed the wish.

"I have enough trouble feeding myself," said Nicholas, "to hell with feeding a greedy brute of a horse. You wait until you pitch camp after a long day in the saddle and then have your encumbrance to groom and water and your harness to clean before you eat. I bet you'll wish to God you were back in the skirmishing line!"

It is doubtful whether Louis ever did pine for the company. He was too happy astride his great, broad-chested Norman mare, which he named, in response to a sentimental memory, Roxy. She was indeed not unlike the great mare Lucy Manaton had ridden through Devon field and coppice, but light brown instead of tan, and with a white diamond on her forehead. Louis fussed over her like a bridegroom. He never tired of combing out the long fine hair of her tail and mane and grooming her shining flanks. Roxy, like every other horse that was put in Louis's charge, soon came to love him and whinnied with pleasure when he lightly slapped her arching neck or laid his cheek alongside her muzzle. He spent hours foraging on her behalf and more than once, during the long, thirsty advance, took foolish risks under the muskets of Russian skirmishers to fill her canvas bag with fresh water. His troop sergeant, who also loved horses, looked on with approval but told the trumpeter that the new trooper would soon get himself killed if he refused to temper devotion with common sense.

"If we lose him I'll lay a hundred francs the horse comes safely out of it!" laughed the trumpeter, who had himself observed Louis's devotion.

The voltigeurs lost sight of Louis for a considerable time. The Danzig Dragoons were attached to Ney's corps but were working on the right wing of the vanguard, more than two miles south of the men of the Ninth. They caught a glimpse of him once outside Vilna and spent an hour or so with him in the smoking ruins of Smolensk, when he rode over to supper at Jean's invitation, the file having had the luck to arrive first on the scene of the half-gutted ruins of a provision shop just inside the walls.

Thus far it had been an uneventful campaign. There was not much fighting, the Russians retreating as the English had done, laying waste the countryside and burning everything that they could not carry away.

It was almost unbearably hot on the plains, even hotter and more windless on some days than it had been during the march down to Portugal. There was a considerable increase of dysentery and some degree of starvation, although in the presence of the enemy the advance guard fared better than the toiling columns in the centre and rear. They just managed to live on what they could find, leaving little enough for their less fortunate comrades.

"This is one occasion when I prefer to be in among the front ranks," said Nicholas, trudging along beside the wagon. The solid strength of Nicholette's team and vehicle enabled her to keep up with the advance with ease, whereas most of the corps' wheeled transport had already fallen more than a day's march to the rear.

There was one sharp engagement before the battle for Smolensk. On the outskirts of Vitebsk, a sizeable town beside the main road, the voltigeurs of the Ninth had the good fortune to distinguish themselves, one and all, under the eyes of the Emperor and the entire army.

Probing forward over broken country between two ranges of low hills, two companies of voltigeurs, numbering approximately two hundred men, were cut off by a sudden charge of Russian cavalry. Columns on the march farther back at once formed square, but the Russians were far too wily to do more than encircle the skirmishers and it looked at first as if nothing could save the column from annihilation. The ground between the voltigeurs and the flat-topped hill occupied by the nearest French was broken up by ravines and dry watercourses.

Old Jean and the others were in this isolated group with two officers, a captain called Delacroix and the young lieutenant to whom the returned prisoners had first reported in Louvain. Both behaved magnificently, as did the men. By the time the nearest Russian lancers and hussars were upon them the stragglers had run in to form square round Delacroix, his lieutenant and the plump Sergeant-Major Soutier.

No one could have supposed that the tiny square would withstand the shock of that charge. The French army waited to see the lancers cut their way through the double ranks and sweep on to the level ground beyond. Nothing like this happened. The voltigeurs were among the finest marksmen in the Grand Army, and after ten minutes' close-range fighting the square was surrounded on all sides by a breast-high wall of dead men and horses. Firing by volley, one rank kneeling, the second standing, the French poured withering fusillades into the troopers as they pranced and cavorted round the isolated infantrymen, stabbing their long weapons into the drifting smoke and jostling one another in a vain attempt to spear their way through at a weak point. The square stood like a rock and the hussars, in the second charge, fared even worse, for their sabres were not long enough to cause a single casualty.

Nicholas, quietly aiming and firing in the front rank, received a long graze on the cheek, but the man who had held the lance went down before Gabriel's musket, fired at a range of less than two yards. Jean accounted for two hussars and Dominique for another lancer.

Throughout the skirmish old Delacroix shouted comic defiance and jocular encouragement to his men. "Give it 'em, boys. Savages! That'll teach them how to shave, the barbarians! Load again, rear rank! This is how we served the Mamelukes at the Pyramids! Steady there! Here they come again! Fire, rear rank! Wash yourselves, you Muscovite monkeys!" And so on, until some of the men, hearing his running commentary above the crackle of volley fire, could hardly load for laughing.

In the end the cavalry were called off. An immense cheer went up from the French army when they saw the little group of voltigeurs moving in square back over the broken ground to the safety of their own ranks. They had lost three men and a drummer boy, all caught on lancepoints before they could reach the shelter of the square.

Among the minor casualties was the dog Fouché, who scurried into the square the moment it formed and emerged with a bullet graze on the shoulder. The dog had followed them all the way from Dresden, and Nicholette encouraged it to sleep under the wagon and growl at prowlers. Gabriel cut away the clotted fur and bathed the wound, the dog submitting to treatment with the resignation of a veteran. When he had finished the dressing Gabriel playfully pulled Fouché's ears.

"That's one back for the nip you gave me on Lobau," he said. The dog grinned and backed away, wagging its plume of a tail. It occupied itself throughout supper by gnawing away at the bandage.

Later that evening Marshal Berthier, the Chief of Staff, detailed a sergeant of Imperial Guard to go out and count the Russian dead. He reported one hundred and ninety-eight, almost a man apiece, together with two hundred and seven horses.

The following day, when the town was occupied, Napoleon held a miniature review. Every man in the voltigeurs' square received a reward of fifty francs; Delacroix, his boy lieutenant, Sergeant-Major Soutier and Jean all received the Cross of the Legion of Honour first class.

The ceremony was impressive. "Napoleon knows how to manage these things," said Nicholas with a grin, but he was as pleased as any of them to see Old Jean stand, tears streaming down his face, whilst Napoleon pinned the coveted insignia on his tunic. Ney was present and this time he recognized Nicholas.

"Found any more stray mules?" he asked and they saw him turn and recount the anecdote to the Emperor, who listened with interest and nodded approval when Ney told how he had settled the dispute.

The Emperor turned to Jean, who was contriving to look down his nose and squint at the cross whilst still maintaining the stiff pose of attention.

"Where did you serve before that?" he asked.

Jean told him, the old familiar recital—Italy, Egypt, Marengo, Austerlitz, Jena, Eylau and Friedland.

"Ah, yes," mused the Emperor, grasping his riding switch with both hands extended behind his back, "at Aspern-Essling as well; I saw you in the churchyard."

"That is so, sire," replied Jean, in a voice suggesting that he would not have been surprised if the heavens had suddenly opened and a golden chariot had swept down to convey him straight to Valhalla.

"One of you played a fiddle!" said Napoleon, unable to disguise the triumph in his voice at such a brilliant display of memory for minute detail.

"My comrade here played the fiddle, sire," said Jean, nodding at the grinning Dominique.

"And where have you all been since Busaco?"

"In England, sire. We were captured in the Peninsula, myself at Coimbra, the others on the Tagus."

Napoleon's eye gleamed and the staff officers edged nearer.

"You escaped?"

"We came back on a smuggler's fishing boat, sire! He was bribed."

"How much?"

"We never knew, sire. The money was not paid by us."

Napoleon nodded. It was obvious that he was deeply interested. Possibly his brain was turning over the possibility of organizing large-scale escapes among the fifty thousand soldiers and seamen held by the British. The exchange system had broken down long ago. It had no chance of success whilst the British held twice as many men as the French.

"Can you write, Sergeant?"

"I regret, not, sire, but my corporal writes well!"

Nicholas gave Jean a sour look, but it was too late.

"I should like a report upon the circumstances of your escape; see that I get it tonight!

The Emperor and his staff moved on and the companies were dismissed. Nicholas spent two hours in the wagon laboriously compiling a report of their sojourn in England and their ultimate escape. It was years since he had written more than a couple of lines, and the effort made him sweat. He cursed Jean at the completion of every laboured sentence. A grenadier of the Guard was waiting to conduct them into the Presence. Jean was fidgety, Nicholas pretended to be bored.

The grenadier handed them over to a staff colonel at the entrance of the Imperial marquee. After a brief delay they were conducted into Berthier's tent, used as an anteroom.

"Straight through, Sergeant!" said the red-headed Chief of Staff, without looking up from the immense map he was studying. They passed through the silken hangings and found the Emperor lying back in a deep-seated chair. Constant, his valet, was shaving him. For an instant even Nicholas felt a trifle awed.

"Read it, Corporal!" said Napoleon, without a glance in their direction.

Nicholas read the manuscript. It was blunt and factual, giving brief particulars of the capture, of the Lisbon compound, the voyage and general treatment of prisoners, the Otter Bank breakwater construction, Louis's engagement as groom and the incident that led to their escape. The only fact withheld was Louis's association with Lucy Manaton. Nicholas tried to give the impression that the incident had been due to a ridiculous fit of jealousy on the part of the returning husband.

The Emperor mused for a while. There was no sound in the marquee except the steady rasp of Constant's razor on his master's bluish bristles.

Presently Napoleon said: "How is it that men like this smuggler Rattenbury are willing to transport enemies of their country out of captivity?"

Jean looked at Nicholas, and the corporal shrugged. It struck the sergeant as extraordinary how composed Nicholas could be in the presence of exalted rank. He seemed to mind Napoleon no more than he minded Sergeant-Major Soutier.

"Well?"

"I can only express an opinion, sire!"

"And what is your opinion?"

"Men will do most things for money. This man was well paid by an old customer."

"Is that all, Corporal?"

"No, sire, the smuggler was a deserter from the navy and like most of the pressed men he had been barbarously treated by officers. He had had his patriotism flogged out of him!"

Napoleon sat bolt upright with disconcerting suddenness. Constant, accustomed to his Imperial master's nervous movements, made a deft sidestep, raising the lather-crusted blade level with his shoulder.

"Yet their navy continues to win victories. It beats our navy off the seas! Can you explain that, Corporal?"

"By another opinion, sire," said Nicholas doggedly.

"Come, come—I'm asking you!"

Jean held his breath and felt his palms sweating. Roustam, the Emperor's gorgeously attired Mameluke, came in with silent tread and stood behind his master's chair, his white eyeballs gleaming in the light of the hanging lamps.

Nicholas spoke slowly, as though considering every word.

"The English are a family, and families quarrel furiously until one of their number is attacked by somebody outside the circle. Pressed men hate the service until they are within range of an enemy vessel. Then the habit of discipline and their own temperament are too strong for them. They fight as well as anyone in the world. Afterwards, if they survive, they persuade themselves that they share the glory with their officers."

Napoleon was silent for a moment, ruminating. Finally he said: "I shall want you to return to Paris and take up duties in the Intelligence Section of the Marine Office. Summon my secretary, Roustam!"

Nicholas set his jaw. Old Jean wished that he could faint.

"With your permission, sire, I would prefer to stay with my company."

A dark cloud seemed to settle on the Emperor's face. The lather dried and flaked on the side that Constant had yet to shave.

"You're a fool," he barked. "I need intelligent, educated men. Thousands of ex-peasants can do your work in the skirmishers' line!" He broke off and studied Nicholas closely. "The transfer would mean officer's rank and a special rate of pay!"

"Both of us have previously refused promotion, sire!"

A tired secretary came in, giving his black breeches a perfunctory dust as he crossed to the desk.

Suddenly Jean spoke up, his voice nervously high-pitched, "We are a unit, sire. We have been together a long time."

His words sounded lame enough, but the shaft was well aimed. Jean might be illiterate but he understood Napoleon's psychological make-up as well as Berthier, Chief of Staff. The cloud on the Emperor's round white face disappeared, chased away by a warm smile. Nicholas recognized the transition, knowing that diplomats from all over Europe and the East had been fascinated by that rapid change of expression.

"Go back to your company, both of you. Roustam!" The Emperor settled back in his chair and by a swift gesture of his right hand indicated that Constant could resume shaving. "Give these men ten napoleons apiece!"

The Mameluke padded over to the secretary's desk and took from the civilian twenty pieces of gold. The money had been extracted from the desk coffer almost before the Emperor had finished speaking. Jean and Nicholas saluted, the former taking the money. Nicholas handed his report to the Mameluke, who passed it to the secretary. Then they saluted, wheeled about and went out, past the bent red head of Marshal Berthier and the silent grenadiers at the entrance of the tent, through the gutted streets towards their own quarters.

Finally Nicholas said: "Divide the money with the others, Jean. I don't want gold from him!"

Jean opened his mouth to speak but closed it again. He had never understood this big, unpredictable schoolmaster. He supposed now that he would never understand him. But he reflected that a few moments since he had felt sick at the prospect of losing him to the Marine Office in Paris.

CHAPTER THREE

The voltigeurs did not take part in the great battle of Borodino,
where the Russians made their desperate stand a few days' march
from the capital. They were held in reserve with the Imperial
Guard and so were spared the decimation that overtook most
of the regiments engaged. Jean, who walked over the battlefield
the following day, said that the slaughter appeared to have been
on an even greater scale than at Eylau. The ground was strewn
with mangled men and horses, shattered equipment, overturned
cannon, drums, helmets and all the litter of a major engagement.
Cannon fire had ploughed up the plain, and in the fresh earth of
the furrows looting of the dead proceeded openly. Here and there
a wounded man called piteously for help.

Jean, who had lost a number of old comrades, shook his head.

"We can't afford these losses at this distance from base," he
told them, "where are replacements to come from?"

"At least the campaign isn't being bungled like the Portuguese
fiasco," said Gabriel; but Nicholas gave a short laugh.

"It isn't over yet!"

They caught sight of Louis, trotting after Murat's squadrons
in pursuit of the retreating Russians. The coachman's son was in

high spirits. He told them he had taken part in the recent affair and had charged the Great Redoubt, where casualties were heaviest. He and his mare, Roxy, had come through without a scratch, although the troop had lost their sergeant, nine troopers killed and a dozen more wounded.

"She behaved magnificently," said Louis, patting Roxy's sleek neck, "minding cannon no more than pop-guns. Up, my beauty, hey, up there!" And, waving his hand, he rode off across the debris, saddle creaking, brass helmet glittering in the early-morning sun, his thickset body rising and falling in the rhythm of a practised horseman.

Jean looked after him regretfully. "We've lost Louis all right," he muttered, and continued looking about for a likely piece of horseflesh to grill. There had been no bread issue since the day after they had left Smolensk.

The old sergeant was immensely cheered, however, when, a day or so later, the voltigeurs topped the rise of Mont du Salut and paused, alongside thousands of others, to look down on the fantastic spectacle of the holy city, its cluster of gilded domes and spires rising in fairy-tale splendour below them. The rays of the afternoon sun fell directly on the gilded onions of the great churches and on the varnished iron roofs of a dozen immense palaces. The whole panorama was unreal and stupendous.

"I've marched into Milan, Cairo, Madrid, Berlin, Vienna and Warsaw, but I've never seen anything like this," said Jean. "It was well worth the tramp!"

"Speak for yourself," said Nicholas, but Gabriel noticed that he too was looking down on Moscow with parted lips and an expression of fascination.

Gabriel would have liked to take out his sketchbook on the spot, but there was no opportunity. The Ninth Regiment, at this time temporarily attached to the Imperial Guard, had received orders to parade within the hour, wearing full-dress uniforms.

"Triumphial entry!" grunted Nicholas with a curse. He was right. The same evening the French marched gaily into the deserted city over the elegant Moskva bridge, a drum-major ahead of each regiment, the advance bands played "Roland à Roncevalles," a patriotic melody of Rouget de Lisle, and the bands behind them striking up "The Marseillaise" and "The Victory Is Ours."

It was a hollow triumph. The battalions' tread resounded through empty streets; no women peeped from the curtained windows of the wooden houses, as at Vienna. The sole inhabitants of the great city seemed to be half a dozen bearded peasants, who stood solemnly at the town end of the bridge watching the progress of the columns with stupid, melancholy eyes.

"I hope those Roman plebs gave Titus a better showing than this!" said Nicholas, with a sidelong grin at Old Jean, but the sergeant grunted and said nothing. He was depressed by the strangeness of their entry—an hour's marching through broad, vacant streets, without so much as a glimpse of a woman, or a vehicle, not even one of the high-slung, two-wheeled carriages they had seen in Smolensk and Mozhaisk.

They were quartered, with some of the Guard, in the vast courtyard of the Governor's Palace. The palace was a huge, rambling building, built in European style and magnificently furnished. In the ground-floor reception rooms were immense pieces of furniture, tables capable of seating two hundred at a time, sideboards where as many dishes might have been set. Fine oil-paintings hung on the walls, including large portraits of the Czar and Czarina. The floor was covered with thick rugs and beautifully woven Ottoman carpets.

Immediately the companies broke ranks, organized looting commenced. The Imperial decree was ignored, first by the Guard, then by the line regiments. Men scattered in groups, ranging through the deserted buildings, turning out drawers and cupboards, scampering down into cellars and smashing off the necks of bottles of wine and vodka that were found there in thousands. The Russians seemed to have made little or no effort to carry away their valuables. In less than an hour the centre court of the palace looked more like an Oriental market than a battalion bivouac. Stacks of furs and costly clothing were piled breast high round the neat pyramids of arms; exquisitely made caskets inlaid with mother-of-pearl lay scattered on a profusion of rugs dragged out to serve as bedding on the flagstones. There were wines of all kinds, cases of liqueurs and boxes of sweet cakes; most of the rich confectionery was only half-eaten and flung down in the straw to be trampled to paste. Stragglers came in with sacks of sugar, large boxes of preserved fruits and garishly decorated ikons. Here and there valuable oil-paintings were hacked from their frames with sword bayonets. The vast courtyard was full of shouting, stamping men, running in and out of the buildings and staggering under the weight of valuables that they could not hope to transport home without teams of oxen. Old Jean looked in dismay.

"We used to be an army," he said. "We've become a rabble of brigands!"

Assisted by a few of the older N.C.O.s, he endeavoured to restore some sort of order in the courtyard. Sentries were posted at various points, but they left their posts as soon as the sergeants' backs were turned and went off looting, terrified of missing such a unique opportunity. Nicholas watched the scene with an expression of amused contempt.

"Gabriel," he said, "observe mankind, whilst you may. Take out your sketchbook and preserve their frolics for posterity. The French, they say, are the most civilized people on earth!"

Gabriel watched two Imperial Guardsmen staggering out of the larger palace entrances, panting under the weight of a huge sandalwood chest, its lid beautifully inlaid with ivory and costly stained woods. He was struck by the similarity of the two men, who might have been twins. The eyes of both were alight with greed, their bearded lips parted with childish excitement. He unstrapped his knapsack and took out some crayons and his book. Sitting down on a pile of rugs, he started to sketch, quickly and decisively, keeping his eyes on the guardsmen, who had begun to attack the lid of the chest with engineers' hatchets.

Dominique watched him sketch, his ruddy cheeks daubed with

the remains of a pastry he had been cramming into his mouth. Nicholas threw himself down on some furs and slept. Jean moved here and there, exhorting and reasoning, but nobody paid him the slightest attention except a corporal of the Second Battalion, who thrust a solid silver crucifix into his hand, presumably with the object of silencing his criticism.

The orgy of looting would undoubtedly have continued all night had it not been interrupted, towards sundown, by the sudden crackle of musketry coming from one of the side streets that branched off the Place du Gouvernement, immediately outside the gilded gates of the palace. Automatically the men sprang for their arms, while Soutier, taking Jean, went off to investigate. They returned within five minutes, dragging between them a figure that looked less like a human being than like a gorilla. The face was almost covered with filthy matted hair, and the lunatic eyes peering out of this tangle resembled the eyes of a trapped wild beast. The man's beard reached below his waist and his sole garment was an unflayed sheepskin, worn in a single piece, holed in the middle to allow the head to poke through, and belted at the waist by a red woollen belt.

Guardsmen and voltigeurs gathered round this hideous creature with lively curiosity.

"He ran right into our arms at the corner," explained Jean. "The rascal was carrying a lighted torch!"

"He's one of the convicts they've left here," said a corporal who had been over the Kremlin earlier in the afternoon. "We bayonetted four over yonder. They were trying to set the place on fire. You'd better kill him."

Jean protested. "I'm not a savage," he said. "Lock him up until we get 'soup' orders!"

"Soup" orders were the instructions issued to companies each evening at about the time the men usually prepared their evening meal. They generally dealt with the programme for the following day.

"We've already had orders to kill incendiaries on capture," argued the corporal.

"I'll wait to be told first," replied Jean. "He's my prisoner!"

He tried questioning the man in French and German, but elicited no reply. The Russian's breath reeked of brandy. While the corporal who had been to the Kremlin was beginning to argue again, the convict settled the dispute himself. Darting out of the group, he grabbed a musket and bayonet from a pile standing against the wall, lunged recklessly at Soutier and stabbed him in the fleshy part of the thigh. The sergeant-major roared with pain and a dozen men sprang at the convict, who went down fighting like a madman. The men, most of whom were half-drunk with liquor they had consumed during the afternoon, got in one another's way in their eagerness to finish him off, but the coarse thicknesses of the Russian's sheepskin prevented him from receiving a mortal thrust.

Suddenly Nicholas burst into the centre of the group. He was holding his musket without its bayonet attached. "In God's name . . .!" he screamed.

The intoxicated infantrymen fell back a step, and Nicholas, standing astride the snarling convict, shot him through the neck. The man twitched a moment and then lay still. His blood spread across the littered paving-stones. Nicholas threw down his musket and, turning, stalked out of the gates into the Grande Place. Gabriel, following, saw him sit down on the low wall that bordered the carriageway. The schoolmaster cupped his chin in his hands and stared straight ahead.

Gabriel went over and, after a moment's hesitation, sat down beside him.

"What is it, Nicholas?"

He noticed that the older man's face was white as chalk. Gabriel wondered why this incident, no more brutal than a thousand occurences that Nicholas had witnessed or participated in during the last few years, should have had this effect upon him.

"It's the abysmal folly of it all," said Nicholas, as though to himself. "We gather together half a million men. We equip them at a fabulous cost. We march them God knows how many leagues to occupy an empty city. And at the end of it what do we do? What *is* there to do? Run about the streets like greedy children squabbling over sweets and drive our bayonets into an intoxicated old man who has probably been turned loose from an asylum. I tell you I'm sick to death of it. What could be worse anyway?"

Gabriel said nothing. There was nothing that he could say. He only wondered whether these remarks had any connection with the insolent bearing that Nicholas invariably adopted towards officers, and with the long gloomy silences that the schoolmaster sometimes maintained in bivouac and on the march.

"We'd have done better to remain in England," growled Nicholas. "I was a fool to let myself be persuaded.

Gabriel, to change the subject, remarked that they ought to walk towards the river and find out whether the baggage wagons had entered the city. Nicholette had kept pace with them as far as Borodino but afterwards had dropped behind. They expected her within twenty-four hours.

"She's going to have a child," muttered Nicholas, and then, with one of his short, contemptuous laughs, "a child! Merciful heaven! In this!"

As he spoke there was an outburst of shouting from some houses on the far side of the Place. They saw several figures running, one of them carrying a torch and others, armed and uniformed, in hot pursuit. The figures disappeared round an angle of the buildings, but thick smoke began to pour from the upper windows of one of the houses. At the same time they noticed a red glow slowly spreading across the sky towards the west.

A party of foot chasseurs doubled by, trundling a hand-cart piled with concertinaed horse buckets.

Jean came out of the palace gates.

"They're firing the city . . . a hussar has just ridden over from the Kremlin; it's fire-piquets for all of us!"

As he spoke a shower of sparks burst from the roof of the house across the Place and more columns of smoke could be seen rising behind. In the stiff westerly breeze the smoke beat across the Place, advancing like a grey sea towards the shining white walls of the Governor's Palace.

They ran, in twos and threes, towards the fire. They were not much interested in the fate of Moscow. It could burn ten times over for all they cared, but there was not one of them who failed to realize what a general destruction of the city would involve. First there would be incalculable loss of loot, loot which they had marched and fought hundreds of leagues to stow in their knapsacks; secondly, a gutted city could offer no winter billets if the army, as it was already rumoured, were to remain in Russia throughout the approaching winter.

The block on the far side of the Place was now well alight, and in several side-streets the flames were already dislodging plated roofs. The heavy sheets crashed down onto the cobbles, sending up vast clouds of sparks. As the infantrymen advanced the wind blew showers of hot ash in their faces and the roar and crackle of an even bigger conflagration came from the direction of the Kremlin. It was obvious that the city had been fired at a dozen different points.

They fought the fire all that night, all the next day and part of the following night. General Milhaud, of the heavy cavalry, had been made governor of the city and organized all regiments into fire-fighting squads, but the unremitting efforts of the men were greatly handicapped by their lack of fire-fighting equipment. Before evacuating the city the Russian Governor, Rostopchin, had destroyed all the hand-pumps so that most of the bigger fires raged unchecked for want of hose and water supplies.

As soon as fires in one part of the town were under control, flames would shoot up in another sector. Bands of armed convicts, turned loose from the city gaols, and led by members of the Russian police unit, furtively roamed the streets applying lighted torches to shops, houses and warehouses. The Emperor and his staff were forced to leave the Kremlin; a huge wooden palace where they found temporary asylum took fire soon after their entry and burned down in less than an hour. All the efforts of one hundred and thirty thousand men, comprising the French army of occupation, could do little more than limit the number of fresh outbreaks and beat out occasional fires before they succeeded in getting a hold. For the rest, major fires burned on until whole streets were reduced to ashes.

Jean, Nicholas, Gabriel and Dominique kept together in the confusion and more than once during the next forty-eight hours were in danger of being cut off by the vast lanes of flame that swept across whole areas of the city with terrifying speed. Gabriel found the burning city a fearsome but beautiful spectacle. From the ramparts of the Kremlin, where they were sent on the evening of the second day, he looked down on a sea of flame, driven by the stiff westerly breeze right across the city. Broad tongues of fire licked into the dark masses of tortuous streets, curving and meeting some other avenue of fire and forming a broad front to sweep eastward towards the outer suburbs. Later, when the voltigeurs accompanied the grenadiers and Red Lancers of the Guard to the palace chosen for headquarters after the Kremlin area had become untenable, Gabriel watched the scene as one records the sequence of a nightmare, awful but none the less fascinating. He saw a party of chasseurs urge a team of captured Russians through an arcade of blazing houses, the prisoners being harnessed by ropes to two-wheeled carriages loaded with provisions snatched from the flames. He watched the French drive the reluctant teams over the scorching débris that choked the carriageway and saw the walls of burning houses collapse on men and vehicles, burying captors and captives in a shower of flaming rubble. Sacks of sugar which had been piled in the carriages flared up in bluish flame, but the men must have perished instantly, for the red-hot débris did not stir and everyone who witnessed the incident recognized the folly of penetrating the burning street and going to the party's assistance.

Nicholas stalked about with a close-lipped, set expression. The others wondered if he was worrying about Nicholette and hoped that she had not reached the city before the fire commenced. They had several encounters with incendiaries and formed part of a firing-party at the execution of a group of nineteen Russians caught in the act of setting fire to the Foundling Hospital. The victims were mostly convicts, of the type shot by Nicholas in the courtyard of the Governor's Palace, but the schoolmaster did not appear to be moved by their stoic acceptance of death. He calmly fired, loaded and fired into the clump of kneeling figures, even wrenched a crucifix from the fingers of a dead policeman and glanced at it before tossing it aside as an article of no value. Something seemed to have happened to Nicholas recently. He was out of reach of their comradeship and conversation. Jean gave him an odd look or two but said nothing.

More than once during their endless tramping from point to point, Gabriel glanced at Dominique and wondered if these appalling spectacles were registered in the slow, patient brain of the Gascon farm-hand. He decided they were not. Dominique had always been a silent, matter-of-fact individual, dealing out and inviting death with no more concern than if he had been forking hay in his master's fields along the banks of the Dordogne. Sometimes Gabriel envied him, although he realized that the boy's intellect was feeble. Dominique seemed immune to physical suffering himself and cheerfully impervious to the sufferings of others outside his own particular circle. He had immense reserves of physical strength in his short, thickset body. He never seemed either tired or cold or hungry, though he slept like a hog in the sun the moment he laid his head on a knapsack, and ate like a famished wolf immediately food was placed in front of him. Now, in this phantasmagoria of smoke and scorching heat, something devilish seemed to animate him. He laughed at the flames and often ran, shouting, into the most dangerous corners to snatch up some worthless trinket he had seen. If he was successful he would stuff it gleefully into an already bulging knapsack.

He reminded Gabriel of the illustrations which he had seen as a child to Dante's *Inferno*, hordes of ghoulish little imps driving the damned into a boiling lake. Dominique continued to match the mad frolics of the fire, darting beneath blazing beams and running down the steps of reeking cellars until Jean, impatient with such childishness, barked an order at him to remain close to his side. Jean was deeply distressed by this orgy of destruction.

"I can't help thinking of all the good food that's going to waste," he told Gabriel. "We shall need every ounce of it if we stay here until spring!"

Here and there they saved what they could. The fire-fighting teams formed themselves into foraging parties, breaking open provision shops not yet reached by the fire and piling goods— sugar, brandy, hams, sacks of flour, mustard, preserved fruits and other foodstuffs—onto the few clear spaces, for collection and transport to the established distribution centres.

At one point they came across a small Russian hospital, and one of the patients, a gunner with both legs broken, implored them in halting French to save him from the flames. The voltigeurs did what they could, carrying a dozen men out of a filthy stable and depositing them in the middle of a garden behind a large private house already demolished. They could do no more and left them there to take their chance. The gunner called after them piteously, but they never discovered whether the injured men survived. That part of the city was afterwards burned to ashes.

"It's their own fault, the barbarians," muttered Jean, as though addressing his own conscience. "They shouldn't have fired the damned city. We shall all suffer for it!"

There were women in some of the churches, hiding down in the crypts in the hope that the dead would protect them. Some of these were persuaded to move over to corps headquarters, where the younger ones were employed as prostitutes and the older as washerwomen or cooks.

Most of the senior officers behaved well, exhausting themselves in efforts to check the fire. Gabriel saw Marshal Mortier, the big, jolly commander of the Kremlin area, working with a party of sappers in a desperate attempt to blow up a section of the wooden houses and create a gap that the flames could not bridge.

The marshal's splendid uniform was singed and blackened and his jovial face smeared with soot. He toiled like a labourer side by side with the N.C.O.s and men of the ranks.

By the morning of the third day the fire had burned itself out. A dense cloud of smoke hung over the city, shutting out the sun. The stench rising from the smoking rubble was almost overpowering. Two-thirds of the city had been completely destroyed.

In the ruins of the Place des Pendus they came across Nicholette. She told them that her wagon and team were intact. The press of vehicles along the main road of advance had been so great that she had been delayed thirty-six hours on the outskirts of the city. By that time fires were blazing in all directions and she had thought it wiser to bivouac on the far side of the Moskva.

Nicholas and the others accompanied her there, loading themselves with the provisions they had set aside for their own use before handing over the bulk of their salvage to the quartermaster. They had set by several sacks of sugar, some liqueurs, a little flour, some pickles and a quantity of fur-lined clothing. Nicholas remained on guard and the others returned to company headquarters, where efforts were being made to rebillet the troops in those sections of the city that had escaped the flames.

Later on, when the company was settled, Nicholette moved in and during the next month the file lived luxuriously. They slept on ermine and there was always something for the cooking-pot. Bread and meat were short, but there was more than enough to drink, so much, indeed, that Nicholette stocked up and did not trouble to sell liquor. They had rum punch every night and occasionally a case of sparkling champagne. Jean soon recovered his spirits.

"This is something like a campaign," he told them, "we didn't do as well as this in Warsaw or Vienna."

They had a comfortable billet in the lower part of a house that had been a doctor's. There was a small library, including some volumes in French. Nicholas read a good deal in his off-duty hours. The doctor had been a devotee of Voltaire and his edition was beautifully bound in red Moroccan leather.

Louis looked in one evening. He had been caught up in the fighting with Murat's column, east of the city. Louis himself looked well enough, but his mare, Roxy, was a good deal thinner than when they had seen her picking her way over the débris of Borodino a month before.

"It's the Devil's own job getting fodder," Louis told them. "I have to pay the Jews for everything I get, and the stuff they sell is too thin for a powerful mare like her. I've had to steal for her on more than one occasion!" Roxy tossed her head and laid her muzzle alongside Louis's cheek, as though she fully appreciated the dragoon's efforts on her behalf.

"You're worse than a woman with that greedy brute!" laughed Jean.

They all noted Nicholette's swelling figure, and Gabriel thought it made her seem even more diminutive than she was. Old Jean pulled a wry face when he discovered that she was expecting a child.

"It'll be well enough if we stay here," he grumbled, "but there are all kinds of rumours going about. I've heard we may be marching on into India to take a look at English colonies there."

"We'll manage," said Nicholas grimly. "I've already spoken to Major Goulard and he's promised to attend whenever it's necessary."

Major Goulard was the surgeon-major of the Ninth Regiment. He was a pleasant, conscientious man, renowned throughout the light infantry for the number of men he had saved after amputations. More than half the wounded who submitted to a surgeon's knife subsequently died of gangrene; Goulard's average of recovery was high and he was also known as a clever accoucheur, having once delivered Madame Lamette, a cantinière of the Gendarmes d'Elite, of twin boys. It had occurred during the siege of Almeida and both infants had survived.

"When do we celebrate?" Jean asked Nicholette.

"Sometime in February," she told him blithely. He observed that she seemed delighted at the prospect, and couldn't imagine why.

"I can't think how it happened," he grunted. "Your mother would have had something to say about it!"

"It happened to her too, didn't it?" replied Nicholette with a smile.

Gabriel was the only one who was not surprised by the announcement. He was convinced, by this time, that the girl was hopelessly in love. He didn't know about Nicholas; the schoolmaster wasn't as easy to read as his wife, but whenever Nicholette was about he seemed gentle and protective, as though he too, despite his outburst to Gabriel on that first day in Moscow, was secretly pleased with the prospect of a son. Of course he was convinced that the child would be a boy. "Not even the gods of the First Empire would be malicious enough to launch another girl into this sort of life," he said.

Old Jean's eyes twinkled. "They were on one occasion," he retorted, looking at Nicholette.

The girl smiled, stretched herself and rose to examine a small portmanteau stuffed with infants' clothing. Gabriel had discovered it in an attic at one of the half-burned palaces and had thoughtfully brought it away with him.

"Ah, well," said Old Jean, sipping his rum punch, "as I said before, it'll be all right if we stay here."

They did not stay there. The following morning the regiment received orders to pack up and be ready to march within twenty-four hours. After five weeks of waiting for peace terms that never arrived the Emperor had ordered a general retreat.

CHAPTER FOUR

The exodus began with an interminable line of wagons, carts and vehicles of every description, loaded down with a variety of loot that ranged from boxes of heavily brocaded church vestments to ear-rings, trinkets and jewellery of all manner of design, plain and intricate, worthless and priceless. In the history of the Grand Army there had never been a baggage train like this one.

The voltigeurs, preparing to leave with Marshal Davout's column and follow on the heels of Prince Eugène's advance guard, massed on one of the boulevards approaching the southern exit of the city and watched the cavalcade trundle past. Carts were piled high with furs, carpets, oil-paintings still in their massive gilt frames, silver plaques depicting scenes from Russian history and Greek mythology that had been torn from public buildings spared by the fire, furniture of all kinds, women's clothing, cases of wine, and old-fashioned ·cannons taken from the Kremlin arsenal as trophies of war for exhibition in Paris. Very little of this spoil travelled more than three days from the capital. It was abandoned by the ton as soon as the rough roads began to take their toll of the vehicles. In the meantime, however, it hampered the line of march and prevented the enforcement of discipline.

Most of the soldiers' knapsacks were similarly laden. Few men in the company had followed Jean's advice to throw away their booty and carry what food was available. Instead they slouched along, bent under the weight of gold and silver ikons, enamelled snuff-boxes, ladies' hair-brushes studded with brilliants, porcelain vases wrapped in soiled clothing, any semi-precious object which seemed to offer compensation for the troubles and fatigue of the long march from the Niemen. In less than a week most of the men would have exchanged the entire contents of their knapsacks for a dozen potatoes. Some made even worse bargains. At one point in the retreat Gabriel saw a hussar hand over a gold crucifix for a raw horse-liver and congratulate himself on having found someone willing to make the exchange.

All that was to come. For the time being the weather was warm and sunny during the day, fresh and dry at night, and there was sufficient food to go round among the infantry. But, even at this stage, at least half the cavalry were unmounted and anxious to buy plain shoes so as to discard their clumsy riding boots. The voltigeurs were adjacent to a vast column of dismounted dragoons and hussars, all faced with the prospect of walking two hundred leagues before they could hope to get remounts in the nearest of the Polish or East Prussian depots.

Old Jean insisted on examining the knapsacks of Gabriel and Dominique, emptying the latter's of a variety of worthless junk and stuffing it with four small bags of rice which they had found in a gutted cellar. Gabriel carried a few potatoes, a little salted beef, a small bag of flour and two bottles of brandy in addition to his linen. He found this heavy enough without the addition of one or two keepsakes that he had intended to carry back. Jean let him retain his sketchbook.

"That's as much a part of us as Dominique's fiddle," he said seriously.

Nicholas travelled with the wagon. He had managed to conceal a limited amount of food, mostly rye and preserves, under the false floor of one of the lockers, but the bulk of the space was used for an ambulance, Nicholette having agreed to transport three wounded officers as far as Smolensk. The officers had enriched themselves during the fire and could afford to pay handsomely for the privilege. Nicholette calculated that she would make more money in this way than by filling the wagon and straining her lean team with the haulage of heavy wine tubs or cases of liqueurs. She had sold all her stock immediately she heard of the impending retreat.

There was no room in the vehicle for the dog Fouché, so Nicholette left it with Jean. The dog attached itself to Gabriel and slouched along at the rear of the company. Jean regarded it speculatively during one of the enforced halts for a transport block on the road ahead. It was lying, head down between its forepaws, blinking into a smoky fire.

"Funny thing about that dog," said the sergeant. "Never seen it prance about like other mongrels. Can't imagine it ever having been a puppy. It knows every bugle call on the scale—look at it now!"

The drum beat a muster and the dog shook itself and stood up, its lean muzzle coming round to Jean for permission to fall in.

Old Jean said that they should stick as close to the wagon as their duties permitted. In case they became separated he arranged a long series of rendezvous between Moscow and Minsk, the supposed magazine town they were heading for. He did not know then that the Staff had decided to attempt a more southerly route passing through districts unwasted by the army's advance. A few days after leaving Moscow, however, this plan had to be abandoned. Prince Eugène's advance guard met a severe check at Maloyaroslavets, on the road to Kaluga. A strongly reinforced Russian army barred the southern route and turned them back onto the old road. The French gave way reluctantly.

It was not long before they approached the plain of the Moskva, where the battle of Borodino had been fought fifty-six days before. Seventy-five thousand corpses lay there, for the most part unburied, many of them gross and bloated in the mud which the rains had washed from their shallow graves. Others had been half-eaten by wolves and birds of prey. The stench was indescribable.

Just ahead of their line of march they saw a knot of men break ranks and crowd round a figure that had dragged itself down a gentle slope near the stream-bed. Hastening forward they discovered the cause of the diversion. The men in the first company had discovered a wounded grenadier, with both legs completely shattered, who had kept himself alive on the battlefield since the previous September.

The poor wretch was quite rational and asked for transport home. He had been sheltered by the body of a horse and had eaten its putrid flesh to keep himself alive, drinking water from a brook foul with the bodies of men and animals. His survival was a miracle and the surgeon-major of the regiment personally supervised the grenadier's transfer to a carriage and ordered him to be carried along with the army. During the days ahead Dominique, who hardly ever spoke, sometimes referred to this man. When things became increasingly difficult he said, with one of his vacant grins, "Ah, but at any rate we've still got our legs!"

They left the battlefield on their right and, as they passed, Gabriel thought of the battle scenes that he had inspected on the walls of art galleries in Vienna and in some of the larger Spanish towns. The men who had painted them must have had a limited experience of war. He recalled a particular painting, a vast canvas representing the battle of Prague. Dead and wounded men were arranged in formal, graceful attitudes in the foreground. Beyond them a team of plumed staff officers, mounted on statuesque horses, were receiving the orders of their chief; the main battle was decently shrouded in lines of battery smoke. There was nothing to suggest bloated corruption, blackened objects that had been heads, acres of filth rotting under grey, drizzling skies.

They were well beyond Borodino when they bivouacked, but Gabriel sat down and sketched a corner of the field from memory. It was perhaps the most graphic of all his sketches.

The following day they began to see signs of the pursuit.

Small squadrons of Cossacks, mounted on swift, shaggy ponies, hung along the line of march, but did not venture to attack the main body. Several stragglers, however, who had lagged behind for one reason or another, failed to return to their ranks at nightfall. It began to grow very cold after dark and the roads became more and more congested with broken transport and abandoned guns. Dead horses, some of them almost hacked to pieces by starving men, lay where they had fallen between the shafts. Grim signs of disintegration were apparent during the earliest stages of the retreat.

"What did I tell you about all this loot?" asked Jean when they passed a white-headed guardsman ransacking an abandoned wagon.

Gabriel jokingly remarked that the older the soldier the bigger the brigand.

"A veteran has rules about these things," said Jean. "With a good soldier it is arms first, food next and loot third. The order of importance should be obvious even to a fool. What good is a knapsack of gold if you can't defend it? What good is a pocketful of precious stones if you die of hunger so that some other rogue can rifle your corpse?"

There was no denying Jean's logic, and Gabriel reflected, not for the first time, that the old soldier was one of the few philosophers who lived by the precepts that he preached. In all their campaigns he had never known Jean to fail to have something edible in his knapsack.

Jean clinched the discussion. "How else do you think I've kept alive all these years?" he asked.

"You'll have the devil's own job to survive this campaign," grunted Sergeant-Major Soutier, who had been plodding along behind him, listening to Jean's sermon with a tolerant grin.

Jean pulled his thin moustache.

"You look to yourself, Sergeant-Major," he replied. "I'll be knocking the neck from a bottle of Rhenish wine when you're still floundering in these birch forests!"

Whenever he remembered the plump, inefficient Soutier in

after years, Gabriel recalled this boast. Soutier, at that time, had four silver ingots, taken from the Moscow mint, in his knapsack, but he had no rice and hardly any flour. Before the Peninsula campaign he had done most of his soldiering in garrison towns.

Marshal Mortier's troops came up with them just as the first snow fell, and the two columns were merged to form a new rearguard. There seemed little hope of overtaking the wagon, which was now more than two days' march ahead, but Nicholas, who should have come back to rejoin the regiment, failed to appear. Jean and the others did not begrudge him his good fortune. It was as well that somebody should stay with Nicholette, and there was something vaguely comforting in the fact that somewhere ahead of them was a reserve supply of food. Their own stock was fast diminishing. In spite of his contempt for their lack of foresight Old Jean could not let old comrades like Soutier, and others, stand by hungry whilst he prepared a meal. There was still plenty of horseflesh, but as the temperature fell men found it increasingly difficult to hack steaks from the frozen carcasses. It was essential that cutting up should take place within a short time of the animal's death.

Still no major attack came from the Russians. The Cossacks stayed out of range and Jean said that they must be confining themselves to observation. After the first heavy snowfalls food began to grow dangerously scarce and they passed by the bodies of a number of men who had collapsed whilst marching with columns farther ahead. At night it was almost unbearably cold, but they found it difficult to light fires with the damp branches of pine and birch. There was always a scramble for the meagre shelters available on the line of march when they stopped to bivouac. The men who arrived first would pack into the few huts and staging-houses, bar the doors and threaten to shoot anyone who attempted to force an entry.

Ten days after the retreat had commenced the real winter came down on them. The temperature fell rapidly to twenty-six degrees below zero and a bitter north wind sprang up, whirling the heavy snowflakes in their faces. Cases of frostbite soon appeared and men began to straggle in search of food, turning off the main road to follow any track that might lead them to a wretched hamlet where a little flour or a few potatoes could be found.

Two days after the first fall of snow the dog Fouché became a problem. It got frostbite in its rear paws, and its progress became so painful that Gabriel and Dominique had to take turns at carrying it. One of them passed over musket and knapsack and slung the dog across his shoulders, where it perched uncomplainingly as they plodded through the drifts.

Fouché was a lean dog, but at the end of the two days' march it became clear that the dog would have to be abandoned. Gabriel argued, but Jean was adamant.

The following morning, when they prepared to march at first light, Fouché tried to struggle to its feet and drag itself a few steps, its paralysed paws making an untidy furrow in the snow. When they moved away from the fire it rolled its yellow eyes up at them and made frantic efforts to stand. As the distance between men and dog began to increase, Fouché set up a frantic whining. Gabriel stopped, cursing.

"I can't do it, Jean. We'd better shoot him."

The dog dragged itself a little nearer and as soon as it saw the three men stop it ceased to whine.

Jean said: "You two move on. I'll shoot him."

He unslung his musket and glanced at the priming, cocking back the hammer with his horny thumb.

Gabriel did not look at the dog again. He and Dominique marched on towards the woods. Before they had left the open they heard a single shot. It rang out on the crisp air like a whip-crack.

They walked slowly and within a few minutes Jean joined them, saying nothing. They had gone nearly a league before the sergeant spoke.

"Nicholette won't be any too pleased. She thought a lot of that mongrel."

Dominique said: "It's a meal for someone."

Jean, Gabriel and Dominique kept reasonably fit. They were

better fed than most and Jean warned them against giving rations to the others.

"We've a long road to travel," he said, "and if I'm any judge the ration stocks at Smolensk will be exhausted long before we get there."

Marshal Ney took over the rearguard from Davout and trudged along on foot with the few battalions retaining a semblance of discipline.

What was happening up with the main body and advance guard could only be guessed from the débris that littered the road. They passed complete circles of dead men, stretched, like the figures on a clock, round the embers of a dead fire. Hopelessly undernourished and worn out with the endless fatigue of marching day after day over soft snow, these men had lain down to sleep with their feet to a fire and, as the night frosts gripped their bones, had stiffened beyond awakening when the time came to resume the march. At one bivouac, after the third day's snow, they came up with an even more terrible spectacle.

All the way along the Smolensk road the Russians had built coach-houses with large barn doors at either end. Here, in normal times, the stages drove in at one end, changed teams and drove out at the other. Most of the buildings had been burned down during the advance, but a few remained and were in great demand as shelters for the night.

Arriving at a wide clearing in the forest, the voltigeurs saw the remains of one of these coach-houses. Smoke was still rising from its burned-out shell. Inside, tightly packed against each other, were several hundred corpses, most of them charred beyond recognition.

They learned what had happened from one of the few survivors, a captain of mounted grenadiers whose hands and uniform bore marks of the fire.

The previous night nearly a thousand men had sought shelter in the building. Their few horses had been tethered outside. When the coach-house was packed to suffocation some crazy fools in the middle of the press lit a small fire to cook their supper. Within a few moments thick trusses of straw had flared up and ignited the dry beams of the roof. There was terrible panic. Men nearest the exits fought to get out, but the doors opened inwards and escape was almost impossible. The captain and one or two others had succeeded in tearing a plank out of the wall, but hardly a dozen all told had escaped death, either from the flames or from suffocation. The voltigeurs went over to look at the pyre.

"God help us," said Jean, turning away.

Others were not so squeamish. They dragged the bodies into the clearing and searched their smouldering clothes for valuables.

The company, now numbering about a dozen, was marching somewhat in advance of the main rearguard. During a blizzard that day they lost touch with the corps altogether. When darkness fell they found themselves alone on the road and Gabriel saw some of the men glancing at Jean as though they realized that their sole chance of getting home depended on the sergeant's generosity. Jean kept Gabriel and Dominique close to him. It was obvious that he did not trust the rest of the men even though they were from his own regiment. He knew that loyalty and comradeship could not be counted on under conditions of extreme privation such as these. Between them Jean, Gabriel and Dominique had more than enough food to see them to Smolensk, but if the contents of their knapsacks were shared among twelve there would be insufficient for another two days' march.

During the last hour of daylight Jean pondered the problem. When they bivouacked he plucked Gabriel's sleeve.

"We shall have to share out tonight," he muttered, "but be ready to give these scarecrows the slip in the morning."

Gabriel nodded, but said nothing. It was a shock to hear Jean referring to his old comrades as scarecrows.

They bivouacked in a birch wood and one of the men brought in a dead raven. They made a fire and cooked a miserable meal consisting of melted snow, rice, a pinch of flour, four sliced potatoes and the frozen bird. After supper Jean carefully measured out a little brandy for each man. After that they built up the fire and lay down on their sheepskins to sleep. Every man had some sort of skin to spread on the snow. They had found a pile of them in an abandoned wagon on the road.

Before it was light Gabriel felt somebody shaking his wrist. He got up, almost paralysed with cramp. The fire had burned low, but there was a faint light in the sky, either from the moon or from the Northern Lights. Gabriel saw Dominique shouldering his knapsack and musket a few paces off.

"March!" said Jean quietly.

The three of them moved into the wood. They marched in silence for a few minutes and then Jean began to justify himself.

"A man can only be responsible for himself under conditions like this," he said. "My first duty is to myself and then to you two; you're all I've got left. I'm too old to start again."

"What do you mean, 'start again'?" asked Gabriel curiously.

"I've outlasted four files like you and the others," said the sergeant as they regained the road. "If you go I'm only looking after myself in future."

It had never occurred to Gabriel that he and the others were mere replacements in Jean's life. He supposed it ought to have been obvious years ago, but somehow it never had been. He had assumed, in some vague way, that Jean had taken charge of Manny, Nicholas and the others shortly before he himself joined the group on Lobau three and a half years since and that this was the first time such an obligation had been placed on the sergeant. He had imagined that before this Jean had served with contemporaries, men of his own age and of approximately the same length of service. He realized now that this was not the case; the middle-aged man trudging beside him had mothered several broods, watching each of them grow up and disappear in the ebb and flow of successive campaigns. It seemed a terribly depressing process. Gabriel became increasingly curious to learn something of his predecessors.

"Who were they all?" he asked Jean.

The old sergeant tucked his musket under his right arm and thrust his mittened hands deep into the pockets of his greatcoat.

"They're all dead," he said. "What else would you expect?"

And, as the wan light began to glimmer through the trees and their numb feet shuffled soundlessly through the soft snow that powdered the frozen road, Jean told them of the young men he had nursed along since the day when he had been made a private first class after the battle of Lodi sixteen years before.

First there had been a batch of boys from Condé, farm lads most of them, sent down into Italy without even the knowledge of how to load a musket. Jean had taken them, one by one, and trained them into soldiers capable of driving the Austrians over the mountains and entering Mantua in triumph, with the young Napoleon riding ahead, dictating peace terms like a new Alexander on behalf of the tottering Directory. The Condé boys were all killed, falling at Arcola, Rivoli and other major engagements, shot and sabred in a hundred skirmishes along the banks of the Adige, shut up in Zurich and Genoa with old Massena, either to starve or to die of plague in one or other of the beleaguered cities.

Then there had been the recruits who went out with the army to Egypt in 1799. Almost all of them had perished in a single campaign. Jean's tuition could not compete with the heat and the flies and the fevers of the march up to Acre, the fruitless assaults on its bastions and the plague-stricken march back into Cairo. The last of the second batch had perished in the battle of Aboukir or died in a native uprising after Napoleon had abandoned the army and sailed home to seize supreme power.

The third batch, Bretons, were recruited after Marengo, and these were the lucky ones. They had at least time to learn their trade in the crowded camps of Boulogne before marching across Europe to fall at Austerlitz and in the Prussian campaign that followed. A few of them lived to squelch through Polish mud to Eylau or to go down under the raking fire of the Russian batteries at Friedland. Jean was alone again, until the new light-infantry regiments were formed for the first campaign of the Spanish war and he was given one-campaign men like Nicholas, Manny and the others. Jean thought a good deal of the final bunch. They had done well, he said, to get through the Saragossa and the Danube campaigns without a fatal casualty, and in the Portuguese adventure they had lost only two, Manny and Claude. They would not have had such luck if they hadn't been captured and shipped overseas. As for the present campaign, he could no longer pretend that any of them stood much of a chance. They were not yet in Smolensk and that was less than half-way along the road to comfortable German billets and a supply of regular rations.

They had marched three to four miles along the road whilst he was talking and were beginning to pick up with the stragglers again. Men walked in twos and threes or hobbled along on their own, eyes fixed on the ground. Some had bloodstained faces, but the blood was not their own. They had been gnawing raw horse-flesh, and the remains of their wretched meal were smeared about their mouths. They walked blindly, frequently stumbling over equipment and dead men strewn in their path, now only half visible under the snow.

It was not quite so cold, however, and a thaw seemed to be probable. As they crossed an open patch of wood to a long stretch of road directly ahead, in the distance they could see what at first appeared to be a skirmish between a single Cossack and a group of infantrymen. The horseman was prancing about in the middle of a knot of figures, dark shapes against the blinding whiteness of the snow.

They did not take a great deal of interest in the scene until they were within a few hundred paces of the skirmish. Then Jean stopped and shaded his eyes.

"That isn't a Cossack," he exclaimed. "He's wearing a helmet and the horse is too big."

As they hurried forward they saw that the horseman was wearing the blue and white of the French dragoons. He was defending himself with sword and pistol against the attack of at least a dozen men armed with bayonets. He had cut down one man and was trying to ride off, but someone was dragging at his bridle and the big animal was plunging wildly on the treacherous surface of the road.

They were within extreme musket range when they saw a flash, then another. The horseman bowed forward over the crupper, and the horse sank to its knees. From a distance the action looked synchronized and graceful, like that of a circus rider. Instantly the attackers closed in, shouting and brandishing their weapons.

All three voltigeurs began to run, slithering over the road and firing as they advanced. The group round the fallen horseman ignored them. They were too intent on dragging aside the dead rider and holding a saucepan to the gashed throat of the dying horse.

CHAPTER FIVE

During the last few days Louis had not been unconscious of the looks given him by stragglers as he picked his way carefully along the road that ran through the endless birch forest. Most of the time since leaving Moscow he had been alone, but his sufferings had been trivial compared with those of the majority of the soldiers. For one thing, he had a good horse under him and was spared the dreadful fatigue of day-long marches through the snow. He felt the cold a good deal, but before leaving Moscow he had taken the precaution of obtaining a long yellow waistcoat of padded silk, which he wore under his tunic. The waistcoat was part of the wardrobe of a Russian count and had been looted by the men of Louis's troop from a mansion a few miles east of the city, in which they were temporarily billeted. It was astonishing how well the odd-looking garment kept out the cold.

Apart from this he was reasonably well equipped for a winter campaign. He had his service tunic, breeches, small clothes and leather top-boots, a pair of red worsted stockings from the wardrobe of the count's valet, a sheepskin cape that laced half-way down the front and left the skirts free to be tucked under the thighs, affording both horse and rider additional protection, and a woollen night-cap, worn inside his dragoon's helmet.

Before joining the artillery convoy that left the city soon after the advance guard, he had been careful to pack his saddle-bags with four days' supply of hoarded rations. The cavalry had not fared well in this respect. Few of them had spent any time in Moscow, having been engaged in widespread foraging expeditions beyond the surrounding countryside, which had been swept clean by the retreating enemy. Louis had a little flour, some rye from which he could make cakes in the manner taught him by Jean long ago, a knot of onions and a small metal flask about half-full of Russian gin. He was a careful young man and had taken Jean's lessons to heart. He ate sparingly and estimated that, in event of there being no ration issue, he could hold out until reaching a revictualling depot at Smolensk.

His principal problem was Roxy's fodder. The cavalry had been extremely short of fodder throughout the entire summer, and after the fire it was practically unobtainable. There was a certain amount of rye, it is true, but Louis had learned from experience that unripened rye was fatal to horses and he was obliged to make extraordinary exertions to gather even a meagre amount of oats and hay for his mare.

When the snow fell and the lakes and streams froze he was presented with another problem. The ice was often so thick that he had difficulty in watering his horse. Sometimes he found a shallow pond and smashed the ice with the butt of his carbine. At other times he foraged around among the litter that covered the roads until he found a bucket which he could use to melt snow; but this was a long, tedious business and he had constantly to be on his guard against horse thieves.

On one occasion, warned by a whinny of protest from Roxy, he shot a man in the act of sneaking off through the woods with the reluctant mare in tow. The thief was an Italian gunner from Prince Eugène's corps and Louis shot him methodically, in cold blood. He knew that without Roxy he would never see France again, and it was this knowledge as much as his love for the horse that encouraged him to take grave risks to keep the animal alive and reasonably healthy.

During the ride from Moscow to Vyazma Louis twice entered the Russian lines for the purpose of stealing fodder. Jean would have considered the risk justified. Without fodder Roxy would have soon joined the thousands of half-devoured carcasses that blocked the Smolensk road, and in high riding-boots Louis would have been helpless to continue his journey on foot. Even if he had been lucky enough to secure a pair of boots from a corpse (and boots were the first articles stripped from the dead) he was now unaccustomed to marching and could not have competed with the tougher infantrymen in their ceaseless battle for food, warmth and shelter. Louis realized this and once he was alone pushed out onto the flanks of the army to fight for Roxy's life and for his own.

He was lucky. Two days after the engagement on the Kaluga road, when the head of the Grand Army was turned back onto the road by which it had advanced, General Milhaud, in command of the convoy, was forced to make an important decision. The transport animals pulling the artillery train were in a lamentable condition and it was obvious to any cavalryman that they could not stagger as far as Vyazma, quite apart from attempting to reach Smolensk and the highroad beyond. Either guns had to be abandoned by the score and teams joined up to pull a limited number onward or a message would have to be sent forward asking for an increased quota of draught animals. The general had no conception of the state of affairs existing in the corps marching ahead of the convoy. He assumed that they were in better case than his own troops, for they had primary access to such depots as existed along the road and were, in addition, that much farther advanced when the temperature began to fall. He could not be blamed for failing to realize that the rearguard alone was maintaining discipline on the march. Such a state of affairs was illogical. It was reasonable to suppose that the rearguard, having suffered the most, would be the most disorganized corps in the army.

Reviewing these facts, Milhaud compromised. He cut the traces of some of the heavier guns and abandoned them on his own responsibility. He then regrouped the teams and sent a messenger forward to contact Marshal Berthier, explaining the dilemma, and ask for fresh orders. He chose Louis to convey the message, for he saw at a glance, whilst Louis was on guard duty outside his billet, that the dragoon's horse was in a far better condition than any of those of his three surviving aides. He contented himself with sending a single rider, since Louis would not be required to leave the line of march and would run little or no danger of capture by Cossacks.

Louis rode off confidently enough, overtaking the wreck of Davout's columns and keeping, as far as possible, to the bridle paths that cut through the forest parallel with the highroad. In this way he made better progress. The main road was choked with abandoned wagons, half-burned carts, dead horses and stragglers from every unit.

Once or twice he was chased by groups of Cossacks, but Roxy soon left their miserable mounts behind. At night Louis made his way back to the main road, for the purpose of gathering information as to the whereabouts of the Chief of Staff and to avoid the dangers of bivouacking alone.

On the third day Roxy began to falter and Louis knew that she must have food if she was to keep going. He had seen, in the distance, Cossack bands walking their horses against the skyline, and a close scrutiny showed him that some of their ponies were carrying fodder. He did not rejoin the army that night, but waited in a wood of dwarf pines for the twinkle of the Cossack bivouac fires out on the flank.

He saw a mass of fires over on the right, but, a mile or so closer, in a copse that sprouted from a shallow valley dividing two bare hills, he saw a more promising bivouac consisting of not more than three fires.

About ten o'clock he walked Roxy out of the pine wood and across the shoulder of the nearest hill, where he reined in, looking down on the Russian bivouac and awaiting his chance.

There was no moon and very little starlight. The temperature had risen slightly and excitement warmed him. By midnight the fires seemed to have burned down and he guessed that most of the Russians would be asleep, their feet to the blaze. Cautiously he descended the slope.

It was far easier than he had imagined. There were two sentries, but they had met to engage in conversation in the middle of their beat. A dozen ponies were tethered to a large birch tree on the outskirts of the wood, more than twenty yards from the nearest fire. Louis whispered a word to Roxy, and the mare stood still. He then crawled forward and, placing the tree between himself and the sentries, took out his knife and quietly sawed through the thin leather reins of three ponies.

He knew that one of the bulging saddle-bags worn by each of the animals would contain oats. Even as he pulled gently on the severed reins Louis experienced a slight qualm of disgust for men who supped and slept without troubling to remove their saddles from the horses they rode all day. The ponies moved off willingly enough and at a safe distance Louis went through the saddle-bags. In two of them he found a small quantity of oats, which he transferred to Roxy's saddle-bag. He then turned the ponies loose and, mounting his own horse, rode back to the pine wood.

He did not remain there, but rode across to the main road, putting the highway between himself and the Cossacks. He fed Roxy by a vast fire lit by a group of stragglers from the Baden Brigade. The men were too exhausted to notice the stray dragoon and his big horse. It warmed Louis's heart to hear Roxy's satisfied champing. Later, in the inadequate shelter of the snow-laden trees, man and beast lay down together on a few handfuls of straw which Louis had saved from the previous day.

When the first thaw came Louis found progress much more difficult. The woods were obstructed by fallen trees and he was obliged to go back to the road. Even here he dared not force Roxy to a trot, although he began to be alarmed by the remarks of some of the stragglers he passed.

At this stage in the retreat, about two days' march from Smolensk, the supplies of horseflesh were giving out and, to make matters worse, men were getting into the habit of killing horses on the spot for the sake of their blood. He saw one wretched animal slaughtered in this fashion by a party of Polish lancers, horsemen who should have had more sense. That same night he shot the gunner who tried to steal Roxy whilst he was collecting wood for a fire.

His own rations were already beginning to fail and he had no opportunity to replenish them. The Cossacks' saddle-bags had contained no food beyond the oats. All the remainder of the space in their bags had been occupied by articles looted from prisoners or from dead men along the road.

Louis hoped that he would overtake Headquarters Staff the following day, but, having seen the disintegration along the road, he doubted if Marshal Berthier would be inclined to send help back to the artillery train. Louis had passed hardly any cavalry and was beginning to wonder if any existed.

He kept a constant eye open for Jean and the others, and once got cheering news of them from a wounded voltigeur of the Ninth who was being transported by sledge. He saw nothing of Nicholas or the canteen, however, and hoped that it was keeping up with the Guard, now well in advance. He looked carefully at every abandoned wagon that he passed and was always relieved when he failed to recognize Nicholette's vehicle.

That night he again penetrated a Russian bivouac and got away with a small truss of hay. This time it was not so easy. He had to stab a sentry through the neck, and only the thickness of the wood prevented his pursuit and capture. Roxy was going slightly lame, but after the hay and a long drink of melted snow she seemed fit enough for the final stage of the journey to Smolensk. Louis judged that the Imperial Guard would reach the city before he overtook them.

He came to a broad expanse of wood soon after starting the next morning. It seemed comparatively deserted and the dragoon passed only an odd straggler or two, who kept their eyes on the ground and limped along oblivious of everything but their own misery.

Soon afterwards, just as it was growing fully light, he entered a long stretch of road and thought that he could discern the towers of Smolensk at the crest of a second stretch, which emerged from woods in the far distance. Between him and the nearest trees there was a party of infantrymen, trudging along the road in a compact body.

Louis would have preferred not to pass them, but he had no alternative. On each side of the road were steep banks inches thick in ice. Louis let Roxy move at her own pace and congratulated himself for the hundredth time on having had the foresight to shoe the mare with frost nails before leaving the convoy's bivouac on the field of Borodino. He wondered whether Roxy was the only horse in the French army with frost nails. He had indeed been fortunate to find a few in a wrecked farrier's wagon close to the battlefield.

As he approached the infantry the men stopped, and one of them, a sergeant, hailed him.

"Got anything to eat, brother?"

Louis shook his head and tried to move through the group. His instincts told him that there was something menacing in the way they stood round, looking up at him. They were a mixed bunch, mostly Bavarians.

Louis groped in his saddle-bag and found his metal flask, now containing about two inches of gin.

"You can share that; it's all I've got!"

The sergeant snatched the flask and, wrenching out the stopper, applied it to his lips. He could not have tasted it before it was torn from his hands and a general scrimmage ensued. Louis thought that it was like a pack of schoolboys fighting over a coloured marble. Nobody had any gin; it was spilled in the snow and one of the men, cursing, fell on his knees to scoop up the patch of snow where it had fallen.

Louis tried to take advantage of the diversion to get through the group and away into the woods. The sergeant, a lean, badly frostbitten man wearing the bedraggled uniform of the Foot Chasseurs, grabbed his bridle.

"What about the horse? She's got blood, hasn't she? Damn it, we're starving, man; you haven't walked a million leagues in this God-forsaken wilderness!"

The other men gathered round, all except the wretch who still grovelled near the fallen gin flask, cramming snow into his mouth.

Louis drew a pistol and pointed it at the sergeant.

"Let go that bridle or I'll blow out your brains!" he said quietly.

Out of the corner of his eye he saw three more infantrymen coming down the road from the woods. He wondered if they were hurrying to share anything that was going.

The sergeant was not frightened by the threat.

"We may as well be shot here as die of hunger nearer Smolensk!" muttered one of the men, but he remained on the edge of the group.

The sergeant looked up into Louis's face. There was murder in his eyes, but also a hint of appeal.

"Let's have the mare to keep us alive, comrade. You shall have your share, I promise you!"

For answer Louis fired in his face and, dropping his pistol, whipped out his sabre.

The sergeant fell, but for some reason failed to relinquish his grasp on the bridle. Roxy reared, snorting with fright at the flash of the firearm so close to her eyes. The men surged round the horse, thrusting with their bayonets. Roxy screamed with pain as one of the points tore her coat, and at the sound of her scream Louis went mad, standing up in his stirrups and slashing down at the shakos with all his strength.

He felt a blow on his leg and then another, terribly heavy, in his stomach. The white landscape seemed to sway and melt, like a snow scene painted on canvas and exposed to a draught. The last thing he remembered was a shout from higher up the road and a blurred vision of three men running and firing as they ran. Then the mare crumpled forward and Louis's face brushed her mane.

CHAPTER SIX

Nicholas and Nicholette had the good fortune to escape the disasters that overtook the greater part of the Grand Army during the first stage of its retreat. Their journey as far as Smolensk was relatively uneventful, despite heavy snowfalls that began to impede the vanguard's progress within a few days of leaving Moscow.

The three wounded officers they carried ensured the wagon against the molestation threatening all wheeled transport once Prince Eugène's corps had received its check near Borovsk and had to turn back to the northern route. Within twenty-four hours of this engagement carts and carriages began to break down and many were looted by the half-starved troops.

Nicholette had a major-general and two colonels in her vehicle, the former officer being a personal friend of Eugène. The Prince lent the equipage half a dozen troopers from his own bodyguard, and the horsemen, all well mounted, managed to keep the wagon on the move and give protection from marauders, which became increasingly necessary after the army had passed through Vyazma and the acute ration shortage grew apparent.

Once or twice, when the road was exceptionally bad and

Nicholette's Flemish horses were unable to drag the heavy vehicle clear of snowdrifts, the Italian troopers harnessed their horses to the team and forced a passage. In this way the wagon improved its position on the line of march until it was close behind the train of the Imperial Guard. Even so, the journey seemed an immense strain, and Nicholette cursed herself for neglecting to carry more fodder. There was never any to be found in the villages once the Guard had passed through ahead of the column.

When the detachments of the Ninth Regiment of light infantry received orders to join the rearguard, Nicholas was under obligation to fall back and find his comrades, but, after consultation with the wounded major-general, he decided to ignore the order and continue the retreat as a transport driver. Nicholette was in no condition to handle the wagon herself, although she still insisted on occupying the driving-box each day. Péliot, the major-general, whose life depended on the unimpeded progress of the vehicle, pledged himself guarantor for Nicholas's conduct.

Nicholas could not help grinning to himself when he listened to the officer's arguments in favour of a corporal absenting himself from his regiment. The wounded man was a cuirassier and Nicholas could well imagine that in normal times, when he could sit his horse, the major-general would be a stickler for discipline. In the circumstances in which he now found himself, however, discipline could go hang. The whole rearguard might be overwhelmed by the Cossacks so long as his wagon kept moving; with Nicholas gone and only a pregnant woman on the driving-box, his chances of reaching the German depots would, in truth, have been negligible.

The major-general did not admit this to himself, as Nicholas might have done. Instead he invented a line of argument in favour of the corporal remaining where he was. He convinced himself and his two companions that a breakdown of the wagon might easily block the whole line of march and thereby delay the progress of the army. After he had expressed this opinion three or four times he began to believe it, and the colonels, themselves at the mercy of the canteen, did nothing to disillusion him.

Eugène's corps maintained its discipline for the first fortnight of the retreat, and on one occasion the Prince rode alongside the wagon to enquire after his friend. Nicholas wondered if Péliot would inform his chief that he was being driven by a deserter, but the major-general made no reference to the fact. He gratefully accepted two bottles of cognac from the Prince's chief of staff and blamed the retreat on the weather.

Eugène was one of the few personalities around the Emperor who had earned Nicholas's respect. He was cool, efficient and kind-hearted; although he was Viceroy of Italy and the Emperor's stepson by Napoleon's first marriage, he did not give himself airs like King Murat. During the retreat Nicholas saw a good deal of Eugène when the army round him was disintegrating and the majority of senior officers were coolly shifting for themselves, and his behaviour did much to confirm the ex-schoolmaster's high opinion of his chief. They had all expected Eugène to sulk when his mother, Joséphine, had been cast aside for the Habsburg woman, but when summoned for the Russian campaign Eugène rode up from Italy with a full complement of men and guns, and displayed his usual cool generalship in all the minor engagements along the road to Moscow.

Watching the Prince dismount and harness his magnificent Arab horse to a floundering gun-carriage in a birch forest outside Smolensk, Nicholas pondered on the vicissitudes of all Frenchmen of his generation. Sixteen years ago Eugène de Beauharnais had been an orphan of the Terror; his father was a victim of the guillotine, his mother the mistress of a corrupt politician. Nicholas wondered if the man's startling change of fortune was due to his mother's sound judgment in marrying Napoleon when the latter was an obscure, hysterical general, or to Eugène's own talents and integrity. He did not pursue the query, his reflections being cut short by the necessity of climbing down from the box and helping to lever a dismounted gun clear of the road.

When he climbed back and warmed himself with a nip of brandy, Nicholas glanced sideways at Nicholette and decided that it was high time that she left the box and travelled inside the wagon. Her pale face was pinched and drawn, contrasting oddly with her swollen figure. She wore a long sheepskin cape and a fur cap pressed well down over her ears, and her hands, thrust into a muff improvised out of a grenadier's bearskin, lay listlessly on her knees. She looked exhausted and apathetic, but she smiled when she met his glance and said: "We ought to be in Smolensk tomorrow!"

She knew that this was a futile thing to say. Even if they were in Smolensk the next day they could not stay there long enough to rest the horses, and, although independent of the revictualling magazines for their own food to continue the journey, they were dangerously short of forage. There was not likely to be any fodder in Smolensk, and even if they were lucky enough to get an issue, the horses needed rest far more than they needed food.

For the first time in her life Nicholette felt vaguely alarmed. She was not afraid of the prospects of losing her wagon and team, or even of what such a disaster might mean to herself and to Nicholas, who would then be obliged to continue the journey on foot. She was worried about the child inside her and the knowledge that the regimental surgeon-major, who had sworn to deliver it, was far behind with the rearguard.

The prospect of having the child did not frighten her. She had assisted her mother on several occasions when Old Carla had acted as midwife to other cantinières. She knew approximately what one must do on such occasions; the certainty of pain and the risks of confinement on the march she accepted as she accepted all the rigours of a campaign. She was afraid only because she desperately wanted the child to live and she knew that, under present conditions, the chance of this was remote. The temperature had dropped each successive day, and despite her thick layers of clothing the cold made her gasp.

She was terrified lest something should happen to Nicholas to take him away from her, and she fussed over Major-General Péliot as the arbiter of his presence and of the child's survival. The boy—she was convinced that it would be a boy—was not due until February. With luck and endurance she could hold out until the New Year, and by that time they must all surely have reached Königsberg and security.

The town of Königsberg became a symbol to her and she began to compose incantations about it, as though the mere repetition of the phrase "Königsberg by Christmas, Königsberg by Christmas," uttered a hundred times before they passed through a patch of forest and emerged into the open, would ensure the life of the child. She could never have imagined that she would feel so strongly about anything, and once or twice she recalled her mother's contemptuous observations on cantinières who bore children during campaigns. Nicholette had been born comfortably in barracks at Lille and it had been summertime. Carla always said that if one did indulge in such folly once in a lifetime one might as well make sensible arrangements about it.

There had been no opportunity to exercise common sense over this child. She had married Nicholas in May and the child must have been conceived immediately. Nobody could have foreseen the fact that they would not winter in Moscow or, alternatively, get out before the snow was expected. The whole campaign had been badly bungled, and Nicholette, considering this, felt the same spurt of anger against the Emperor as her mother had experienced when they were kept hanging about outside Genoa instead of marching at once to the city's relief and the extrication of the Irishman who owed Carla four hundred francs.

"You'd better go back into the wagon," Nicholas advised her. "We'll have another blizzard within an hour!"

She turned and rubbed her chin on his epaulette, and he winked encouragingly, taking one hand from the reins and throwing it across her padded shoulders.

"We'll get there all right, Nico, don't worry!"

It was odd that his presence should be so comforting to a woman who had grown up surrounded by men of every type and temperament. Nicholas puzzled her as he puzzled Jean. Like the sergeant, she had never understood why this cynical schoolmaster should have captured her fancy and held it so strongly that she trembled with excitement at the prospect of bearing his child.

She wondered if her mother had felt like this about Big Hervé, her favourite, and, if she had done so, whether it was virtually certain that Big Hervé had been her own father.

The wagon crunched on, its wheels grinding the army's débris into slush. They passed frostbitten men who looked after them piteously, but Nicholette noticed neither them nor their wretchedness. She crawled back into the wagon and doled out the brandy ration to her passengers. Bald-headed Péliot cursed, and one of the colonels, who had neither moved nor spoken since they left Vyazma, muttered the name of a woman and turned feverishly in his blankets.

Nicholas managed to buy some oats from the Jews in Smolensk. The price was fantastically high, but it would have been worth all the money they possessed. They stayed in the ruined town two days and saw the wreckage of the divisions stagger in, too weak and too frostbitten to fight for the inadequate supplies of flour left by the Guard. Late arrivals were lucky to secure a handful apiece; senior officers stood by and threatened to shoot any man who helped himself to the rearguard's allocation.

Discipline was now virtually at an end. Imperial Guardsmen consumed bottles of vodka and died raving in the streets. Groups of men huddled in the cellars, too exhausted to rejoin their ranks when the survivors mustered to continue the march. All that remained of the cavalry was formed into a few squadrons for personal attendance upon the Emperor, and a few thousand of the Guard still kept their ranks. Infantry and cavalry combined did not total ten thousand men.

The army was saved from complete annihilation only by the timely arrival of Marshal Victor's corps, which had not advanced beyond Smolensk. The divisions still on the road, including Ney's rearguard, were considered lost.

The escort of Italian troopers left the wagon at Smolensk and were enrolled in the Sacred Band, the name given to the remnant of mounted men. Nicholas saw that they would have to face the next part of the journey alone, and took the precaution of cleaning his musket and laying in a good stock of cartridges. There were plenty lying about in abandoned knapsacks, and he also emptied the holsters of a dead cuirassier whose saddle had been flung on one side when his horse was dismembered by a horde of famished Badeners.

One of the wounded colonels they carried died during the halt, and Nicholas tumbled him into a ditch, not even bothering to search the body for valuables. There would be plenty to perform that office, and Nicholas was no longer concerned with anything that would not contribute to their chances of getting home. He went through the wagon inch by inch, stripping it of everything unlikely to be of service. Spare harness and farrier's equipment were thrown out as useless weight, and Major-General Péliot was moved from the top of the locker he had occupied since Moscow and placed on the floor, beside the other passenger. Nicholas then sawed the locker in pieces in order that they might have dry kindling for the bivouac fires. Their dwindling stock of food was augmented by a pound of coarse meal. It cost Nicholette one hundred and fifty francs in gold.

The cold was not nearly so intense when they left Smolensk and set out along the road for Orsha, but the sudden thaw had made the going difficult and their progress was painfully slow. A mile or so beyond the town they overtook a lame grenadier whose right foot was badly frostbitten. His boot had gone and he limped along in a sheepskin pad. As they passed, the man begged hard for a lift and offered to pay handsomely for the privilege. In other circumstances Nicholas would have passed him without a glance, but he reflected that without an escort he might need another musket and the man looked fairly sound apart from his feet. He told the grenadier to climb up beside him, Nicholette having permanently transferred to the interior of the wagon.

The guardsman's name was Joicy and he came from Tours. He told Nicholas that he believed himself the sole survivor of his company. He was a man of Jean's disposition and believed in travelling light.

"The other fools clung to their ikons and silver plate until they fell dead in the snow," he said. "If it hadn't been for my cursed boot I'd have kept up with the Guard; there's sure to be fighting ahead."

Nicholas asked why, supposing the Russians to have been too busy attacking the columns in the rear to be anywhere in the neighbourhood of Smolensk.

"They've moved up on both flanks," Joicy told him. "We'll never get out of this."

Nicholas reminded him ironically that the Emperor was still in the van.

The veteran spat, or tried to, for his lips were cracked and encrusted with frozen blood.

"Napoleon's a conscript," he grunted. "Who else would have hung on in Moscow for so long?"

Nicholas shrugged and said nothing. He found it interesting to hear a veteran of Jean's class cursing the Emperor, but he was not impressed, knowing that at the first sound of gunfire the man at his side would hobble into the snow and instinctively make his way towards the firing. As likely as not he would shout, "Vive l'Empereur!" when he presented his bayonet at the Cossacks. They were all like that, Nicholas told himself, incapable of logical thought, guided solely by the impulses of their emotions and ready to have those emotions exploited at a moment's notice.

The following day they discovered that the grenadier's information had been correct. A wedge of fifty thousand Russians had overtaken the vanguard south of the line of march and occupied the hills on each side of the approaches to Krasnoe. The remnant of the Grand Army would have to fight its way through or else surrender en masse. The Emperor decided to fight.

Nicholas was not very sanguine as to the result. The enemy had cannon posted on all the ridges, and their infantrymen were able to pour an enfilading fire into the thin columns of Frenchmen strung out along the main road. The army closed up and moved forward, Napoleon marching on foot, surrounded by veterans of the Guard and a group of senior officers. What remained of the transport halted to await the issue of the battle.

The cannonade was murderous and the wagon train came under close fire, a four-pound ball tearing through the taut canvas of the canopy, within a few feet of Nicholette and the two wounded officers. The guardsman, Joicy, as Nicholas had prophesied, slipped off the driving-box during the action and moved up to take his place in the ranks. He returned the following morning in the best of spirits. Nicholas had already heard that the road had been cleared.

"We went through them like a bayonet through pork," Joicy told him.

"How did the conscript behave?" asked the schoolmaster, with a sardonic grin, as he cracked his whip, setting the wagon in motion once more.

The veteran Joicy rubbed his nose.

"Ah," he said thoughtfully, "it was like the Sierra de Guadarrama all over again!"

"What happened at the Sierra de Guadarrama?" asked Nicholas, glad of a chance to talk and thrust his immediate worries into the back of his mind for an hour.

"Didn't you hear about that?" said Joicy, helping himself to a swig of brandy from the bottle wedged between the leather cushions of the driver's seat.

Nicholas reached out and grabbed the bottle before Joicy could empty it. "No," he said, "tell me."

Joicy smacked his cracked lips, the tip of his tongue seeking a stray dribble of liquor.

"We were chasing the Englishman Moore out of Spain. He was bolting for the coast and we were hot on his track. Hot, did I say? Hell, it was worse than this." He gazed round the dismal landscape. The vast snowfield was broken only by yellow wheel-ruts where the Russian guns had been hastily evacuated in the face of the French advance. Here and there a blue, inert mass, already half-covered with drifting snow, marked the farthest limit of an

Imperial Guardsman's retreat. Joicy interrupted his story to say that the break-through had cost the Guard several hundred men and that almost all the wounded had been abandoned. Behind him, in the wagon, Nicholas heard the persistent coughing of the surviving colonel and the clumsy movements of Nicholette rearranging blankets. He thought how lucky Péliot and the other man were to have made a bargain with his wife back in Moscow. No other cantinière would have adhered so rigidly to the terms— transport, with service, over a journey of six hundred miles —under conditions of this sort. He wished that she wouldn't exert herself so much on behalf of her passengers.

With an effort he pushed Nicholette from his thoughts again and addressed the grenadier beside him.

"Go on, finish telling me about the Sierra."

The veteran was not unwilling and Nicholas reflected that all these old soldiers liked the sound of their own voices.

"Ney got over the mountains with the cavalry, but we were caught in a blizzard and the wind bowled us over like skittles. I saw several men blown over precipices. The Emperor was there, helping to dig the snow from the track. I saw him at it, with his old grey coat streaming out like a swallow's tail. Afterwards we all linked arms and marched up the pass in a body. I forget what we sang, but it was something to help us along."

"You didn't catch the English, did you?" put in Nicholas, who now realized that he had heard the story before from Old Jean.

"Of course we didn't," said Joicy. "The Emperor left us and cleared off to Paris. He put Soult in charge, and Soult couldn't catch a cartload of horseshoes with a squadron of light cavalry!"

They jogged along in silence for a few minutes and passed over a wide area of churned-up white snow piled with the previous day's dead, now frozen into grotesque attitudes.

"I heard music between the gunfire yesterday," said Nicholas. "What was it?"

"The fifes," Joicy told him. "The fools began to play 'Safe in the Bosom of the Family,' but the Emperor soon stopped that.

He ordered 'Watch Over the Safety of the Empire' and played it right up to their bayonets!"

A memory stirred in Nicholas, bringing a picture of the idiot youth Dominique scraping away at his fiddle in the churchyard at Essling, playing the same tune to the same man. That had been only three years ago, but it seemed like fifty.

They bivouacked that night in a wretched little village on the road to Orsha. A few battalions passed them on their way back towards Smolensk, and Nicholas heard that they were being sent to extricate the remains of Eugène's and Davout's corps, cut off by the army that the Guard had pushed on one side the previous day. The men were sullen but resolute, and for a brief moment Nicholas was tempted to join them. He was worried about Old Jean and the others. Perhaps they were back there, struggling against terrific odds, without food or brandy. The impulse passed. He had Nicholette to look after, and for once in her life she was in no condition to look after herself.

During the night Nicholette awakened him. In spite of the intense cold she seemed feverish. She said: "I think the child's coming, Nicholas."

He was petrified. "That's impossible!"

He used the word because he wanted it to be impossible. He was not concerned, as she was, whether his child lived or died. He had long since resigned himself to the child dying within a few hours of birth. The important thing was to get Nicholette to a place where she could be delivered in reasonable comfort and safety. Here, in this village, which would be evacuated at first light and might be occupied by the enemy almost immediately, the dice were loaded against all of them.

By morning Nicholette's pains had ceased and he began to hope again. He moved off after the infantry without waiting to make soup. Stragglers from the corps in the rear began to come in. There had been a night battle in the snow and once more the French had had the best of it.

They struggled on towards Orsha, but one of the horses went

lame and the wagon began to lag. Men passed them in twos and threes, walking blindly along the road, dragging frostbitten feet, not even glancing at the slow-moving wagon.

Soon after midday complete disaster occurred. The lame horse collapsed and dragged its floundering companion into the soft snow beside the road. Nicholas and the old grenadier wasted an hour in efforts to get the animal to rise again. The horse lay on its side with flanks heaving and eyes glazed, its mouth frothing in distress.

They agreed to bivouac and hope for a sledge to overtake them. If they had such luck Nicholas decided that its owner must be bribed with half of all they possessed to convey Nicholette as far as Orsha. If they reached a town there was certain to be someone who could be hired as midwife.

As soon as it began to get dark her pains began again. This time Nicholas could no longer doubt the implication. Prolonged exposure and the endless, jolting journey had brought on the birth.

They lit a big fire and Nicholas posted Joicy beside it to accost every straggler in the hope of finding a man from a medical unit. He informed Major-General Péliot and the colonel that they would have to evacuate the wagon temporarily. Péliot grumbled, but he realized that there was no alternative. The two officers were lifted out and placed on sheepskins near the fire, whilst a party of stragglers, men of the Mounted Gendarmerie whose horses had died as far back as Vyazma, consented to erect the old hooped tent as a shelter.

The wind had got up again and more snow was expected. The dismounted gendarmes considered themselves lucky to have found shelter and a share of horseflesh at a bivouac. Some of them set about killing and cutting up the horse. The surviving animal was covered with a blanket and tethered in the shelter of a small fir coppice near by.

Nicholas went about his tasks automatically, refusing to consider the immediate future. He made some soup out of horseflesh, meal and a few onions, and shifted Nicholette's couch to the far end of the wagon, wedging it sideways between the remains of the lockers, in order to give himself plenty of room to work. He knew that no other stragglers would pass them now and that he would have to act as midwife himself.

When the tent was erected Péliot and the wounded colonel shared it with the gendarmes. Nicholas had confided in the guardsman, Joicy, and the old fellow promised to remain awake all night and do anything in his power to assist. He sat on the tailboard, watching the steaks which he had set himself to grill. The odour of roasting horseflesh filled the wagon.

From time to time Joicy went into the wood to collect more fuel. It began to snow, lightly at first but more heavily as time passed. The road was deserted, but from his seat in the wagon Nicholas could see the glare of one or two big fires to the east. The sight relieved him of one of his principal worries. With men strung out behind them, they should be comparatively safe from the Russians.

After he had eaten his supper he went in to Nicholette. She lay on her back, staring up at the smoking lamp that swung in the biting draught from the holed canopy. He followed her glance and tore a piece of rotten canvas from Péliot's empty hammock, going outside and standing on the side of the wagon with a vague idea of repairing the hole. He soon abandoned the attempt. The canvas was threadbare, and in any case his hands were too numb to use a needle. He went in again and sat down beside his wife, waiting.

Joicy stirred up the fire, and the glare, penetrating the wagon, threw Nicholas's shadow on the shuddering canopy. He blew on his fingers and took hold of Nicholette's hand. She shivered at his touch and he saw that she was sweating. She drew her knees up to her chin as another spasm seized her. He felt sick, dazed and helpless.

Presently she said: "Do you know what to do, Nico?"

They called each other Nico; it was a name that had come to them naturally during their first week together in Königsberg.

"I'll do anything you tell me. The baby can't live, Nico!"

259

She shook her head. "Perhaps another time; we never have any luck."

"We've been lucky so far," he reminded her.

Just before another spasm contorted her body her mind sought refuge in the practical. All her life she had been grappling with hard facts, and even now, in the face of intolerable pain, she was able to think in terms of the commonplace.

"We shall want plenty of hot water and a warmed blanket, Nico. Turn out those children's clothes that Gabriel found for us and get your hands clean; you'll find some yellow soap in the tail-board locker."

He got up, marvelling, and found the soap, then climbed down from the wagon to give Joicy the soup kettle and two well-scoured saucepans. Even under these conditions Nicholette had kept her pans clean, scrubbing them after every meal with a stiff brush that hung under the tool box.

The guardsman Joicy filled the pans with snow and put them on the fire. Nicholas waited until the water in the smallest saucepan was lukewarm and then set about scrubbing his hands, digging into the blue furrows of dirt beneath the fingernails and filing the rough edges on his teeth. Between them they managed to erect a frame to hold the blanket up to the flames. They hung it on the windward side of the fire to protect the blanket from the showers of sparks that were whipped up by every gust of wind.

When this was done Nicholas went back into the wagon, turning to lace the thongs of the stiff curtains. The big vehicle rocked in the wind and the fire glowed red. Drifts of snow piled up against the hooped tent where the two officers and the gendarmes slept in a confused huddle.

The guardsman Joicy had no difficulty in keeping awake. With his back against the spokes of the big wheel and his bloodshot eyes fixed on the heart of the fire, he sat on, occasionally shifting his position when the snow piled up too thickly or he felt a twinge of cramp in his gaitered legs. He could sit like that for hours, his memories making light of physical discomfort. They were good memories, like Jean's and Old Carla's. He never remembered the bad times.

From time to time he heard sounds in the wagon behind him, the clump of boots (good boots, he thought, remembering Nicholas's feet, braced against the dashboard all that day) and once or twice a choked cry and a long, hissing noise, like a man beginning to whistle and uncertain of the tune.

A long time seemed to elapse before he heard a single scream, rising clearly above the wail of the wind. It broke off suddenly, and he heard the big voltigeur calling.

"For God's sake . . .!"

A hand fumbled with the lacings of the tailboard curtains. Joicy got up, unhurried, and lifted the soup kettle from the fire. The curtains flapped and he saw Nicholas standing at the back of the wagon, looking as though he was going to faint and fall forward into the fire.

Joicy handed up the kettle and the blanket. Nicholas steadied himself and took them, then disappeared again, muttering something which the guardsman failed to catch. Joicy stood by the tailboard waiting, with another saucepan in each hand. The woman inside cried again and he heard the voltigeur curse.

The guardsman's curiosity was aroused and he concentrated the whole of his attention on the sounds issuing from the wagon. Close as he was, it was not easy to hear anything. The east wind moaned a long, monotonous note and the vehicle rocked, straining every bolt and setting up a continuous creaking, like an inn signboard in a gale.

Once he thought that he detected a low moaning as of an animal in a trap, but it might have been imagination. The suspense began to irritate him; he staggered round to the front of the wagon and groped for the brandy bottle among the leather cushions. Finding it, he pulled out the cork and put the bottle to his lips. At the first taste he thought of the man and the woman in the wagon and, with an immense effort, resisted an impulse to take more than the merest sip, re-corking the bottle and blundering back to the fire, where he lifted the saucepans from the spit and thrust them through the flapping curtains.

He saw the man standing in the centre of the wagon, holding something in the blanket. Beyond him the woman lay inert, her pallid face staring up at the swinging lamp.

The man said, "Give her some brandy, Joicy," and moved past him, jumping down from the tailboard into the snowdrift and moving off with long, clumsy strides towards the fir coppice where the horse was tethered.

Joicy mixed some brandy and hot water in a metal cup and climbed into the wagon. The woman's face looked yellow in the uncertain light, and he had difficulty in holding the cup to her mouth. Its rim chattered against her teeth like castanets, but she drank greedily, wasting hardly a drop and whispering something that might have been thanks when he withdrew the mug.

He noticed that she was shuddering violently and he made an attempt to straighten the blankets. His frostbitten fingers moved with rough tenderness, for he felt an immense warmth for these two individuals.

Nicholas had only glanced at the child to make quite certain that it was dead. It looked, he thought, like a shrivelled monkey and not at all as he had imagined during the hours he had sat awaiting its appearance. Nicholette had been right; it was a boy, but he found it difficult to associate the bundle that he held with people like himself, the guardsman, or the men huddled together in the hooped tent on the far side of the fire.

He was incapable of thinking of the future, of whether Nicholette would survive or whether he and these others would ever get as far as Orsha. The task that he had just accomplished, a task he had never dreamed himself capable of accomplishing, had stupefied his faculties. He walked stiffly, blundering in and out of the drifts, carrying the bundle loosely as though he were moving across the field with a spare box of cartridges for a hard-pressed sector of the skirmishers' line. He could think back but not forward. Odd impressions of the last few hours stood out clearly like patches of a landscape illuminated by lightning: a stray lock of hair plastered across Nicholette's damp forehead, the paleness of her lips, the staccato booming of the wagon canopy in the wind—trifles remote from the business occupying his clumsy fingers.

He wondered how clumsy he had been and if any other gross amateur could have done any better. Probably his very tenderness for the woman had increased his awkwardness. He reached the trees and stumbled against the motionless horse crouching in a hollow, half-buried in drifting snow. The collision reminded him of his immediate task and he went down on his knees, placing the bundle beside him and scratching in the light snow like a terrier. He dug furiously for about a minute before placing the bundle in the shallow grave. It occurred to him that he ought to pray, but he had forgotten any prayers that he had known as a boy or a student. Instead he said aloud to himself: "We'll get away from it, Nico, the two of us, we'll get away from it. I promise, I swear we'll get away from it!" It was not so much a prayer as an oath, to himself and to Nicholette. Then he shoveled the child into the snow with his hands and beat it flat with his palms, emphasizing each word with a blow. Crouching there in the storm, he looked like a primeval savage in the performance of some grotesque rite. Icicles formed on his beard as he fought for breath in the ever-increasing violence of the wind.

He might have died there if the guardsman Joicy had not come and dragged him back to the fire, forcing a cup of brandy and water down his reluctant throat. The spirit made him drowsy and he fell sideways in the snow. Joicy put one arm round his shoulders and another under his knees, lifting him with a titanic effort onto the tailboard and rolling him into the wagon. He climbed in after him, having tossed the last of the wood onto the fire. Nicholette was sound asleep and her rigour seemed to have left her. Joicy foraged around until he found Nicholas's sheepskin, placing a corner of it, the hair inside, under the schoolmaster's buttocks. Then he lay down beside him, throwing the other end of the skin over his own shoulders and tucking it beneath him. He was warm and drowsy after his long watch by the fire. He put both arms round the voltigeur and hugged him as he hugged his favourite memories. In a short while he sensed an answering warmth in the other man's body and his breathing became more regular.

The wind drove shrieking over the plain like an army of Cossacks, and the lamp danced in the violent draught from the hole torn by the four-pounder.

CHAPTER SEVEN

It was fortunate for the men who killed Louis that Gabriel and Dominique had discharged their muskets on their approach. Had they arrived on the scene with loaded weapons, two of the group round the dead dragoon would have been shot out of hand. As it was, running up breathlessly and identifying Louis at a glance, Gabriel retired to the frozen ditch and immediately commenced to reload. His example was followed by the farm-hand.

The men round the horse did not take the slightest notice of the newcomers, but went on drawing off the blood in a tin saucepan and hacking away at the more tender portions of the flesh. The rider was pulled clear and laid alongside the sergeant whom he had killed at the commencement of the struggle.

Old Jean watched the scene for a moment and then went over to Gabriel, just as the latter withdrew his ramrod and stepped towards the stragglers.

"Let be!" said the sergeant. "Louis was nothing to them."

Gabriel stared at him. He was so surprised that for a moment he could not reply. Then he pushed Jean aside and, raising the musket to his shoulder, pulled the trigger. Jean calmly knocked up the barrel, and the ball passed over the group kneeling beside the horse.

"Damn you," shouted Gabriel furiously, "they killed Louis, didn't they?"

He began to struggle, Jean still holding firmly to the end of the musket. The stragglers were not disturbed by the shot. Engrossed in their work, they barely glanced at the two men wrestling beside the ditch.

Jean suddenly lost his temper. He released his hold on the barrel and grabbed Gabriel by the shoulders, shaking him furiously.

"I tell you they were starving! They had a right to the damned horse!"

Dominique took no part in the struggle. He stood close at hand, looking indecisively from one to the other and holding his loaded musket poised, ready to point it in any direction. Finally Jean got the best of the tussle and managed to drag Gabriel clear of the group. He began to push him, still half-resisting, a short distance up the road towards the woods.

"I don't understand you," Gabriel was shouting. "They killed Louis in cold blood. They didn't have to kill him; they're worse than the Cossacks. Why don't we exterminate them? It's your duty, isn't it?"

"Don't talk to me about my duty," growled Jean. "Here, calm yourself with this!"

He thrust the metal brandy flask into Gabriel's hand, and the three of them fell into stride again and moved into the fringe of the wood.

"At any rate we're entitled to our share," said Dominique, grinning.

Gabriel looked at the half-wit with disgust. The incident made him feel strangely alone, as though the two men with whom he marched were mere stragglers picked up along the road, without a common background that made them comrades. He drank a mouthful of brandy and sullenly returned the flask, not trusting himself to speak. It was the first time in three and a half years that he had quarrelled with Old Jean. He could not understand the sergeant's lack of concern at Louis's murder; it flashed across his mind that perhaps the rigours of the campaign had done more than break up corps and regiments. It looked as though hardship and suffering were reducing tiny units such as their own to individuals concerned only with their own survival. He would never have imagined that Jean could have acted like this. He had seen the sergeant step out of a square whilst they were being harassed by English cavalry during the fighting along the Coa in Spain and risk his life to bring Louis, stunned by a spent musket ball, back into the ranks. He marched on in silence, and Jean must have guessed his thoughts, for he began to talk.

"You think we ought to have revenged ourselves on them. Well, that's a lunatic's action in the first place. They were more than a dozen to our three and they'd have cut us to pieces without so much as interrupting their meal. But even if there had been only two or three of them, I wouldn't have fired the first shot. Louis must have had the Devil's own luck to get a horse this far. He was bound to kill it sooner or later, and they'd as much right to it as anyone. After all, Louis didn't pay for it; it belonged to the army."

Dominique nodded, as though he at any rate saw logic in the sergeant's argument.

Gabriel muttered: "Louis fought them at longer odds, didn't he?"

Jean shrugged. "Louis was a fool. I don't know what came over him after he left us for the cavalry. They're all fools in the cavalry. 'Why wear out your feet, Sergeant?' I've had them say to me often enough, but what good did a horse do Louis? He's back there with a musket ball in his belly and we, we're still alive and in sight of a depot. Louis ought to have got down and handed over the horse. He could have fought for his share of it; there would have been sense in that!"

They tramped on and presently Gabriel's anger cooled. He reflected that in all these years Jean had never been wrong about anything, and, in spite of himself, Gabriel began to wonder if, after all, the sergeant wasn't right about this. Supposing they themselves had been without rations for days, trudging over snowfields on frostbitten feet, and supposing a sleek dragoon had trotted by, mounted on a horse that looked uniquely well-nourished in the circumstances of the retreat. The more he thought about it, the more convinced he became that he would have been a party to shooting the rider and eating the horse. The men who had shot Louis had no bond with him. He was just another dragoon, riding while they walked, eating while they starved, and likely to be holding out his kettle in a Smolensk revictualling store long before they had dragged themselves into the town to scratch about for stray crumbs. Jean had been right: Louis's death was due to his own folly—just like Manny's, who had stayed behind to search for a man whose escape he had engineered, and was crucified for his pains up in the sierra.

Gabriel was an honest young man. When they stopped to warm themselves by a fire, he said: "You were right about Louis, Jean."

The old sergeant grunted, spreading his hands to the blaze.

"Recruits never learn until it's too late!" he said.

They got into Smolensk that night and were just in time to collect a minute ration of flour at one of the Guard's depots. Almost every house in the town had been burned during the advance and they searched for a cellar in which to bivouac. It was too dark to look for Nicholas and the wagon, but near one of the huge fires in the main street they encountered Sergeant-Major Soutier. Old Jean was shocked at the man's appearance. He had lost every ounce of his fat, and his uniform hung about him grotesquely, looking a dozen sizes too large.

Soutier's cheeks had fallen in and one of his feet was frost-bitten. He had been lucky enough to buy a lift into Smolensk on one of Davout's caissons. Without it he must have perished days ago. He told Jean that the ride had cost him every sou and every article of value that he possessed.

"So you see the loot was of some use to me after all," he said, with a wry smile.

Jean worried his moustache. "It's too early to say that. What are you going to do now?"

Soutier said nothing and Jean felt a slight pang of sympathy for the man. Soutier was unused to this kind of campaign. Before entering Spain he had never heard a shot fired but had mooched about putting on flesh in German billets. Jean reflected that a man's luck didn't last forever.

"I'll crack a bottle in memory of you when we get into Prussia," said Jean.

Soutier hestitated, as though trying to make up his mind to say something. When Jean moved away he reached out and caught his arm.

"I did fairly well for myself in the old days, Jean. I got married after the Jena campaign, and my old woman, she's got a good farm near Erfurt. What would you say to a thousand francs for taking me along? We've lost touch with our own transport."

Gabriel looked at Jean. The sergeant's face was expressionless. Soutier watched it as a deserter might study the face of an officer presiding over his court-martial.

"It's company I need more than transport," said Soutier.

"Can you walk?" Jean asked at length.

"I shall have to. I'm better now, anyhow; the rest did me good."

"You'd better trail along after us, then, but we'll make short work of your old woman's stock when we do get to Erfurt!"

Soutier was so voluble in his thanks that he almost choked. He kept repeating his offer of a thousand francs over and over again until Jean cut him short.

"We don't want your money, Sergeant-Major; we'll take the geese, fat, tender geese, cooked with onions in a litre of dripping!"

Soutier sighed and poked about on the edge of the fire for a place to rest his kettle. They pooled half their rations to make soup, and Dominique brought in some horseflesh. There was no salt and so they made do with powder. It was a good meal, their best since leaving Vyazma.

Before it was light a section of the Guard held a muster in the principal street. Gabriel heard that they were recruiting a rear-guard, and Jean told them all to keep out of sight. A few officers went round routing the stragglers out from the cellars, but the column that marched out of the east gate was barely two hundred strong. They were sent back to replace Marshal Ney and his corps, now given up as lost.

That morning the three voltigeurs tried to get news of Nicholas and the wagon, but all transport had moved out the previous day. Jean thought it probable that Nicholas was well ahead. He heard nothing to suggest the contrary and there seemed to be no sign of the vehicle among the mass of broken carts and carriages that were being used for firewood in the main streets of the town.

They left Smolensk after a twelve-hour halt and marched all that day and all the next, crossing the battlefield of Krasnoe with the remnants of Eugène's corps. The blizzard caught them again in the forest and they weathered the storm in a crowded coaching-house. Towards evening of the third day Soutier began to lag. So far he had kept up remarkably well, but his right foot was causing him acute pain and several times Dominique had to go back for him. Jean was carrying his knapsack and musket.

Shortly before dark they saw a big village ahead of them, and as stragglers made very determined efforts to reach shelter before every building was occupied, Jean detailed Dominique to assist Soutier and hurried on with Gabriel to see what could be done to find a billet for the night. They came up with a party of artillerymen and joined them in a fight with men of Eugène's guard, who had barricaded themselves in a single-storey hovel on the outskirts of the village. Unsuccessful in their attempt to storm the hut, the gunners began to pull it down from the outside, determined to have a fire if they were forced to sleep in the open. The Italians resisted bitterly and several were wounded in the fight. More stragglers came up to assist the gunners, and the hut was soon torn to pieces and converted into firewood. Jean and Gabriel established themselves on the inner ring and awaited the arrival of Dominique and Soutier. They cooked a couple of oatmeal cakes and thawed four potatoes, giving nothing away.

The men round the fire began to move on before it was light. There were Cossacks in the neighbourhood, and all who were able to continue the march were anxious to keep as close as possible to the Guard, now making for the Berezina. There were rumours that Marshal Oudinot's fresh corps was covering the crossing, and every man who had struggled thus far made his best attempt to reach the river before the Russian armies hovering along each flank were able to concentrate.

Dominique and Soutier had not yet appeared, but Jean showed no anxiety until mid-morning, when he and Gabriel were alone at the fire except for two or three dying men unable to move another step. Jean said that he supposed Soutier had collapsed and Dominique, obeying his sergeant's orders to the letter, had remained with him throughout the night. Dozens of stragglers passed the bivouac during the morning, but neither Dominique nor the sergeant-major was among them.

By midday Jean was obliged to make a decision, either to push on and abandon the other two or to go back along the road and look for them. He considered the problem carefully. If he and Gabriel moved on to Orsha, Dominique must be considered lost. Jean knew that the farm boy would never abandon Soutier without orders; he would remain with him until both of them died or were taken prisoner. He felt certain that they were close at hand, for when Jean and Gabriel had pushed on into the village the previous night they were barely an hour's march behind. The sergeant felt no qualms about abandoning Soutier. He and the sergeant-major had come to an understanding, but if Soutier could not walk any farther the arrangement was automatically cancelled. Regarding Dominique the position was quite different. Jean had never yet failed in his duty towards the men placed in his charge. After some thought the sergeant decided to return. He explained his reasons to Gabriel, at the same time releasing him from any military obligation to join in the search.

"It's my own fault," he told Gabriel gruffly. "I told Dominique to look after Soutier and I owe it to the boy to go back and give him permission to abandon the old fool."

Gabriel observed that anyone except Dominique would have left the sergeant-major long ago, notwithstanding any instructions that he might have received from a sergeant.

Jean shook his head. "Dominique's not like us," he said. "He may be a bit weak in the head, but he's a first-class soldier. I've got to go back, confound them."

Gabriel understood Jean's motives. He had not served with him all this time without discovering how the veteran's mind worked.

"I'm coming with you, Jean," he told him.

"Don't be a fool; I'll pick you up at tonight's bivouac."

"I'm not losing sight of you," said Gabriel, and although he was jocular he meant it, for Old Jean had become a sort of talisman to them all. As long as the sergeant was marching alongside him Gabriel did not doubt their prospects of getting home. Jean possessed a toughness and ingenuity that no amount of privation and hardship could impair. Gabriel found it impossible to imagine Jean lying dead or Jean a prisoner, and his instincts told him to hang on to Jean even if the sergeant's quixotic sense of duty impelled him to march east instead of west.

So they set off together, marching through the slush towards the wood where they had parted from Dominique.

They had not gone very far before they met an old chasseur blundering along, head down, and carrying his left arm in a sling. As they came abreast the chasseur looked at them with surprise.

Jean stopped, recognizing an old friend. "This is a bad business, Albert."

They enquired after mutual friends, and Jean told the old soldier their reasons for retracing their steps. The chasseur shrugged.

"He must have been rounded up in the ambush. The Cossacks closed in on one of the fires about midnight and grabbed more than a score of them. I got off with this." He glanced down at his arm and Gabriel saw that it was clumsily splinted with a pine branch. "Most of our fellows threw down their arms. You wouldn't have a mouthful of brandy for an old comrade, would you? I could get on if only I had some brandy."

Jean took out the flask and a small piece of sugar from his pocket; pouring spirit onto the sugar, he handed it to the delighted chasseur.

The man put it to his lips, sucking noisily. "This means twenty leagues to me, Jean," he said.

"We'll pick you up at the next bivouac," Jean told him.

The chasseur grimaced. "It's suicide to go back, comrade; the Cossacks are herding them all back to Smolensk. I got under cover and watched the column move off. They'll all die en route. They might just as well have shot the prisoners on the spot, but you can't expect the laws of war from savages."

"How many hours have they been on the march?" asked Jean.

"Four to five; you won't catch them now."

"They'll be marching at a snail's pace," Jean said and motioned Gabriel to move.

The chasseur re-addressed himself to his sugar, wincing as the brandied morsel touched his cracked lips. He looked mournfully at the empty road.

"This is the craziest thing we ever did," he muttered, sadly but without rancour.

Jean blew on his hands, one eye cocked at the ribbon of the Legion of Honour sewn on the chasseur's tattered tunic.

"We got back from Acre, didn't we, Albert?"

"Ah, Acre," said the chasseur, with a rueful grin. "We were young bones in those days!"

He moved off slowly, picking his way over the hummocks. Jean and Gabriel unslung their muskets, looked at the priming and entered the wood.

They found the tracks easily enough, a wide area of trampled snow round a dead fire in a clearing. Beyond, a broad path of footprints curved off to the south through the more open portion of the forest. On each side of the tracks were the hoofmarks of escorting horsemen.

They followed the tracks for the better part of two hours, and just before it got dark they came out of the wood and looked down on a small town huddled in a shallow valley a long musket shot from the last of the trees. Fires were already twinkling along the single street that ran between lines of one-storey log huts. More than a hundred Cossack ponies were tethered to a palisade of lances erected round a frozen pond close to the first house, while an incessant murmur of voices reached Jean and Gabriel in their cover on the edge of the wood. Jean guessed that the prisoners were all locked in one of the cabins and that their captors were busy getting drunk. The Cossacks were not popular with the peasantry. Their impact on a civilian community was usually as disastrous as that of the Guard had been in the heyday of the Empire, before the Emperor adopted conciliatory methods of ruling conquered territory.

"There's the nut," said Jean, biting his moustache. "All we have to do is crack it!"

Gabriel would not have given much for their chances of success. A company of well-armed and well-nourished infantrymen would be needed to storm a town held by two troops of Cossacks, whether they were drunk or sober.

"We'll give them an hour or two," said Jean, "and I hope one or two stray from the fold. It's time we had some luck."

They did have luck. Less than an hour after dark, when Gabriel was thinking that he would be unable to endure the torture of lying still in the snow a moment longer and was about to suggest that they go back into the wood and cook a meal, a single Cossack came out of one of the huts and untethered his horse, mounting and riding directly towards them. They saw him silhouetted against the rising moon as the pony walked leisurely up the slope towards the wood. The man was apparently setting out on some errand, perhaps to acquaint a larger body of troops with information or to ask for orders regarding the disposal of prisoners. As he came nearer they noticed that he swayed slightly in the saddle and they heard him crooning softly to himself as he let his horse find its own way through the drifts in the path leading to the forest.

The night was very still and they dared not risk firing a shot. Ordering Gabriel to remain where he was, screened by bushes on the edge of the path, Jean wriggled back towards the trees and regained the track where it was obstructed by a fallen tree. Jean had noted the spot before they settled down, and chose it now because he knew that the Cossack would have to dismount at this point. He crawled to the far side of the trunk and groped around for a piece of wood heavy enough to use as a club. Finding nothing but rotten twigs, he drew his sword bayonet and waited.

The Cossack seemed to take hours to cover the short distance between the fringe of the wood and the fallen tree. As he approached, Jean heard his heavy breathing and once or twice the pony snorted. The sergeant had forgotten cold, hunger and the twinges of pain in the joints of his right hand, certain forerunners of frostbite. For the first time for days he felt warm, and he waited impatiently for the Russian to climb from his saddle and cross the log. As he did so, turning to urge his pony over the obstacle, Jean rose up beside him and drove his bayonet into the Cossack's neck with the full strength of his arm. The hilt jarred against the base of the skull, and the man gave a loud hiccough. For a moment he stood there beside Jean, the reins still grasped in his right hand. Then he fell sideways, tearing the bayonet from Jean's grip and crashing among the brushwood that sprouted round the fallen tree. His fall startled the pony and the animal reared, its forelegs slipping from the trunk and plunging into the drift. Jean grabbed at the reins but missed them, and the pony turned, slithering down the path towards the fires.

Gabriel heard it coming and ran into the open, waving his arms. The pony hesitated and a moment later Jean, leaping the trunk, had secured it and led it back into the wood.

It was no simple business to strip the dead Cossack. Here, among the trees, there was hardly any light, and Jean's bayonet was so firmly wedged in the man's neck that it required their united strength to extract it. The man wore a prodigious amount of clothing. They stripped off a sacklike jerkin and half a dozen waistcoats, some of them made of silk. He wore two pairs of breeches, one of serge and one of leather, a fur cap and a good pair of cuirassier's riding-boots fitted with heavy spurs. In addition to his lance, which they recovered from the drift, he carried an ivory-hilted dagger of Oriental pattern and two long-barrelled old-fashioned pistols. Strapped to the pony's saddle they found a leather portmanteau and a greasy blanket, but they had no leisure to examine the portmanteau and left it where it hung on the crupper. The Cossack was short and fat, and his clothes fitted neither of them. Gabriel, as the shorter of the two, struggled into the leather breeches and some of the waistcoats, belting the smock over his tunic and cramming the fur cap low on his forehead. They hardly spoke whilst the change was being made. All their plans had been worked out in detail whilst they lay in the bushes looking down on the camp.

The Cossacks kept notoriously bad watch. Once inside the village, Gabriel was able to move about unchallenged. It did not take him long to locate the hut where the prisoners were confined, a long, low building, probably a communal storehouse, situated at the extreme end of the street. It was negligently guarded by two or three Cossacks, stamping about on the platform outside the main door. Gabriel was able to effect a thorough reconnaissance, passing round to the rear of the building and probing the rotten planks. The hut had probably been chosen as a prison because it was the most ramshackle in the village. He found a section of the rear wall where one plank had fallen away from another, leaving a gap about the breadth of his hand. He peered inside, but the hut was in complete darkness. Gabriel then guessed the reason for the inadequate guard. Every prisoner was probably in the last stages of exhaustion. Every man except Dominique, Gabriel reflected.

Farther down the street the Cossacks were singing and Gabriel waited until the chorus reached its crescendo before tearing at the loose plank. It gave slightly, but the cracking of the rotten wood made him shudder. He waited for a moment and then tried again. By the time the Cossacks had roared their way

276

through the next chorus a section of the plank was loose in his hand. He called softly through the small aperture.

"Dominique!"

There was a rustle in the dark interior. Somebody cursed in Italian.

Gabriel paused again, uncertain of what to do and wishing that Old Jean had not been too gaunt for the Cossack's clothes. He was just about to make an attempt to wriggle into the hut when he heard a giggle, and instantly recognized the sound. Dominique always tittered when he wanted to express emotion. It was his way of saying: "Don't look any farther, Gabriel, I'm here!" Gabriel had often heard Dominique's giggle when they had been crawling through undergrowth together in the skirmishers' line.

Gabriel said: "Is Soutier with you?"

Again the giggle, an odd combination of glee and excitement.

"Fetch him," said Gabriel, "and for God's sake keep quiet!"

The Cossacks began to sing again. The men on guard at the front of the shack joined in. Gabriel remembered hearing Russian prisoners sing the same song in Moscow.

Somebody dragged himself over the floor of the hut, colliding with someone who cursed. Presently Gabriel heard Soutier's voice.

"Who is it?" The whisper failed to disguise the man's weakness.

"Private Colonna, Sergeant-Major; you can get out if you're quiet."

"Is Jean Ticquet there?"

"Waiting in the wood. We've got a pony. Get Dominique to push you through."

Six months ago Soutier would have laughed at an invitation to squeeze through a hole twice as large, but now it was a possibility.

There was silence for a moment and Gabriel heard Dominique titter again. Then Soutier said: "It's no use; you'd better get off without me. I shan't leave here in the morning."

"I tell you we've got a pony!"

Something scraped against the edges of the hole, and Dominique's head and shoulders appeared. Soutier was pushing from behind. Gabriel grabbed the farm boy by the stuff of his epaulettes and eased him gently to the ground.

The sergeant-major spoke again. "Tell Jean to call on my old woman. He'll get his geese all right and maybe something for his trouble." Then they heard Soutier drag himself away, and someone whom he disturbed began to babble in delirium.

Gabriel and Dominique led the pony through the drifts at the rear of the cabins and recrossed the plain towards the trees where Jean was waiting. The Cossacks were drunk and they got away unchallenged.

The three of them headed due north, taking turns to ride the pony and travelling by the stars. They kept away from the main road and emerged from the forest only at night. What was left of the French army was now far in advance, and Jean supposed that the rearguard had been overrun long ago. No word of it had come through since before the Smolensk halt.

Twice they saw Cossack detachments pass, and once they almost ran into a column of Russian infantry driving a horde of scarecrow prisoners. Watching from cover, Jean swore savagely.

"After Austerlitz I saw French staff officers dive into a freezing lake to bring a couple of wounded Russians ashore," he told them. His face twitched and for a moment Gabriel thought that the sergeant was going to fire, but he controlled himself and lay still, waiting for the column to pass.

On the fourth day they had a stroke of luck. Crossing a frozen lake, Dominque shot a bear, and they ate the best meal since leaving Moscow. They were too weak to carry much away and had to leave the bulk of the carcass to the wolves.

When they had leisure to ransack the Cossack's portmanteau they found a bottle of gin and a variety of cumbersome trinkets, looted from Frenchmen killed or captured along the road. Jean threw most of the spoil away, filling the portmanteau with bear's meat.

"It's still a long way to Prussia," he muttered.

On the fifth day Jean became doubtful of the direction they were taking. For forty-eight hours they had seen neither Cossack nor Frenchman, only a monotonous expanse of snowfield and forest. Soon after setting out that day they crossed a shallow stream and Jean cracked the thin ice with the butt of his musket, noting that the water ran south.

"We must have crossed the main road in the dark," he said. "From now on we follow this stream, no matter how difficult; it's bound to flow into the Berezina."

They followed it all that day, climbing over fallen trees and slithering down the banks, covering less than a league after each two-hourly halt. They built a bivouac before it grew dark and, because they were ravenously hungry, ate the last of the meat. Jean was particularly sparing with the Cossack's gin.

Before it was light Gabriel was awakened by Jean shaking his shoulder. In the wan light he saw the sergeant's face glowing with excitement.

"Listen!"

Gabriel listened. Presently, clear on the east wind, he heard the sound of gunfire and understood the cause of Jean's excitement. Firing must mean that a French army still existed.

They packed up and turned the pony's head into the wind. About midday they emerged from the forest and looked down on a shallow fold between two hills. A small column of men, marching in close order, was toiling up the valley. Gabriel saw that the rear files halted every now and then and fired at a cloud of horsemen hovering just out of musket range. Beyond the horsemen, in the far distance, were black smudges of infantry.

Old Jean's eyes shone and he swung himself from the saddle. "It's the rearguard, by heaven!"

A sudden excitement seized them. They stumbled down the hill, shouting and waving; some of the men at the head of the column waved back. The firing continued, but none of the horsemen rode within normal range and the column was allowed to proceed virtually unmolested. When it reached the outskirts of the forest it halted and the three voltigeurs joined it, sobbing for breath. The pony followed more leisurely.

A man in a cocked hat and a tattered fur-lined cloak approached. Gabriel saw that he hadn't shaved for weeks and his lined face was covered with stiff red bristles. His grey uniform was nondescript and only his hat betrayed his high rank. He wore no sword, but carried a musket. There were powder smudges under his eyes, and his right wrist was bandaged. He called over to Jean.

"Who are you? Where are you from?"

Jean came to attention. "Voltigeurs of the Second Battalion, Ninth!"

The officer scratched his stubble. "The hell you are; whose corps?"

"Viceroy of Italy's!"

"When did you last see the main body?"

"The day after we left Smolensk, nearly a week ago," said Jean.

"How did you get here?"

"We returned for a comrade and lost our route."

A young officer in a filthy uniform sauntered up, blowing on his hands. "Eugène's corps! Then they're over the river now, what's left of them. We're better off in the rearguard, Michel!"

Only then did Old Jean recognize Michel Ney and, beside him, his only subordinate, General Maison. He looked down the column as the men broke ranks to search for firewood. It was the most tatterdemalion body of troops that Jean had seen since they routed the regular Spanish army, back in 1808. There were men of every unit and half a dozen nationalities. Many were wounded and all were in rags. They were about eight hundred strong, and a glance told Jean why Ney and his second-in-command were carrying muskets. There was no artillery and no transport. The carts carrying the wounded and such baggage as had remained had gone down when the column crossed the Dnieper on thin ice.

The men had only one thing in common. Everyone, from the marshal downwards, was under arms.

A few days later the rearguard entered Kovno and recrossed the Niemen. It was composed of Old Jean, Gabriel, Dominique, thirty-eight grenadiers, a few Germans from the Kovno garrison, General Maison and Marshal Ney, whom some called Duke of Elchingen.

Half-way across the bridge one of the Germans staggered and dropped his musket. Ney bent and picked it up, taking careful aim at a swarm of partisans closing in on the bridgehead. Standing there on the parapet, his cloak bellying in the wind, he fired the final shot of the campaign. It was a characteristic gesture, half genuine defiance, half bravado.

PART FIVE

The Elster

CHAPTER ONE

Nicholette closed the door of the sickroom very softly and paused on the landing, waiting until the surly Prussian landlord had mounted the stairs and gone to his own room.

Nicholette had avoided the Prussian ever since she had bribed her way into the house. She distrusted both him and her own powers of self-control. It had cost her nearly a thousand francs to buy her way into the merchant's house. The little town of Elbing was crammed with troops. Every family had its quota, and the civilians were seething with a rage which they disguised as re-awakened nationalism. They went about telling one another that Prussia would soon be free again and secretly contributed to the Tugenbund, Lützow's and the poet Körner's underground organization which specialized in assassination and was already improving on the methods of the Spanish and Portuguese guerrillas. But the real reason for their discontent was commercial. The exclusion of British trade was ruining the German towns, and the Grand Army, since its return from Russia, had degenerated into a diseased rabble. The French commissary was temporarily unable to honour the billeting slips, and the conscripts of the line were too poor to spend freely in the shops.

Nicholette's landlord was a wealthy silk merchant with political influence. He had been excluded from the billeting list and Nicholette paid him privately. She knew that Nicholas's chances of recovery would be negligible if he went to the hospital, and had established contact with a Danzig Jew to draw sums on her Frankfurt banker. The silk merchant's terms were prohibitive, but she had no alternative except to pay what he asked and take it out in silent hate. Nicholas grew neither worse nor better. He slept restlessly, for days at a time, muttering and staring at her with vacant eyes when she tried to feed him with broth that cost her ten francs a bowl. She wondered whether he was blind or incurably insane.

The guardsman Joicy had long since rejoined what remained of his unit, and gone over to Danzig, where Davout was recruiting. All Europe was simmering, and there would be more hard fighting in the spring. Péliot, the major-general, had been patched up and sent home, an incurable cripple but thankful to escape with his life. He had promised her three thousand francs when he could get to his banker in Paris, and she knew that he would pay. In the meantime she could manage, although the Jew charged her a high rate of interest for the Frankfurt drafts, and she writhed under the iniquity of his demands.

She felt her loneliness acutely. Her body was strong enough now that she could buy sufficient food, but her mind was weighed down by anxiety. She did not know what she could do if the silk merchant turned her and Nicholas into the street. No French officer in the town would dare to enforce hospitality where the landlord was locally powerful. She wished with all her heart that she could get news of Jean and the others.

January passed, with snow turning to sleet. She went down to the barracks every day and enquired for stragglers of the Ninth. She had heard that the light infantry were concentrating in Elbing before marching back over the Elbe for a refit. New drafts of conscripts trickled in from the west, rosy-faced boys of sixteen and seventeen, most of them still in farm smocks and leggings made of sackcloth. They were housed on the stone floors of the barracks with less than one blanket apiece. They could not even begin their drill, for Elbing had no muskets in its arsenal. The Grand Army had emptied it on the way to Moscow.

February went by and Nicholette drew another thousand francs at fifty per cent. Nicholas still lay and stared at the ceiling, and the Prussian landlord ceased to answer her greeting when she came downstairs for her daily visit to the barracks.

On the first day of March a short column came in from the north. Nicholette saw them approaching and immediately recognized them as veterans. They marched loosely, their arms slung anyhow, and they did not sing like the boy recruits.

She watched the lean men swing by, but there was not a face she recognized until the rear file drew level, two men and a sergeant, the latter in the centre, limping badly on the right foot and helped along by his comrades. The sergeant looked straight ahead; the others, bowed under his shared pack, had their eyes on the ground.

"Jean! Jean Ticquet!"

She ran, leaping, across the rutted road, and the three men stopped, staring at her, amazed and slightly embarrassed.

"Thank God you've come . . . it's Nico . . . he doesn't get well!"

They fell out by the roadside, and the sergeant hugged her delightedly. Gabriel stood by, fidgeting with his pack, while Dominique's mouth hung open in his habitual grin.

They did not know what to say. Neither of them had ever seen Nicolette weep before.

The first thing Nicholas saw when he opened his eyes was a thin veil of snow on the large latticed windows. He watched the flakes settle on the diamond panes and saw them melt a moment after and slide, like watersnakes, to the sill.

The high ceiling was full of dancing shadows, writhing about the heavy crystal chandelier; it was some time before he realized that the shadows were kept dancing by the spluttering log fire on the other side of the room, farthest from the window.

He lay there a long time, his eyes moving slowly about the room as his brain made feeble attempts to account for his presence in the high canopied bed.

He was like a man suddenly awakened whilst sleep-walking, who finds himself confronted with doors and walls that he fails to recognize. Time and again his consciousness returned to the attack only to recoil in miserable bewilderment from the wall of alien factors confronting it. Soon the effort exhausted him and he abandoned the attempt, shutting his eyes tightly and fixing his mind on his identity as the one mooring post in an ocean of unaccountable cross-currents.

At last he was able to remember the wagon and the birth of the dead child on the road to Orsha. The recollection comforted him; he determined to begin from this point and push forward, gingerly, like a skirmisher leaving cover and advancing, belly down, over the plain towards enemy piquets.

He remembered going out in the blizzard and burying the child in the soft snow. After that there was a gap until the guardsman Joicy had brought him some stew and he had found himself under the sheepskin beside Nicholette.

He became excited by his ability to remember so much, and his mind advanced with more confidence into the shadowy past. They had been marooned beside the road for two days, and by that time the wagon had been snowed in up to the floorboards, making it impossible for their one horse to drag it back to the packed snow of the highway. The gendarmes in the hooped tent had moved on; the colonel, one of the two surviving passengers, had died in the tent, raving of a wife in Picardy and whimpering like a frightened child when they had tried to force the brandy bottle between his clenched teeth. Major-General Péliot survived, crawling back into the wagon and making himself a nest in the cavity beneath Nicholette's palliasse.

The guardsman Joicy had solved their immediate problem

by tearing off the tailboards, fashioning a rough sledge and fitting it with a canopy made from the rotting canvas of the tent. Nicholas had stood by, marvelling at the man's ingenuity and iron resolution, watching him straighten nails with frostbitten fingers. Joicy had been apprenticed to a carpenter in Condé when he was a boy. He had never forgotten his trade and there remained in him, after fifteen campaigns as a guardsman, the old pride of craftsmanship. He apologized for the ungainly object when the sledge was finished.

"I could do something better, if only I had sound hands."

All this time Nicholette had lain on her pallet and nursed her returning strength. It was incredible how quickly she rallied from the shock of Nicholas's unspeakably clumsy delivery. Nicholas himself seemed the weaker of the two when at length they started out. It was the woman who did most of the reassuring.

"We'll get back all right and winter in German billets. If Annette holds out we'll be in Danzig for the New Year," she kept telling him.

Annette was the surviving mare, and in spite of her miserably inadequate fodder she plodded along, dragging Nicholette and Péliot on the sledge, with Nicholas and the guardsman taking turns to ride on the runners. Nicholette said that Annette was the best draught horse she had ever seen. Old Carla would have been mad about her.

They followed the wreck of the army to the banks of the Berezina, where Victor's corps held off the Russian attacks until the greater part of the fugitive mob had crossed to the west bank. Nicholas saw the engineers building the two bridges, standing waist deep in icy water and driving the piles down into the slime. Almost every engineer engaged in the work died on the job, but countless stragglers had crossed before one bridge collapsed under the weight of the transport and the other became little more than a flimsy jumping-off place into the black current that swirled the débris downstream.

Thousands died on this bridge, fighting for handholds on the planks, screaming for help where no help could be given, not even by one's own brother or oldest comrade. Whole groups of men and women spilled over the parapet, clutching at one another in despair, clinging to the uprights and stray ends of binding rope, hanging on sometimes for an hour before another avalanche tore their fingers from the hold and whirled them downstream. And all the time the Russians closed in on both banks, while Victor and Oudinot fought them off, savagely and sullenly, as though from habit.

The sledge passed over during the night, when the eastern bank was studded with the bivouacs of hungry wretches too engrossed in cooking horsemeat to make the precarious crossing. They passed through Smorgonie, where the Emperor boarded a fast sleigh and headed away for Paris, leaving the rabble to the reluctant Murat. The indignant King of Naples, looking faintly ridiculous in the shreds of his tattered finery, stamped about in the snow bewailing the loss of his splendid cavalry. The troops heard of the Emperor's desertion with indifference. They were far too immersed in their personal problems to question the wisdom of Napoleon's decision. To the survivors of the Grand Army the Emperor Napoleon had ceased to act as a rallying-point. They were more interested in plundering the pay wagons of the Imperial Guard, which they passed, overturned, on a slippery hill outside Vilna. Some of the men, who had long since abandoned their arms, stopped to fill sacks with forty-franc pieces.

Several times the fugitives beat off Cossack attacks, but after Smorgonie Nicholas was hardly conscious of incident. He fired mechanically when Joicy fired, and reloaded behind the sledge canopy when he saw the old guardsman drop a ramrod into the barrel of his musket. He no longer talked to Nicholette, and sometimes the four of them travelled the whole morning without exchanging a word. When they got into Kovno, on the Niemen, Nicholas realized that he was partially blind. The discovery came as a violent shock. He found he had difficulty in focussing his eyes on the buildings, while the streets seemed to merge with the snow-covered plain beside the broad river. He remembered looking with interest at the round bald patch on the crown of Major-General Péliot's head when the officer took off his fur cap for a moment to adjust a muffler. He recollected noticing that the pinkness of the bald patch was of the same shade as the clouds behind the setting sun over the river. Then the clouds and the water, the town and the plain and Péliot's bald patch dissolved into one broad sheet of blinding white and he stopped suddenly in the tracks of the sledge and began to scream.

He lay still under the stiff linen sheet and watched the shadows dancing on the ceiling. The door opened and a woman came in, carrying a tray and a steaming bowl. She went over to the fireplace and he was able to study her back. She was short and sturdy, moving with a certain tautness that was not without grace. She busied herself at the hob for a moment and then turned towards the bed. He recognized Nicholette and tried to smile.

She stood quite still for a moment, gripping the tray, her lips parted, her eyes looking into his. He thought that she trembled a little, but he might have been mistaken. She came over to the bed and set down the tray on a bedside table. He tried to speak, but she stifled the words against her tightly stretched bodice, fingering his hair and his beard and crooning inarticulate words.

"You've been terribly ill, Nico. I kept telling myself that you'd come back, but I didn't believe it and Jean didn't believe it, either, even if he always pretended to."

After the soup he fell asleep again, his face on her shoulder. She lay there until the fire began to go down and cramp racked her body. When his breathing was quite regular she wriggled free and replenished the fire, afterwards going out softly and quickening her step down the stairs, across the wide hall and into the rain. She did not stop to put on a cloak, but made straight for the crowded barracks in the old town. She ran swiftly, for that morning the morose Prussian had presented his three-day ultimatum. He had communed with his conscience and would not continue to house brigands for all the gold in the Imperial treasury.

On the third day Jean, Gabriel and Dominique came to the house. They entered the room quietly and stood round the bed, grinning. A faint colour had returned to Nicholas's cheeks, and Nicholette had made an attempt to shave him with a notched razor. Gabriel thought that he looked years older than Jean, and his long hands, white as a woman's, rested listlessly on the counterpane.

"How's Louis these days?" he asked.

Jean exchanged a swift look with Nicholette, who nodded and smiled faintly.

"Gone after Manny and Claude," he said.

There was silence for a moment. Dominique scratched his nose, and his eyes roved round the room.

"Got yourself a good billet," said the farm boy.

They stood about, not knowing what to say, while Nicholette, conscious of the general embarrassment, pretended to busy herself at the fire.

Presently Nicholas said: "How about yourselves?"

"Well, we're here, aren't we?" answered Jean.

Nicholas's eyes smiled. Old Jean looked uncomfortable for a moment. Presently he coughed and looked hard at Nicholette's back.

"We've got to get you out of here, Nicky, and we've got to take risks to do it, d'you understand?"

Nicholas nodded. "You can tell me. What is it?"

Nicholette spun round, her eyes blazing, her mouth clamped in a hard, savage line. "I offered the German pig another five hundred. I can't get any more until the Jew comes in from Danzig next month. I held the money out to him, five hundred in gold, and all he did was to spit on my hand!"

She wiped her palm on her thigh and shrugged her thin shoulders in a gesture of despair. Dominique looked out the window and Jean dropped his eyes. He knew that Nicholette hated them to see her tears.

Gabriel took up the tale. "It's the Prussians, Nicky; they're turning against us. Nico's been paying a ransom to keep you here all these weeks and now she's been told to move out by tonight."

Nicholas stirred in the bed.

"What did you say about risks, Jean?" he asked.

"I've got a plan. It's for you to say if you'll take the chance of it. You can't walk and you can't even stand, but we could get a stretcher and come in here to fetch you." The sergeant was at ease again. He was always more comfortable when discussing action. "We could jolt you down to the general hospital, of course, but you'd die there. They're dying there every day; it's not a hospital, it's a pest-house. We haven't got a billet; we're in barracks and you'd die there just as surely. This rain, it's ten times worse than the snow."

"Well?"

"There's an officers' hospital in the convent at the far end of town. We could take you there and you'd stand a good chance."

Nicholette suddenly put a finger to her lips and Jean broke off, looking at her with a puzzled expression. She made a sign to Dominique, who was standing nearest the door, and then tip-toed across the room, tearing open the door and standing swiftly to one side. The Prussian fell into the room, and, as he passed, Dominique beat him down with a shrewd blow on the back of the neck. He lay with his head in the wide hearth, gasping.

They looked at one another for a moment. Then Jean spoke very slowly.

"We've got officer's papers and kit. Dominique here has been an orderly for a captain. He's got a new outfit and he won't want his papers until we move again. Get Nicholas ready, Nico."

The Prussian tried to raise himself on his hands, edging back from the heat of the fire. Dominique drew his sword bayonet. For a moment longer there was stillness in the room. Then Gabriel took an involuntary step forward.

"Can't we gag him and leave him somewhere outside the town?" he said.

Nicholette turned on him furiously.

"The swine's had two thousand five hundred out of me and he still wants to turn us out in the street. Stick him through the belly, Dominique, or I'll do it myself!"

They all waited, their eyes on Jean. The Prussian struggled to a sitting posture and began retching, too dazed as yet to be afraid.

Jean said quietly: "I've never yet killed a man in cold blood. Twenty years in the field and every man I've sent on his way was trying to send me on mine. There aren't so many who could say that."

The Prussian stopped retching and stared at Jean, his eyes revealing that he was suddenly aware of his position. He tried to say something, but immediately checked himself as though he felt that the first word would be Dominique's signal to lunge. His gaze left Jean and fixed itself on the point of the sword bayonet.

"You don't have to kill him," said Nicholette. "Dominique's itching to do it!" Her voice rose to an hysterical scream. "He was listening, wasn't he? You smuggle Nico into the convent as an officer. Forged papers, stolen kit! How long do you think he'd be there before this pig rooted him out? What about the rest of us? Is what happens to him more important than what happens to us?" She snatched at Dominique's bayonet.

Jean moved suddenly and slapped her hard on the face.

"Hold your tongue, you silly bitch, and leave this to me!"

Nicholette recoiled from the blow and fell against the bed. Nicholas, propped up on an elbow, did not move, but the heavy bed canopy shook under the impact. Suddenly she began to whimper and Nicholas turned on her impatiently. "Leave it to Jean, can't you?"

"There's a safer way than killing him," pursued Jean thoughtfully. "He can go into the lock-up on a charge of robbery. Gabriel and I can swear him in and it'll be weeks before they get to the bottom of it. He'll most likely die of gaol fever."

Terror faded from the Prussian's face and his eyes travelled round the group.

Gabriel said, "Maybe Nico's right, he'll only blab about us to the provost." But he felt immensely relieved by Jean's decision.

"The provost is an old comrade of mine," said Jean, "and nothing this hog says will get any farther than the gaol door." He seized the landlord by the scruff of his neck, and the man cowered at his touch. "We'll have that money off him first, though. How much did you say, Nico?"

The girl remained silent, holding her cheek. Nicholas spoke from the bed.

"Two thousand five hundred, Jean."

Jean addressed the man in German. "Take us to it," he said.

They fetched a stretcher from the hospital and loaded Nicholas onto it, wrapping him in the Prussian's blankets and throwing an officer's greatcoat over his legs. Gabriel noticed that Nicholas was as thin as a lance; his thinness accentuated his height and made him seem incredibly long in the leg. His patched boots projected over the edge of the wicker stretcher.

They recovered most of the money and trussed the landlord with some of his own bell cords, kicking him downstairs and into the street. Dominique walked immediately behind him with drawn sword bayonet, and all the way down to the gaol the man did not open his mouth. He was signed in and handed over to the acting provost, a sergeant-major who had served with Jean in the Eylau campaign. The arrest cost Nicholette a handful of silver, enough to keep the silk merchant behind bars for months.

They begged a lift up to the officers' convent on a powder wagon, and there Jean entered Nicholas on the rolls as Captain Grénard of the Third Infantry of the line. Marshal Davout, the only marshal who interested himself in the welfare of disabled men, had recently re-organized the officers' sick quarters and there were sufficient medicines and plenty of food. The sisters kept the building spotlessly clean, and Nicholette was able to buy herself a billet at a neighbouring farm. Once Nicholas was off their hands the four of them gathered there for supper.

When they had finished the meal Jean wiped his mouth with the back of his hand and cocked a humorous eye at the girl.

"Your mother would have hit you harder than I did," he told her.

Nicholette finished off a chicken bone and laid it beside a pile of others on her plate. She ate fastidiously and it occurred to Jean that the only characteristics she had inherited from her mother were Old Carla's steadfastness and her curiously inconsistent avarice.

"My mother would have sawed through that Prussian's throat," she replied. "It's no wonder we don't win any more."

CHAPTER TWO

There was talk in the ranks of setting stars and twilight over empires.

By the end of April, 1813, the whole of Europe was under arms, Russians, Prussians, Swedes marching west, the French and their lukewarm allies marching east. The French, as ever, were attacking, threading the forest paths of Franconia and debouching into the open country of Saxony, bad terrain for an army with barely fifteen thousand cavalry and matched against the most powerful international alliance since the Crusades.

Most of the marshals were there, exhausted in mind and body after nearly two decades of unremitting active service. Napoleon himself was there, tense and eager for decisive battles. But the day of decisive actions had passed and the men who had established Napoleon were dead, gone to gild the eagles of half-forgotten triumphs.

There is a limit to any nation's exertions, and some said that the limit of Bonaparte's France had been reached on the far side of the Niemen the previous autumn. Napoleon, however, did not think so and in those hot, sunny days of late spring it seemed as if he were right once again. France and her satellites had found nearly a quarter of a million men for the final struggle on the plains of Germany, and in the May fighting these men, four-fifths of them raw conscripts, had stood up to the cannonades of a hundred army corps and the charges of the heaviest squadrons east of the Elbe.

The initial spurt, however, did not last very long. As the summer advanced Austria came into the coalition against France, and the men of the West were outnumbered by four to one, and by ten to one in cavalry.

There were marches and counter-marches, long dusty crawls across the plains, an endless straining of muscles up the steep, tortuous paths of wooded country, the taking and the retaking of towns and villages at the point of the bayonet, senseless artillery duels in the night, gun firing at gun by the light of bivouac fires. Later came weeks of drenching summer rain that kneaded the dust into a sea of mud and beat down any corn that had survived the passage of a hundred artillery trains.

Murderous battles were fought in that long, indecisive interim, battles in which boys from Picardy and the Vosges stood row on row, white-faced and resolute, whilst their squares were harried by Cossacks, by Prussian hussars, by eight-pounders that ploughed the ranks in even furrows and built the raw infantry a human rampart against the inevitable cavalry attacks at the end of the cannonade. Early victories at Lützen, Bautzen and elsewhere were turned to no profit, could not be turned to profit even by the best captains in the world, because there were never enough reserves, never enough cavalry and always some position lost that should have been held if a theoretically perfect plan were to fulfil its object.

Some of the legendary figures were there when the corps commanders rode into headquarters for conferences: Marshal Oudinot, with his twenty-six scars, recently repulsed before Berlin; Ney, haggard after his five-hundred-mile walk from Moscow to Kovno; Victor, the fussy ex–drummer boy; Davout, silent and meticulous; divisional commanders like the resolute Souham and the roystering Vandamme. But the pace was too hot even for Invincibles, and they failed, collectively and individually, to stem the flood. They were tired, like the veterans, like their Commander-in-Chief.

Bessières, chief of the Guard, was the first man to go down, walking, like any green conscript, into the range of a laid gun on the morning of Lützen and dying like Lannes, but more mercifully. The veterans mourned him as an old comrade, but some of the men, like Jean, could not help wondering if things might have turned out differently had Bessières made the same fatal mistake a year ago. It was the Guard commander who had held back reserves in the battle outside Moscow, when the Russians were on the run and a decisive victory was essential.

Even the countryside had changed. In the old days Germany had been a popular campaigning ground. Men like old Soutier, who left his bones on the road back into Russian captivity, had once grown fat in Saxon billets and German fortresses. Now it was different, the French found hostility everywhere. Food and forage were hard to buy and had to be pillaged, and every veteran knew that pillage did not pay in a protracted campaign. It embittered the countryside and soon recoiled on the marauders.

During the short nights the veterans sat in their bivouacs and talked about setting stars and twilight over empires. It was their own empire that they referred to now, not those that had crumbled before their battery smoke at Rivoli, Austerlitz and Jena.

Nicholas had made a good recovery in the convent, and the four voltigeurs concentrated at Erfurt in late April, when Marshal Victor was making up his light-infantry battalions for the great advance. The Eighty-seventh Regiment was re-formed, but Jean knew none of the men and only one or two of the officers. The four sharpshooters were the only seasoned troops in their company, and even so it had cost them money to stay together. Victor's plan was to stiffen his square with the few veterans at his disposal.

Nicholette had acquired another wagon, second-hand, of much

lighter construction than its predecessor. She had learned her lesson in Russia and would never again invest in a heavy vehicle that required two horses to drag it over bad roads. The new wagon was hardly more than a cart, but it was well sprung and canopied. She joined up with the Eighty-seventh again, and Nicholas, still too weak to march, got permission to ride with her providing that she could maintain the pace of the general advance. He could have gone back into the garrison over the Rhine if he had wished. All convalescents discharged from the convent at Elbing had been issued a six months' second-line voucher, but Nicholas shed voucher and false identity the day he left hospital, to sneak back into the line barracks as a returning straggler. Hundreds of men were coming in from Polish and Lithuanian hide-outs, and his return went unquestioned. As a veteran he was worth his weight in roundshot.

He did not talk much to Jean and the others. They would have liked to question him about the child, but, beyond informing them that it had been born dead on the road home, he volunteered no information and Gabriel got the impression that it was a subject which neither he nor Nicholette wished to discuss. Nicholette told them about Major-General Péliot when that officer rode over from Oudinot's headquarters to pay his passage money. He was one of the few officers well-mounted, for he would never walk again, although he had volunteered for staff work in the field rather than sit in Mayence counting paper divisions. In addition to the money, he gave Nicholette a jewelled locket worth as much again as the sum she had charged him.

"A gift from a disappointed godfather!" he told her and galloped off across the lines, his fat buttocks rising and falling comically as he tried to master the art of riding with a single stirrup-iron.

Nicholette looked at the locket a long time before putting it away in the wagon chest where she kept her few personal belongings and her one change of underclothes.

The voltigeurs got through Lützen without a casualty, but the company as a whole was decimated in the afternoon cavalry charges. That night Gabriel saw Nicholas and Nicholette talking together in the wagon and he fancied that both of them looked unnaturally startled when he climbed the tailboard to collect the communal kettle for supper. Jean also noticed their absence and grumbled over his cooking. Dominique played his fiddle, but neither Nicholas nor Nicholette came out to join the bivouac circle. After calling once or twice, Jean divided their suppers among half a dozen famished conscripts who had been attracted to the bivouac by the music.

About eleven o'clock, just as Gabriel and Dominique were rolling themselves in their greatcoats and preparing to lie down feet to the fire, Nicholas and Nicholette jumped from the wagon and approached Jean. The old soldier was sitting cross-legged, cleaning his musket with rag and linseed oil.

Nicholas said: "Nico says that we must tell you, Jean!"

The sergeant did not look up. He went on oiling the hammer-spring and squinting down at the polished stock.

"Well?"

"Nico and me, we're pushing off!"

Gabriel and Dominique moved nearer, watching Jean's lowered eyes.

The sergeant laid down the oily rag and picked up a scraper, gouging away at the fouled touch-hole.

"Where are you aiming for, Nicky?"

"Switzerland. We've worked it out, the two of us. I was a student in Berne and Zurich and I know most of the cantons. There's a place behind Lake Thun—Spietz, it's called—I stayed there all one summer and, if the same people are there, they'll have us so long as we pay our way."

The sergeant looked up. "That was a long time ago, Nicky; supposing the same people aren't there?"

"We'll chance that and, in any case, we'll be safe enough. A year from now the Bourbons will be back in Paris and they won't waste time hunting down a corporal."

Gabriel avoided Nicholas's glance. The announcement shocked him and he expected it to shock Old Jean. He was amazed that

Nicholas should have the temerity to inform a senior sergeant of intended desertion, especially a sergeant like Jean in whom the habit of loyalty was ingrained. But the matter did not seem to strike Jean in this way; he mused awhile, his scraper circling the priming-pan.

"It isn't the future you'd have to fear, Nicky; it's the present. Switzerland? How far is Switzerland? A good step, even in that." And he jerked his grizzled head in the direction of the wagon. "Maybe you'd get there, maybe not; I don't know. It depends on the number of provosts patrolling down south. But if you are stopped and can't talk your way through the barriers, they'll hoist you back here, both of you, and she'll be a widow this time."

"We've got our story by heart," said Nicholas, "I speak canton German like a Bernese goatherd. We're travelling in watches; Nico's laid in a chest of them."

Old Jean put aside his musket and began gathering the accessories together and packing them away in his cotton hold-all.

"I'm not going to tell you to go or to stop, Nicky. That's a thing a man's got to work out for himself. I'd say if I hadn't gone when we were winning I wouldn't go at all, but I'm not you or Nico either; you've got the right to look at it your own way."

"I never believed in it all; you must admit that, Jean," said Nicholas defensively.

"I'll own that," replied Jean. "You always said that we should break up and it looks as if you're right, though we've had a longer spell than your reckoning gave us. I suppose, if it does come to the Bourbons again, you'll have earned the right to be out of it, making your own way, teaching school again maybe and taking it easy by one of those blue lakes I've heard you talk about. You could do that, I reckon, better than most of us, because you're a man who knows more about things than any of us. But what of Nico? She'll never take to it, not if she lives to go deaf and silly. You'd better make up your mind to that now, Nicky."

Gabriel, watching, saw Nicholette flush in the firelight.

"I'll take to it all right, Jean; you don't understand."

"I reckon I understand all right," said the sergeant, "a piece more than you think."

"You don't," said the girl, stubbornly, "you don't understand me and Nicky. Ours isn't the usual canteen marriage. All the time we've been different. We're like . . . like the people in towns who live ordinary."

She blushed furiously as she said this and looked down at the ground. Gabriel had a notion that she had forced herself to say it and was wretched at having to go to such lengths to justify herself.

Old Jean stood up.

"You'll go off thinking that I blame you for going. I don't want that. You asked me what I thought and I told you; but it's me talking, remember, and I never knew any life but this. I'll say good luck, and so will Gabriel and young Dominique. You've been a good comrade, and we've been a long way together. It was good of you to tell me, Nico; I'd never have forgiven you going off saying nothing. But I'm a sergeant and I ought to stop desertions; so go quietly now; pack up when me and these others have turned our feet to the fire. That'll give you six hours' start before I report to the provost. One other thing—don't try to take that wagon any farther than the army lines. If you reach the frontier they won't bother a man and a woman walking, but they'd look into a wagon. I would if I was the frontier provost."

The two men embraced formally, and Gabriel saw the sergeant's face over Nicholas's shoulder. His expression was stony and vacant. Nico kissed him lightly and climbed back into the wagon.

Nicholas stood silent for a moment longer before turning uneasily in the direction of Gabriel and Dominique, who had remained sitting by the fire, quietly finishing their soup.

"There's these two, Jean; they're young enough to start afresh. I wondered—"

Jean interrupted and Gabriel thought that his voice trembled a little. "I tell you I'm a sergeant. If you're determined to go I won't stop you, even if I should, but that doesn't mean that I can stand by and listen to you persuading others!"

Nicholas understood. He had understood from the beginning, when he and Nicholette had first discussed their project and the girl had stubbornly refused to leave without telling Jean. He shrugged his thin shoulders.

"Good-bye, Jean. Good-bye, Gabriel, Dominique!"

Gabriel said good-bye, but Dominique, who was never able to concentrate upon more than one thing at a time, perhaps had not fully heard or understood the conversation, for he contented himself with a nod, as though Nicholas were going to the ammunition park for a brief spell of guard duty. The sergeant said nothing as Nicholas followed the girl into the wagon.

Although the night was warm and the supper had been adequate, Gabriel could not sleep. He lay listening to the muffled sounds from the wagon and to the voices of Nicholas and Nicholette conversing in low tones. Gabriel's mind kept returning to his first conversation with the schoolmaster, in the churchyard at Essling on the evening after his first battle. It was difficult to realize that four years had passed since then and that almost every day of those years had been spent in Nicholas's company. The departure depressed him as the deaths of Manny, Claude and Louis had never done. These three were ordinary casualties of war. Premeditated desertion was different, cold-blooded, somehow more final. Gabriel had always admired Nicholas for his learning and power of detachment. The schoolmaster too had taken a genuine interest in Gabriel's painting, casting an eye over each new sketch and making clear, incisive comments on its merits and demerits. Gabriel had learned a good deal from him, particularly during the months of captivity in England, and he knew that he would miss him as much as he had missed Manny or as he would miss Old Jean.

He lay there and wondered what their life would be like in Switzerland, what occupation they would choose and whether they would have any more children. It was fantastic to think of

Nicholette as a housewife, cooking meals in a kitchen and sewing children's clothes. She did not fit into any civilian pattern and he knew that Jean had been accurate in his forecast. He tried to imagine what would happen when eventually the monotony of her existence drove her to urge Nicholas to make a change, and what the legal position of the pair would be if they ever returned to France.

He was still musing when he heard the thud of boots and the rattle of the tailboard. Over by the wagon a spare figure moved against the moon; Gabriel, propping himself up on his elbow, looked again and noticed that Nicholas was wearing civilian clothes. Instead of a shako he had on a soft felt hat, of the sort worn by drovers who came into the camp with fodder. It looked so ridiculous that Gabriel stifled an impulse to giggle. Then Nico's voice called to the horse, the vehicle lurched forward and they moved off slowly along the bivouac lines. For a long time Gabriel heard the rhythmic creak and the soft jingle of the harness. As he rolled over and looked at the two sleeping men beside him, he felt immeasurably grateful for their presence on the edge of the fire.

CHAPTER THREE

Old Jean got a good deal of gloomy satisfaction out of the muddled campaigning of that summer. He liked to sit by the fire when the company had bivouacked and lecture to conscripts on the errors of divisional and corps commanders. Doubtless it was bad for morale, but it was good for Jean. After an hour spent in explaining where the army had gone wrong, he would lie down to sleep in the best of spirits, determined to prove that tomorrow's blunders, once they had been committed, would be even more fatal to the success of the campaign.

Jean's reasoned pessimism became a byword in the ranks. Recruits, faced with an order to march five leagues in the rain and make a feint at a village occupied by twice as many Prussians, would say to one another: "This is all part of the plan. Sergeant Ticquet says that we always win if we don't start fighting until we're exhausted." Or, "This must be the right road. Sergeant Ticquet says it's the longest way round, and the general always prefers the longest way round."

Gabriel wondered if this was Jean's method of keeping the youngsters comparatively cheerful.

After the worthless victory at Bautzen, the logic of Jean's

favourite cliché, which had once been Napoleon's own, "Pursuit is more important than the victory," was clear to the least experienced conscript. The tired, half-starved French hurled themselves at ninety thousand Prussians and Russians and levered them out of a strong position, but for all the good it did the Imperial cause the men might as well have stayed in their hutments. The victors possessed no cavalry, so that the beaten enemy were able to withdraw at a leisurely pace and calmly await reinforcements. There were always plenty of reinforcements for Coalition troops. The French were employing cripples as transport drivers.

A temporary truce saved the French army from virtual collapse. Jean's comment that the respite was of far more use to the enemy than to themselves fell on indifferent ears. Three months of interminable night marches and constant hand-to-hand encounters with a numerically superior enemy had taken the fight out of youths who stood up to point-blank discharges of grape at Lützen. They had ceased to be interested in the acquisition of glory or decorations. All they wanted was to get home with a whole skin, and once the guns were silent desertions began to multiply alarmingly.

It was not long before an order came round to shoot one out of every ten men caught away from the regiment, but punishment was a matter of luck. Twenty men would be driven in by provost and mounted gendarmes, two to face a firing squad the following morning. The other eighteen would be cautioned and sent back to the ranks. Nevertheless desertions continued unchecked. The conscripts were agreed that this chance of survival was more favourable than if they remained for the renewal of hostilities in the autumn.

When there were no deserters to shoot, corps commanders resorted to all manner of stratagems for the sake of maintaining discipline and cohesion in the regiments. General Milhaud, the cavalryman, engaged a private to play the rôle of a man condemned to death for sticking a pair of shears into the belly of his horse. The regiment formed a hollow square to witness the execution. A grave was dug and the intended victim walked towards it, escorted by regimental drummers beating a solemn tattoo. The squad discharged their muskets and the man fell, but he must have imperfectly understood his instructions, for a moment later he climbed out of the grave and demanded his money. Dominique thought this the funniest thing he had ever witnessed and was helpless with laughter for over an hour. Jean, on the other hand, was furious at such a display of official buffoonery.

"We used to be soldiers," he told Gabriel, "then we became brigands, now we are mountebanks!"

After the expiration of the truce Austria joined the enemy Coalition and thousands of men in flat little shakos trooped across the plains to the Prussian cantonments. Bernadotte, once a French marshal, now Crown Prince of Sweden, was already there, and with him General Moreau, who had once led the ragged French republican armies to victory in the days when the distant strains of "The Marseillaise" tumbled professional armies back from the French frontier.

Just before the resumption of hostilities, when the company was back on the outskirts of the Saxon capital, a provost of the Alsace Gendarmerie came into camp asking for Sergeant Ticquet. He found Jean by the fire, skinning an undersized rabbit that he had trapped on the banks of the stream. The gendarme presented a roll of papers from his saddle-bag.

"I want you to come over to regimental headquarters," he said. "You're needed for identification!"

Jean handed the rabbit to Gabriel and told him to finish preparing it for the soup. He then climbed up behind the provost and trotted off through the lines.

Corps headquarters was established in a large farmhouse. On their arrival the gendarme was joined by two others, and the trio escorted Jean along a flagged passage to the buttery, a small whitewashed room lit by a single barred window too small to admit much light. In the buttery, which was being used as a detention cell, Jean saw a single prisoner sitting on his hams teasing a cockroach with a piece of straw. As the gendarme shut and relocked the door the man stood up. It was Nicholas.

The senior gendarme said: "Recognize him, Sergeant?" Jean said nothing. The prisoner smiled grimly.

"Hullo, Jean?"

The gendarme chuckled softly. "I've wasted your time, Sergeant!"

"You've wasted your own, Provost," said Nicholas. "You'll be sending me back to the battalion tomorrow and any officer, from the colonel down, would step up and kill the fatted calf for me. Are fatted calves still on the menu, Jean? I hear you've been having a bad time." He turned to the guards. "Why don't you ask the sergeant to sit down, Provost? I've killed most of the beetles!"

"Can I talk to him alone for a minute?" asked Jean. The provost hesitated a moment and Jean went on, "We've been together a long time, ever since Eylau."

The provost swung his keys. "All right, Sergeant, but no monkey tricks; I've had special orders about this joker!"

Jean nodded and the gendarmes retired, locking the door behind them.

The two men regarded one another silently for a moment. Finally Jean said: "What happened, Nicky?"

The schoolmaster gave one of his characteristic shrugs. Jean thought that he looked much fitter than when they had parted on the field of Lützen. His lean cheeks had filled out and his skin was tanned and healthy.

"We tried to be greedy," said Nicholas. "You were right, Jean, we shouldn't have taken the wagon as far as the frontier. I ought to have insisted, but Nico, well, you know what she's like about property!"

Jean began to prowl up and down the tiny room, two steps east, two west, biting savagely at the rough skin on the edge of his thumbnail. Finally he stopped and opened his mouth to speak, but Nicholas checked him with a wave of his hand.

"Too late for belly-aching, Jean. We tried and we had bad luck. I always have bad luck when I leave you. You'll die in your bed when all these pranks are ancient history."

"Where's Nico?"

"Looking for you." Nicholas grinned ruefully. "We always start looking for you when it begins to get dark!"

Jean ceased prowling. "For heaven's sake stop joking and think, man. There must be some way out; you've got a first-class record. I might even get hold of Ney!"

"I'm in debt to the marshal already, Jean. Remember the late Sr. Carolini and his mule at Busaco?"

A series of desperate plans jostled through Jean's brain: to return that night and file the window bars; to find Nicholette and bribe the provosts; to appeal to General Bonnet, to Bertrand or to any of the high-ranking officers under whom he and Nicholas had served in former campaigns. After all, Nicholas was no conscript whose place in the ranks anyone could fill. He was a veteran, and veterans were growing scarcer every day. Jean mentioned this, but Nicholas only grinned.

"It's because I'm a veteran that they'll shoot me. I don't have to tell you that; you knew it the moment you came in here. I've got a romantic last request, Jean."

The sergeant looked at him shrewdly and saw that although Nicholas was still trying to speak lightly, all trace of flippancy had gone.

"If it's about Nico, don't worry. She'll tag along with us again."

"It's not that; she can always look after herself, Jean. It's something more immediate."

"Well?"

"After the drumhead has passed sentence they'll pass me to the company for disposal. You'll have a sergeant-major round, picking a firing-squad."

"You aren't dead yet," growled Jean, but he stopped pacing nevertheless.

"Will you, Gabriel and Dominique volunteer? I'd like to be shot by somebody who can hit a cow at ten paces. Those conscripts you've got would puncture me in half a hundred places."

Jean turned and hammered on the door, which was hurriedly

308

unlocked. "I'm going to Michel Ney," he said and went out past the gendarmes, without looking back.

Gabriel was alone at the bivouac when Nicholette finally located the company. He looked up from the turning soup-kettle and saw her staring at him through the eddying smoke.

He had never seen her look so haggard and pale, not even when she ran up to them as they marched into Elbing in the spring. She looked as if at any moment she might fall forward into the fire. He jumped up and went round to her.

"Where's Jean?" she demanded.

"Over at the Sixth Corps headquarters; he's trying for Ney!"

Gabriel noticed that she had developed a nervous habit of jerking her head sideways, and with each jerk loose strands of hair tumbled across her cheek. She began sentences and forgot to finish them; all the time she was talking she clasped and un-clasped her long fingers. Sometimes their joints cracked under the pressure. The woman who had sat in the circle of firelight on Lobau and had driven down the main road from Burgos in the blinding heat of the sun was a thousand miles away. Standing there, squirming and twitching, she looked now more like an epileptic child.

"It was my fault . . ." she began. "Nicholas said sell the wagon . . . we couldn't get a good price . . . they aren't so short of trans-port down there . . . down on the frontier they're questioning everybody. . . ."

"Jean's gone for Ney," repeated Gabriel. It was all that he could think of to say.

She picked up a billet from the brushwood pile and tossed it onto the fire. It was a mechanical action, but to Gabriel it seemed at the same time grotesque.

"We planned all this at Elbing," she went on. "Nicholas thought of it long before that . . . outside Smolensk he first talked about it . . . I had the baby then . . ."

She turned on him eagerly. "You didn't see how good he was delivering that baby. I couldn't help much . . . he gave me a

309

cartridge-box to bite on . . . I left marks on it; his cartridge-box it was, but none of you could have done it so well; just like The Drummer, he was."

Gabriel knew about The Drummer. He had heard Old Jean and Nicholette discuss her round the camp-fire in Spain. She had been a cantinière who followed the Eighty-fifth and specialized in midwifery. They called her "The Drummer" because one of her husbands had been drum-major and when he was killed in the fighting round Landshut she had marched into action beating his bass drum, heading a charge that broke clean through the triple ranks of the Croats. Old Carla had often acted as an acolyte at The Drummer's confinements.

Gabriel poured the girl a measure of Danzig gin and sat beside her on Dominique's spread greatcoat, putting his arm across her thin shoulders. She shivered at his touch, but quietened a little. They sat there for a long time, saying nothing.

Just before dusk Old Jean limped in from the main road, and they saw by his face that his errand had been unsuccessful.

"Michel Ney isn't there," he told them. "That bastard Joubert had his adjutant kick me out."

He fumbled in his tunic pocket, pulling out a canvas bag. "I stole some coffee from the guardroom. That'll teach them not to leave it lying around."

Nicholette said nothing and Jean scratched his nose. His embarrassment made his voice harsh and querulous.

"Come on, Gabriel, let's get some water and make a brew."

They gathered up their mess tins and went off down to the stream. On the way Jean said: "Nicholas wants us to volunteer for the firing-squad."

Gabriel stared at him. "He's crazy!"

"He's not crazy; he's afraid of being holed in a dozen places by the conscripts."

They walked in silence as far as the stream. Finally Gabriel said: "I couldn't shoot Nicky!"

"Somebody's going to. I've seen firing-squads formed out of

recruits before. It's worse than killing pigs. Those babies can always take fire better than they can give it. You and Dominique have got to help me out; it's the last thing we can do for him."

"But Nicholette . . .?"

Jean swished the water round in his tin, watching the grit settle.

"Nicholette needn't know. They won't let her into the square."

Nicholas was lying on his straw, his hands clasped behind his head, when he heard the music. He recognized it instantly. It was a variation of the tune that Dominique had played on the British transport when they were going to England.

Nicholas smiled to himself and wondered how the farm boy had located the buttery window. He had probably pitched some yarn or other to the gendarmes and they had sent him round as a joke. The prisoner got up to look out, but it was dark now and he could see nothing more than a pattern of bivouac fires on the hillside opposite. It occurred to him that he would never see that familiar pattern again.

The tune squeaked on; Nicholas wedged his face between the short bars and called. Somewhere out in the darkness the fiddle stopped and Dominique hailed him. Nicholas could see the outline of a sentry's shako and shoulders a few feet from the aperture. The man shuffled and grounded his musket stock.

"It's an old comrade of mine playing the funeral march," said Nicholas as Dominique's dim figure doomed up. Then he called: "It's at reveille tomorrow, Dominique; better tell Jean!"

"Are they going to shoot you, Nicky?"

"You are, Dominique, and see that you aim straight. No gin tonight and get to sleep early!"

Dominique grinned in the darkness and Nicholas heard the snick of a musket sling. He called sharply: "You go back home, Dominique; you can't do anything. Go back to Jean, d'you hear me?"

The sentry shifted his position and Nicholas wondered if the man was aware that he stood in acute danger of losing his life. Apparently not, for he said drowsily, "Play that fiddle again; it sounds good!"

There was silence for a moment; then Nicholas heard the sling snap back on Dominique's shoulder. He stayed to play a few bars and then slouched away in the direction of the outbuildings.

"Plays that fiddle well," said the sentry, and, turning back to the window, "You wanting tobacco?"

"I've got some," replied Nicholas, "more than I've time to smoke!"

He settled back on the straw and lit up his short pipe. Deliberately he went back over the years—boyhood, university days in Berne and Zurich, lean days in Toulouse, the idyll at Cicero's, Camilla swimming in her lake, the night sky over Poland, sultry afternoons by the Danube, Nicholette's canteen wedding, the thirsty road down into Portugal, fragrant Devon hedgerows beside the Otter, the steady slop of the Channel wavelets against the smuggler's prow, the smell of despair in Moscow, east wind humming through the canvas as he bent over Nicholette on the road to Orsha.

He envied no one, regretted nothing. His review of the years was like a walk through a wood, with no one tree distinguishable from the others. He did not resent his sentence that afternoon; it was no more and no less than he had expected. He knew that Nicholette loved him as much as she could love any man, and was grateful for it, but he was unable to feel anxiety about her future. It had been a mistake to try for Switzerland. He knew before he had gone a league that Jean had been right; she could never settle to domestic life. He wondered if it would have been any different with himself, whether he could have gone back to teaching after shooting and bayonetting his way across Europe for so many years. He felt no sense of disgrace at the manner of death they had chosen for him. It was much the same as that he had courted ever since he walked into the Toulouse depot on the night he left Cicero's, and it was sure to be more certain and painless than the ends awaiting most of the men squatting round those pinpoints of light on the hillside. The majority would either be cut down in the cavalry charges of the future or receive a shower of grapeshot that knocked them aside and left them to gasp out their lives in the mud or on the operating tables of improvised clearing stations. He was no more ashamed of dying for deserting the Empire than he would have been of dying to sustain it a few more months. He saw clearly now that its collapse was a matter of time, possibly only of weeks, and he felt that the men who had condemned him were equally aware of this irony, all save the few diehards like Jean who would stamp about shouting *"Vive l'Empereur!"* until somebody told them that the Bourbons were back in the Tuileries. Then they would have to make their peace with the new régime or else sit playing at conspirators on half-pay in faubourg cafés.

Lying there in the foul straw, Nicholas had an odd sense of oneness with the dark sky, the stars and the night breeze blowing in from Bohemia. He wished for only one thing: he wished that Jean and Gabriel and young Dominique were coming with him. He had no real hope of finding Manny and Claude and Louis.

The sky was red behind the city roofs as the regimental square formed up in front of the crude hutments. The troops shivered in the early-morning ground mist, for the camp was pitched on marshy ground and until the sun rose men walked about shrouded to the knees in vapour.

Somewhere a drum was beating, the tattoo sounding soggy and indistinct as the drummer hammered a damp skin. Over by the town, cavalry trumpets brayed and thin smoke spiralled from fires built of damp wood.

The firing-squad, Jean, Gabriel, Dominique and two others, white-faced boys of barely eighteen, had assembled outside the barn used as headquarters and now stood about restlessly, awaiting the adjutant-major, who was inside drinking coffee—the officers were all new to the regiment and they did not think Jean's request to be included in the firing-squad a strange one. The sooner the tiresome business was over the better. The troops were restless during this period of inaction; the officers wished the campaign would either end or begin again.

The provost and his gendarmes conducted Nicholas to a broken-down wall that had once bordered a pigsty. The sergeant-major, who knew Nicholas only slightly, offered him a bandage for his eyes.

"Take the damned thing away," Nicholas told him. "I've brought my own bandage; it's in my pocket."

The sergeant-major felt in his prisoner's pocket and pulled out a dirty white handkerchief, puckered by needle and thread into a clumsy rosette.

"Pin it above the heart," said Nicholas. "There's a mist about and I can't swear to the marksmanship of all the firing-squad!"

"Veterans are doing it," the sergeant-major told him as he fumbled with the rosette.

"I know," said Nicholas. "They're comrades of mine."

The man looked surprised but said nothing. He made a tail out of a loose end of the handkerchief and tucked it firmly into the breast pocket of the prisoner's tunic. Nicholas glanced down.

"They ought to hit that at ten paces," he said.

The companies started to fall in round the pigsty, sullen at being ordered to parade before they could get their bivouac fires bright enough to cook breakfast. Nicholas saw them dimly, massed in close ranks on three sides of the crumbling wall.

Ahead of him, in the low mist, somebody shouted an order and the firing-squad tramped into view, marching in step with Old Jean in front. They formed up quite close to the sty and grounded arms. Then the adjutant-major and his drummer took their places at either end of the file.

Nicholas exchanged a single glance with Jean, but Gabriel and Dominique looked away, over the prisoner's shoulder towards the hills. The sun struggled to break through the mist, but soon abandoned the attempt and crept blindly along the eastern horizon, flickering for a moment on the spires of the town.

Sentence was read, a jumble of words indistinguishable to all but the principal actors. Nicholas shivered slightly and thought of accounts of executions that he had read in Cicero's library, where brave victims donned two sets of underclothing on the morning they were to suffer lest the witnesses might think they shivered from fear.

At last the adjutant-major stopped mumbling; the provost took over, barking the order to aim. The five men in the squad glanced at their priming, and their barrels went up reluctantly, their eyes squinting along them towards the rosette.

Nicholas wondered if he had acted wisely in wearing his tunic. He had cut off the brass buttons in case they deflected the balls, but most men were shot in their shirts. Involuntarily his mind went back to the executions in the square of a Spanish village, when he had stood where Jean was standing now, centre man in a file of five.

At that moment the sun triumphed unexpectedly over the mist, breaking through in thin rays and catching points of light on the levelled musket barrels. Five distinct jewels sparkled like a necklace girdling the squad.

Suddenly Nicholas felt winded, as though he had run full-tilt into a solid obstacle level with his stomach. The five jewels multiplied until they seemed to cover the distant city in a mantle of brilliant lights. . . .

Before the smoke had cleared away, before even the echo of the volley was lost among the hills, the right-hand side of the square bulged and a one-horse wagon forced its way through into the enclosure.

Jean's dull eyes left the man on the ground and swung round on the vehicle. The provost sheathed his sabre and ran towards the wall. The adjutant and his drummer crossed over to the woman driving the wagon.

Jean saw the officer exchanging words with her. Gabriel and Dominique had already moved away towards the bivouac. Out

315

of the corner of his eye Jean saw that Gabriel walked unsteadily, leaning on Dominique's forearm, dragging his musket by the barrel.

The adjutant came back to the provost, who was certifying the death of the man stretched on his side at the foot of the wall.

"She's his wife and she has an order for the body. Do you know anything about it?"

The provost nodded. "It's all in order," he said. "She saw the Old Man last night. Here, you!" he called to a group of conscripts who were slouching away from the fringe of the square. "Nobody's told you to dismiss; get the body into that wagon. Move to it!"

The conscripts obeyed clumsily, the man nearest the head turning away his face as he took hold of the shoulders. They lifted the body and carried it across to the vehicle. The woman had already let down the tailboard and spread a brown regulation blanket on the plank floor.

Jean slung his musket and touched Nicholette on the arm just as the conscripts jumped down and began to lift the tailboard back into position.

"Better come back to the bivouac, Nico."

She turned and looked straight at him. Before he could drop his gaze she spat, firmly and accurately, hitting him just above the mouth. Then she turned away, went round to the front of the wagon and called shrilly to the horse. Jean stood there dully, watching the vehicle pick its way through the dispersing groups of men, and his fingers brushed the sparse hairs of his grey moustache.

CHAPTER FOUR

The Grand Army was at bay on the outskirts of Leipzig.

Earlier in the campaign General Moreau, chatting at Allied Headquarters with another distinguished renegade, Crown Prince Bernadotte, had likened the French army to a maimed bear striking blindly at a pack of lithe wolves; but Moreau, because he was French, did not underestimate the bear's powers of recovery once it broke from the ring.

Moreau and Bernadotte sought one another's company a good deal at Allied conferences, neither taking much part in the discussions. Moreau was already regretting his decision to join the Coalition against his countrymen. Looking across at the French lines, he sometimes wondered whether any of the men he had led to victory twenty years ago were still in the bivouacs. Bernadotte's memories were much more green. Less than four years ago he had been leading a corps against his present allies at Wagram.

The veterans found it hard to forgive either man.

Moreau's doubts as to his wisdom in joining the Coalition were soon to be set at rest. A stray cannon ball ricochetted into a group of staff officers outside Dresden one morning and laid the ex-Republican general mortally wounded at the feet of the Czar. Moreau died like Turenne and Lannes and Bessières; but, unlike these men, he was not wearing a French uniform when the cannon ball cut away his legs. Bernadotte rode away thoughtfully. After that he was even more silent in the Allied council chamber.

By mid-October the French army had withdrawn to the villages ringing Leipzig.

Jean, Gabriel and Dominique lay in Mockern with the second company of the Eighty-seventh. They were strongly entrenched and did not doubt but that they could hold out against a dozen assaults of the Swedes and Blücher's Prussians camped in the plain beyond. For this was to be a defensive battle, at least until the edge had been worn off Allied enthusiasm. The voltigeurs were a mixed company now, half veterans, half conscripts, a unit differing from that of the early summer, when there were ten recruits to every experienced sharpshooter in the ranks. Most of the conscripts had disappeared during the summer fighting. Some, who had survived Lützen and Bantzen, had simply gone home, travelling by night with the instinct of homing pigeons, unchallenged for the most part by military police and gendarmes, whose units had now been swept into the firing-line. Many of the deserters reached their farms and cottages before the New Year, keeping out of sight until the First Restoration coaxed them into the open. The conscripts had stood the initial cannonades well enough, but they learned more quickly than the preceding generation, and those that had been eager for glory soon decided that one cannonade is very much like another.

Thirty days' marching and fighting in drenching rain had accounted for others, whose graves were dotted about the German fields. Phlegmatic ploughmen turned them up from time to time after the armies had trailed off to the west and spring crops were being sown. They were buried naked, for there was a serious shortage of draught horses in the Grand Army and thousands of new uniforms were still stacked in the Rhine depots awaiting distribution to the corps in the fields.

318

Gaps in the ranks were filled by veterans from the German garrisons. Ever since the end of the September armistice little columns had been trickling in from Bohemia, Württemberg and Bavaria, consisting of men who had fought well in the early campaigns and had earned their luck to settle in fortress towns. Many of them openly cursed the obstinacy of the Emperor, and as they sat round the fires at night there was talk that Jean would have considered blasphemous a year or two ago. Now even he said nothing, but spent most of his time foraging in the vegetable patches behind abandoned farms. He and his file lived extremely well by the standards of the Imperial infantry in the autumn of 1813.

Gabriel began sketching again during the lull, and several pictures from this period survived. There is one of a team of horses tugging a field-piece and its caisson up the slopes of a shallow ravine. The horses are thin and the gun is of small calibre. Artillerymen of the Coalition armies would have thought it hardly worth while bringing into action. Gabriel also sketched a memory impression of Nicholas facing the firing-squad, but this odd piece of work is obviously unfinished. The artist has shown the five musket barrels radiating like the spokes of a wheel, while the man in the hub of the picture has no features to identify him as Nicholas. The only clear part of the sketch is the background, showing the spires and battlements of Dresden. It is difficult to understand why Gabriel left it in the book. The sketch has a laconic title—"Dresden Parade."

The night before the first day of the final battle they talked about Nicholette. They had not mentioned her since she had driven off with Nicholas's body. Gabriel suddenly demanded to know where she had buried her husband, and Jean, without looking up from his soup, replied: "She bought a plot in the little churchyard near the Gross Garten. I went there, soon after she'd moved off."

Gabriel had heard from some of the men about the incident

at the tailboard when Nicholette had spat in the sergeant's face. He said nothing, but he wondered how Jean felt about it, whether he was enraged or philosophically indifferent. The girl had as completely disappeared as if she had been shot and buried with Nicholas. Gabriel wondered, as he had wondered in England, whether they would ever see her again, or if she had driven off to find peace in Switzerland by herself.

He felt curiously depressed by Nicholette's departure. The gradual whittling down of their group, its reduction now to a mere trio, seemed to him symbolic of the process that was going on in every battalion. New faces appeared and disappeared; the old spirit of unity that had existed right up to the day when they marched out of Moscow was gone, sped on the wings of triumphs that had once been yesterday's bivouac topic and now seemed as remote as the epic of Roncevalles.

Across the fire Dominique still fiddled, while the recruits lay listening apathetically. The veterans cleaned their firearms, methodically still but without the conscious showmanship that had been a feature of earlier eve-of-battle scenes. It occurred to Gabriel that Dominique's doleful tunes and Jean's drooping moustaches were all that was left of the past, these and the eternal undertones of a hundred thousand men living in the open.

The Grand Army was awaiting extinction.

Soon after dawn on October 16th, 1813, the Allies attacked all along the line. Blücher, who flung himself on Mockern, saw his leading files carried away by the murderous volleys of the French, firing from behind cover. Time after time the furious Prussian infantry recoiled while Napoleon brought up the Guard, determined to break the enemy centre and snatch a victory before weight of numbers or shortage of ammunition compelled the French to withdraw over the Elster and cut their way back to the Rhine. He must have known that the effort would be useless. In spite of substantial gains during the first day's fighting, the second found new wedges of Prussians and Austrians advancing over the ground piled with the previous day's dead.

Russian and Austrian reserves arrived by the thousand and Bernadotte's Swedes moved up to support the hard-hit Blücher. The Emperor drew in his lines and sent Bertrand over to Weissenfels to secure the line of retreat to the Elbe.

The French withdrew sullenly, leaving the villages they had occupied piles of smoking rubble. Jean stayed behind for a few moments to fill his haversack in a field of unripened beetroot.

On the third day the Allies put over a quarter of a million men in the field, and the French positions on the edge of the city became untenable.

Jean, Gabriel and Dominique fired until their muskets were too hot to hold. Conscripts lay on their backs to load for the three veterans, and no enemy came within twenty yards of the low stone wall they occupied in the garden of the elegant suburban dwelling-house to which they had retreated. Soon after noon there came a short lull broken by confused shouting to the right.

"Maybe they've got through; crawl over and find out," Jean told Gabriel, addressing him over his shoulder.

Gabriel ran along under the garden wall and through the house to the street. He was just in time to see thousands of the Saxons who had been guarding their right wing march into the enemy skirmishing points firing their muskets in the air. The entire corps had deserted.

He hurried back to the garden and told Jean what had occurred. The sergeant wiped the powder sweat from nis forehead and slung his musket.

"That's good," he grunted. "At least we know where we stand!" He addressed the staring conscripts, "Get back out of here and make for the city wall where our reserves are mustered!"

Gabriel went after the recruits, reflecting that Jean's comment had been made by almost every soldier in history when faced with the consequences of an ally's desertion in the field. At least they knew where they stood! It seemed poor consolation for the loss of an army corps.

Making for one of the town gates, they saw Nansouty's cuirassiers ride out with the Young Guard, the last available reserves, launched with the object of remedying the Saxon desertion. Inevitably the counter-attack was beaten back, but the survivors withdrew in good order, filing through the narrow streets towards the single bridge over the Elster. As dusk fell, the Allies closed on the town, firing from the windows and roofs of houses that had been barricaded by citizens against the French, but were opened to the first Allied troops to cross the city boundaries. The confusion in the city centre was indescribable and the din hellish. Soon after sunset fighting virtually ceased, since no man had sufficient elbow-room to ply the bayonet.

The French columns began to defile across the bridge, horse, foot, artillery and baggage, moving slowly, interminably, like a ghost of the ragged cavalcade that had recrossed the Berezina less than a year before.

The survivors of the second company bivouacked on the eastern bank, secure for an hour or so from the advance of the enemy. Not even artillerymen firing grape could have forced a passage just then through the main streets approaching the bridge.

Jean drew Gabriel and Dominique aside. "We'd better get out of here. Alone!"

Gabriel listened incredulously, finding it difficult to believe that Jean was proposing to abandon the wretched conscripts and dodge away in the darkness towards the bridge. The sergeant must have divined his thoughts, for he snapped: "I told you in Russia that I wouldn't start it all over again! These children are nothing to me. Suppose I did get them over the river? How long do you think they'd last?"

Gabriel said nothing. Dominique slung his musket decisively. "Let's move!" he said.

They edged off into the darkness and Gabriel followed, casting a last look at the miserable little fire around which the half-dozen conscripts were trying to boil a saucepan of rice and sliced beetroot. They were working quietly and methodically in the manner taught them by Jean when they had first joined the company four months ago. Their deliberation now was pathetic, for they behaved as though they were preparing supper at home

322

after a hard day in the fields. Behind them the ear-splitting discharges of artillery moved regularly nearer and a dull roar of despair rose from the embattled city.

The three voltigeurs left the boulevard and crept cautiously along the river bank, heading for the column that surged around the first span of the bridge. Bomb-shells, fired from a battery in the Halle suburb, had set fire to a row of houses facing the river gardens, and in the light of the flames they saw that the mob of men between the bridge and themselves numbered several thousands, stragglers of all units. Baggage wagons abandoned by their drivers blocked the approaches and had to be manhandled into the river. It took the three men the greater part of the night to reach the bridgehead.

At first light the tumult multiplied from the direction of the city centre, and enemy skirmishers began to infiltrate along the river bank. Stragglers from Poniatowski's corps and Macdonald's rearguard, left behind to cover the remainder of the army's passage over the Elster, joined the vast press of men waiting to cross.

About an hour after dawn, when stray shots were beginning to fall into the crowd, the voltigeurs heard a deafening explosion immediately to their front. A wave of panic seized the men around them as, within seconds, the truth became known. The engineers, alarmed by the rapid advance of Austrian and Prussian skirmishers, had blown the bridge. When the smoke cleared away Frenchmen on the town side of the river looked across the water to see a ragged gap in the centre span of the structure.

Old Jean was unmoved.

"We'd have done better to stay with our unit," he grunted.

Dominique spoke and even this disaster could not efface his habitual grin. "I was in Halle hospital once," he said. "I used to walk up the river looking for fish. I never found any, but there's fish there, they told us, up by the ford!"

It was a long speech for Dominique and when he had finished he looked slightly embarrassed and glanced down at his feet. Jean swore.

"Ford! Are you sure there's a ford?"

Dominique nodded.

"How far up?"

"Short march."

Jean reflected a moment, then began to bellow at the top of his voice.

"March north to the ford! Get to the ford, all of you!"

The men nearest Jean stopped cursing. The crowd began to surge slowly along the river bank, passing the end of the broken bridge and scattering a knot of Austrian grenadiers who had worked their way round the French rearguard and appeared from the far side of the town. Progress was easier when the crowd thinned. Dominique led the way, musket at the ready, slopping through the mud at the water's edge and scaling the network of slime-coated breakwaters and mooring posts.

There was little or no opposition for the moment. The bulk of the enemy advance guard was still battling in the centre of the town. Word had got through to Macdonald's companies that the bridge was blown, and they were staying on, half-crazy with rage, to fight it out in the houses of the town. So the shambling procession moved along the bank until Dominique stopped, a short distance past the second curve beyond the bridge.

"About here," he told Jean.

They stared across the river and saw the tattered columns of the French moving slowly along the road parallel to the bank. Gabriel could guess what confusion existed among the men over there; but they were the lucky ones, they had at least put a river between themselves and the enemy.

It did not look much like a ford. The river was not wide, but the current flowed swiftly. Men began to throw off their equipment and toss aside arms, and when the first few entered the water, watchers from the bank saw the water rise over their shoulders. Soon they were swept off their feet and only two strong swimmers reached the farther bank.

The crowd behind began to curse again, while some of the

stragglers who had followed the voltigeurs roundly abused Dominique.

"It's a good enough ford for a porpoise!"

They moved on upstream, occasionally wading out waist deep and sounding the river bed with their muskets.

Dominique became sulky. "I tell you I forded here, Jean," he complained.

"Maybe you did, in high summer," said Jean.

Suddenly there was a burst of firing from houses close to the river, and a body of horsemen forced their way through the indecisive crowd to the water. Gabriel recognized two of the marshals, Prince Poniatowski and the Scotsman Macdonald. Poniatowski had been wounded and was supported in his saddle by an aide-de-camp. A troop sergeant of the Polish lancers rode up to Jean.

"How deep is the river at this point?" he demanded.

Jean shrugged. "My comrade here says there is a ford, but several men have been drowned trying to cross."

"It's either that or the Prussian bayonets," said the lancer, turning back to the two marshals. After a moment's deliberation the group moved forward, coaxing their exhausted horses into the stream. At the same instant volley-firing commenced from the houses about half a musket shot along the embankment, scattering the fugitives between the river and the town in all directions. The horsemen bunched into the stream, the two marshals and their staff in the lead. Jean chewed his moustache for a moment, glancing upstream and then towards the town. He made a rapid decision.

"Into the water, both of you, and get hold of a tail!"

The three of them plunged into the current. Several of the horses, terrified by the uproar immediately behind them, reared in the shallows, resisting the shouts and spurs of their riders. The three voltigeurs seized a tail apiece, other infantrymen followed their example, and the struggling mass blundered forward. Jean and Gabriel were lucky in their choice. Their horses fought the current to midstream, then settled down to swim diagonally across. Dominique's horse floundered and lost way, but the farm boy hung on, turning and twisting in an effort to dodge the thrashing hooves. Its rider lost his seat half-way across, and, freed of his weight, the horse quickly recovered, breasted the flow and finally struggled up on the far bank. Dominique staggered clear of the shallows before collapsing. He had been kicked twice, once in the shoulder and once in the chest. He lay on his face in the ooze, and a party of dragoons who had forded the river lower down dragged him up the bank, hailing Jean as the sergeant waded ashore.

About half the Poles had succeeded in crossing, but among the missing was Marshal Poniatowski. His aide-de-camp cantered about in a distracted manner, while Marshal Macdonald collected a party and rode off downstream in an effort to recover the body. Over on the other side the fugitives had disappeared, but Austrian skirmishers were standing on the embankment taking potshots at swimmers. Jean saw them as he ran over to Dominique.

"Look at those bastards," he shouted. "They've run away from us forty times since Lodi!"

On the French side the confusion was scarcely less than in the town. Men of all units scrambled up to the road and joined the rabble pressing westward. Here and there a field officer stood on the bank, trying to infuse some sort of order into the retreat, but all such attempts were hopeless. Three days' continuous fighting and the pitiless slaughter in the town had demoralized the battalions; their one thought was to put distance between themselves and the Prussians. A new note had entered the war since the resumption of hostilities. With the whole of Europe now on their side, the Prussians were determined to make it a war of extermination. They hated better than the Austrians and the Russians, and the poet Körner's songs were showing grim dividends.

They found Dominique where the dragoons had left him. He was unconscious, blue in the face. Jean forced some brandy down his throat, and the farm boy's eyelids fluttered. He looked up at them stupidly, unable to speak.

They stripped him and examined the huge purple bruise on the right side of his chest. Probing cautiously, Jean's thick fingers found a displaced rib. Dominique began to shiver violently, and the movement seemed to cause him intense pain. Blood flowed freely from the gash on his shoulder, but Gabriel saw that this was a mere flesh wound; the injuries meant that Dominique would be unable to march.

Old Jean began to fume again. He cursed the medical orderlies for never being where their services were in demand, cursed the engineers for blowing the bridge so precipitately, abandoning a third of the army to the enemy's bayonets, and cursed Nicholette for driving off with a dead man when her wagon would have been of inestimable service to the living. Gabriel had never seen him in this mood before. Throughout all the disasters of the Peninsular and Russian campaigns he could not once remember the old sergeant losing his temper and that characteristic sense of balance which made him such an efficient N.C.O. He bent down and dressed Dominique as gently as he could. They had no bandages, no salves, no hope of getting the man on his feet to continue the march towards Erfurt.

Gabriel went up to the road and watched the rout. He had been there nearly an hour before a small convoy of wagons lurched past. He approached them hopefully, but a glance showed him that the interiors were already crammed with wounded of all ranks. The drivers looked neither left nor right, but sullenly flogged their horses through the press. At each jolt screams came from the men under the canopies.

Presently a riderless horse struggled up the bank. Gabriel saw from its saddle-cloth and beaded holsters that it had belonged to a cuirassier unit, probably Nansouty's, which had made the futile charge after the Saxon desertion the previous day. He caught it listlessly and led it over to Jean, who was plying Dominique with more brandy. The injured man tried to rise, but fell back with a sharp yelp of agony, clutching at his side.

"It's his ribs," said Jean, more calmly. "He'd be all right if he could lie up for a week or two."

"There's a farm higher up," said Gabriel. "Maybe we could find a cart or something."

"Stay here and watch him," muttered Jean. "I'll take the horse!"

A doubt pricked Gabriel like the point of a dart. Two days ago the possibility of Jean taking the horse and moving off down the road by himself would have been absurd, but now it was different. Jean's conscripts were still somewhere on the other side of the river, most likely dead round the ruins of their fire, at best prisoners being herded in batches through the reeking streets.

The doubt passed and Gabriel felt as though he had been caught out in a schoolboy lie. Jean swung himself into the saddle, trotting off towards a group of buildings on the far side of the road. An hour later he returned, towing a two-wheeled cart of the type used by German farmers for the transport of pigs and manure.

It was an ungainly little vehicle with solid wheels. Gabriel thought that it looked like one of those war chariots used by the barbarians against Roman legions. He had seen a crude illustration of one in an old pictorial history that Nicholas had found among the books in the doctor's house at Moscow. The cart had no springs, its axle creaked monotonously, but it nevertheless seemed to be the means of restoring Jean's confidence in himself. He bustled about making a litter and wedging it against the unplaned sides of the chariot. When this was done he checked the rope harness; then, between them, he and Gabriel lifted Dominique onto the stretcher. They joined the stream of fugitives with their faces towards Erfurt, Jean leading the horse, Gabriel marching in the rear, trying to keep his eyes from the contorted features of Dominique whenever the wheels crunched over a pitted section of road. There were many pits. The Saxons had not been greatly interested in road-making.

The beaten army trailed across the territory of its former ally, the King of Saxony, rallying somewhat at Markrundstadt before traversing the field of Lützen. No effort was spared by the marshals to help forward the process of reorganization. Macdonald, with a fresh uniform and a borrowed charger, galloped up and down the line of retreat promising rest and refit in Erfurt. They crossed the Saale at Weissenfels and crawled towards the arsenals of the Elbe, where the grumblers were disappointed for once. There were clothing, rations and ammunition in abundance, enough for an army of two hundred thousand.

Dominique did not get as far as Erfurt. For five days he lay groaning in the chariot while they pushed on, Jean beating off all stragglers who attempted to board the vehicle. Perhaps Jean's diagnosis had been correct and Dominique's injuries were limited to a cut on the shoulder and a couple of broken ribs; or perhaps the blow of the iron-shod hoof had caused a more serious internal injury. Gabriel never knew the truth, but marched stolidly along behind the cart and watched the farm boy grow weaker each day. His rational periods became rarer and by the time they trundled into Weissenfels they had ceased altogether.

The two voltigeurs held a conference, weighing chances and eventualities as they had done when there were seven voices to contribute to the discussion. Gabriel was inclined to agree with the sergeant as to the futility of conveying Dominique any farther along the road to the west. In his present condition it seemed doubtful whether the wounded man would survive another day's journey.

The pursuit was slackening, and here and there along the road dressing-stations were being organized. At this distance from Leipzig it seemed unlikely that the fury of the Prussians would extend to wreaking vengeance on abandoned wounded. Injured and sick men, gathered together in barns, were left in charge of such of the medical staff as were still with their regiments. Surgeons and orderlies accepted this desertion as part of the luck of the game. They scoured the small towns and farms for vegetables and medical supplies, resigning themselves to the inevitability of being made prisoners when the Allies moved on the Elbe. To stay with the army meant more fighting in the spring; to remain behind meant life, at least for the time being. The war could not last forever; few thought that it could even last through the winter.

They left Dominique in a barn at Weissenfels. The tall building was crammed with wounded, and field amputations were going on in the yard outside. There was straw and a soup issue—more than Jean and Gabriel could provide in the chariot. They cut the harness ropes and sold the horse to a major of the chasseurs for a pound of tobacco and twelve potatoes. Neither Jean nor Gabriel was at home in the saddle; they had been marching for too many years.

The remnants of the second company, remustered on the banks of the Saale, were lumped together with other fragments, the whole forming a regiment of quarter-strength. Just before the column moved off, Jean and Gabriel went over to the barn to take a last look at Dominique.

He was lying flat on his back between a hussar with his right leg shorn away and a cheerful old corporal of Flying Artillery, whose head wound did not prevent his relishing the pipe of tobacco Jean handed to him. Dominique's breathing was noisy and his face heavily flushed. Gabriel, looking down at him, thought it odd that the boy should have survived all the rigours of the Russian retreat to go down under the kick of a horse and a wetting in the Elster.

The philosophic artilleryman nodded towards the oilskin bulge in Dominique's pack.

"What's in there, comrade?" he asked hopefully. "More tobacco?"

"A fiddle," Gabriel told him. "He was good at it!"

The artilleryman rolled over and pulled the bundle from the knapsack. The oilskin had preserved it from the water. He drew the tiny bow once across the strings, laid it down, adjusted the bridge and the squat pegs, then tried again.

"I used to fiddle myself," he told Jean.

He began to scrape an army ditty, a jerky little melody that Gabriel had never heard Dominique attempt, although he had often heard it sung on the road. Dominique had usually preferred his own music.

"You can have the fiddle if they bury him," Jean said and turned abruptly for the open door, Gabriel following.

The tune went on and someone across the barn began to sing in a high, cracked tone. Dominique stirred, but his eyes did not open. One or two other voices took up the words, and the song followed the voltigeurs out across the yard, past the busy surgeons and their orderlies, down to the river bank where the tatters of the Eighty-seventh were waiting, blowing on their hands amidst their piled arms.

Neither Jean nor Gabriel saw or heard of Dominique again. After the unit had defiled over the bridge and was moving briskly along the broad metalled road towards Erfurt, Jean spoke.

"He might have been short of wits, but he was a damned good soldier. With a few thousand like him we could hold the Rhine forever."

Gabriel thought the comment as good an epitaph as any.

CHAPTER FIVE

They had been marching along French roads for a long time now and for the past three days had been camping in the woods of Fontainebleau.

Jean found it strange after all these years to be using his own language to local peasants and billet-holders. It was twenty years since a battle had been fought on French soil.

The odd thing about this campaign was the fact that they had won half a dozen victories in a row. Every engagement seemed to end in the rout of an enemy, but there always came another battle within forty-eight hours. It seemed to Jean that every able-bodied man from the Rhine to Moscow was in arms against them. They sought out and dispersed columns of Russians, Prussians, Bavarians, Saxons, Swedes and, of course, the inevitable Habsburg troops with the low-crowned shakos. They hardly troubled to fire at these last, who still ran into the woods at the sound of a French trumpet. The Bavarians and the Saxons were not much trouble, either, only the Russians fought with the old, familiar obstinacy of Eylau and Friedland, while the Prussians were as murderous and vindictive as ever, particularly when they had the advantage of numbers.

Jean, who sometimes tried to estimate the strength of the French battalions, could never make them total more than fifty thousand, despite an occasional trickle of reinforcements from the south or the north-east. He supposed Paris to be strongly held, and old Augereau was said to be lurking down in Lyons with another veteran corps. If this were true Jean felt it time that the seedy old rascal shook off his torpor and marched north again.

Then there was conscientious Davout, locked up in Hamburg, and erratic Saint-Cyr, surrounded in Dresden, both with thousands of men who might have forced a decisive action here at home. Jean could not imagine why these corps had been abandoned, unless it was due to the speed and unexpectedness of the Leipzig retreat. In the old days the Emperor had never left his columns sprawled about Europe in this fashion; he had always sacrificed everything for the sake of concentration. Jean himself recalled marching a day and a night with Davout's corps in order that it might be present at Austerlitz.

At the same time Jean was certain that there was nothing wrong with the manner in which the Emperor was fighting this final campaign. On the contrary, the Old Man had never been so nimble in taking advantage of clumsy dispositions. Time and again the French troops were turned out in the night, hustling along roads that seemed empty of the enemy, until the rattle of musketry advertised their presence just ahead. When this happened, there was always a successful charge by the Grand Army's laughably small force of cavalry, resulting in enemy withdrawals all along the line. In this way the little army tumbled the invaders out of town after town, position after position, but still no decisive result was obtained. After searching the slain for cartridges, they were always off again the following day to find a fresh column to trounce.

Jean had no illusions left about the ultimate end of it all. Here in Fontainebleau a persistent rumour circulated the fires to the effect that the Czar was already in Paris, but most of the men had gone beyond depression. They had enough to eat, since the countryside was friendly, and that meant a great deal after the Russian and German campaigns of the two previous years. European politics had long ceased to interest them.

Someone who came into the camp announced that Paris had definitely surrendered, and that the English were driving Soult over the Pyrenees and up into the Dordogne area.

Gabriel and the other Gascons were mildly interested in this piece of news, wondering what the girls in Agen would think of the Highlanders' kilts and the pink, clean-shaven faces of the redcoats.

In the meantime the tired infantry were glad of their rest in the forest. Spring had come to the deep glades of Fontainebleau, and the trim gardens surrounding the old palace were bright with flowers. After the winter rains dry firewood was difficult to find, but Old Jean remedied this by ordering the demolition of some outbuildings close to their bivouac. Painted summer-houses were torn down, and the boarding blazed cheerfully. The men sat by their fires, idly speculating about the future.

One morning early in April, orders came round to parade for an Imperial review. Most of the troops did not grouse, preferring a review to another night march, and they all spent an hour or two patching clothes, polishing tarnished brass or cleaning their arms.

The second company of the Eighty-seventh had long since ceased to exist. It had melted away for the third time in two years at the battles of Brienne, Montereau, Craonne, Laon and a dozen other engagements. During March all the surviving light infantrymen had been embodied in the Guard. Old Jean made a joke about it when they took up quarters alongside the famous bearskins.

"It's taken me fifteen campaigns to get into this outfit," he told Gabriel, "and now it's too late. I think we've fought our last battle."

Gabriel celebrated the occasion with a sketch—of Jean sitting on a drum talking to two grenadiers, who are regarding him cryptically, as though they are not quite sure whether incorporation with line infantry can be justified even by national disaster.

The uniforms, even of the grenadiers, are much the worse for wear, while Jean looks more like a brigand than a sergeant of the Guard. Through the trees, beyond the trio, one catches a glimpse of the old palace. The sketch is dated "March 30th, 1814."

The review was a great success. Napoleon, riding his famous Arab barb Marengo, passed slowly along the shabby ranks, smiling faintly at the shouts of *"Vive l'Empereur!"* There was nothing ironical about the cheers. Perhaps they were even more spontaneous than in the past, for most of the men realized that they were unlikely to have another chance of acclaiming a man who was still popular with every one of them. The veterans did not hold the Emperor responsible for the present disasters, but found scapegoats, each according to his disposition. Some blamed blundering marshals; some accused men like Murat and Marmont, who were already recognized as traitors; some thought that Napoleon's own family had disgraced him, while others, like Old Jean and most of the veterans, were content to write off the invasion of France as the result of overwhelming odds. A nation, they said, could fight a continent for ten years, but not for twenty. There was a limit to its supplies of manpower, which had been reached and passed in Saxony the previous summer. The veterans forgot the Russian campaign, forgot their grumbling round the Dresden camp-fires when it became known that the Emperor had refused to compromise. Napoleon had cleared himself by his masterly handling of the current campaign and they felt that his obstinacy the year before was more than justified in view of the recent treachery of those whom he had raised to exalted rank. Many of the men present at the review wore the Legion of Honour; their crosses would be treasured until they died, no matter what happened to Napoleon and his Empire.

All men are reluctant to destroy their own idols. It is so much easier to make excuses for them.

Cavalry piquets brought them definite news—of Marshal Marmont's surrender to the enemy. There was talk of marching south, of picking up Augereau at Lyons, Soult in the south-west, and continuing the fight behind the Loire or the Alps, but nobody really imagined that this course would be followed. Augereau would not stir, Soult was too far away and in any case Fontainebleau was almost surrounded.

The troops heard about the abdication, but took the news calmly. One or two whose memories reached back to faubourgs of Paris during the Terror were a trifle alarmed at the prospect of a Bourbon restoration, but their comrades soon put these fears to rest. It had all happened so long ago that the Bourbons would be certain to grant a general amnesty. France might be exhausted and the Grand Army practically non-existent, but both had such a formidable record that even the Bourbons would have to exercise tact in dealing with veterans.

The men sat about, smoking or chasing the small game which abounded in the woods. Somebody issued an order announcing the entry of the Bourbons into Paris, and the older men chuckled when they heard of the enthusiastic public welcome. So many of them could remember the grey January day, twenty-one years before, when the same Paris boulevardiers had gathered in the Place de la Révolution to acclaim a king's execution.

"This is the best life after all, Gabriel," said Jean. "We do the same thing every day and I'm too old to change now."

But even Jean had to change as everything changed about him.

One morning in late April the Guard was mustered in the palace courtyard and the Emperor rode along its ranks on horseback. It was not a review, but a parting ceremony. Napoleon embraced the commanding officer and made a brief farewell speech. Old Jean wept, while beside him Gabriel stared straight ahead, his eyes fixed on the extraordinary scene that was taking place. He found himself quite unable to decide whether Napoleon's emotion was genuine, assumed or merely self-induced. After the Emperor had kissed the eagles, Gabriel glanced beyond Jean towards the serried ranks of veterans. There was hardly a dry eye. The men looked far more tense than they did when facing fifty squadrons of cavalry.

Gabriel's fingers itched for pencils and brushes. Here, he thought, is something of the answer to it all. They crowded round the main gate and cheered the Emperor on the first stage of his journey to exile. It was a curious end to all that marching and fighting from Moscow to the Tagus.

They were paraded again the following morning and moved off along the road to Paris. Gabriel, who had marched into four capital cities, had never visited his own. His senses thrilled with expectation, but Old Jean was not in the mood for talking and they marched, for the most part, in gloomy silence.

Outside the Paris barriers, when some of the bystanders gave them a cheer, Jean momentarily brightened. He turned to Gabriel. "What now? Will you go home?"

Gabriel glanced at the lean face beside him. The cheekbones were so prominent that they appeared to be pushing through the taught skin. The moustaches, as meagre as ever notwithstanding his enrolment in the Guard, drooped with the same touch of melancholy. Something rose in Gabriel's throat, a full tide of affection for the scarred veteran at his side. Memories fell into position like the figures running to join a parade, recollections that buckled their belts and adjusted their haversacks as they took their place in the muster of the years: Old Jean handing out his first bowl of soup in the Lobau bivouac. Jean rejoining the column on the Burgos road, with a haversack full of onions dug from a cottage garden. Jean swinging a pick in a Devon trench, Jean rallying the company when it had been isolated by the Russian light cavalry outside Smolensk. Jean, always resourceful, always cool, always able to produce a handful of rice and a pinch of salt for the communal kettle; Jean shepherding his file through the burning streets of Moscow and brushing the ashes from his bloodshot eyes. Jean plodding through the snow with the blood of a half-cooked bear on his moustaches. Jean at a loss on the banks of the Elster, Jean standing with his back to Dresden's spires and aiming at Nicholas's rosette. The others had come and gone. Gabriel recalled and cherished their characteristics, Manny's gay laugh, Louis's good temper, Nicholas's quiet cynicism, Dominique's doglike fidelity, but Jean was different, he was

337

the epitome of them all, of all they had endured, of all the leagues that they had tramped together in the last five years.

Gabriel reflected that the man had been grafted onto him, like flesh onto a wound, had become a daily habit like the weight of a musket on his right shoulder, the smell of burned powder and the shuffle of infantry on the march.

Home? How much did the people of Agen mean to him when measured against Jean?

Gabriel considered his own future. If they were discharged, as was currently anticipated, what could he do? How could he earn a living? He had a small amount of his aunt's money left, enough to keep him a year, perhaps two, in moderate circumstances. He knew Jean to be penniless.

Jean said: "I can't get over that gipsy I met in Brabant when I was a boy. She insisted that I'd die on a battlefield, and here I am, with the war over and nothing but scars to support a pension claim!"

They marched down towards the incomplete Arc, raised to commemorate twenty years of unbroken triumphs. The bourgeois stared at them curiously, as if they had been a circus troupe, and Jean noticed that everyone sported a white cockade, emblem of the Bourbons.

"We'll stick together, Jean, no matter what happens," said Gabriel.

As the battalion swung down the Elysée a group of bystanders shouted at the bandsmen.

"Play 'Henri Quatre'!" called someone.

But the drums and fifes of the Guard were silent. The bandsmen did not know any Royalist tunes.

PART SIX

The Sambre

CHAPTER ONE

Old Jean became a silent spectator of the Paris festivities when he and Gabriel settled in the lodging they had found behind the Invalides. Jean thought that the crowds in the street might have been celebrating a national triumph instead of a national disgrace. He did not pretend to understand the air of gaiety that pervaded the capital during the first two months of the Restoration. He had been in the ranks far too long to realize that soldiering is abhorrent to most men and that, whilst they will cheer lustily for every victory gained in a far-off country, the prospect of donning a uniform themselves and of charging a battery needs somewhat more compensation than a few evanescent monuments and a wagon train of pilfered art treasures. The average Parisian was quite willing to restore pictures and statues to Venice and Vienna, even to find another name for the Bridge of Jena, if it meant that the shadow of conscription would be lifted from himself and his family, and that he could talk of glorious campaigning days without having to contribute to their lustre.

The Bourbons made every mistake it was possible to make. They renamed the Imperial Guard the Royal Guard and forced soldiers, most of whom had never been to church in their lives, to attend mass every Sunday. They distributed the cross of the Legion of Honour, coveted by every veteran who had the luck to win it, to unblooded young popinjays of ancient houses who gaily donned the brilliant plumage of the Household troops. They were miserly with pensions for the crippled and the orphaned. They placed thousands of the finest officers in Europe on half-pay, standing by when returned émigrés sneered at soldiers who had marched into half the capitals of Europe during the last twenty years. They imported a glut of English goods, throwing whole populations of manufacturing towns like Lyons out of employment. Despite all this, the ageing King Louis had good intentions, but he could do little to curb the arrogance of the aristocrats who had sulked in exile whilst Frenchmen were tumbling down autocracies north, south, east and west.

Even so, the Bourbons might still have been welcomed had it not been for the action of the Allies in sending home one hundred and fity thousand prisoners of war within a few weeks of Napoleon's abdication. From the Allies' viewpoint it was a stupid policy; from the point of view of the Bourbons it was suicidal.

The freed veterans tramped and begged their way to the frontiers from every direction. They came from the fortresses of Germany and Austria, moved like a tide of scarecrows across Central Europe from Russia, marched down from the north with Davout's hardbitten infantrymen and up from the south with the wreck of Soult's Peninsula divisions. They came in by boat from the English hulks, with old scores to pay and plenty of questions to ask. When they met and mingled with the men who had fought in the final campaign, the sum total of their conversation over the café tables was, "Ah, but this could never have happened if we had been there!"

Gabriel, a realist by now, knew that it would have happened in any case. Six corps of veterans could not have expelled the invaders from France whilst there were traitors like Talleyrand and Marmont scheming in Paris. But Gabriel knew better than to contradict the veterans, especially when Old Jean endorsed their arguments.

It was a difficult summer for the men of the Grand Army. The civilians called them brigands, and all but the marshals, who were flattered and courted, found it difficult to avoid a round of duels. High-ranking officers like Vandamme and Drouet were insulted almost daily in the salons, and the crowning folly of the Bourbons was to appoint General Dupont Minister of War. The veterans smashed glasses in the cafés when the *Moniteur* announced this appointment. They remembered that Dupont had been the first French general to surrender, as long ago as 1808 when the eagles were untarnished, and that his incompetence or worse had condemned thousands of Frenchmen to rot in Spanish prison camps. Too late the mistake was made known in the Tuileries and Marshal Soult was given the post. By that time the damage had been done; every man who had served in the army regarded the preferment of Dupont as a personal insult. The unemployed men of the Grand Army were very sensitive in the summer of 1814

Gradually the mood of Paris changed. The Cossacks and the Uhlans went home, but the rancour their presence had occasioned remained. Soon it was unpatriotic to smile and the atmosphere of the city became oppressive. People who could remember said that it was similar to the atmosphere of the capital in the last days of the Monarchy, when the Bastille was still standing.

The secret police of the Bourbons were painstakingly active.

It was during this period that Gabriel, with time heavy on his hands, taught the old sergeant to read. It did not occur to Gabriel that Jean was safer as an illiterate. In July the pair obtained employment in a bakery kept by an old Imperialist called Grinard who had lost his right leg at Auerstadt, where Marshal Davout defied the bulk of the Prussian army while his master was crushing the remainder at Jena. The baker whose premises were in the Faubourg St.-Germain, was an active Bonapartist, and his low-ceilinged bakery soon became the rendezvous of a group of old soldiers, some of them officers. These latter were glad to eat the crisp rolls that Grinard distributed from his ovens when the old comrades gathered to discuss old times. Gabriel, although he did not worship the past, soon found himself infected by the trend of their conversation. There was no real treason talked in Grinard's bakery, but the latest Bourbon outrage was the topic of every session.

Then one day Grinard disappeared and his bakery was closed. There was no explanation, no charge preferred. The employees were merely told that the baker had left Paris and that they must seek work elsewhere. It was not easy to find employment now; the two ex-voltigeurs had to dip into their reserve for more than three months before Gabriel found a badly paid post at a coach-builder's on the other side of the Seine and ultimately succeeded in getting Jean there as night-watchman. They did not see much of each other after that, for Jean worked at night, going off duty at sunrise when the workshop opened. In the New Year, during one of many robberies commited by the discharged soldiery, Jean got a crack on the head which kept him in bed for a week. During this period Gabriel brought him in some papers to read, among them old copies of the *Moniteur*, now a violently royalist publication. He came home the following night to find Jean in a state of violent agitation. The old sergeant flung a crumpled copy of the *Moniteur* in his direction.

"Read about Colonel Debussy; go on, read about it and then think about it! This is how they treat men of honour! This is our reward for pouring out our blood for twenty years!"

Gabriel, who had heard too much of this sort of talk since the abdication, was not impressed, but he glanced through the newspaper, finally coming across a column dealing with a lawsuit. Its introductory line, printed in insignificant type, read: *"Debussy versus State."* Half-way down the column Gabriel had to shift his position in order to turn his back on Jean's sullen gaze. The younger man felt an overwhelming desire to chuckle, the lawsuit was so typical of the times and Jean's reaction was so typical of the current mood of the Imperial soldiery.

It seemed that the Debussy in question was a well-preserved

corpse, pickled in a barrel of rum nine years before, after finding a glorious death at the head of his infantry column on the field of Austerlitz. The Emperor, with his characteristic touch of showmanship, had decreed that the remains of certain field-officers who had fallen at the head of their troops should be embalmed and ultimately entombed in a Hall of Heroes that he intended to build in Paris. The embalming never took place and pressing affairs constantly delayed the building of the Hall of Heroes. Meanwhile, however, Debussy and the officers on the list were preserved in spirit and sent home to France. Nobody seemed to know what had happened to the other bodies—presumably they were buried by their families—but the barrel containing the remains of the infantry colonel was placed in a storeroom of the War Ministry. It had remained there for years, the relatives knowing nothing of the proposed glorification and supposing Debussy to have been interred on the field of honour.

Events thereafter succeeded one another with such rapidity that the Emperor's plan was shelved and ultimately forgotten. One day, however, soon after the Allies had entered Paris in the spring of 1814, the barrel containing the colonel's remains rotted through and fell to pieces. A startled War Office janitor who had gone into the storeroom came face to face with an unusual spectacle. Colonel Debussy's corpse was excellently preserved, but the spirit had caused the officer's whiskers to grow to enormous length, so that he now leaned nonchalantly against the storehouse wall, with his feet in the wreckage of the barrel, looking more like a monstrous caricature of a Viking chief than a deceased colonel of the Imperial infantry.

The colonel's story did not end there. The War Ministry notified a surgeon, and the body was taken over to the Anatomical College for dissection. Unfortunately this reached the ears of the relatives; they immediately obtained an injunction against the surgeon and he, in turn, appealed to the Ministry. The result was a tedious lawsuit in which the final verdict went against the family. Colonel Debussy's last service to humanity was to act as a means of instructing medical students.

Gabriel put the paper down on his truckle bed.

"It's no more than you would expect," he began, but Jean interrupted him with a snarl.

"I served under Debussy in two campaigns and he was one of the finest officers in the army. At Raygern, when we were rounding up the Coalition, I saw him carry a wounded sergeant across an open field swept by crossfire. I was not ten yards from him when he was killed below the Pratzen heights. We had just broken through three battalions of Russian grenadiers. Get your brains blown out for your country, then come home to be cut up and served out to a pack of young sawbones. I tell you it's monstrous, Gabriel, and it can't go on. I shall send a protest to the *Moniteur* myself!"

"You can't write," Gabriel reminded him.

"Then you shall write at my dictation. Come, fetch pens and paper or else I shall run into the streets and shout for the Emperor this very moment!"

Gabriel sighed, knowing that Jean's threat was no idle one. He fetched pens, paper and ink and began a laborious composition into which Jean intended to introduce a massed protest from Imperial ex-servicemen.

Gabriel finished the address at two in the morning, Jean having forgotten all about his duties at the coach-builder's. The following morning when Gabriel awoke, Old Jean was gone and Gabriel guessed that he had already commenced his tour of the Bonapartist haunts in search of signatures. There would be no lack of names on the petition if Jean handled the matter.

The inevitable happened. Jean was arrested and taken into custody. Gabriel bribed his way into the St-Germain lock-up to give the old sergeant some tobacco and chocolate. Jean looked happier than he had looked for months. The fact that he had been arrested as a Bonapartist seemed to restore to him much of his self-respect. He lay in prison all through February of that year, cheerfully awaiting trial with other Bonapartists, both civilian and military. Gabriel did not waste much sympathy on him. There were so many old soldiers in the gaols that sentences were sure to be light when the massed trials opened in April. In the meantime the old fellow was in good company.

As it turned out, the trials were never held. Early in March an incredible rumour circulated the cafés. Napoleon was said to have left Elba and landed at Cannes. Within hours of the rumour's first circulation Paris was in turmoil; Gabriel, in common with all other infantrymen on the reserve, received a curt notice to present himself at the Guard's barracks in the Ecole Militaire. He went blithely, having missed Jean and grown tired of coachbuilding.

The column was marching down the Lyons road. It was smart, new and well-equipped. Labédoyère rode at its head and the men stepped briskly, as though they were going into garrison after a successful campaign.

The early-spring sunshine had dried the neglected roads, and the scent of wild flowers came from the woods. Peasants at their ploughs stopped to line the banks and stare down at the troops as they passed, their muskets slung easily on their shoulders, neatly squared knapsacks bobbing between their shoulder-blades, bayonet scabbards swinging, lively fifes playing only, the drums strangely silent and no one asking why. Through the Paris barriers and for a few leagues south the men had sung "Vive Henri Quatre" and "La Belle Gabrielle." But down here, where there were few white cockades to be seen, they reverted to the old songs and sang them lustily. Labédoyère rode ahead, making no comment, and his staff glanced at him curiously.

Gabriel, as a light infantryman, had been seconded to the Seventh of the line, being sent with the first Royalist troops to make head against the Usurper, who was reported to be progressing rapidly towards Grenoble. Marshal Ney, who had boasted that he would bring Napoleon to Paris like a wild beast in a cage, was following up with heavier metal, guns and cavalry. Macdonald, at the head of another army, guarded the approaches to the capital. Nobody in Paris thought this kind of nonsense could last very long. That was what they told one another; it gave them confidence. None the less, King Louis's head coachman had had orders to overhaul the harness of all the carriage horses in the Royal stables. The Bourbons were not a family to leave anything to chance.

Gabriel felt curiously light-hearted. He had a new sketchbook in his knapsack, together with a good supply of drawing materials, and the rythmic movement of the line of aigrettes on the shakos of the men ahead made him itch to reach bivouac and start work.

As they passed through Lyons the Lyonese looked at the Royal troops sulkily. Lyons was a town that had prospered under the Empire. Beyond Grenoble they saw a cloud of dust approaching, and Labédoyère abruptly halted his men. Red wine was served in leathern buckets, being paid for by the paymaster with newly minted louis-d'ors.

The dust cloud advanced and the men drained their cups, idling about on the highway, waiting. No orders were issued to prepare for either attack or defence.

A small column of men came into view, marching briskly. As it drew nearer one of the infantrymen in the Royalist column grabbed his musket and ran shouting down the road. Others followed, catching the man's excitement. The oncoming column halted within musket shot and, in the brief silence that followed, a short, thickset figure came on alone.

Suddenly tumult broke out. Men tore off their shakos and rushed in two and threes towards the lonely figure advancing to meet them. The men behind him broke their ranks and ran forward also. A confused uproar arose with shouts of *"Vive l'Empereur!," "Vive la Garde!," "Vive Napoléon!"*

The man who had first detached himself from Gabriel's column fell on his knees in the highway, and the two columns mingled, men capering, laughing hysterically, embracing one another in the ditches and stream-bed beside the road. Gabriel edged forward, fascinated by the sheer drama of the scene, to hear Napoleon address the old infantryman.

"Well, old moustache, tell me honestly, were you really going to shoot me?"

The man rose to his feet and, whipping his ramrod from its sockets, dropped it into the barrel, where it fell home with a metallic clang. At this the Emperor and the men close by roared with laughter. The musket was unloaded.

Labédoyère now stepped forward and saluted, Napoleon embracing him. Ringed by grinning Polish lancers, the younger officer produced an eagle from under his cloak; its appearance was hailed with renewed shouts of laughter. Two drummers provided another surprise. Smashing the skins of their drums, they up-ended them and a stream of tricolour cockades poured out onto the road. There was a mad scramble for the emblems as the two columns formed up together in line of march and took the road back to Grenoble.

That night Gabriel sketched the scene from memory. On this occasion, apparently, he did not feel that a date title was adequate. He called the picture "Reunion, Grenoble, March, 1815."

The troops marched north, and on the way they encountered Ney's troops, who joined them en masse. Ney came, too; there was no more talk of the iron cage.

The army entered Paris without firing a shot and Old Jean was turned out of his prison cell. He blinked in the strong sunlight and asked his way to the nearest arms depot. He could wait for a uniform and kit issue.

CHAPTER TWO

Old Jean lay in the green corn, his back to a bank, his short pipe gripped between broken, discoloured front teeth. Overhead the rainclouds had drifted off to the north and the sky was a brilliant blue, Vienna blue; a warm, drying wind blew in from the sea. The old sergeant shifted his position slightly and grunted with contentment.

"This suits me, Gabriel," he said, and Gabriel was aware of his utter sincerity. The sergeant seemed to have shed twenty years since they had rescued him from the St.-Germain lock-up.

Gabriel sketched, slowly and thoughtfully. He wanted to capture Jean's benign and satisfied expression, his bald head gleaming in the June sunshine, his narrow shoulders framed in the riot of cow-parsley and speedwell that clung to the bank.

Round about them the men of the Forty-fifth Regiment, Donzelot's division, sprawled in the trampled corn. A few smoky fires fought a sulky battle with the breeze, but the brushwood was damp and the preparation of soup was a slow process. Jean and Gabriel had not troubled to cook. During the previous day's march they had half-filled their knapsacks with bread and goat's-milk cheese found in an abandoned farm. Jean had his usual brandy flask and they had fared better than most of the infantry.

Notwithstanding their lucky find at the farm, the previous day had been a great disappointment to Jean and he had laid himself down to sleep in a querulous mood. The Emperor had been heavily engaged by the Prussians at Ligny, while Ney had fought a drawn battle against the British at Quatre Bras. Gérard's corps, to which Donzelot's division was attached, had marched aimlessly to and fro between the two battlefields, arriving too late to participate in either action. The army of two years ago would have considered itself fortunate thus to have evaded pitched battles, but the army of 1813 had been composed of conscripts whereas the men in the cornfield were veterans to a man. Most of them had waited years in British and German prison camps for this, and they were eager to teach the enemy that they had not yet forgotten how to use the bayonet.

Propped up against the bank, puffing contentedly at his pipe, Jean felt his spirits improve. He was convinced that the Emperor would give battle again within the next twenty-four hours, for it was known that the Prussians had been hurled back on the Wavre, while the British army, with its feeble Dutch-Belgian allies, had been cut off from Blücher and was said to be making a stand along the ridge which they could see on the skyline. Jean wondered idly what the next battle would be called.

Gabriel, having put the finishing touches on his sketch, passed the book to the sergeant. Jean examined it critically.

"There's flesh here that I haven't got," was his comment, "but the face is good!"

He closed the book and returned it to Gabriel, rolling over to tap his pipe on the heel of his muddy boot.

"This is a good life, Gabriel," he said. "If I live to my dotage, I'll never hanker for peace again."

Gabriel studied him affectionately. With the sun in his face the old sergeant looked more Mongolian than ever. Gabriel said with a grin: "Peace wouldn't have been so bad, Jean, if you'd learned how to keep your mouth shut!"

The sergeant spat and began refilling his pipe from the same sealskin pouch that Gabriel had seen him use on the Isle of Lobau.

"Not bad, eh? Well, maybe you're still young enough to shape yourself accordingly. But me, I'm like one of those donkeys we used to steal from the wells in Spain, fastened to the bar and going round and round to draw the buckets up. You remember them? They were never any good harnessed to transport. They kept stepping out more to the right than the left and dragged the wagons round in wide circles. You can have peace, Gabriel. What was it for me? Two months of living on your charity, a few weeks cooped up in a bakery hotter than Egypt, three more months taking my share of bread without looking for it, and a few weeks defending myself against pickpockets and me armed with a club! Then gaol, until you came for me, and gaol was the best time of all. In there we could at least talk and expect our food regular!"

Across the field a drum began to beat, and Jean shambled to his feet, buckling his knapsack, easing the sling of his musket and swinging it onto his left shoulder. The men, cursing, began to gulp down their half-cooked soup. The breeze had dropped and the smoke spiralled vertically upwards; behind the bank an artillery train rattled by, the drivers shouting hoarsely as their teams plunged up the muddy incline.

Far away in the direction of Charleroi the sun sparkled on a slow-moving column, cavalry advancing at a walk. Jean shaded his eyes and glanced in that direction.

"Cuirassiers," he told Gabriel. "Their casques always catch the sun like that. Well, we can't have enough of them for tomorrow. I wouldn't care to change these boots for those of an English dragoon."

They picked their way through the trampled corn towards the ranks that were forming up on the lower slopes. There was a smell of summer, of wet leather and human sweat.

CHAPTER THREE

The two armies faced one another across the shallow valley, the French massed in columns on either side of the Brussels road, the British and their allies crowning the ridge of Mont St.-Jean, their front presenting a short mile of bivouac fires behind a few advanced field batteries crowning the edge of the plateau.

Half-way down the slope, on the right of the enemy's position, lay a huddle of white and grey buildings, the farm and château Hougomont, with a small orchard, a few barns and low stone walls reaching out to the edge of a sparse copse. It was occupied by the English. Here and there the watching French skirmishers caught sight of a flash of scarlet as the Guards garrison moved about the yard, loopholing, digging, barricading.

"A hard nut to crack," said Jean, but he knew that he and Gabriel would not be asked to crack it, for their place in the line of battle was farther to the right, opposite the higher bastion of the English line, the smaller, more open farm of La Haye Sainte.

The Forty-fifth had moved into position late the previous evening, passing the Imperial staff outside the farmhouse of La Belle Alliance. The Emperor himself had been standing by a fire talking to Marshal Soult and Gérard, their own corps commander.

When the tired men greeted the Emperor he had acknowledged their cheer with a perfunctory lift of the hand and one of his pale smiles. Round about him the grenadiers of the Old Guard were cooking their evening meal; Gabriel noticed that all traces of Ligny mud had been removed from their long white gaiters. They looked as trim and elegant as on the day he had seen them reviewed in the courtyard of Schönbrunn, after the Wagram campaign.

There was an air of confidence about the camp, and divisions moved into position without fuss or flurry. No one would have supposed that Marshal Berthier was absent, his time-honoured place as Chief of Staff being filled by Soult. There were guns everywhere, and between the batteries were ranged masses of cavalry, more than Gabriel had ever seen on a single battlefield.

As they bivouacked beside the road Gabriel wished that Dominique had been present to play them a tune. Before they rolled themselves in their greatcoats beside the fire Jean and he discussed old times and old comrades. The sergeant summed up his last file.

"They were good boys, all of them—even old Nicky, until he went crazy!"

Neither of them mentioned Nicholette, but after they had thrown fresh wood onto the fire and Gabriel had rolled on his back and looked up at the few stars, he wondered whether the girl had rejoined the army after the Emperor's return. He would have asked Jean his opinion on the matter, but the old sergeant had already begun to snore. Jean was never more than a moment in getting to sleep.

The battle opened with a murderous artillery duel. From where they were standing to arms, near the main road, the light infantry-men saw something of the havoc created by the French guns among the red-coated artillerymen on the ridge. After a spell the more advanced batteries withdrew behind the skyline, but for more than an hour the French continued to pepper the ridge, screening the entire battle line with battery smoke that hung like a fog on the light air.

About eleven o'clock the division received orders to march and moved off down the main road towards La Haye Sainte. On their right three other divisions of Gérard's corps advanced along parallel lines of march, whilst on the road itself a few squadrons of cuirassiers clattered forward in support.

Then the British artillery opened fire and balls began to plough into the column. As it approached the farm the crackle of musketry was heard and a line of flashes picked out the loopholes. A few men dropped, but the column marched on up the slope, driving in the British skirmishers and striking out for the crest, which appeared to be empty of anything but guns. One battalion inclined to the left to surround the farm, where firing soon rose to a climax. The other, with Jean and Gabriel in the van, skirted a sandpit manned by British riflemen, won the crest and advanced with fixed bayonets against a double line of troops lining the hedgerow. The enemy did not wait for the collision. Badly shaken by the long cannonade, of which they had borne the brunt, an entire division of Dutch-Belgian infantry broke and fled, sweeping back into the second line and making no attempt to rally until they were out of range.

The French infantry threw themselves at the hedges, and Jean, turning to Gabriel as the latter jumped down onto open ground, shouted for joy. His elation was premature.

Advancing in column, the Forty-fifth had lost much of its momentum in the act of crossing the hedge. Its officers rushed along the edge of the ditch, shouting orders to deploy into line, but the movement had hardly commenced when the breathless men heard the thunder of hooves on their immediate right. A mass of cavalry bore down on them, squadrons of the royals and dragoon guards, an avalanche of grey and black horses, their riders leaning right and left as they lashed out with their sabres, scattering the disordered ranks in heaps and hurling the survivors back into the hedge. There was no time to form square.

Hundreds of men went down under the fearful impact; others, seeing what was happening from the French side of the bank, turned and fled downhill, the dragoons streaming through a gap lower down and cutting obliquely into their line of flight.

Jean and Gabriel rallied a dozen men and fought back with the bayonet, their feet in the ditch, but once the gap had been found the dragoons galloped away to find less resolute victims on the slopes of the incline. Jean took advantage of the respite to shepherd his half-company back over the hedge; then he bullied them into forming some sort of square to fight a way back to their starting-point. Furious at the repulse, he began to curse the officers.

"God in heaven," he shouted above the roar of artillery, which had opened fire on the fleeing column, "fancy trying to deploy us in the face of the enemy. We might as well sit down and blow our own brains out! Is this what they learned in the Peninsula?"

British cavalry, life guards and dragoons, was still pouring down into the valley, overturning the few cuirassiers who tried to oppose them on the fringe of La Haye Sainte. Jean's square, shaken now into a defensive formation, attracted more and more fugitives. A sergeant of the 105th joined them, his face bleeding profusely from a sabre cut.

"They've taken our eagle," he growled, dashing the blood from his eyes. "Who in hell would have expected cavalry at that point?"

"Wait a minute and then watch our own people present the bill," replied Jean; and indeed, within seconds, the rallying in-fantrymen began cheering. From their side of the declivity they had a good view of the opposite slopes. There they saw the British cavalry, carried away by its own impetuosity, storm up the valley towards Gérard's guns and wheel to sabre the gunners as they fled towards the reserves. At that moment a long streak of green and silver lunged from the solid ranks of the French cavalry reserves as whole squadrons of cuirassiers and lancers plunged down the slope into the disordered masses of redcoats.

The execution was fearful. Caught in the flank, their horses blown by a long gallop over soft ground, the dragoons did their utmost to turn and race for their own lines, but hardly one of them escaped the long, straight swords of the heavy cavalry or the points of Jacquinot's green lancers. Within five minutes the valley was dotted with scarlet, while riderless greys reared and cavorted in the mêlée. Only a few well-mounted survivors galloped past the retreating infantry and rode for the plateau; the jubilant French infantry gave them a scattered volley as they passed.

"So much for that," said Jean, as they re-formed behind the cavalry screen.

Over at Hougomont a terrific battle was in progress. Orchard and wood were veiled in drifting smoke, and a confused roar spread right along the valley from the sector where Reille's infantry battered impotently on the château gate, falling in heaps before the well-directed fire of the British Guards.

Before La Haye Sainte there was a short lull, men of the light-infantry companies occupying the time by rifling the bodies of the dragoons. Jean pocketed a silver watch but gave its owner, a trooper dying from a lance thrust in the back, a few swallows of brandy. The man thanked him with his eyes. He did not appear to grudge the loss of his watch.

The din from the direction of Hougomont had increased; the artillery exchanges were deafening when Ney, attended by a group of staff officers, rode up to the regrouped battalion.

The marshal had just led an unsuccessful attack on the château gate, and his face was smudged with powder. He pointed towards La Haye Sainte with his sword.

"We're going to take that!" he shouted. Then, clapping his spurs into his horse, he cantered towards the head of the column and took his place in the front rank.

The division was set in motion, up the slope once more, this time heading directly for the farmhouse.

A storm of roundshot and grape struck the column; Gabriel saw Ney's horse stagger and fall, throwing its rider from the saddle. Donzelot having helped the marshal to his feet, he continued to advance on foot, breaking into a run and turning to urge the leading files forward.

"Good old Michel," cried Jean as he too hurried towards the head of the column, Gabriel following.

They stormed into the courtyard, to be met by a feeble spatter of musketry. Inside the farm a British major and his German garrison crouched behind the barricades. They knew that there was no hope of holding the position against this fresh assult. Their cartridge pouches were almost empty.

All the farm buildings, however, including the great barn, had been manned by light troops, and for a brief space there was a fierce struggle for possession of the sheds and byres, the French closing in at the point of the bayonet and fighting their way through fires started by their own field artillery. The door of the great barn resisted all attacks until some of the voltigeurs clambered onto the roof, tore loose sections of the tiles and fired into the interior, shooting down the garrison to a man.

Inside the main building the British major in command, seeing that further resistance was useless, cleared the back door for a retreat into the garden and across the fields to the plateau. He and a few others succeeded in getting clear, but the French soon smashed in the front door, carrying the fight into the narrow passage that ran the length of the farmhouse.

Jean and Gabriel were among the first over the threshold, lunging at the Germans packed in the narrow space. The struggle could not last long, for the French, with full pouches, fired volleys into the struggling mass jammed in the passage. Gabriel shot a sergeant at point-blank range and Jean took another man through the throat. The din was hellish, the passage reeked of powder-smoke. In the uncertain light Gabriel saw a young officer, his shoulder shattered by a musket ball, reel into a room branching off the corridor. He was quickly followed by two of his men. A crowd of skirmishers, shouting "No quarter," followed at their heels, and when Gabriel forced his way into the room the two men were being bayoneted. One of them, a boy of about eighteen, screamed for mercy, but the other, a veteran, continued to lunge at his assailants' feet until he died. There was no sign of the German officer and Gabriel guessed that he had crawled under the broad four-poster bed that occupied the centre of the room. It was clear that Gabriel was the only man to have witnessed him enter. The Frenchman took a single step towards the canopy, then stopped; a vivid memory seared him, revealing another bed, in another violated dwelling on the banks of the Danube.

For a second he stood quite still, staring down once more at the first man he had killed more than six years ago and suffering the same revulsion. There was the same patch of sunlight on the floor, the same dust motes hovering in the beam, the same dark pool of blood spreading round the body of the young bayonetted German. Nausea gripped him and he leaned heavily against the smooth surface of the massive bedpost.

One of the voltigeurs, casually wiping his bayonet on the patchwork quilt, glanced at Gabriel. "You wounded?"

Gabriel shook his head, and the man looked round the room. "Any more in here?"

In his fancy Gabriel heard the German officer's heart beating, felt the man's sweat beading on his forehead, choked with the effort of controlling laboured breath. He made an immense effort to push himself away from the bedpost.

"Come on, there's more outside!"

They went out into the passage and Gabriel closed the door. In a strange way it seemed an act of atonement for murder done long ago.

Jean joined them in the yard, where the column was re-forming. The old sergeant was sweating and the muscles of his face twitched. Gabriel saw that Jean's tunic was coated with white dust and blood; it crossed his mind that the sergeant had become more savage since the last campaign. He had never formerly been a man to kill in cold blood. During the years that they had fought side by side Gabriel had seen him spare a dozen men whom most veterans would have despatched without a second

357

thought, but today Jean was as vicious as any of them. This was a different war, more relentless and unforgiving even than Leipzig. Gabriel remembered something that Jean had said when they were crouching in the pine forests of Russia, watching the convoy of prisoners being driven along the road: "After Austerlitz I saw French staff officers dive into a freezing lake to bring a couple of wounded Russians ashore." That act of mercy now seemed remote and absurb, like a chivalrous exchange at the barriers in the Middle Ages. Men were dying on all sides of them, piled on the manure heaps in the yard, crawling painfully away from the blazing byres, crying out for help and getting none. The elation of yesterday had gone. Today it seemed incredible to Gabriel that he had contributed to this slaughter, that some of the men at their feet had fallen before his musket and his bayonet. He glanced at the bayonet tip and saw that it was as red as any man's in the yard.

A shower of grapeshot whipped the only instinct that mattered into awareness again, the instinct of self-preservation, of keeping alive as long as possible. As they dived for cover officers began shouting and pointing towards the plateau. Now that La Haye Sainte was in French hands the British gunners on the ridge had opened fire once more and the shots were flailing down on the shattered buildings, splintering tiles, pitting the cob walls of the farm and sending out spurts of choking dust. The battalion poured from the yard, fanned out in the field between farm and plateau, and advanced in skirmishing order, kneeling, firing and loading, closing in on the emplacements, where little red figures crouched and ran, sponged, sighted and died.

For the second time the French infantry gained the flat crest, leaping over still figures of men who had marched into bivouac with them the previous evening. Gabriel ran behind Jean. In this tempest of sound he found comfort in fixing his eyes on the sergeant's bouncing cartridge-box, dreading to lose sight of the one sure reality in a succession of terrifying nightmares. He felt like a small child pursuing his mother's apron across a crowded fairground peopled by screaming lunatics. But, just as they reached the guns, Jean's cartridge-box ceased to bounce; it seemed to hover for a moment before falling sideways and rolling over and over into the shallow emplacement beside a stationary field-piece.

Gabriel went over to the gun and fell on his knees, turning the sergeant onto his back and staring down at the lean, contorted face. The lips twisted in agony and the moustache about which they had made so many jokes jerked comically, as though determined to maintain the joke to the last moment. The battle rolled past them as they crouched in the trench; over the lip of the little crater Gabriel could see a red, compact square of British infantry, stationed well back, a hundred paces from the crest of the plateau. He immediately understood why they could never win this battle.

He stripped off Jean's equipment and tunic, appalled by the pallor of the sergeant's face, but the wound was not mortal—a musket-ball graze along the right side of the neck, a near-miss leaving a thick red weal but hardly drawing blood.

He began to laugh, semi-hysterically, with sheer relief, but Jean continued to writhe and pointed down at his left leg. Then Gabriel saw that a second ball had passed through the lower part of the thigh, a clean wound the size of a thrush's egg, blue at the edges and pumping blood steadily.

Gabriel took out his knife and cut away the upper half of the breeches. Picking up his musket, he slashed at its leather sling, twisting it into a tourniquet with the knot facing inwards a hand's breadth above the wound. There was only a ramrod to complete the appliance and he turned Jean onto his side, slipping the ramrod under the sling and twisting until the steady pumping subsided as the tourniquet bit into the flesh. He tucked the end of the ramrod into Jean's boot and then set to work on his shirt, tearing off strips of the coarse material and bandaging swiftly. That done, he remembered something else and, after groping in the pocket of Jean's greatcoat, found the brandy flask and held it to the sergeant's mouth. Jean swallowed twice, jerked back his head and coughed, speaking for the first time since they had left the farmyard.

"You're left behind, Gabriel."

The younger man glanced round and saw that the fighting had ceased on the plateau. The red square was still in position, and over on the left he caught a glimpse of a similar formation, three-parts shrouded in smoke. Looking behind, he saw the remains of the French assault column pouring down the incline towards La Haye Sainte, with a brigade of the King's German Legion in hot pursuit. From the edge of the emplacement Gabriel could see the greater part of the battlefield. Facing right, on the lower slopes of the incline, the upper storey of Hougomont was visible, its garden and farm buildings wreathed in smoke, an unholy din still rising from beneath the pall. Hougomont continued to hold out against Reille's frantic assaults. On the opposite side of the valley were masses of French troops, mustering for a fresh attack, while to the left, higher up the incline, La Haye Sainte could be seen burning furiously. In the field behind the farm squadrons of cuirassiers were cutting down the men of the German Legion that had just put their own column to flight. The entire valley was dotted with casualties, red and blue about equally divided, with here and there the green of a French lancer or the silver grey of a hussar. Riderless horses were everywhere, wandering aimlessly among the dead or standing patiently beside their former riders. Over the whole valley hung an immense cloud of smoke, drifting lazily towards the north-west. Apart from the minor scrimmage behind La Haye Sainte there was no sign of a battle. All the fighting about Hougomont remained invisible, reaching the plateau only in the form of a confused roar. The sound reminded Gabriel of the crash of breakers on the Devon coast.

Jean said: "See if you can find my pipe."

Gabriel found his pipe, filled and lit it and stuck it between Jean's teeth. The sergeant puffed contentedly. The pain did not seem nearly so intense now that the tourniquet was beginning to numb the lower half of his leg.

"How's it going?" he asked. From his position on the floor of the emplacement he could see nothing but sky.

Gabriel told him, gauging numbers, making guesses at probable movements.

"We'd better stay here awhile," Jean said presently. "If the English gunners come back they won't harm us; I never heard of the English mauling wounded. Maybe you'd better play wounded as well."

Gabriel glanced at the field-piece just above his head and saw that it had been spiked.

Jean said: "They're good troops, these Englishmen, but they deserve better allies. If Marshal Grouchy turns up before night-fall we'll roll them up like a row of skittles."

An eight-pounder screamed over their heads to pitch within a few paces of the square, causing an officer's horse to rear violently. The ball ricochetted off to the rear.

A moment later a battery opened fire on the far side of the valley, then another, then a third, until the air immediately above them shuddered with the passage of the projectiles, bomb-shells and small-calibre balls mostly, as Gabriel could tell by the pitch of their whine.

They crouched in the trench, heads pressed down to the soil.

"That had to happen," grumbled Jean. "Lie here and be murdered by our own artillery! How's their range?"

Gabriel took a series of cautious peeps at the square. It was still in formation, but every now and again, as a ball tore a gap in the closely dressed ranks, the sides of the square billowed like a regiment of poppies in a soft breeze. The French range was excellent and improving all the time.

After about half an hour there was a lull. Jean twisted onto his side and peered across the plateau.

"They're waiting for our cavalry, poor devils," he said, "otherwise they wouldn't keep square."

Gabriel crawled across the pit and looked over the outer edge. Jean's guess was correct; masses of French horsemen were moving down the opposite slope and heading for the plateau. The

361

guns were silent whilst the squadrons moved from the French crest, but they opened up again immediately the mass of horsemen had dipped below the muzzles of the guns. Within five minutes more than two hundred guns were in action. Shot tore into the British ranks, while from time to time a ball fell short and struck the soft bank of the voltigeurs' emplacement, sending a shower of earth and stones into the pit.

"I picked a lively place to get a ball in my leg," grunted Jean, who, although he was curled in a grotesque position, went on puffing at his pipe.

Presently the cannonade ceased altogether and another sound replaced the thunder of the guns, a wild rippling cheer heard above the beat of five thousand hooves. The duet grew louder and louder until Gabriel could see Jean's mouth opening and closing without being able to hear a syllable that the sergeant uttered.

Suddenly the first horsemen gained the plateau, and went racing past the abandoned gun. The next moment Jean and Gabriel cowered under the wheels while an avalanche of cavalry swept over them. Milhaud's steel-clad cuirassiers, Lefebvre-Desnouette's chasseurs, Piré's and Jacquinot's lancers, mounted grenadiers of the Imperial Guard, a sea of blue, red, yellow and green uniforms, shouting and screaming, at the enemy and one another, as they crouched over their horses' necks, heading directly for the squares, pouring across the level ground like the vomit of a volcano, overturning everything in their way until they recoiled from the wall of bayonets jutting from the square or piled up under volleys discharged at point-blank range by men who seldom missed at a hundred paces.

For more than an hour the struggle continued, a contest of weight and speed against stolidity, of impotent sword and ill-aimed pistol against steady crackle of musketry, wave on wave of the finest cavalry in the world hurling itself upon the most dogged infantry in the world.

There was no danger now from French artillery, nor dared the reserve batteries of the British open fire. The small force of British cavalry did not ride out to try conclusions with the twelve thousand horsemen cavorting round the squares. Gabriel stood up in the emplacement, leaning against the gun, while Jean, lying on his side with his face towards the squares, forgot the pain of his wound in the grandeur of the spectacle. Rifts in the all-enveloping smoke showed them fleeting facets of the struggle, a redcoat dragged from his place by the sidelong thrust of a lance, an officer of the chasseurs towed round and round the square by his stirrup iron, the maddened horse overturning others in its frenzy, a wall of dead men and horses piling up at the corners of the square where the volleys were fired into close concentrations, wounded cavalrymen trying to crawl clear of the mêlée, and once a glimpse of Ney himself, astride a huge grey horse, endeavouring to rally the shattered squadrons on the edge of the plateau.

More than once during the struggle Gabriel contemplated lifting Jean on his shoulders and starting off down the decline in the direction of La Haye Sainte, but each time he was about to propose the move fresh squadrons of cavalry poured up the slope, barring the way of retreat. It would have been a matter of extreme difficulty to make his way back to the lines alone. Carrying a wounded man, the attempt would have been quite impossible. So they stayed where they were, in comparative safety, and watched the French cavalry batter itself to pieces against the squares.

Jean raged helplessly. "Why don't they send infantry? In God's name why don't they send up the Guard?"

Gabriel suspected the reason, but said nothing. From his position against the gun he could see what Jean, lying prone, could not see, a line of advancing puffs of smoke moving towards the French right from the direction of the woods that covered the Wavre road. Jean had said Grouchy must come that way, but the smoke puffs could mean only one thing—the advance of another enemy division, Prussians or more British, forcing the French right back on its centre and pushing towards the main road to the south.

The last of the cavalry drew off, hustled from the plateau by thin squadrons of British dragoons, whose ranks had been decimated by the morning encounter in the valley. The squares shook themselves and cleared away the wounded. Blue-uniformed artillerymen ran towards the abandoned pieces on the crest, where some of the guns quickly opened up on the retreating French.

A British sergeant jumped into the emplacement, but after scanning the spiked touch-hole of the gun jumped out again without so much as a glance in their direction. Gabriel ate a few mouthfuls of bread and tried to coax Jean to eat. The sergeant shook his head sadly.

"It's all over with us, unless Grouchy moves in," he said. He settled lower in the pit, wincing, and Gabriel asked if his wound was giving pain.

"I've had worse," he replied. "There's nothing to a clean bullet wound. This one matches the hole they made in me in Spain. I'm unlucky against the British; the Austrians never left a bullet in me."

There was activity now behind them. The squares were breaking up, deploying into line. Gabriel wondered if the moment had come for a general advance and glanced across at the distant villages on the French right. The puffs of smoke were still no nearer, but they seemed infinitely more numerous. The whole area between the two patches of woodland was shrouded in smoke. Over at Hougomont the air had cleared a little, while the fighting round the château seemed to have died down. The din was transferred to the opposite side of the valley.

All at once Gabriel stared at the French centre. Two teeming columns of infantrymen were moving down the hill into the valley. The setting sun rippled along the line of shouldered arms, but there was no wide sparkle as there had been when their cavalry flooded the slope. Two solid wedges of bearskins were in motion. The Old and Middle Guard were advancing to carry the plateau, moving obliquely across the valley, heading straight for the enemy's centre, half-way between Hougomont and La Haye Sainte.

CHAPTER FOUR

The advance of the Guard in the early twilight of Waterloo was more than the final act in a battle or campaign; it was an iron door slamming on the epoch. Nobody was better aware of this than the pale, plump man standing on the knoll before La Belle Alliance. He knew as he gave the order he was asking the Guard to pass from actuality into legend.

There were men on the French side of the valley who looked upon the Guard's advance as a final card that might, by some extraordinary chance, yet win the game. It was because of this that thousands of exhausted infantrymen with half as many cavalrymen on jaded, sweat-lathered horses took their places alongside the column and marched up the hill, not hopefully but steadfastly, buoyed up by the knowledge that the men in the bearskins and white gaiters had never been defeated, had never failed to sleep on the field of battle.

Nobody in the Imperial army grudged the Guard their right to stand to arms throughout a battle and then march forward at the final moment to gather the first fruits of victory. It was for this reason that the Guard existed; this was their place in the scheme of Imperial conquest. The fact that during the last decade the Guard's share of fighting had been individual rather than collective excited no rancour in the line regiments. Neither did the guardsman's special rate of pay, which was accepted as a privilege earned. For without the Guard the Empire could not exist. Ever since Consular days it had been the corner-stone of French strategy.

There were some staff officers around Napoleon that evening who would have held the Guard back in order to cover a retreat, but the Emperor, who had been strangely apathetic since the failure of the first assault, was alert enough now. He knew that there could be no retreat for an army engaged in this gigantic gamble. A retreat would have meant more battles, more campaigns, and, before the summer had passed, a dozen Continental armies would be over the frontier, driving him this way and that, forcing him south of Paris, playing last year's game again for even higher stakes. It was then or never, but with the Prussians hammering at his flank, and unbroken British squares still on the plateau, the chance of decisive victory was so slim as to be no real chance at all.

It was because he saw this so clearly that he ordered up the Guard and watched, impassively, as the two massive columns marched over the brow of the hill and down into the valley of annihilation.

Along the crest of the plateau the British artillerymen gauged their range as the first of the columns began to mount the slope. The British held their fire without much anxiety. They had been doing this all day, alternately firing and retiring; even if the Guard gained the crest, contemptuous of losses, the gunners could always return to the squares and watch the infantry fight it out in the dusk.

The columns advanced deliberately, marching erect, their officers in the leading files, two solid wedges of white and blue winding across the valley like two lonely tribes of migratory automatons. They marched without hope, but without fear, the sons of pre-Revolutionary peasants who understood nothing but war, who acknowledged no loyalties but to the man who had created them, no family but the House of Bonaparte, no homes but the barracks, men who in twenty years' campaigning had never once lost their nerve and who even now, under the point-blank discharge of many batteries, did not lose their dressing.

The English artillerymen knew that they were fighting for their lives, but they touched off their guns with reluctance. They had their own traditions, but nothing like this one.

At the first discharge the stragglers broke and ran, horse and foot pouring back into the valley, carrying their officers along with them. The Guard marched on, directly up to the muzzles of the guns lining the plateau.

They got within a few paces of the crest before melting away, raked by crossfire, by a hundred guns firing grape, canister and roundshot, and ten thousand muskets, almost all in the hands of marksmen as good as the best of the French tirailleurs.

A dense column of sulphurous smoke rolled into the valley; with it went the tatters of the Guard, reeling, shattered, reduced by two-thirds, groping blindly in the smoke for a place to rally and form square against the tide that would now sweep down from the level ground the moment the redcoats had leisure to deploy.

Facing the Prussians at Planchenoit, the Young Guard still clung to the churchyard, dying among the grey headstones, until their battalions were reduced to a hundred and fifty men. Then, under irresistible pressure, a square moved slowly towards the Charleroi road, its commander, Count Lobau, shouting defiance at Thielmann's Prussians, who hung on to the fringe of the square like dogs prancing at a tied bear. At the crossroads Count Lobau halted, while his veterans looked dully at the tide of fugitives streaming down the slopes, shouting to one another that all was lost—as indeed it was.

A madman stood on the low bank, steadying himself against the trunk of a scarred tree, waving the stump of a broken sword and screaming at the fugitives to rally, to stand firm, to join the Guard and hold open the road to the south. In the extremity of their despair some of the fugitives threw a passing glance at the madman standing there on the bank, his grey uniform in tatters, his epaulettes blasted away, his face black with powder, and an infantryman, hurrying past, shouted, "Long live Marshal Ney!" The crowd took up the cry, but nobody stopped. After the Guard had fallen back no one wanted to die with Ney, except the men in the square, who were keeping off the fugitives with their bayonets. The tide of men and horses surged past them like a spring torrent cleaving on a granite spur.

Gabriel came upon the square as he blundered along in the ditch, carrying Jean in his arms. The sergeant's leg was the source of a hundred furious curses, for the ramrod kept it rigid and his protruding foot constantly came into collision with the press. Each time a man fought his way past, Jean snarled, drawing back his lips and twisting in Gabriel's grip. Where the square stood in the centre of the highway there was a bottleneck; everyone who recoiled from the bayonets flung themselves at the banks and tried to pass the obstacle by way of the fields.

Gabriel, on the point of exhaustion, saw that he would have to put Jean down and wait until the crowd thinned. It could not be long in thinning, for the Prussians were already driving fugitives up the byroad from Planchenoit. He put Jean down into the ditch and unslung the sergeant's musket, glancing automatically at the priming. While he was doing this somebody took a firm hold on the skirts of his greatcoat, and, turning round, he saw Jean drag himself to his feet and reach authoritatively for the musket. Gabriel tried to pull it away, but the sergeant began to shout, his high-pitched voice overtopping the uproar.

"Give it to me, it's mine, damn you; you left yours on the plateau, didn't you? Give it to me, conscript!"

He was beside himself with rage, his jaw muscles working convulsively. Gabriel gave him the musket and immediately received a push that sent him sprawling, face foremost, into the ditch. Men ran over him and he struggled to his knees dazed and half-stupefied by the pummelling of their boots. He saw that Jean had fought his way into the square and was standing facing him, his bayonet in line with the guardsmen on either side. Jean saw Gabriel, too, and shouted something, but this time his words were carried away on the uproar. As he regained his feet Gabriel caught a fleeting glimpse of the sergeant's discoloured teeth before a fresh avalanche of fugitives lifted him and hurled him against the rigid bayonets at the corner of the square. His right hand, stretched out instinctively to break his fall, was transfixed on a point and he hung there a moment, his feet off the ground, the bayonet protruding from his knuckles, before another convulsive lurch of the crowd carried him past the square and out on the comparatively open ground beyond.

After that there was no stopping, for the column of men poured irresistibly through the tiny gap and streamed up the hill towards La Belle Alliance. Running up the hill, the last of the fugitives once again heard the roar of artillery. It was a battery of field-guns playing on the Guard's square.

When the smoke had drifted away, a party of Prussian horse artillerymen found the bearskins lying in ordered ranks; the artillery major, looking down on them, remarked on the strange uniformity of the features of the dead. A few dazed survivors of the discharge were rounded up to be sent back along the road to Waterloo. Jean was not among them.

The same night, however, a British camp-follower who was systematically rifling the pockets of the dead mused for a moment on the body of a sergeant with the shako numerals "105" who had died with a ramrod tied to his leg. The young moon shone faintly on a pallid face, its drooping moustache in startling contrast with the heavy bristles of the guardsmen, fierce even in death. Assuming that the dead man was a senior non-commissioned officer, the transport thief ransacked the pockets very thoroughly; he found little enough, only an army pay-book, the English watch, a short clay pipe and a quid of tobacco. An expert looter with years of Peninsula experience, he next tore open the shirt and laid his hand on the thin chest. After a few moments he found what he expected to find, a thin cord encircling the neck, and tugged at it. The frayed cord snapped and gratefully he slipped the Cross of the Legion of Honour into his breeches pocket.

Jean Ticquet, voltigeur sergeant of the infantry of the line, lay where the non-combatant had thrown him, his head resting on the stained waistcoat of one guardsman, his boots in the blood of others, tumbled with a hundred dead, in the middle of the Charleroi road. This was his bounty for twenty-two years' service in the field, and Jean would have judged it a generous one.

A troop of Prussians cantered by, pressing the pursuit down the road to Jemappes; their hooves trod on the comical moustache.

CHAPTER FIVE

The pursuit roared away to the south, through Jcmappes, through Charleroi, through Philippeville, no longer an army in flight but a disordered rabble, its former chieftains making their own decisions about the best way to save their lives.

The Emperor abandoned his carriage and made off on a borrowed horse, Bertrand and Gourgaud being among the few field officers in attendance. The Imperial escort consisted of perhaps forty men riding jaded horses.

Soult made for his own country; Ney, miraculously alive, went into hiding, lurking here and there until the Bourbons caught him and dragged him to Paris.

The others, rank and file, did what they could to dodge the sabres of the Prussians, hurrying down the broad road in a compact mass, fighting off the jubilant hussars, snatching what food they could find until the harrying ceased and the solid battalions of the Allies re-formed and moved on the capital.

Gabriel marched in his sleep, beyond exhaustion, beyond conscious thought, stepping along with the tide of fugitives until he approached Jemappes, where he saw some infantry officers trying to organize a rearguard. Then he turned off, crossing the fields behind the town and losing himself in a stretch of broken country to the right of the main road. When dawn broke he was alone and his normal instincts began to reassert themselves. He felt ravenously hungry and was suddenly conscious of a searing pain in his right hand. Not until the pain shot through his palm like a hot blade did he remember the bayonet at the rout of the square or realize that he had been wounded. He knew then that he must both rest and eat, and his skirmisher's training came to his aid. Looking round for cover, he saw a thick fir coppice on his right. Stumbling towards it, he fought his way a short distance into the tangled undergrowth that grew round the base of the young trees. There, in a tiny clearing, he sank down and tore at the flap of his knapsack, taking out a few crusts of stale bread. While eating them, he fell asleep.

He did not awaken until late afternoon and for some moments was unable to recollect how he came to be lying under the briars. Somewhere near at hand blackbirds were whistling. He listened absently to their carolling until a burning thirst assailed him, and he crawled forward through the bushes in search of a stream whose murmur could be heard behind the constant twitter of the birds.

He found the brook a few yards from his glade and plunged his face into the shallow water, gulping until he was satisfied. Then he washed his hands and face and began to unlace his boots. The act proved difficult with his left hand and, when he had loosened the laces, his feet throbbed a dual accompaniment to the agony in his hand. Looking carefully at his wound, he saw that the water had washed away some of the congealed blood, but he was unable to flex his fingers and that not solely on account of the pain which the effort caused him. The bayonet had cut through the tendons of the two middle fingers and, apart from the thumb, his right hand seemed to be paralysed. He unbuttoned his tunic and began to tear at the tatters of his shirt, puzzled at first to find that it was already in ribbons. Then he remembered Jean and the application of the tourniquet on the slopes of Mont St.-Jean.

Sitting back against a tree, he tried to realize that Jean was dead. For a minute or two he attempted to persuade himself that the sergeant might have been taken prisoner. Then he recalled the merciless sabre-cuts at stragglers all along the Charleroi road. If the Prussians were so engaged several hours after the battle, it seemed highly improbable that they would have paused to take prisoners on the battlefield. The English might, providing that they saw Jean was badly wounded, but the artillery firing into the square had been Prussian and, in any case, how could Jean, standing erect in a square, have been recognized as a wounded man?

Gabriel dabbled his feet in the water, finding the slow current delightfully refreshing. For the moment he was not only physically exhausted but spent mentally as well. He knew that in a day or two he would begin to mourn for his old friend, to curse himself for surrendering Jean's musket and failing to drag the sergeant out of that absurd square, but for the moment he was unable to focus his emotion. He could only look on the events of the last forty-eight hours as a series of pictures seen in a book, like those illustrating the large leather volumes that Crichot had lent him when he had called upon the ex-priest on Sunday evenings long ago. Then he abandoned recent recollections and began to think of things more remote, finding them strangely satisfying, almost comforting.

Memories flowed by like a long chain of bubbles on the surface of a stream, steering their own way down the years, sometimes breaking almost as soon as he caught sight of them, sometimes sailing round the stones and twigs of fixed events in his life and riding on out of sight. Tiny, unimportant details stood out with great clarity—the pattern of the leaves when the noon sun beat down on their bivouac in Lobau, the odd, upward curve of the dog Fouché's tail, the smell of burning corn at Wagram when they had dragged Nicholas from a ring of flame, the softness of Karen's hair as he had sat stroking it on the hillside the night before the fire.

Once he checked himself, thinking that he was growing light-headed with hunger and fatigue, but the memories still came back, building up like floodwater until he stood aside and surrendered himself to them once more. Manny, the Jew, speculatively regarding the plump breasts of Karen's sister as she bent over the kitchen table to prepare their supper; Claude sitting in the firelight beside Nicholette on the night of the canteen wedding; Louis heating the iron for the branding of Carolini's mule. And through the memories came a rush of unanswered queries that could never be answered or even guessed at, now that Jean was dead. What had happened to the surviving Carolinis? What fate overtook the English woman, Lucy Manaton, who had made such a fool of herself over horses and Louis? How long did poor old Sergeant-Major Soutier survive after they had abandoned him in the Cossacks' hut? What were the feelings of Nicholas when he looked down the musket barrels of his three comrades? Where now was Nicholette?

His memory took a byroad and he began to concentrate on Nicholette, on her strained look, her white, even teeth visible only when she gave one of her rare smiles, her hair that was constantly working loose from the confines of its coils to fall down across her ears like a dark curtain. He knew then that he had always wanted Nicholette, knew also that she had hardly ever been aware of his existence, even before she took up with Nicholas, yet now that Jean had gone he felt an overwhelming desire to be near her, if only to hear her harsh, male voice shouting to the team. His yearning was sexless, but this made it even more urgent. He wondered, if Nicholas had not been there, if he had been drowned with Claude when they were all plunged into the Tagus on that autumn day, whether Nicholette might not have chosen him as the best of the survivors and a better proposition than changing her file in the middle of a campaign. He thought it possible, even probable, for her manner had never been cordial with any of them except Nicholas. He knew that something had gone sour in her that night by the fire in the Dresden bivouac, when Jean had come into camp and told them that there was no hope of a marshal's reprieve.

Across these meditations a single musket shot suddenly cut like a whiplash. He leaped to his feet and stood with his back to the tree. Groping blindly with his injured hand for the sling of his musket and not finding it, he realized that he was unarmed and a fugitive. He had jettisoned his sword bayonet when he left the plateau.

The knowledge sobered him, jerking his mind from past to present. He slipped into his boots, treading his rotting socks into the stream, and bent, cursing softly, to fumble at the bootlaces with his left hand.

He listened for a moment, then dropped on hands and knees, dragging himself cautiously forward until he reached the fringe of the plantation and an open patch of fallow land covered with coarse grass. Cautiously he rose to his knees and examined the country. Across the field ran a winding byroad, leading to God knew where, and stationary on the road, less than two hundred paces from the spot where he stood, was a solitary two-wheeled wagon to which was harnessed a single horse.

A muffled thumping came from the interior of the vehicle and a riderless horse stood by the roadside, cropping the long grass. As he watched, another horse, small but strongly built, ambled from behind the wagon and moved along the edge of the field, looking for richer tufts. There was no sign of the riders and Gabriel guessed that they were both inside the wagon.

His first impulse was to crawl back into the wood. From the distance at which he stood he recognized the horses as those of a light-cavalry unit, but was unable to read the regimentals on the portmanteaux fastened to the back of the saddles. He felt reasonably certain that the horses belonged to Prussians, while the single shot he had heard indicated that they had met with some sort of opposition from the carter. There were stronger reasons, however, that encouraged him to leave the wood and creep forward through the tall grass. With a horse under him he could get clear of the battle area within two or three hours, and he saw from the saddle holsters that both horses carried pistols, which meant that he would not be at the mercy of the first trooper who overtook him. In the circumstances there was no great risk. If the Prussians came out of the wagon he could easily bolt back into the woods before they could remount to ride in pursuit. He knew that they would never try to follow him on horseback through the dense undergrowth of the coppice.

He could still hear indeterminate sounds coming from the wagon and it occurred to him that the two horsemen had probably disposed of the carter and were now engaged in ransacking the interior. This would improve his chances of catching one of the horses and of making his escape. He approached the wagon from the side, moving very cautiously and glancing over his right shoulder towards the road to ensure that no other horsemen were in sight. The road, and the heath around it, was bare. It was so quiet in the grass that he could hear the chirrup of crickets. The scent of clover reminded him of summer afternoons on the banks of the Dordogne.

Suddenly he stopped crawling. Just ahead of him, through the forest of slender green stems, appeared the body of a Prussian hussar, lying flat on his back. In his right hand was a carbine, of the type used by some of the Prussian cavalry. The man was quite dead, and as Gabriel moved into the area of crushed grass where the body lay, he saw that the hussar had died from a shot through the chest. His brief inspection emboldened him. It meant that there was only one Prussian in the wagon.

He had risen to his feet and was about to make a dash for the nearest horse, when a thought struck him. The Prussians had killed Jean and all through the night they had been cutting down unarmed fugitives. Gabriel hesitated only a second; then he went down on his knees and cautiously drew the hussar's sabre from the scabbard that hung on the man's embroidered belt. A sabre was better than a carbine for this sort of job.

His left hand closed round the hilt. Gabriel had never struck at a man with his left hand, but he felt that his disadvantage was more than outweighed by the element of surprise he would enjoy.

At that moment the scuffling in the wagon suddenly increased; a woman's scream, loud and penetrating, shattered the drowsy silence of the afternoon. In ten strides Gabriel was beside the dropped tailboard, tearing aside the canvas flaps that screened the interior. He saw a man and a woman huddled together on a thin mattress laid between two rows of lockers. They were struggling, the man uppermost. The woman screamed again, then began to shriek curses in French. The hussar laughed and grasped at the woman's free wrist.

Gabriel struck first at the man's foot, holding back the tailboard flaps with his injured hand and slashing with all his might at the calf of his leg, just above the furred top of the short riding-boot. The hussar howled and rolled over onto his side, crushing the woman with his weight. The next moment the point of the sabre was in his throat and he slumped, coughing, into the narrow space between the edge of the mattress and the lockers. Gabriel clambered into the wagon and stood over him, his weapon poised for a second jab. There was no need; his blade had penetrated four inches into the Prussian's neck, severing the jugular vein.

The hussar levered himself into a sitting position to rock to and fro, supporting himself by his hands pressed down on the wagon floor. Convulsively he heaved himself forward, his body bending like a bow, and died, crouched, as Gabriel had seen men die before the bivouac fires on the Moscow highroad. His shako slipped forward over his forehead, revealing thick greying hair plaited into a neat pigtail and tied with a black ribbon.

The woman too struggled into a sitting posture, leaning back against the rear of the driving-seat. She was breathing heavily and her bodice was torn down the middle, revealing one of her small breasts. Her dark hair, which had broken loose in the struggle, framed a face as pale as the paint on the lockers beside her.

The woman was Nicholette.

She stared at him stupidly, screwing up her eyes in the glare of sunlight that beat through the join of the tailboard curtains.

For nearly a minute they stared at one another, neither making any effort to move.

Finally Gabriel said: "I'd better throw this fellow out, Nico. His blood will damage your stock."

He turned and stepped down from the wagon, dragging the dead hussar over the tailboard. As he bent over the body the woman got to her feet and walked unsteadily to the rear of the wagon, casually rearranging her disordered clothes and flinging back the mass of hair that fell across her eyes.

"I wouldn't bother to search him, Gabriel," she said. "I've plenty of money and there's sure to be more of these pigs on patrol!"

Gabriel went round to the front of the wagon and climbed to the box.

"Have you a musket?" he asked, addressing her through the canopy.

"Pistols as well. I settled with the first one, but the other swine came at me from behind, climbing up over the shafts." He heard her opening lockers. Then, "Come on, let's move; head away from Charleroi and we'll pick up the Rheims road in less than an hour!"

Gabriel gathered up the reins and called to the horse. The wagon began to trundle softly along the dusty road.

After a while Nicholette spoke again from the interior. "It's a pity we couldn't take their horses, but that would be asking for trouble now that they're heading for Paris. Nobody would be such a fool as to buy a Prussian horse after yesterday's business."

Neither of them remarked on the oddness of their reunion.

They continued a desultory conversation until they came to the junction of the byroad and the Rheims highway. When the wagon stopped, Nicholette jumped down and came round to the box. She was wearing a different dress of plain grey cotton and her hair was bound up under a red silk handkerchief. A little colour had crept back into her cheeks, but Gabriel noticed that she looked a good deal older than when he had last seen her,

378

sitting beside the camp-fire outside Dresden. She threw a neat parcel of clothing onto the dashboard.

"You'd better change into those," she told him. "Then we can head back north as a couple of carriers travelling to Brussels."

He climbed down and stripped off his uniform, reflecting that no fundamental change had taken place in her since they had all taken turns to ride on the box-seat during the long march acrosss Spain. She was still as tough and matter-of-fact as the hardiest infantryman; she still had an inexhaustible supply of common sense and logic when confronted with an everyday problem. He wondered whether the years had taken the edge off her avarice and if constant brooding over the circumstances of Nicholas's death had converted her stoicism into bitterness.

Gabriel climbed up beside her again and she jerked at the horse. The wagon turned north, heading into enemy territory.

Presently he said: "Jean and Dominique have gone, Nico. I'm alone now."

She did not appear to notice the huskiness of his voice, but merely asked: "Since yesterday?"

He told her, briefly, of the manner in which Dominique and Jean had followed the others. She said nothing for a while, holding the reins loosely and staring vacantly up the white road towards a gleam on the horizon.

When she spoke again her voice had an odd jerkiness, as though she felt that some explanation was required of her but was not giving it willingly.

"After Nico went I got tired of it all; I went back to France and set up a canteen in Nancy."

"Were you there through the Peace?"

She ignored the question. "Jean used to say that if you once started moving when you were young, you never stopped again, or not for very long. Jean was no fool except when he caught sight of Bonaparte's hat." She paused and he made no comment. After a moment she went on: "When the army marched out again I couldn't stay there any longer. So I bought this outfit and stocked up with civilian clothes. I kept a day or two's march

379

behind the army and sold three parts of my stuff within a day and a night. I knew that you'd be beaten, and men will pay anything for civilian clothes when they're on the run."

Gabriel was obliged to grin; the scheme was so typical of Nicholette.

They jogged along in silence again for a few minutes. All the horror of the past two days had ebbed from Gabriel and he felt as tranquil as a child.

He busied himself bandaging his hand and it occurred to him that he might never paint again.

For a long time he tried to frame the words that he wanted to say.

Finally they came, haltingly. "I've always wanted you, Nico, ever since Lobau. Couldn't we stay together after this?"

She smiled grimly, remembering they were the same words Nicholas had used years ago in Königsberg.

Her left hand slipped from her lap and fell lightly across his mangled fingers. The gesture was so unexpected, so uncharacteristic, that he had to glance down to assure himself that it had really happened.

"You came at the right time, Gabriel," she said.

He made no answer, staring ahead, wonderingly, at the static gleam in the distance. It might have been a stationary squadron of cavalry, their cuirasses reflecting the evening sun, or simply a shining curve in the Sambre, winding across the plain towards Namur.

Nicholette said: "The horse needs watering. Look out on your side for a pond."

EPILOGUE

When Madame Friant came into the veteran's room in the morning carrying her lodger's coffee, she found him asleep, his face laid sideways across a folio of drawings that he appeared to have been examining. She set down the tray and shook him by the shoulder.

After a few attempts to awaken him in this way, she passed round to the far side of the table and looked at him more closely. She was a stolid woman, not given to sudden outcry. After she had satisfied herself that he was quite dead, she went out and fetched Father Pavart, standing by whilst he and Peltier, the ostler, carried the old man over to the bed. As the priest intoned a short prayer she glanced furtively at the books on the table. She had never seen them before and wondered how the old fellow had got them. Father Pavart asked her a few questions, of when and how it happened, whether the old man had been failing recently and what his appetite had been like during the past few weeks.

Madame was faintly irritated by his queries. "You saw him alive as often as I did; you were here with him yesterday afternoon," she said, and went out to make arrangements about cleaning the room and advertising for a new tenant.

The priest stayed a while longer, rubbing his long chin and idly turning the pages of the grubby sketchbooks. Presently he gathered the books together, tying them round with a piece of string that he found near the hearth. He was a methodical man and went downstairs to inform the landlady that he had borrowed the books and would keep them whilst they were checking over the old man's effects. He did this because if there was an inventory anywhere he did not want to be accused of stealing them.

Presently the doctor went along to certify the death. He was not very explicit about the cause and, when questioned by Father Pavart on the subject, used a number of long words and said something about old soldiers occasionally dying in middle age as suddenly as their younger comrades had died on the battlefield. The doctor was not particularly interested, and neither was anyone else except Father Pavart, who went away musing. He could not know that, soon after he had left the veteran the previous evening, the man had fallen asleep and dreamed a strange dream.

He had seen himself walking rapidly along a rutted track enclosed by tall hedgerows, and as he rounded a bend he had caught sight of a one-horse wagon travelling slowly along the lane in the same direction. When he first saw the wagon it was about a hundred paces ahead, and as he hurried forward to catch up with the vehicle he saw six men sitting on the tailboard, their legs swinging free.

A great joy flooded his heart. He began to run, calling the men's names one after the other, until they ceased chattering among themselves and began to shout back at him and to wave their hands.

Although the wagon did not seem to be moving at more than a walking pace, it proved extraordinarily difficult to catch; but the veteran made every effort, pounding along on the sparse grass that grew between the ruts of the track, coming a little nearer with every stride and reaching out to touch the hands of the men that were stretched towards him.

At last, with an immense feeling of relief, he drew near enough to be grabbed by the wrist and pulled into the wagon. The six men squeezed together to make room for him on the crowded tailboard. They shouted and laughed, thumping him between the shoulders, and one of them, a man with a grey, drooping moustache, wrung his right hand. Even in the excitement of the moment Gabriel could not help noticing that the fingers of his hand were straight again and that the palm no longer showed a puckered scar.

The speed of the wagon increased as, somewhere in front of them, a girl's harsh voice shouted, "Hup, hup!" to the plodding horse.